[redacted]

A Silent Prayer

A Prayer Series 1

Always chase your dreams

AWARD-WINNING AUTHOR

SAMREEN AHSAN

Samreen

A SILENT PRAYER - 10TH ANNIVERSARY EDITION
Book 1 of *A Prayer Series*

This is book 1 of the series and ends with a cliff-hanger. This book is intended for mature audience and not suitable for the readers who do not enjoy suspense endings.

Cover Design by @ammarasartbox (IG)
License Cover Image by Adobe ©
Print and Distribution by IngramSpark
ISBN 978-1-989893-10-4 (Hardcover)
ISBN 978-1-989893-11-1 (Paperback-Large Print)
ISBN 978-1-989893-09-8 (Paperback)
ISBN 978-1-989893-08-1 (eBook)

@authorsamreenahsan

To the memory of my brother,
Mohammad Ali.
You will always be my baby brother.
Miss you always!

PLAYLIST

1. *Les valses de Vienne* (The Viennese Waltz) — François Feldman
2. *Deliverance* — Yanni
3. *It's the Most Wonderful Time of the Year* — Andy Williams
4. *Haven't Met You Yet* Michael Bublé
5. *Waltz No. 2* — Shostakovich's
6. *Serenade* — Schubert's
7. *Since I Fell for You* — Lenny Welch
8. *Iris* — Goo Goo Dolls
9. *Uninvited* — Alanis Morissette
10. *Amazed* — Lonestar
11. *Save the Last Dance for Me* — The Drifters
12. *She Bangs* — Ricky Martin

CHAPTER 1
AN ENCOUNTER

ADAM
FEBRUARY 2012

"No DEAL," I SAID, slamming the file on the table. "I'm sorry, but what you ask is impossible."

Having an uncomfortable business dinner on a Saturday night in a French restaurant wasn't a wise idea. The restaurant was in an old district of downtown Toronto—the servers milling about, carrying fancy dishes. Mr. Groston, who sat across from me, rambled on, but my mind wandered. I was already bored with his company. I had better things to do at this hour than sit across this old man.

Like what? Sit home and paint?

I looked around, noticing people engrossed in conversation. As if I had too much time on my hands to contemplate philosophically, I wondered how each person had his own story to tell—everyone had a past, a present and a future to look forward to. I didn't want to dwell on the past; my present was an open book, and I hadn't given much thought to my future.

"Mr. Gibson?" He broke my trail of thoughts.

"No, it's not possible." I took a sip from my glass of whiskey. I didn't pay attention to what he'd just said, but agreeing with him didn't seem wise.

"Come on, Mr. Gibson. You've built half of Toronto," argued Groston, "And you're saying this hotel project is not possible? Have you suddenly decided you no longer want to make money?"

Xavier Groston was a businessman in his late fifties who knew how to exploit any situation. That's what made him a god in the construction business on the American West Coast. To him, everything started and ended with money and power.

"Mr. Groston, I understand your situation," I answered, expressing mild irritation, "but the property you're interested in has been given to the local community center. Every day, underprivileged people go there to eat, sleep, and receive food and clothing donations. Now, you want me to kick them out?"

I was quite frustrated by this meeting. This business tycoon wanted me to demolish the community center and its surroundings and build a five-star hotel. The man was either much too greedy or too high. I understood his aggressiveness. The property was a prime location for a hotel, and it would bring both of us money and more business.

But this was not about money.

Over the past five years, underprivileged and homeless people have found a safe place at the community center, regardless of any religion or ethnic background. Despite being an atheist, I couldn't play with this. I was not a saint, but I still had some fragments of reverence. I gave my word to the mayor of Toronto and the people of the community that the property would be theirs to use. Now, Mr. Groston was asking me to destroy my credibility and take back my so-called altruistic donation.

"I can offer you better properties all around Ontario, Mr. Groston," I suggested. "I have a staff who is dedicated to finding the best land. I'm sure they'll come up with a deal that will be fruitful to both of us." I tried to distract this stubborn man, but he failed to acknowledge me.

"So, you are refusing my proposition?" He glared at me. "You cannot relocate this center elsewhere?"

Yes, he is definitely high because his brain fails to understand the basic thing: it is inhumane.

"Mr. Groston, as much as I intend to do business with you," I said, leaning forward, "I protect my own reputation as well." He had my undivided attention. "You may own half of the West Coast and millions of dollars worth of properties, but the Canadian market is quite different. That community center serves hundreds of people daily—providing food and shelter and a venue for community and religious activities. In fact, without it, many seniors in the area would have no place to attend religious services. In America, it may be the almighty dollar that rules, but here in Canada, we try to remember that communities are for the people living in them, not merely those who make money off them."

My empathic values with *O Canada* were finally surfacing.

"My staff will get in touch with you," I continued, "to show you some of the finest properties, but I'm afraid this one is off the market."

Finishing his whiskey, Groston finally got to his feet. He agreed to look at other properties, though he still wanted this one. I joined him and shook hands, then sat back, thinking about his proposal. It would make a lot of money, but sometimes, other things are far more valuable.

Five years earlier, on Canada Day, I was invited to an event—a government-funded function for underprivileged residents. A group of seniors approached me, asking about my contribution to this community. Their actual question, which they could not ask openly, was: *what the hell was I doing here?* This was a kind of blow to my ego. For a moment, I had nothing to answer. Just because I'd once been homeless didn't mean I understood their sufferings.

I had recently acquired a vast land to build a five-star hotel. Out of nowhere, a sense of humanitarianism had emerged in me, and I donated the land and even promised to make a community center. Within a year, I made the headlines about the generous donation and how the community center was thriving, helping the homeless and even new immigrants who were low on funds. The land was still under my name. No one bothered about the legality. I could do as I pleased, including Groston's hotel project. But people trusted me, and I didn't want to break their trust. I wouldn't say I was unpretentious, but I was loyal to my work. Anything I do or commit to, I stick to it.

The server appeared, bringing me back to the present, and quietly replaced my empty glass with another one. I looked around. This was one of the earliest construction projects that my company had done—an early nineteenth-century building, and I was proud that we preserved its original beauty. It reminded me of a restaurant in Marseille where I once had dinner with a client. I took inspiration from that restaurant and added a medieval and renaissance touch, frescos reminding people of a bygone era with a display of deceased kings and queens with biblical references. The vast Swarovski chandelier hung proudly in the centre, and one could see the perfection in the artwork that covered the ceiling. The wall sconces created an impression of a medieval castle, and the furniture was made of dark wood, transporting the patrons back in time.

Downing my whiskey, I closed my eyes to concentrate on the music. It was a French song, a man declaring his love for a woman, his heart aching for her. How could a woman change a man's heart like that? How could you crave someone so severely that nothing made sense without her? I've read all this in books but never understood this feeling. How could your soul depend on someone so hopelessly? It sounded like a miserable state, bringing yourself to this point.

I finally left the restaurant located on the top floor. The building had six levels, each with a different kind of business. All of them earned well and paid me rent on time.

Heading to the elevator, I caught a glimpse of the door with a fire exit. Something propelled me to go this way. But when I opened the door, I noticed stairs leading to a higher level. I thought the restaurant was on the top floor. It had been a long time since I renovated this building. Did it have any stairway access to the roof? If I remember correctly, the fire exit led to the metal stairs going down from outside the building. And if there were a rooftop, it would be an absolutely absurd idea to check it out in harsh February weather.

I climbed the stairs anyway.

Outside, a stunning view of the Toronto skyline made me pause. I see this view daily from my work and home, but today, how it was covered in snow... was breathtaking. How everything glittered on the white winter night, how the diamonds and crystals had been spread all over, was magical.

I approached the railing and admired the view of the nearly frozen lakeshore on one side and the CN Tower on the other. A lot of junk was piled here as if no one had come here in ages. It was freezing, but I was glad to take a chance.

After my massive donation on that Canada Day, I had been in the limelight for every news channel. Since then, I've had very few moments I could call private where I could breathe in the air and think of nothing.

And right now, I thought of nothing. It was just me and the winter night.

As I stared out over the city, a sound caught my attention. I looked back, but the door was shut, so there was no way the music was coming from the restaurant. And since it was upscale, they didn't play the music so loud.

I concentrated on the music, wondering if this track was

Western Classical, but I hadn't heard of it before. It was magical. I tried to figure out where it was coming from. Another building was connected to this one, sharing the wall. If I recall, during my renovation days, there was no building connected to it. How much has this changed in the past few years?

The wall in between was low. I climbed over and jumped to the other side. I looked sideways, checking for a *no-trespassing* sign, but I ended up wetting my clothes with dirty slush. The music was getting louder.

I approached the door and tried to open it, but it was bolted like it had never been used. After a bit of struggle with the rusted knob, I finally managed to open the door. I'd expected another set of stairs, but instead, a passage led ahead. Nothing was there on either side except darkness, but the music was so enchanting that I was compelled to follow it.

A sensational warmth spread through me as the music penetrated my every pore. I no longer felt cold. As I followed the passage, there was something very comforting yet disturbing about it. I have frequented many clubs where the loud music beats with your heartbeat, but it was nothing like this. Like a drug, this one was slowly entering through my veins.

Groping a few more steps in semi-darkness, the sight froze me, just like the weather outside had. This piece of architecture had no doors, windows, or stairs. Like an abyss, it was nothing but a spiral passage leading down to the ground level.

I am an architect, and this didn't make sense. No pillars held this spiral passage together.

I looked down at the floor, and my heart wedged in my throat.

A girl was dancing to the music.

From my vantage point, I couldn't see her face clearly on the sixth level, but how she moved took my breath away. I felt like the dance and music had cast a spell on me. She was lost in her dance, not caring about anyone watching her. Or perhaps she didn't even know she had an intruder here. Others were dancing with her, but I couldn't see more than shadowy figures since the spotlight was on her.

For the first time, I felt my soul pulling me toward something...toward her.

Unable to resist the temptation, I started trotting down the winding passage. The music became clearer and melted in my ears...in my body...in my soul. I'd never heard of anything like this. Who was the composer?

On the second-to-last level, I was able to see her more clearly. It looked like a masquerade as the girl had a Colombina mask tied over her eyes. Clad in a long, pink ballerina skirt, her body moved celestially as if she was not carrying any weight.

I looked around, but the shadows still weren't clear to me. I knew I hadn't had enough drink to make me this heady. But a dance session with so many shadows and no faces didn't make any sense.

Then, one shadow lifted her up in the air, swirling her around with lights and music as if she, herself, were the light and melody. I inhaled sharply, trying to make some sense, but it was impossible to take in.

The shadows kept on dancing around her, but it was her presence that was only visible. The rest was just a blur of movements. I thought again. Did I drink too much tonight? Why couldn't I see the other people? Or was I so awed that I couldn't see anything other than her?

I'd never been drawn to anyone like this before. A mystical power was drawing me toward her, but at the same time, a presence was pushing me away from her.

I must see the girl more closely, meet her, and tell her how captivating she was when she was dancing. *What is she thinking right now?* Was she dancing for her missing lover, or was it a dance to ward off her pain?

Chasing a girl was very unlike me. I hadn't even acted like this in my adolescence. Something deep within me was screaming not to make a move, warning me not to cross the forbidden territory.

I ignored the cry and kept moving. Why couldn't I look away? This had never happened to me before. Or perhaps I had never seen anyone like her.

The intensity of the music augmented my fascination. Under the colourful lights, she moved like a dove borne by the wind. My heart rejoiced the way people write about the rainbow appearing after the endless rain.

Upon reaching her level, I noticed she was dancing alone.

Where did the other people go, whose shadows I saw from above?

I watched her in a trance, admiring her body and movements. The violins behind me accelerated, and so did her body. She twirled around and around with the music. If it had been a few millennials in the past, I could have called it a dance with pagan gods. Though I saw no one around her, I could sense the presence of something powerful helping her move this way.

It was magic.

It was unreal.

She was unaware of my presence as she twirled around. As if someone had pushed her, she suddenly crashed against me.

I held her by the waist firmly to support her. The music stopped, and so did her dance. She exhaled heavily, catching her breath, her breasts moving and touching my chest as the air filled her lungs.

Our eyes met. Under the pink mask, her big, darker-than-ebony eyes caught my attention. She looked at me as if she were looking directly through me. The madness in her eyes ripped my existence apart, peeled off my flesh and bone to search my soul. Their darkness drew me to let her devour my presence, insanely and willingly. If I had any slightest doubt that she was my imagination, it melted away after touching her.

I hadn't been dancing, but my heart kept pace with hers. My gaze moved to her rose-pink lips, and I had this painful urge to kiss them, to find out if they were as soft as they looked. Her fragrance was diffusing in me like a drug, slowly and venomously. Never have I smelled such a perfume—one that could take me to another world, where there was no pain, where only pleasure existed.

I wanted to touch her skin, but its softness and tenderness scared me in a way I'd never experienced before. Instead, I raised my hand to remove the mask from her beautiful face, wondering if it was as perfect underneath as it looked.

As if reading my thoughts, she pulled away instantly, releasing herself from my grip. I felt my hand moving away from her waist. I knew I was not doing it because I didn't want to leave her, but I could not oppose. The lights slowly dimmed around us. Though my gaze was fixed on her, I knew no one was around. It was just two of us staring at each other in consternation. We were both stuck in a moment where perhaps she felt I was an intruder in her magical world, and I could not evaluate the reason why and how I was here.

A gravitational force weighed me down, my feet rooted to the ground, and I was so utterly entranced that all I did was watch her pick up her bag. I knew she was about to leave, and I must say something to make her stay, but I just stared at her. Time and some unseen powers had frozen me in this moment.

She paused and looked up.

I inhaled sharply as she dared to dive into my soul again. She got to her feet in a heartbeat and disappeared into the darkness. That last look moved me to the core.

I stood there, numb, for endless beats, when I realized nothing was around me.

Where were the others who were just dancing with her? Where was the music coming from when there was no sound system here? Where was the light coming from when only one light fixture was behind me?

What I saw from above was either my imagination or a hallucination. No, I could not have imagined it. I felt her in my arms.

Befuddled, I sprinted out of this place to catch my breath. My heart skipped from one place to another, eager to find the answers. As if I'd caught a high fever, my body trembled vigorously, and I couldn't even stand properly.

I leaned against the bike stand installed at the corner of the walkway. A shiver jolted through my spine as the cold rain fell brutally from the sky. I *would* catch a fever if I stood here for another minute.

I turned to look back.

An intense cold invaded my body once again when I noticed no spiral structure behind me. The restaurant building stood alone, with no other building connected to it. The ground melted under me, so I grabbed the handrail firmly. It muddled my mind that the place I came out just now wasn't anywhere in sight.

Beside the restaurant building, an alley winded down and disappeared into darkness.

What just happened to me?

Now, all the practical solutions were coming to my mind. I had a phone with a camera. Why didn't I record her while she was dancing?

I had never seen such an alluring woman in my life. She was a refinement that surpassed all levels of beauty and grace—an artistic existence so pure that even the angels would envy her. How could someone make your heart run so fast without touching, kissing, or making love? If this urge to see her again stayed with me, I would go crazy.

I had never hesitated to talk to people my entire life, but this woman struck me mute like a lightning bolt from above. I had never felt so paralyzed.

My trance was broken when my chauffeur honked the horn at the corner of the street.

Ice-cold rain still poured down on me, drenching me from head to toe.

I ran toward the car as my heart called out William Wordsworth's poem:

She was a phantom of delight
When first she gleamed upon my sight;
A lovely Apparition, sent
To be a moment's ornament;
Her eyes as stars of Twilight fair;
Like Twilight's, too, her dusky hair;
But all things else about her drawn
From May-time and the cheerful Dawn;
A dancing Shape, an Image gay,
To haunt, to startle, and way-lay.

CHAPTER 2
ONE FINE DAY

RANIA
NOVEMBER 2012

MY PHONE ALARM JOLTED ME out of a deep sleep. I checked the time: 6:15 a.m.

Still feeling tired, I set my alarm to snooze. Then suddenly, I recalled I wasn't going to work today. I had been invited to a breakfast meeting at Gibson Enterprises headquarters on King Street.

Shit!

I forgot to check the subway route last night. Sleep vanished like a ghost, and I flung myself out of bed and headed to the washroom. I came out in no time and blew my long hair dry. I definitely needed a haircut in winter, as this blow-drying process took a long time in the mornings.

Finishing my morning prayers in ten minutes, I rummaged through my closet, not sure what to wear. I had never attended a breakfast meeting except those in my office. I wasn't sure why I'd been invited to this one—my boss hadn't told me much. But as a Senior Creative Designer for Greenway Advertising, I couldn't skip it. And I had to look professional.

I settled on a long navy-blue sweater dress with matching

leggings.

Born and brought up in Beirut, I had collected all the usual values of Muslim families. Offering my prayers on time. Not exposing my body parts for men's attention. Refraining from strangers. And most importantly, no sexual relationships outside marriage.

I wasn't really an exemplary Muslim girl, though. I don't wear a hijab. Although I am Lebanese, I'd inherited my mother's Egyptian features: dark eyes and black hair. She was an exceptionally beautiful woman, and despite having the same looks, I lacked her grace. I never understood why men kept offering me relationships and friendships I was not interested in. Did I have an *available* sign on my forehead?

My mind wandered away into the past, but I shook it away. This was not the right time to dig up old memories. I was seven seas away from that nightmare.

I gave myself some final touches and looked one last time in the mirror before leaving.

Taking my necessary travel paraphernalia—my bag, phone, umbrella, and jacket, I locked my apartment and took the elevator. My apartment was on the sixteenth floor of a high-rise condominium on Yonge Street, close to the Finch subway station. I simply adored my neighbourhood. Everything was close to my place—the theatres, restaurants, subway station, and the mall. Just outside my building was a bakery from where I'd always bought breakfast. They sell the best pumpkin bread in the Fall season.

After twenty minutes of subway travel, I reached my station. Even without snow, the morning of November was still cold and wet in Toronto. I headed toward my destination—the headquarters of Gibson Enterprises. Across the street, a tremendously tall building, at least fifty stories high, touching the skies above, stood proudly. Outside the building, there was an ostentatious stone and marble entryway with the company's name etched on it.

I continued toward the main entrance, the umbrella under my right armpit, the travel mug in my hand, and the bag swaying in my other hand since I found it hard to carry it on my shoulder with a jacket on.

Suddenly, I felt a pull and noticed that the strap was stuck on one of the decorative bolts sticking out of the wall. Everything spilled out of it like spring showers.

Damn! Why don't I ever close my handbag?

I disentangled the strap from the bolt and bent down to pick up my belongings.

Thank God it wasn't raining anymore. Otherwise, my gadgets would have been soaked by now. Amid my misery, I sensed someone was watching me. I looked up to meet the most beautiful dark green eyes I had ever come across. I looked away and continued picking things up, cursing my handbag and the decorative bolts and grudgingly wondering how ungentlemanly the men of this generation are that they don't bother to help anymore. He could have at least asked to hold my umbrella.

I looked up again, and the emerald eyes were still on me, apparently flabbergasted.

They were not just eyes. They were two precious gemstones with all four Cs: Colour, which was composing my soul. Cut, which was ripping me off to expose me. Clarity, as if he was looking through me. And Crystal, like he was an open book with nothing to hide. Each emotion was visible in his eyes as if he had not seen anyone like me. It was as if I were the only woman on this planet at that very moment.

Or is he enjoying my misery?

I got up, ignoring his curious gaze, and headed to the door.

Two days earlier, we were told that since the main office of Greenway Advertising was also located somewhere in this building, we were authorized to go through the turnstile by swiping our badges. I checked the time: 8:55 a.m.— still five minutes to show up on time. I would have arrived earlier if not for the bolts.

When I reached the turnstile, I slipped my hand into the front pocket of my bag, where I'd always kept my badge.

It wasn't there. *Damn!* Where was it? Did I lose it when I dropped everything?

Cursing, I turned back to avoid blocking other people's entrance. My body slammed into a tall, strong, masculine form, causing me to lose my balance. His hand gripped me firmly by my waist. I met those amazing eyes again as he swiped the badge and propelled me through the Plexiglas door into the building.

Whoa! What was that?

He released me, a silent smile curving his lips. He had not spoken yet. The security guards were looking at me with 'it's okay' expressions on their faces. What kind of security did they have here? I was here for the first time, and they let this gorgeous man bring me through the high-security door without any questions. Why didn't they check his ID?

He finally bothered to speak, hiding his smile. "You dropped this when you were struggling with the bolts." He handed me my badge.

And you didn't have the courtesy to give it to me earlier?

"Thank you for picking it up for me." I didn't hide the sarcasm in my voice. I moved from the entryway and let the people pass. It was inappropriate to stand there and gaze at this alluring man.

I headed to the elevator and took out my phone to confirm where the breakfast meeting was held. The invite said, "The Maple Room," but no floor was mentioned.

I read the email repeatedly to ensure I didn't miss the floor number. I must ask the concierge if they knew.

"May I help you?"

I looked up from my phone and met those green eyes again. This time, he didn't hide his smile. His bright, shiny teeth looked like they belonged in a toothpaste commercial. For the first time, I noticed he was not only the owner of beautiful emerald eyes, but I could imagine he had a well-toned body under an expensive suit.

Magical eyes, stunning physique, tailored suit, and neatly trimmed stubble. This overall combination made me realize he was *hot*, just like a book boyfriend.

Control yourself, girl! I put my diva back to sleep.

He was still waiting for a response.

"You work here?" *What am I asking?* Of course, he worked here. The guards knew him. That was why they let him in without a question.

He closed his eyes momentarily. "Yes, Miss Ahmed, I… work here."

Oh! He knows my name.

"I read your name from the badge you dropped."

Of course!

"Okay..." I answered. "Then you can tell me where The Maple Room is. I'm already running late, and my meeting invite doesn't show me the floor number."

"The Maple Room?" he asked as if hearing it for the first time.

"Yes, The Maple Room. You know where it is?" I wasn't sure if he was sure or not.

Once again, he briefly closed his eyes.

"Yes, I know where it is. I can take you there." He looked at me as if searching for something. No man had ever looked at me like that, as if I were some puzzle he wanted to solve. I felt his gaze travelling through my heart, unlocking all the doors to my soul.

"Well, thanks, Mr.…?" I didn't know his name.

"Adam," he said.

"Thank you very much, Mr.—"

"Just Adam." He pressed.

"Okay...Adam. I don't want you to be late for your work, but if you can tell me the floor, I can go by myself."

"No, Rania," he objected. "I don't have anything particular to do right now." He took a step toward me. "Consider it my pleasure."

With an alarmingly warm gesture, he read my face again. It made me conscious, and I shifted, taking a step back. *What's going on?* But I was already late, and I didn't want to start an argument.

"Thanks for your help. I really appreciate it." I had to say something nice; this was the best I could come up with. I put my finger on the call button for the elevator.

"SHIT." *Shit.*

We both cursed together. Our hands met on the call button, my hand over his, and I felt a sudden spark as if thousands of watts had surged through my veins. We both took a step back, electrocuted and stunned. Did he feel the spark?

Don't overthink, girl. It's November. The heating is on. It's just static and not a spark. And when was the last time you felt a spark?

What was I thinking? If he said he'd show me the room, then it was obvious he should call the elevator. Embarrassed, I said a silent prayer to either disappear from here or give him amnesia for a while.

Ting.

The elevator door opened, and we both stepped in, trying not to get electrocuted any further by each other's touch. I had not noticed earlier that there were others standing behind us, waiting with us.

As the elevator started to fill, he shifted to stand behind me. I could hear his breathing. His heart was beating loudly—or was it my heart? I couldn't tell. The elevator ascended, stopping at each level. Every person who entered the elevator smiled at the man behind me.

So, people do know him here.

When we reached the 45th floor, the elevator was vacated, except for the two of us. I noticed his reflection on the mirrored wall on my right. His eyes were closed as if he was trying to analyze something. He was still breathing hard, and I wondered if he was claustrophobic. He opened his eyes and met my gaze through the reflection.

I think I broke his concentration.

"We have almost reached the top," I said. "You forgot to press the floor." I tried to remain polite, not to undermine the situation.

He brought his head closer, behind my neck. "*Pleasures!*" he whispered. *What? What is he talking about?* I gaped at him. He closed his eyes again, tilting his face toward the ceiling. "You are wearing *Pleasures*. Right?"

My perfume? All this time, he was evaluating my perfume? Ignoring his olfactory skills, I finally gathered the courage to turn around and voice my frustration.

"Do you even know where to go?"

He looked down at the floor. "No."

"So, you were wasting my time?"

Unbelievable! He was entertaining himself all along.

First, he was enjoying my misery outside while I fought with the bolts, and then he kept my badge purposely and, without even asking me, grabbed me and pushed me through the security door. Was he playing an April Fool prank with me in November?

For a moment, I thought he was a gentleman when he offered to guide me, but all he could do was sniff behind me to figure out my perfume.

He just stared in return.

Without wasting more time, I pressed the ground-level button to return to where we started. I would ask the management for help or call someone from my team to find out where I should go. I shouldn't have trusted him.

He pressed the sub-basement button without a word. Luckily, the elevator descended from the 45th floor to ground level without stopping and wasting any more time. His eyes were still reading my face, trying to discover something.

The doors at the ground level opened, and without a backward glance, I moved forward. He held me by the elbow and pulled me back inside. The door closed again within seconds, the elevator descending to the lower level, the sub-basement.

What the hell!

"I told you I'll take you to your meeting," he grumbled. "Why can't you trust me?"

The doors of the elevator opened again at the lower level.

I was so struck by his act that I let him lead me out. At the end of the corridor, he gently released his grip.

"I'm sorry to delay your arrival, but I was preoccupied. Let's go. It's closer from here." Having no choice, I followed his lead, unsure what to say.

During our short walk, I noticed his expensive suit fitted elegantly on his masculine body. It was navy blue with an ice-blue shirt, accented with a matching tie. The outfit looked pricey, perhaps equivalent to my whole month's salary. His movement was elegant, as if he'd been raised as an overprivileged boy in a very expensive private school and had never seen hard days. His watch, wrapped on his left wrist, also looked very valuable. He must be spending a lot of money out of his salary just to look good. Perhaps he was not even on a payroll. Perhaps his daddy must have owned a company here, and he was here just to flaunt his wealth.

Stopping by another glass door, he swiped his badge on it

and headed toward another corridor.

It was quiet, and the only audible sound was our footsteps on the dark green carpet. We didn't speak at all.

At the end of the long passage, a double door opened to a very large room. The name 'The Maple Room' was written outside on the hardwood board, embossed with bronze letters. Both doors were wide open, and I spotted my team in there.

"Finally," he said with pride as if he had discovered a new country.

"Yes, finally. Thank you." I smiled at him.

"So, what is this all about?" Peeking inside the room, he asked with curiosity.

"It's a breakfast invitation for my team."

"Can I join you?" he asked bluntly. "I haven't eaten anything this morning." He took a gander inside the room again to check out the food. He looked quite serious.

Is he really hungry?

"I don't know if I'm supposed to bring people." He studied me intently, so I added, "I'm not sure what the protocols are at Gibson Enterprises."

I followed his gaze, wondering who he was looking for. With this suit and watch, I doubted he was telling the truth. But guilt and my values began to wage a war inside me. My grandmother would never have let anyone go on an empty stomach, and it was very rude of me to refuse breakfast to someone who confessed he was hungry.

"I'm sorry," I continued, "if you had come to my office, I'd have invited you for breakfast, but this place is new to me, too." I gave him an apologetic smile. "But…umm…" I started digging in my handbag and took out my travel mug and pumpkin bread from the bakery, which I hadn't had a chance to eat at all. "You can have this meanwhile. It's tea, though. Not sure if you take tea or coffee, and this is pumpkin bread, which I'm sure you'll like.

It's the best in town." He gaped as he looked down at the items. "And I haven't drank any tea," I added. "It is still hot, though. You don't need to warm it up. I already have this breakfast invitation, so you can have it."

Still stunned, he took the food from me.

"You don't need to apologize," he finally said. "I completely understand." He gave a boyish yet shy smile, which I found intriguing. "And thank you for breakfast. I really appreciate it. I'll return your mug soon." He peeked into the brown paper bag.

I turned to leave, but then I stopped, curious to know something. "If you don't mind, can I ask you something, Mr.—"

"Adam," he pressed. "Just call me Adam, please."

"Yes…umm…if you knew this place, why did you let the elevator go all the way up?"

He searched my face intently again.

"I don't know…" He shook his head. "I really don't know. You made me…" his gaze dropped to my lips, "lose my mind." He took a step forward. "I got carried away by your presence… by your…fragrance."

Huh?

I stared at him, baffled. No words of argument formed in my mouth.

"It was really nice meeting you, Rania," he added. "Enjoy your breakfast." He smiled—not shy this time and turned around.

Within seconds, he was out of my sight.

What the hell just happened?

CHAPTER 3
AT FIRST SIGHT

ADAM

W*HAT THE HELL JUST HAPPENED?*

"Sylvain, get in here immediately." Groaning at my personal assistant in a very unpleasant manner, I barged into my office.

"Is something wrong, Mr. Gibson?" she asked in a motherly tone.

Something wrong? I'm fucked up!

"There is some breakfast meeting or get-together in The Maple Room. Find out all the details about it—who is holding it. What it's about. Ask the security department to fetch me the list of invitees and the pictures from their security badges." I had never been so insistent about anything.

Sylvain scurried out of the room on high alert. Taking my seat behind the huge dark wooden desk, I swivelled the leather chair to face the view outside. My office was on the fifty-fourth floor. It felt powerful to take in the view and own a place so high, yet I felt so weak before her.

It had started raining again. It reminded me of that winter night, how the snow and light had glittered the city. That feeling hadn't occurred again. But the way my heart danced that night by meeting that mysterious girl, it danced again after seeing Rania.

She was undoubtedly the most beautiful woman I'd ever seen, and it was quite unsettling to me that she didn't give a fig about who I was. Was she truly an enchantress from some other world, or was she a part of the fantasy I had conjured in these past months? And all this time, in her presence, I was under a spell, unable to do or say anything sensible. Had we been in the Middle Ages, this would undoubtedly be witchcraft.

At the sight of her, my heart began racing like a pinball stuck in the arcade machine. It was the same feeling I had nine months earlier when I met the woman dancing. I could never forget how those ebony eyes looked at me from behind the mask.

Is she the same girl?

No, she couldn't be. That woman was celestial—the way she moved was not humanly possible. Rania was just a girl doing a regular job. There was magic in that enchantress, in her eyes, in her presence. Yet the same magic existed in Rania's eyes, too. And her fragrance, it was so familiar. The same scent that intoxicated me earlier when I had lost my mind. I lost it today, too. But wasn't it possible that so many women use the same perfume?

And the spark I felt when her hand touched mine, did she feel the same sensation?

I'd slept with so many women but never felt anything except fulfilling my bodily needs. I wondered how every part of my body ignited with the touch of her hand. What would it be like to be close to her? The explosion would surely kill me. And that death would be so much sweeter than this life.

What must she be thinking about me, a rude, self-centred man who didn't have the courtesy to help a woman? I could have called her back and given her the badge. What the hell was I thinking?

A knock at the door brought me back into the world of reality. I wasn't sure how much time had passed.

"Come in, Sylvain." I was expecting her.

"Mr. Gibson, I have the details," she began. "The meeting is organized by Ben Dynham, CEO of Greenway Advertising. Their office is on the thirteenth floor of this building. It is just a regular holiday breakfast for their creative teams. Their sales and marketing departments work from here, whereas the other departments, like *Creative Graphics* and *Creative Minds*, work at the Inwood International head office on Bloor Street. The meeting room is booked until 12:30 p.m., under Mr. Dynham's name." Sylvain looked proud to have delivered the information so quickly.

She handed me the list of invitees, which I immediately scrutinized. It included their employee and badge numbers, as well as their headshots.

"Is this why you texted and inquired about The Maple Room?" I looked up and met her soft gaze, but I couldn't say anything in return. As if reading my mind, she changed her words, "Anything else, Mr. Gibson?"

"Yes, send Ali in."

I studied the list. *There she is—Rania Ahmed.* It was very easy to locate her. How could someone look so pretty on a security badge? The rest of us looked like criminals on the loose.

Her eyes carried the same magic. Utterly and miserably lost in her beauty, I didn't realize when Ali stepped into the room. He must have knocked on the door, which I didn't hear in my trance. Dragging my eyes away from the paper, I placed it on the desk.

"This girl." I tapped my index finger on her picture. Ali looked intently, reading out her name. "I want her complete background check, where she lives, where she goes, her hobbies and activities, her job details, her weekly schedule, her relationships, her shopping interests. I want to know everything about her."

Surprised and dubious, Ali regarded me, probably considering me a psycho stalker, but he didn't say it.

Ali bin Moosa had been working with me and for my father for twelve years, almost as long as Sylvain. He was my father's right hand, and after his death, he started working for me. He was kind of a brother to me, although he was ten years older. An ex-army officer of Moroccan background with a tall, broad physique, he was a trained fighter and knew how to handle the most critical situations. He knew all my habits, my secrets, my interests. I always had my employees' backgrounds checked, but I had never been so aggressive about it. Not even about my clients with whom I do million-dollar deals.

"Adam," he said firmly. "You're asking things as if she's a spy. We are not in government security—"

"I know." I sighed and rubbed my eyes. "I just want to know her."

He smiled and pulled the chair opposite me. "I'm all ears." He placed his laptop on the table.

"I want you to find out about her first." Why was I nervous even confessing to Ali?

"By looking at the sheet, I assume she works here?"

"Not here." I glanced at her picture again. "She is attending some breakfast meeting in The Maple Room."

He sat back and smirked. "And you can't muster the courage to confront her."

"I'm not invited to that breakfast, Ali." I seethed. He wasn't making it any easier.

"Oh, now Adam Gibson," he said, looking around, "the CEO of Gibson Enterprises and apparently the owner of this building, cannot do what he pleases."

"It's unethical."

"And stalking her is?"

I rolled my eyes and got to my feet to look outside the window.

"Where is this all coming from?"

I took my time to answer. "I met her today outside the building. She and I were in the same elevator."

From the window reflection, I noticed Ali opening his laptop and typing something. "I'm listening," he said without looking up.

Sometimes, I wonder why I once hired a therapist if I had him to talk to. Would he understand that I had met someone who looked like Rania last February at a place that had never existed? Would he think I sounded like a madman?

"Don't think too much, Adam." He read my silence. "You don't have to carry this weight alone."

I shook my head. "She was so beautiful, Ali." I noticed his smile in the reflection, but he didn't meet my gaze. "And I stayed like a dumbass. I couldn't say anything."

"So, she made you nervous?"

I turned around and took the seat again. "I could not say the things I wanted to say."

"You can confess the girl made you nervous."

"You're not helping," I groaned.

"I'm trying to evaluate your state, Adam." He paused and looked up. "You haven't sounded like this before." I stared at him, speechless. "Now, think again. Were you nervous?" *Was I?* "Did your heart run fast at the sight of her?"

I looked away. I didn't know what to say, but I tried to form the words.

"I felt the world stopped," I recalled the moment when she looked up at me while she was collecting her stuff. "Everything else ceased to exist. I couldn't see anyone...anything...beside her." I exhaled a heavy sigh. "She was picking her stuff from the floor, and I just...I just stared and did nothing. I had this paralyzing feeling where my mind could not comprehend what was happening to me."

Ali pursed his lips to hide his smile.

"What?" I asked with irritation.

"Adam Gibson est en amour," he said in his French Moroccan accent.

"What nonsense!" I got to my feet again to avoid his attention. "There is no such thing as love at first sight."

"Then what's the rush?" He objected. "You know where she is right now. Be a man. Go and talk to her."

I turned to glare at him. "Are you even looking for what I asked?"

"Yes." He waved me to sit. "She works at Greenway Advertising as a creative graphics designer. It's her third year here. Before that, she'd worked with Gibbs & Gills as a software developer. She is a Software Engineering graduate from the University of Toronto. She had done some courses in digital media and printing."

"I could have found it from LinkedIn," I snapped.

Ali said nothing in return but looked intently at the screen. I didn't know what was taking his time.

"She lives in North York near the Finch station, in Archeries Condominiums. Apartment number 1609. The apartment is owned by Ben Dynham, which means she is renting it."

The name caught my attention. "What did you say? Who owns the apartment?"

"Ben Dynham. CEO of Greenway. Her rent is deducted from her salary. That's what it shows here."

I wonder what relationship she had with Ben Dynham to rent his apartment.

"She is originally from Lebanon," Ali continued. "Her father's name is Ahmed Al-Bari. He is a UN Secretariat, who now resides in Dubai."

I raised my eyebrow with surprise.

"It might please you that she has no siblings. She lives here alone."

Did it truly please me? That she lived on her own?

"She'll be turning twenty-six this January," he carried on. "I'll print her information if you want, but considering your state, I think you'll remember everything."

I rolled my eyes at his words.

"She isn't a Canadian citizen yet. And…" he trailed off.

"And?" I leaned forward.

"She doesn't have a driver's license, either."

"Really?"

"Not everyone can afford a car, Adam," he reprimanded.

"She can afford to live on her own," I objected.

"Yes. But look at the rent. It's not even half of what others pay in that building."

I pondered at Ali's words. Why would Ben Dynham rent out a place to his employee at a subsidized rate? "But she should have a photo ID."

"She can use her health card as a photo ID. Maybe she doesn't go anywhere."

"How is it possible to stay in one city and not go anywhere?"

"There are buses and trains."

I sat back at Ali's words. He had answers for everything.

"You may also find it interesting," he added, "that she attends a dance school in the evening."

"I assume you have the address?" He nodded. "Just text me then."

Ali closed his laptop. "Can I ask something?" I waited for him. "What's the point of all this? If you like her, go and introduce yourself and get to know her. She isn't your employee. You don't need to do her background check. Wouldn't it be simpler if you asked her out?"

I knitted my eyebrows.

"Take a conventional approach. A dinner invitation, perhaps?"

"Do you think she'd say yes?"

He chuckled. "Have you ever been rejected before?"

"But I haven't asked out anyone before."

"Point."

"What if she says no? I didn't leave a good first impression."

He gave a short laugh. "You are afraid of rejection." He sat back. "My god, Adam, you're in deep shit."

Just thinking about the idea of confronting her again made my heart race.

Ali waited for me to say something, but I didn't. He got to his feet, picking up his laptop as well. "Is there anything else you want?"

"Yes. Inform Mr. Dynham that I'll be joining the breakfast shortly."

Ali nodded and walked out of the office. I must go down before the meeting is over.

Showtime!

CHAPTER 4
STRANGER IN DISGUISE

RANIA

After that mysterious man left, I had a quick restroom trip before joining my team.

Ben Dynham, my boss, was engrossed in the conversation when I entered the room. He was one of my father's closest friends. They studied together at the University of Glasgow. Ten years ago, Ben moved to Canada and started his advertising firm. With many years of hard work, he had achieved the highest-profile corporate clientele in Canada, from large telecoms to winery businesses. I was proud of him. He'd always considered me as his daughter since he never had one of his own. Besides my father, he was the first man who held me after I was born.

As I took my seat, Ben came over to me.

"Good morning, princess. Where have you been?" He asked. "You missed my speech." He gave me his fatherly smile, reminding me of Baba so much.

"Oh, I…" I looked away. "I got stuck…in…umm…a situation." I wasn't sure if I should tell him about my accident.

"Did you take anything to eat?"

I shook my head.

"No skipping breakfast, okay?" He pressed like Baba.

"I'm not hungry right now," I answered. "But I'll have something in a while. Thanks for asking, Ben." I lost my appetite when I heard: *You made me lose my mind.*

A call on Ben's cell phone distracted him.

"Dynham speaking." He paused. "Yes. Okay." He listened to the person on the line. "Yes, of course. The pleasure is all mine. He is most welcome. Thank you for letting me know." Smiling, Ben shoved the phone back into his jacket pocket.

"Good news?"

"Oh, yes," he answered. "It was from Gibson Enterprises. Mr. Gibson will be coming here shortly to join us for breakfast. I'm delighted." He took a vacant seat next to me.

"That's nice. You have tried so many times to reach out to him." Having a client like Gibson Enterprises was a dream for Ben.

"Exactly," he conceded. "I'm surprised he's finally agreed to meet me. He is a very private man, and he doesn't go anywhere unless it benefits him. If he is coming, I'm sure he's considered giving us some projects."

I smiled at his optimism.

"Have you considered attending the seminar in New York?"

"I haven't applied for the visa yet," I answered.

"Do it this week."

Ben wanted me to attend a seminar where private business owners and entrepreneurs gather yearly to showcase their work and contributions to the advertising world. It had always been a big event, and Ben made many contacts for his company. Last year, it was a conference on animation in the media world. This year, they would showcase graphics in e-magazines and e-catalogues, which was my expertise. Ben was doing me a big favour to boost my career.

When Ben left the seat, I began chatting with my colleague about the current project. Suddenly, I sensed someone standing by the entrance door.

It was him.

What is he doing here?

I got to my feet and met him at the door.

"What are you doing here?" I grumbled, evidently annoyed. "I told you I can't bring people in here."

"Oh, I'm sorry," he said, "I came to return this and say thank you." He handed me the mug, his sweet, husky voice melting all my annoyance. "The bread was really good, like you said."

"You didn't have to. It was okay."

"Rania..." Ben appeared from nowhere, putting his arm around my shoulder. "You know Mr. Gibson?"

I looked up at the green-eyed man with an open mouth. *Shit.* I wanted to disappear. God must have a weird sense of humour.

"Adam Gibson." He extended his hand to me for a friendly shake.

God, bury me, please.

Speechless, I gave my hand to him.

I imagined the CEO of Gibson Enterprises as an old, bald man in his late sixties. But he was...

"Yes, Mr. Dynham. We met recently...in a...very interesting situation." Adam winked at me wickedly, still holding my hand in his.

Ben shifted his gaze from Adam to me, his eyes carrying thousands of questions. I pulled my hand from Adam's firm grip, returning Ben a foolish smile.

"I was looking for the meeting room," I explained to Ben, glancing at the overly sexy man. "Mr. Gibson was kind enough to guide me here." I looked down at my shoes, wishing to disappear.

"You're very welcome here, Mr. Gibson," Ben added, sounding hospitable yet nervous. "It is a great honour for our firm that you joined us for breakfast. Some journalists and photographers are also here. I hope you don't mind if they cover you for this event." This handsome young man, who was holding my hand a minute ago, was a gold mine to Ben. He wanted to make the most of this acquaintance.

Though our firm had an office here in Gibson's building, Ben had never gotten a chance even to meet Adam Gibson personally. He'd been trying to get Gibson's company as a corporate client for years, and this seemed to be his only chance. I already knew from his expression what he would ask me in the future.

"I wouldn't mind at all," Adam answered, "But before any photographs, I'd be honoured if Miss Ahmed accompanied me for breakfast." He looked at me. "You owe me one." *Good, Lord!* "I asked earlier if I could join, but she refused. You should be proud your employees follow all the protocols."

Could this be more embarrassing? I just wanted to vanish from here.

Ben looked at me horridly at how I'd dared to prohibit Adam Gibson from attending the breakfast as if it was a major offence to say *no* to this man.

"I apologize on her behalf, Mr. Gibson—"

"You don't have to," Adam interrupted.

"Of course, Mr. Gibson," Ben said. "Rania, why don't you escort Mr. Gibson to the buffet table?" He forced a smile at me, silently passing an order like a boss. "Mr. Gibson, please enjoy your breakfast. I'll see you shortly."

Ignoring Ben's order, I left the conversation without bothering to look back. Adam followed me like my shadow. I handed him an empty plate with the cutlery. I could feel him watching me intently.

What does he want from me?

I had nothing to offer him. Whenever our eyes met, I felt he wanted to ask me something.

"Would you like some pancakes, Mr. Gibson?" I asked without turning to him.

"Yes, thank you. And please call me Adam." He moved up close behind me, whispering in my ear. "I insist."

Space! I need some space.

He was so close that if I dared to turn around, we would end up touching each other. I pretended to ignore this closeness. I didn't even have the courage to look around to see if anybody was watching us. I knew how the media scavenge like vultures, seeking for gossip.

"I thought you ate the pumpkin bread," I mumbled, turning to meet his gaze.

"I'm always yearning for more," he answered in an undertone. "You have no idea how greedy and voracious I am." He searched my face. I averted my eyes and moved a few steps to the side, creating distance between us. He closed the gap again, watching me intently.

"You're not eating anything?" He inquired, perhaps noticing that I wasn't taking anything for myself. Did he think my stomach wouldn't have knots after all that had just happened?

"I had it already, but thanks for asking. Do you want a muffin?" I picked a blueberry muffin.

Glancing at the muffin, he smiled. "You don't need to ask every time you pick something. Fill me with whatever your heart desires."

Okay!

He was too much to take in. I had met many flirtatious men, but no one had ever talked to me like that. They could all read the 'not interested' sign on my face. Why was this man different? Why couldn't he read that sign?

"Are you sure you'll finish all this?" I added a scone. "It is not nice to waste food. There are some parts of the world where people are dying of hunger."

When he didn't say anything in return, I turned my head to look at him. He was just staring—stunned.

I looked away and picked a croissant. "Still want it?"

He blinked as if coming out of a trance and shook his head.

I should have realized that he ran this empire. He owned this place. He could come and go anywhere he wanted. No wonder the security guards didn't question him. And I pushed him away when he *got carried away.* I realized he didn't lie. He spoke his mind.

"Can I ask you something, if you don't mind?" he asked, his voice dipped in honey. I remained quiet, pouring coffee for him. "Please look at me, Rania. I'm talking to you." I looked up, meeting his inquisitive gaze. He was standing close to me, very close. I didn't say anything; just let him continue. "Have we met before?"

"You think so?" I looked away.

"You look so…familiar. Your eyes… I've seen those eyes before," he added, leaning against the corner of the buffet table.

"That's cheesy." I rolled my eyes at him.

"I'm serious," he scowled.

"Mr. Gibson. There are almost seven billion people in this world. You think God will not repeat the eyes?" He opened his mouth to say something, but I continued, "And a theory suggests that there are seven more faces similar to each of ours."

He moved from the table and closed the distance between us. The coffee cup started to shake in my hand.

What's he going to say?

"The eyes holding a thousand secrets…" he whispered, out of everyone's earshot, "they cannot be in a population of seven billion. This maddening darkness doesn't exist anywhere else. Please tell me if we've ever met before."

Noticing my hand shaking, he took the cup from me.

"I didn't even know your name. How can you ask if we've met?" I picked up another cup and poured tea for myself. "We are not in a club, Mr. Gibson, where you use your pickup line."

He handed me the milk pot, his eyes still studying me. I added milk and sugar to my tea and turned around.

Ben was looking at us skeptically.

Oh, crap!

I wasn't interested in any more interrogation. As Ben approached, Adam took two steps back to give us space. I took a deep breath, relieved.

Ben asked me to join him and Adam. I didn't have a bloody choice, did I? He led us to an empty table, and we sat down, me facing Adam across the table.

"Why are you skipping your breakfast again?" Ben asked as he noticed I didn't sit with a plate. "Let me bring something for you."

He was about to get up again when Adam pushed his plate toward me. "Don't bother, Mr. Dynham. She'll share it with me."

All eyes in the room turned in our direction. If somehow my cup of tea could become a well, I wished to drown in it. I had no room to reject his offer, so I quietly picked a scone.

When Adam made sure I took a bite, he began. "So, Mr. Dynham. How come your marketing team is here, and your creative team is operating from another location?" He looked at me specifically when he said *creative*. Did he already know which department I worked for?

Ben tried to read my uneasiness, curious if he was missing something.

"Mr. Gibson, I always wanted my company to operate from one location," he answered, "I mean this one. But the office space is all occupied here. We have half of the thirteenth floor, and the Petersons Law firm has the other half. If they ever vacate, we'd snap up that space."

Adam took a sip of his coffee. His posture was slightly tilted toward Ben, his right elbow resting on the table. He rubbed his lower lip with his index finger, thinking something. I guess this was his habitual gesture of contemplation. He finally looked up with a slight curve to his lips.

"I want your creative people to work from this location, Mr. Dynham," Adam announced. "If you're interested in doing business with us."

Ben's jaw dropped in surprise. I blinked at Adam for what he was saying. It seemed that if Ben wanted Gibson's business, we must all move in here. He and I, working under the same roof—unbelievable! His presence had already made me a nervous wreck. *How can I…?*

"How soon can you move in here?" asked Adam. "I can vacate the entire floor for you. We can sign the lease later. Move in first, and then we will further discuss business prospects and—"

A phone call interrupted him.

"Excuse me, please…" He accepted the call, showing his mild irritation. Absently, I twisted my ring around my index finger, but when I looked up, I noticed him studying me and then my ring, though he was on the phone.

Ben had apparently noticed the way he was staring.

"Yes? Good. I'll see you shortly." He ended the call. He was smiling. Something pleasant had obviously happened.

"Please excuse me," I announced as I got to my feet. "I need to use the ladies' room." I needed an excuse to get the hell out of here.

"And please excuse me, too. I've got to attend an urgent meeting," Adam said and joined me. Ben walked us to the door.

"Mr. Gibson, thank you very much for joining us," Ben exclaimed as if it was still unbelievable for him to meet Gibson. "It is an absolute honour to have you with us. If you don't mind, can we have a photograph together?"

It was a perfect time to slip out of here. So, I moved toward the door.

"Miss Ahmed, please join us," Adam said.

I closed my eyes for a moment and turned. Both the men were waiting for my answer. I must smile back. I had no other option, did I?

Ben waved at a photographer from some business magazine. I stood between Ben and Adam. The photographer asked us to move closer. Adam shifted slightly toward me, crowding me, and I lost my balance. He grabbed me by my waist as if he knew I was going to fall.

"Hey, you okay?"

I didn't expect him to be this considerate.

"Yes. Thanks." I straightened my posture. His hand was still on my back, and it didn't seem like he was planning to move it. It wasn't fair that he could send electricity up my spine with just his touch.

The photographer did his work and left.

"Thank you again, Mr. Gibson." Ben shook hands with Adam. "We will not take up any more of your precious time. We all look forward to working with your prestigious company." He was *really* looking forward to this opportunity, and I knew he would never put it at risk for any reason.

"I also look forward to it, Mr. Dynham." Adam's eyes met mine briefly. *Is he checking me out?* "My secretary will get in touch with you for the next step." Before I decided to step away, he turned to me. "Can I have a word with you, Miss Ahmed?"

Good, lord! He is so blunt.

I glanced at Ben, who nodded with approval and yet sent a silent warning not to disappoint him.

"Please come." I forced a smile. I had a feeling that Ben would use me to get this business, like bait. I didn't like this idea. He had always treated me like his daughter.

I headed quickly toward the elevator, where Ben could not see me.

"What do you want to talk about?" I folded my arms over

my chest, showing my annoyance as I leaned against the wall beside the elevator. "Weren't you late for your urgent meeting?"

He put one hand on the wall over my head, blocking the view from The Maple Room should anyone happen to be looking at us.

Diving into my eyes as if searching for something, he said, "Why are you doing this to me? What have I done to deserve this?"

Our eyes locked, and at that moment, I realized he was really desperate to know me.

"What did I do, Mr. Gibson?" I kept my tone very professional.

"You know what I'm talking about. If it's about the elevator incident, then I'm sorry."

I blinked at him but didn't say anything.

"Or if it's about how ungentlemanly I acted and didn't offer to help…"

I rolled my eyes.

"Is it because you don't like me?"

I looked away.

"You are purposely ignoring me. You don't look at me when you talk. I feel like you're trying to run away from me. Do I intimidate you?" His appeal sounded more like a silent prayer.

I didn't realize at first that his other hand was on my face, lifting my chin so I could look him in the eye. There was no sexual intention. No lust. Just a request.

At his touch, my heart started to beat very loudly.

"I'm not comfortable talking to strangers, Mr. Gibson," I mumbled. "I hardly know you."

"Then let's get to know each other," he answered hurriedly. "I want to know you. Everything about you. How about lunch together today? Let me take you out somewhere."

Is he asking me out? Say something, Rania, before…

"We just had breakfast." I moved away from him, and this

time, he took his hands off me.

"How about coffee… umm… juice?" Noticing my silence, he added, "Ice cream?" He sounded really desperate.

"I have work, Mr. Gibson. I cannot delay it." I looked around the corridor and saw Ben standing in the doorway. Perhaps he'd been watching us all this time. I didn't care what he might be thinking.

"How about dinner tonight, then?" He was unstoppable. *Why doesn't the day end at lunchtime?* Was he incapable of hearing rejection? I hardly knew him, and there was no reason why I should let him. I had handled many in the past. I knew how to push men away. I was good at it.

"I have plans," I answered, looking down as I twisted the ring on my finger. I didn't want him to catch my lie.

"What plans?" His tone changed immediately, scowling.

"I have my personal life as well, Mr. Gibson. Goodbye."

And I escaped from his gaze and ran into the ladies' room. I didn't even care if Ben had seen us. I was sure Adam wanted me. There was desperation in those green eyes. He'd ask me out to dinner, and then he'd lure me to visit his place, and eventually, he'd use me as his fucking toy and toss me aside. By now, he should know I was not that girl, one who would drool over his bank balance and kiss the ground he walked on.

Not a chance!

BEN WAS WAITING FOR ME AT THE doorway when I returned from the washroom.

I took a lot of sweet time to brace myself. I had a feeling that Adam wouldn't take rejection easily, and on the other hand, I feared Ben would be expecting something preposterous from me.

"Would you care to tell your uncle what just happened?" He scowled.

"There is nothing to say."

"You didn't have the courtesy to tell me he was coming here?" Anger simmered in his eyes.

"I didn't know." I averted my gaze, glancing down at my boots, hoping to disappear once again. "I thought he only showed up to return my travel mug."

"He came all the way here to return your mug?" He raised his eyebrow, clearly not buying this. "That's it? And how did he get it?" I felt like I was back in high school when my father learned about my prom date.

"We met in the lobby," I explained, wondering if he could read my chaotic thoughts. "I told you. I was searching for the room location in my email, and he offered to guide me. When we reached here, he asked me if he could come in. Since he was a stranger, I told him I had to abide by corporate policy and that I could not bring him in without permission. So, I offered him my tea and bread in case he was hungry." I skipped the entire embarrassing situation at the turnstile.

"Are you kidding me, Rania?" Ben gaped. "You were trying to feed someone who feeds thousands of people daily?" I opened my mouth to argue, but he continued, "Come and sit. We need to talk." Taking my hand, he guided me to the corner table close to the doorway. "I'll not ask what happened between you two. I figured out you were unaware that he is Adam Gibson." He smiled. "I guess your kindness has smitten him."

"Smitten? I—"

"You didn't notice how he was looking at you? Open your eyes, girl," he added, not sounding like my father now. "He looked like a lovestruck fool." *Oh, come on!* "Now, listen to me very carefully." Ben scooted forward, his voice lowering a few decibels. Feeling a chill down my spine, I had some intuition about what he wanted to say. "You know how much I wanted Gibson's name on my profile. This opportunity has come to me on a gold platter. A single mistake from you could have ruined everything." His tone was threatening. When it came to business, Ben was uncle to no one.

"What did I do?" I snapped.

"I saw what you were doing in the corridor. You were pushing him away—"

"What exactly are you expecting from me?" I interrupted, suddenly angry.

"I'm not asking anything. Just go with the flow." Ben had never spoken to me like this. I stayed quiet, regarding the table, while he continued, "Rania, you're like my child. I know my son loves you, and I've always accepted you as my future daughter-in-law. But I can see you don't feel the same for Mike. He is no more than a friend to you."

Ben's words were nothing but the truth, but they still twisted something inside me.

"I've seen how miserable Mike gets when he is drunk and cursing your name some nights," he continued. "I don't blame you for breaking his heart because you never made any promises to him. It was always one-sided." I looked up at him to understand what he was trying to say. "I have been quiet, but I won't now." I tried to grasp his meaning. "This business is my baby, more than my son. Mike is a grown-up, and I know he can look after himself emotionally. But this baby needs me. I've given my heart and soul to it."

He sat back.

"You refused to go out with Gibson. Why?"

Why? He, of all people, is asking me this? Like he doesn't know why I push men away.

"He doesn't like to be treated like that, Rania," he added. "He is a private man. He never approaches women. He never had to. If this is his first time pursuing a woman, you should give him the benefit of the doubt." He paused for a moment.

"And he could be dangerous. If you provoke him, it could hurt my business. Do you understand me?" I nodded. "So, if he asks you out again, would you agree? For your Uncle Ben?"

I looked down at my lap, noticing Ben holding my hand. "He will not ask me again if he is a man of principles." I looked up past Ben to the corridor, ignoring his watchful gaze.

"You don't think he would? What if—"

Ring ring!

A phone call on Ben's Blackberry interrupted us. He answered it.

"Ben Dynham speaking. Yes? Really? That sounds great. Yes. I'll check my email…sure, I'll forward…thank you…" Ending the call with a smile, he shook his head with amusement. "You were right, Rania. He *is* a man of principles." He studied my baffled face. "You spurned him, and he took another route, a very prudent one." Ben was still shaking his head in bewilderment.

"What are you talking about?"

"He has arranged a party in honour of Greenway and Gibson doing business together. Can you believe it?"

What? It was ridiculous to throw a party just to see me. Why not just ask me out again?

"When is the party?"

My curiosity brought a smile to his face. "Tonight. Fairmont Royal York. 7:00 p.m. They will be emailing us shortly. I'll forward the invitation to all my employees. We are *all* invited." He emphasized just to ensure I didn't make an excuse.

Without arguing, I pushed back my chair to stand up. Collecting my travel mug and my jacket, I headed to the door.

"Leaving already?" he asked.

"I'm taking the rest of the day off."

Without waiting for his response, I left the room to clear my head.

I STEPPED OUTSIDE THE GIBSON BUILDING, embracing the cold November breeze. After this morning, I needed some time alone.

I looked around, examining Gibson's stones and decorative bolts, where I'd first glimpsed those green eyes. Some extraordinary messages had emitted from them. I had never felt like that—the fluttering in the stomach, the tingling nerve endings, the quickening of the heartbeat. What was happening to me?

With his big emerald eyes, dark brown hair, sharp features, and extremely seductive appearance, he was an angel in the guise of a man. There was something pulling me toward him. He was affectionate, so why did I push him away? There was no harm in asking out someone. He didn't know my past. He didn't know my reservations, so he didn't hesitate.

I'd tried to avoid him, but his scorching gaze had wrecked all the doors in my heart that I had closed long ago. He did not even knock at the doors. He was battering them down without my permission, and it was very hard for me to let him do such a thing.

He was like a forbidden fruit, attracting everyone around him into the paradise of pleasure. I knew the consequences of trying this fruit, but still, I was tempted to take the risk.

Inhaling the cold air, I headed to the Starbucks at the corner of the street. It was about time I did some research on Adam Gibson. I purchased hot chocolate, sat in the corner, and opened my phone. I searched for his name on the browser, and lots of interesting results showed up.

A source mentioned that he had disparate views about women. In one of his interviews, he claimed that a woman's body is only meant for a man's pleasure and nothing else. *What a bigot!* Why should a man entangle himself in the complexity of a relationship if women are readily available to him? I couldn't believe they published all this nonsense.

I closed my eyes, recalling his eyes on me, and it sent shivers down my spine.

Was he looking at me to satiate his hunger? To charm me with his wealth and then take me to bed.

The thought filled me with abhorrence. I would never let him seduce me. I swore in my heart.

He is a very dangerous man. Ben's words rang an alarm in my ears. I searched more about his personal life, but I believe it had been kept very private. He'd been spotted with some women at the parties and leaving with them, but not a real date. No blog or article showed he ever had any steady relationship.

One newspaper mentioned that he was the youngest business magnate in Canada, a mogul in construction and development. He built houses, high-rise condominiums, resorts, five-star hotels, schools, and community centers throughout Ontario.

I didn't know why I was interested in his personal life, but I wanted to know if he was a self-made man or if he'd inherited this business. Going through his public profile, I learned that his father started his career as a builder of private homes. He wanted his son to be an architect so he could expand the business. Adam's father died of a heart attack when Adam was twenty-three, just as he'd finished his university studies, leaving an immature business to his son. With his creativity and intelligence, Adam rode his father's dream to the highest level, and in nine years, he touched the skies. His father must be proud of him from up there.

Another article mentioned that he was only six when his mother left his father and married another man, taking their younger daughter, who was two months old at the time. I felt sorry for Adam. How did he live without a mother as a six-year-old? Who would have been there to tuck him into bed? Who would have been there to tell him bedtime stories? Who would have comforted him when he woke up frightened in the middle of the night?

I had been trying to cope with my mother's loss all these years, but losing your loved one is a grief that chases you like a shadow. It goes everywhere with you. And in Adam's case, his mother was here but not here for him.

He was Adam Gibson now—a man with attitude, power, and unlimited wealth. I wondered if he ever met his mother again.

As I slid through my browser, one link caught my attention. *"A man with an altruistic soul."*

I opened the link, and the article flabbergasted me. A few years earlier, he donated fifty acres of land to the municipality of Toronto and constructed a vast state-of-the-art community center to provide shelter to the homeless. More than three hundred people come and eat daily at Gibson's expense. In addition to the shelter home, the community center holds all kinds of religious activities, whether it is Christians' prayers, Muslims' Salat, Jews' Siddur, or Hindus' worship services—it accommodates all.

Putting the phone down, I sat back, thinking about him. He was donating an extreme amount of wealth from his treasure box to the needy and afflicted. It was heartwarming. My perception of him was beginning to change. He was creating his own space in my heart.

It was too much information for me to absorb in a day. No matter how dangerous he was, I wasn't afraid of him anymore.

He had a heart.

He had a soul.

I LEFT STARBUCKS TO TAKE A LONG WALK. The flavour of the Holiday Season was already filling up the city, adorning it with beautiful decorations of garlands and Christmas trees. Since I told

Ben I was taking the rest of the day to blow off all my agitation, I decided to be a kid once again and visit Santa Parade.

University Avenue was crowded with hundreds of families who were waiting for Santa to arrive. Groups of senior citizens were singing Christmas carols with jingle bells and giving away candies. I agreed with the song being played from somewhere close by—it was truly the most wonderful time of the year. The whole street was blocked in honour of the parade. People were standing on the sidewalks, kids riding in strollers, couples walking hand in hand.

I closed my eyes to engross in the atmosphere. I inhaled the sweet scent of pine, baked cookies, and all the flavours of Christmas, recalling my childhood days when Mike and I used to visit malls to see Christmas décor back in Lebanon. How beautiful those days were. My mother made sure Mike never felt sad for not having a mother.

I time travelled back in the past, with beautiful, innocent days. As time passed in my memory, a dark shadow invaded my thoughts. But Adam's face appeared out of nowhere, and the shadow dissipated in a flick of a moment.

Before I could open my eyes to end my daydreaming, something hit me, knocking me to the ground. But I didn't land on the pavement—strong arms held me tight as I landed on something that cushioned my fall.

I was so lost in my other world that it took me a moment to fathom my surroundings.

"Are you fuckin' blind?" I heard a very familiar voice. When I opened my eyes, I found myself lying on Adam Gibson.

We were both on the concrete sidewalk, his arm around me. *Where did he come from?*

I stared at him, speechless and disoriented. He shifted to a sitting position, still holding me tight.

I tried to take in my surroundings. He brushed my hair

away from my cheeks and gently cupped my face with his warm hands. There was never enough space for me to breathe when he touched me.

The last thing I recalled was that I had closed my eyes and wandered off in my fiction fog when someone pushed me. Now, I was in his arms.

How did it happen?

"Are you okay?" There was pure gentleness in his voice. I tried to catch my breath. He tucked my hair behind my ears. "Talk to me. Are you hurt?"

He was treating me like a toddler lost in a parade, and now her father was here to rescue her. He released me as I shifted away from him. He was still concerned, his eyes observing my every expression.

"What are you doing here?" I asked, annoyed.

That's rude, Rania!

He gaped in disbelief. I could have said something better.

"Didn't you see the biker coming your way? You were standing right in his path. He could have hurt you." His expression changed again back to concern. I wonder why anyone would be biking in November here, but students find many ways to commute. I'd been there.

"No, I…I didn't see anything…I…" I looked around, trying to avoid his worried look. How could I tell him that he invaded my thoughts?

"He was calling you to move. Didn't you hear him?" With mild agitation, he got to his feet and grabbed my arm to haul me up. I didn't know what to say, so it was better to shut up. Noticing my knees shaking, he held me by the elbow. "Come, sit here." He guided me to the bench, where we sat together.

I closed my eyes momentarily, trying to calm my tattered nerves. What was I thinking? Why was I standing in the bikers' lane with my eyes and ears closed? And on top of that, I reacted like a spoiled, mannerless woman.

Knowing he was still there, I opened my eyes and turned to him. "Are you following me?"

"Yes…no…I mean…I…" he stuttered. "I saw you standing there as if you weren't aware of your surroundings. Then I saw the biker coming your way and heard him warning you to move. But you weren't listening, so I moved you out of the way. I hope you're not hurt." He checked my elbows and turned his head to check my back for injuries.

"But what are you doing here?"

Oh, Rania, is that all you can say? Have you forgotten to thank the person who saved you?

"You're very welcome," he said, pursing his lips to stifle his smile, making me realize that I was a rude and stubborn girl, and instead of having the courtesy to thank him, I was asking a dumb question and scowling at him. After all, it's a free country. He could visit any place. It was his damn right.

I looked around the parade, noticing how people stared at us as if we were some celebrity couple.

"Umm…I'm sorry," I mumbled, sounding evidently nervous. "Thank you…for saving me." Lips still twitching in a smile, he regarded me with his intense green eyes. "But really, what are you doing at the Santa Parade? I thought you had a meeting."

"I came to…see you."

Why?

"I thought you were still at work," he went on, "And then Mr. Dynham told me you took the rest of the day off." He checked my every single expression as if trying to wrack through my mind.

"How in the world did you know I was here?" I slid away. "Wait! Are you stalking—"

"No, no, please, don't think like that." His mouth slacked as he mumbled in an apologetic manner. "I came down to the room to talk to you and apologize for my behaviour in the corridor. So, I met your boss on my way and inquired about you. He told me you have taken a day off, so I—"

"But I didn't tell him where I was going."

Is he stalking me?

"Oh." He looked away. "I tracked your phone and—"

"Rania! Hey, look here!" I heard my name being called from somewhere in the crowd. I looked around to see where the familiar voice was coming from. Ignoring Adam, as I was seriously pissed, I searched for the voice. Was this the way to apologize to someone? Tracking them down through their phone?

I headed to the voice.

"Oh my God! Mike?" I shrieked and cut through the crowd. My best friend was standing there, and I hadn't seen him in three months. He had gone on some special police training to Calgary. I missed him so much, and the happiness in his eyes told me he'd missed me, too. Feeling like an elated toddler, I ran to hug him tightly.

"Oh, Mike," I exclaimed, "it's so good to see you. How come you're here?"

"I missed you so much," he answered, returning a warm bear hug that always feels like home. "I came this morning, and they assigned me to monitor the parade. I saw you sitting with a guy, so—"

"I'm so happy to see you. Does Ben know you are here?" I interrupted before he asked me about *him*. I hope he didn't see me and Adam lying on the ground. That would be too embarrassing.

"No, Dad doesn't know yet. I was caught up at work." Mike's gaze shifted, noticing Adam standing next to me.

Ben's words rang in my head like an alarm—that I should be easy on Adam, or else I'd end up spoiling his business. I glanced at Adam, forcing an awkward smile. He returned the gesture, his eyes inquisitive.

"Mike, sorry," I said. "This is Mr. Gibson. And Mr. Gibson… this is Mike, my friend." Looking at each other curiously, the two men shook hands.

"Pleasure meeting you, Mr. Gibson. You look very familiar." He studied Adam. "Are you the one who donated—"

"Yes, I assume you're talking about the one who builds houses?" Adam interrupted.

"Your reputation precedes you, Mr. Gibson. The donations—"

"Pleasure meeting you," Adam interrupted.

I wonder why Adam didn't let him finish the donation part. I wanted to know if it was true, if he truly donated such a large tract of land.

"It's surprising to know you've cops as your friends." Adam turned to me. "I should be more cautious, then."

I could sense Mike's curiosity. He was only waiting for Adam to leave.

"I didn't know Rania had friends other than me," answered Mike, showing his disapproval.

Friends? He thinks Adam is my friend.

Could this be more embarrassing than the morning accident?

"Ah!" Adam chuckled. "I hadn't been much lucky to gain her trust."

His gaze read me like an open book from head to toe. Whenever he looked at me like that, I felt a thousand watts of current running down my spine.

Pride was evident on Mike's face, whereas Adam looked like a wounded dragon, whom I had stabbed directly in his heart with a big sharp dagger.

Or is it just my poor imagination?

"I know I'm the luckiest man on this planet," Mike conceded.

How do I explain Mike? He'd been good to me all these years. He was my only friend and perhaps my only family now.

And the cherry on top, he was good-looking and sexy. Whenever I hung out with him, I noticed many feminine eyes on him with desperation. Girls asked him out for a date, but he never gave someone a second chance. I knew he loved me, but the kind of love he expected in return—I couldn't give him that. He knew I could not love anyone. I could not *afford* to love anyone.

I had never seen Mike jealous of a man because he knew me. Today, I could sense his jealousy, but what was more interesting was the same jealousy in Adam's eyes, too.

Am I thinking too much?

"Let's hang out tonight, baby," Mike said with a sexy tone, pulling me in his embrace. "It's been so long. I missed you so much." He'd never used that tone to me before. I noticed Adam's obvious glare, but I didn't know why he was jealous. He was famous as a womanizer, and there was no way I was letting myself be one of his extra flavours.

I shifted away from Mike, taking his hands off me.

"Tonight would not be possible." I glanced at Adam. "I have something official to attend. But tomorrow night? I promise."

"Sure, girl. Anything for you." Mike kissed my forehead lightly. "I'll call you. I must get back to my duty now. See you." Mike's friendly kiss didn't affect me, but Adam's eyes on me burned me from the inside. "Pleasure meeting you, Mr. Gibson."

Adam forced a smile as they shook hands. Mike disappeared into the crowd, leaving Adam and I and our words hanging in the air.

Before we could say anything to each other, I heard the crowd cheering. I turned around, noticing people welcoming Santa. In all this chaos, I missed the entire parade. It was sadly about to end. Ignoring Adam, I joined the crowd, taking my phone out to make a video.

When the crowd started to disperse, I shoved the phone back in my pocket and turned to Adam.

"You looked like an innocent child when you were looking at Santa." He stepped closer, lowering his head as he smiled. "As if you had a secret wish to tell him."

Is he a mind reader?

His question made me nervous as I twisted the ring on my index finger.

"Santa Claus doesn't exist. It's a fiction created for children's imagination to make wishes." I looked toward the parade.

"And I feel you also have a wish?"

He was totally oblivious that people passing by were noticing us. It was too obvious. I wasn't going to share any wish with him, though the wish did exist.

Not waiting for my answer, Adam continued, "You seem to like all this?" He looked around the area.

"I enjoy everything about the Holiday Season. The colours, the décor, the glitter, how the trees and houses light up in the dark." I took a deep breath, inhaling the aroma of fresh cinnamon and hot chocolate from the nearby cart. "The lights at night tell us that no matter how much darkness there is, only the light can dispel it." Adam listened with undivided attention. "Everyone likes it, Mr. Gibson. Can't you see everyone here, already in a festive mood?"

His gaze turned a darker shade of green.

Taking a few steps back from me, he closed his eyes briefly, shaking his head. "No, Rania, I can't see…I can't see people…" He shook his head again.

What is he saying?

Regarding me again, he continued, "When you're around…I can't see anything…other than you."

Stepping back further, he turned around and disappeared into the crowd.

Shit! What was that?

CHAPTER 5
THE PARTY

ADAM

"THE PROPERTY WE PURCHASED last year has made us an enormous profit." Our corporate lawyer, Tom McKenzie, clinked his champagne glass with mine.

"Toast to the Abyss resorts," I announced. "The Northern Ontario market is booming higher than our expectations. We should look for more land to build high-end luxury resorts. I want to promote more tourism in the province."

Glancing at the doorway, my heart stopped beating. Time froze as she entered the room. *Beautiful!* She looked around like an innocent child entering a magical kingdom for the first time. But the truth was, all the magic was in her. A gorgeous Christmas present, wrapped in a demure red lace dress, she was a holiday treat I'd want to hold on to forever.

I tracked her heading toward Ben Dynham. As he checked his watch, he asked her something. She was almost an hour late. I wanted to ask what took her so long, but it was better to ask Ali later. I texted her a few hours ago but got no response, which was an untold rejection on its own.

After a minute, I realized I wasn't the only one who was

attracted to her. She was a head-turning beauty. Men were gazing at her like hawks, and I felt like kicking all of them out of this party.

A man approached her, asking for a dance. She refused. I was pleased I wasn't the only one being turned down, though I hadn't even tried my luck.

What am I? A fucking teenager?

A few minutes later, some other prick asked her for a dance. Then another, and a few minutes later, another. *I should start counting.*

Chuckling, I invested my attention in finding out how many men she would reject tonight. Among the four hundred guests, no woman was as captivating and alluring as she was. I was too afraid to try my luck. She finally noticed me and excused herself from the conversation she was in to come over and say hello.

"Hi." She offered a handshake with a charming smile. For the first time, in all those dazzling lights, I noticed she had dimples on both cheeks.

I realized I'd never seen them this morning because she never smiled at me. My heart bounced like a ping-pong ball in my chest. I hoped she didn't hear it.

"You look…" I failed to find the appropriate words. "You look… beautiful… I—"

"Thank you, Mr. Gibson, for your hospitality," she replied. "And thank you for sending your special man to pick me up." She looked around nervously at the other guests.

"The pleasure is all mine, Rania. And please remember my name. It's Adam." That seemed to make her more nervous. We were interrupted by a server carrying a champagne tray. "Would you like something to drink? We have some special—"

"I'm sorry, I don't drink," she interrupted, glancing at the server.

"Sure. Tea then?" She smiled, shaking her head, perhaps

recalling what I'd wanted her to remember.

"No, thank you, Mr. Gibson… umm… I mean, Adam. I'll certainly ask if I need something later. Thanks for offering, though." She gave me another smile, looking away.

So, she is shy!

The music changed in the background, and the crowd moved to the dance floor. She watched the couples dancing with admiration, oblivious that I was admiring her.

"Your fragrance…" *will screw me one day.* I closed my eyes momentarily to breathe and continue, "…is heavenly." She gave me a bashful smile, looking past my shoulder. "Rania." She met my gaze. "If you don't mind, can I ask you for a dance?"

I embraced myself for the rejection. *Don't say no, don't say no.* I recited the mantra in my head.

"Sure. My pleasure." She forced a smile, but it didn't reach her eyes. Although I was surprised, her behaviour was much friendlier than this morning.

Placing her gold clutch bag on one of the tables, she followed me to the dance floor. I placed one hand behind her waist, holding her hand with the other. Her other hand rested on my shoulder.

"Mr. Gibson, I must warn you in advance. I don't know how to dance. If I trip—"

"I won't let you fall." I wish I could tell her that I knew she attended dance school. She'd been taking classes every day. But confessing to her would prove that I was stalking her.

"Thank you for saving me today. I'm sorry I was rough on you. I shouldn't—"

"You are very beautiful," I exclaimed.

"You already mentioned it, Mr. Gibson. Thank you." Utterly unaffected by my compliments, she glanced at me once before averting her eyes as if there was nothing new about it.

"Don't you like to be complimented?"

“Who doesn’t?” She forced a smile. “But false praise leads to nowhere.”

“You think I’m lying? You don’t realize how beautiful you are?”

She shook her head with mild amusement.

“Seventeen men approached you for a dance tonight, and you doubt—”

“You were counting?” She laughed openly. The sound filled my heart with contentment.

“Yes, I was. I saw you rejected the first three, so I entertained myself by counting the number of heartbroken men.”

She continued laughing as she dabbed a tear from the corner of her eye.

“No, seriously, there were seventeen men,” I said. She met my gaze, and this time, the smile reached her eyes. “On a serious note, can I ask you something?”

She pursed her lips, focusing on my words. “Yes, please, Mr. Gibson. No one has made me laugh like this in a long time. Humour me.”

“I notice you keep men at arms’ length. I mean, strangers. I’m still a stranger to you, so I wonder why you’d agree to dance with me.” She looked up at me. The smile was gone from her lips and eyes. “It’s okay if you don’t want to tell me.”

“Oh no, Mr. Gibson. I don’t think you’d like to hear the truth!” Looking nervous, her gaze raked the room, avoiding my eyes.

“What do you mean?”

I tracked her gaze and noticed her looking at Ben, who was already looking in our direction. “Nothing,” she said quietly.

“Has Mr. Dynham asked you to…”

“Please, Mr. Gibson, don’t complicate it.”

Her request rendered me speechless. It was because of her boss.

Fucking bastard!

I cursed Ben Dynham at this moment. She was still looking miserably at the floor. I felt my heart sinking into a giant pool of emotions. All this time, she was smiling because of my fucking power. I halted the dance and released her. It looked like her pride had been torn into millions of pieces; I didn't know my wealth could crush someone like that.

"I'm sorry, Mr. Gibson, I didn't—" She trembled with fear but still managed to reach her hand toward me to continue the dance.

"I'm so sorry." I took a step back. "You should have told me earlier." She glanced at her boss nervously, who was watching us intently. *Don't get her in more trouble.*

I took out the phone from my pocket, pretending to receive a call. With a dreadful look, she stood quietly, noticing my action. Faking a smile, I made an excuse to leave the dance floor. She stood there momentarily, then returned to where she left her clutch and leaned on the back of a chair, taking deep breaths. I wanted to hold her in my arms and comfort her, but I understood she needed some space. She grabbed her clutch bag and headed to the doorway.

Is she leaving?

She didn't even eat anything. If I stopped her at the doorway, Ben would notice, and I didn't want to create any more trouble for her. Instead, I chose wireless technology to communicate.

> *Adam: I never wanted our first dance to end this way. I could never imagine putting you in this challenging situation. Please stay for dinner. Adam.*

I joined the people at the bar for the drink. My eyes were locked on the main door, hoping she would return. I shouldn't have chickened out of the dance like that. But she was dancing with me against her will. She refused to dance with other men because no power was involved; she could make her own decisions. In my case, no one asked her what she wanted. I couldn't even confront Ben about why he forced her to do such a thing. That would complicate things more at her work. I remembered Ali telling me that her apartment belonged to Ben. It means there was more between them than just a boss-employee relationship.

I checked my phone again to see if I'd missed a reply from her. Then I saw her coming back inside. We gazed at each other silently, sharing unspoken words. She blinked softly, her eyes thanking me for my actions and my eyes apologizing in return. I called a server and asked him to offer her something to drink. She looked at me again as I toasted my drink from a distance. She picked up a glass of orange juice and returned me the same gesture. She took a seat with some of her colleagues, I noticed at breakfast.

Standing beside me, Ali watched me, watching her.

"I've never met anyone like her. And this alarming beauty…" I sighed.

"Yes," he conceded. "Beauty with brains." I noticed he was holding a document. He followed my gaze and, perhaps noticing that I was in no mood to talk business, tucked the paper in his jacket pocket. He faced the bar and asked for a drink. He took a sip from his glass and continued. "You were right, Adam. She is not like other women you've been… umm… dealing with in the past. You'll have to work really hard."

I turned around completely to face the bar as the bartender offered another drink. "What took you so long?"

He chuckled as he looked into his drink, swirling it. "Your tricks of sending a chauffeur to impress a girl didn't work on her." He took a sip. "It took me an hour to convince her that weekend nights are not safe for a girl to travel in public transport, and she took an hour in arguing that she can afford to travel in a cab."

I stared at him in return.

"If you think you tried to impress her by sending a ride, she was genuinely agitated."

"What made her change her mind?"

"I offered a brotherly ride. Spoke some words in her mother tongue—"

"Oh, for fuck's sake!" I grunted.

He laughed and shook his head. "Don't do that next time. She won't be impressed by your wealth. Her father is a UN secretariat. This isn't new to her. I'm sure she has a more affluent lifestyle back home."

"Then why doesn't she have a car?"

"What I think," he took a moment to answer, "she is running away from something. Or maybe from that culture." He shrugged. "Or maybe she never bothered to apply for a driver's license." He turned to me. "Why does it even bother you if she isn't driving?"

I blinked at him for a moment. "Because..." I thought for a second. Yes, why? Why was it bothering me? "Because I know what people do in subways. And she is so beautiful."

He snorted at my words. "And you are a very insecure man."

I glared at him, but there was nothing to say in my defence.

"I saw you made her laugh. You are going to hit the news tomorrow." He smirked behind his glass. *"Toronto's most eligible bachelor is finally captivated."* I shook my head and continued with the drink. "By the way, I found out who her boyfriend is. I mean the young cop." He put his glass down, his voice clipped. I waited for him to continue. "He is Mike Dynham. Son of Ben Dynham."

Is that so? Apart from being her boss, Ben was her boyfriend's father. Mike looked utterly besotted with her. She was living under his roof. But if he intended to marry her in the future, why was Ben pushing Rania toward me? Was he nothing but a greedy monster, a person who couldn't see his son's emotions? Then how would I expect him to consider Rania?

I still wonder if Rania and Mike were in a live-in relationship. But if that were the case, then why would Rania be the one paying rent? Or had they split the rent? Ali's limited information was enough for me to understand Rania's position. She was doing Ben a favour because of Mike.

I turned around, my eyes searching for her. She was busy talking to some people.

I put my glass on the table. "I've to make an announcement. Excuse me." I left the bar, headed to the stage, and picked up the microphone.

"Ladies and gentlemen! May I have your attention, please?" The conversation died down, and everyone turned to me, including Rania. "I would like to express my gratitude to everyone who has honoured us with their presence here tonight. I hope you're all having a good time. Dinner will be served shortly. But before that, we have a special performance. I recently learned that most people around us are already in a *festive* mood." I glanced at Rania, her lips parting in surprise. "But there is something I'd like to mention before the entertainment starts." I paused for a moment, letting my words sink in. "We light our homes and our surroundings at night during this season, yet we forget to light our hearts, which remain in the darkness." I glanced in her direction again. "Someone told me a very nice thing, which I'll remember always. The lights at night tell us that no matter how much darkness there is, only the light can dispel it. I hope we will keep this light in our hearts to warm others. Thank you all. Please enjoy the evening." I put the microphone down, and people clapping filled the ballroom. Rania looked utterly baffled. I decided not to approach her right now and stood beside Ali to wait for the performance.

Black curtains dropped behind the stage, providing a backdrop. As soon as the song: *Les valses de Vienne (The Viennese Waltz)* started, twelve young girls appeared, dressed in light pink ballerina dresses with pink masks over their eyes, and began to dance. The black background curtains were covered in stars and sparkles, providing a magical experience for the audience. The lights in the ballroom dimmed to enhance the shine of the stars onstage. Rania was engrossed in the performance, tapping her feet to the music. It warmed my heart to see how much she loved dancing. I'd arrange the whole performance just to see that look on her face.

When the performance was about to end, I decided to approach her. But as I got closer, I noticed how blanched she looked, as if the blood had been drained out of her face. She looked so stunned that one might take her as a wax statue. I closed the distance between us and realized she had the same darkness in her eyes as the woman I met a few months ago. Despite the warm indoor temperature, I suddenly felt intense cold, as if the time were locked in a freezer. No matter how hard I tried to move, my feet remained rooted to the ground—the same feeling I had that day.

It seemed like we were both suspended in a spell which could not be broken. The voices behind me receded, the music faded and was barely audible, and for a moment, I sensed no one around me.

Suddenly, she blinked and shook her head to break her trance. Just then, I realized the performance had ended. When I was a few steps away, I noticed her dabbing tears from her eyes. She looked around to check if anyone was noticing her and headed to the exit.

I was about to follow her when Ali grabbed my arm. "Don't push your luck, Adam." I inhaled sharply and watched her leave. "You are the host. You must stay here," he reminded me. Before I could ask him about the cold feeling, he continued, "Let me drop her home."

Her tears had drawn a high boundary between us. I knew

I couldn't yet invade her territory. My trance also broke when everyone applauded around me. It was as if, for a moment, I was teleported to some other world.

I grabbed a drink just as a server passed by and sat back at the bar to calm my nerves.

After a few minutes, when my patience ran out, I texted Ali.

Adam: Is she with you?

Ali: Yes.

Adam: How is she?

Ali: She is quiet. I'd rather not disturb her.

I sighed heavily at Ali's words. But I was an impatient man, so I opened another chat and texted her.

Adam: Hey. It's me!

Adam: Did I do something wrong again?

Three dots emerged. I waited for her to finish the message, but after a few seconds, they vanished.

Disappointed, I tucked my phone back into my pocket and faced the bar. As I took the sip, I heard a voice behind me. "Mr. Gibson." I turned again to find Ben Dynham. "I was looking for you."

"Good evening, Mr. Dynham." I faked a smile and cursed him in my heart. *It's all because of you, you prick.*

"It's a wonderful party, Mr. Gibson. Thank you for the lovely welcome dinner. I look forward to our prosperous business relationship." The bastard couldn't talk about anything besides business. He didn't care if his son's girlfriend left a while ago without dinner. "I wanted to come earlier, but you were occupied." His eyes wandered around, perhaps looking for someone. "Have you seen Rania?"

"She left," I grumbled, taking another sip.

"Left? So soon?"

"She wasn't feeling well."

"Oh. I didn't know. I'd have given her the ride." He showed

his faux concern. "Actually, she doesn't attend parties. A recluse, I must say."

It was a pathetic idea to throw a party. I should have known.

"She skipped her dinner," I seethed.

"Ah!" He exclaimed. "She does that all the time. She's always been like that. Avoid eating in public. Even as a child, she used to skip lunch at school." Had he known her since childhood? When he noticed my sour expression, he added, "I apologize on her behalf. I assure you this shall not happen next time." He took his phone out. "Let me check how she—"

I swore to myself that if he even thought of pushing her at me one more time against her will, I would take his balls off.

"Don't worry. I gave her the ride."

Surprise etched on his face. "Ah! Thank you. She is actually—"

My phone pinged with a message. "Excuse me."

Rania: Please, don't embarrass me

A smile sneaked out of my lips. "Sorry." I looked up. "You were saying something about…"

"Yes," said Ben. "She is like my daughter. I am her godfather, actually." I knitted my eyebrows. "Not in a Christian way," he elaborated. "Her father and I are childhood friends. Our kids practically grew together."

Another text grabbed my attention.

Rania: I should be the one to say sorry

"Yes." I looked up from the phone again. "I had the privilege of meeting your son today."

"Is that so?" Ben blinked with surprise. "When?"

"At Santa Parade," I replied. "He was on duty, I believe. Rania introduced us."

"She did?" Why was he surprised? "I didn't know you attended Santa Parade."

I sensed him mocking me, but I ignored him once again and texted her.

Adam: Why are you apologizing?

Adam: If it's about performance, just think it never happened.

Rania: I shouldn't have left without a word. I know you went to so much trouble…

The dotted bubble popped up again, but no text came after this.

"I'm sorry." I looked up at Ben again. I know it was rude to use the phone when someone was talking to you. "I have some urgent messages to respond to."

"Take your time." He smiled broadly. "We will chat later. Whenever you're available."

I nodded and dove back to my phone to text Ali.

Adam: Stop by at some drive-thru and ask her to eat something.

I texted Rania again.

Adam: I thought you'd like a dance performance.

Rania: How do you know I like dancing?

Rania: Oh, I get it. Your stalking talents :)

Rania: I'd like to know someday how your secret spying agency works.

And I'd like to tell you, someday, how I feel about you.

Adam: You left without dinner.

I changed the subject.

Adam: You owe me one now.

Rania: :)

Rania: You're a good host, Adam.

Her praise sent warmth all over my body.

Adam: Thank you, but I'd really like to take you out for dinner. Perhaps tomorrow night?

Rania: Are you asking me out, Mr. Gibson?

I chuckled at her words.

Adam: Yes, Miss Ahmed. I am asking you out.

Adam: But no pressure. I'll understand if you refuse.

She must know I was not trying to exercise my power. It took her a minute to respond.

Rania: I'm busy tomorrow.

Oh yes, I forgot. With Mike, of course.

Rania: How about Sunday?

A group of men approached me and asked me to join them at the dinner table. As the dinner was served, they started talking about the new investments and how government policies were changing to impact businesses. I tried to focus on their words, but I itched to text her back. No one had the slightest idea of what was on my mind. And knowing she left without eating, I couldn't force myself to eat.

Another text grabbed my attention.

Rania: I should mention once again that you're a good host. Ali insisted that I eat upon your order :) I appreciate your concern.

Rania: I'm enjoying my chocolate shake right now, but I'd like to let you know that I've reached home safely.

Rania: Thank you for what you did and for everything you tried.

I sat here frozen, reading her message again and again. So, she did realize I was trying something. She did get my hidden messages, which I couldn't say. Suddenly, I realized I was smiling stupidly over a text, and people were watching me.

Calm down, Gibson! You're not a fucking adolescent.

Adam: Chocolate shake is not dinner. I still owe you one.

Rania: Then let me be the host.

My heart started pounding again. I decided to cut the crap

of sending messages and waiting for them endlessly, and better to call her.

"Excuse me, gentlemen. I need to make an urgent call." There was too much noise in the party hall, so I scurried to the lobby, dialling her number, my heart pumping frantically.

After three rings, I heard her beautiful voice. "Hello."

"Hi. This is… umm… this is me." *You don't have a name, moron?* "I hope I didn't disturb you." I could hear the hesitation in my voice. *The oh-so-Mr. Confidant is finally shaky and nervous.*

"No, you didn't. Your party is over?" I could hear her sipping her chocolate shake.

"No, it's still going on. Listen! Umm…" Why was my heart racing so fast? "About your last text. I couldn't understand it."

"Really? It's a simple message. I'm inviting you for dinner."

For a moment, the world ceased to exist. Everything receded to the background: the party, the people, the grandeur. I stayed silent as I didn't know what to say.

She continued, "You've been really kind to me today. I have been thinking about…" She paused momentarily and then continued hesitantly, "*Us*, and I found myself at fault. You proved to be a perfect host tonight, and I ran from there like a fool."

"That's all right. It was your wish not to stay. I had no right to ask you—"

"No, please, Adam. Let me finish what I've to say." Her voice warmed me through the phone. "I don't want you to think that I'm some rude, self-centred girl. It's just that I'm not comfortable with strangers. This morning, when you asked me out, I didn't know what to say, as I never expected that. I didn't know how to deal with you, so I ran away. I'm still surprised you wanted to see me again after my rude behaviour. Yet, you found another way to meet me and arranged a party." She paused for a moment. I heard her breathing. *So, she knows I threw the party for her.* "I'm not blind, Adam. I can see your kindness and…feel it, too. But what I don't get is that even when I was not good to you, you were concerned that I left without eating—"

"You still consider me a stranger?" *We are not strangers, Rania. We were never meant to be.*

"I don't know. I just want to say I'm very sorry about my rudeness. And I want to make it up to you. I know you went into a great deal of trouble for me, and I left the party in the middle without giving any reason." I wanted to ask her if she felt frozen in time for a moment, but then I decided to remain quiet. "You were kind enough to understand me. I have no words to thank you."

"Please. Don't mention."

"No, Adam. Please let me thank you. Let me be a good host. I know it is not enough to reciprocate, but I really want to invite you for dinner. Can you take some time out of your busy schedule…on Sunday evening?"

I inhaled sharply at her words.

"And if you're wondering I'm asking you out, then yes, Mr. Gibson, it's a date." I could sense playfulness in her voice. She seemed to be in a cheery mood. "A date with *no* benefit."

I chuckled at her words. Of course, it was just a dinner, but at least I could hope for more.

"Umm…" I cleared my throat, suddenly feeling nervous. "Wow!" I chuckled again. "I must confess I'm nervous."

"Ah!" She said playfully. "I get it. You don't do dates."

"No. It's not that," I said immediately. "Rania…I really don't know what to say. I'm… speechless. Let's make it the other way around. Let me take you out to dinner."

We both stayed silent for a moment. As soon as I thought of saying something, she interrupted me. "But *I* want to thank you."

"You don't have to thank me for anything, but if that's what you wish, we will meet at the place of your choice. You can offer me your hospitality there." I couldn't stop smiling, and I felt she was, too.

"Please, Adam. Don't complicate it. It would be on me. And you need to choose the place. I don't know what kind of food you like."

"I'll eat anything you choose. Whatever pleases you, pleases me." I imagined her cuddled up in bed, wearing her nightdress. I wish I could have seen her when I made her smile.

"Okay! I'll text you the address tomorrow. We'll meet there at seven." I didn't want this conversation to end so soon. "Then, we'll decide who is hosting who."

"Can I pick you up from your place?" My heart raced again, embracing yet another rejection.

"I can come by myself. Please don't bother."

"If you're not comfortable with the idea, I'll send Ali to give you a ride. But please, no cabs or subways. Consider it a way of thanking me…if you really want to." I was literally bargaining with her.

She paused for a moment, thinking. "But then, how would you get there?"

"Rania, I own more than one car," I mumbled. I heard her giggling on the other end.

"Of course, I almost forgot. I'm talking to Mr. Gibson." Her giggle sent a jolt through my body. People passing by gave me strange looks, as no one had ever seen me smiling over a phone call. She continued with a hint of humour in her voice. "All right then, I'll see Ali at seven on Sunday. If not tomorrow, I'll text you the address on Sunday afternoon." She was still sipping her chocolate shake.

"I'll wait for your message." *And you don't know how desperately I'm waiting to see you again.* How would I pass these forty-eight hours? *Rania, you're sending me on an endless journey of time.*

"Good night, Adam." *Say something, you moron.*

"Good night, Rania." *I am fucked!*

She disconnected the line, leaving me with hope. A hope of a journey to a magical kingdom with my enchantress.

CHAPTER 6
THE VERY FIRST DATE

ADAM

ONE OF THE THEORIES OF TIME suggests that the faster a clock moves, the slower time passes.

In my case, I was trying to avoid looking at my watch, but it seemed like my time had stopped. I had been waiting for Rania to arrive, but every second felt like an eternity.

I was taken off guard when she called in the afternoon and switched our dinner from Sunday to Saturday. She sounded urgent, but I was already desperate to see her. We decided to meet at a Persian restaurant on Bay Street. Ali had gone to pick her up, and they should be here any minute. It was a simple, warm and welcoming restaurant. Soothing Persian music blended perfectly with the ambience. Surprisingly, all the tables in the restaurant were private, each encircled with a wooden gazebo. I was relieved because we needed to talk, and I didn't want anyone to take our pictures today. All the patrons were seated on floor cushions, relaxing in the cozy environment and low-height tables.

I liked her choice. It was different from where I usually go.

I unlocked my phone and went through the article again—

the reason that made it all so urgent.

The headline read **TORONTO'S BACHELOR CAPTIVATED!**

A picture of us at the office meeting was posted this morning. The thought made me smile at how she'd tried to ignore me and leave the situation. I wonder what kind of first impression I had created on her. Perhaps I should ask her today.

Another picture of us, sitting on the bench before Santa Parade, was posted. I was holding her by the elbow.

Adam Gibson was spotted on Friday afternoon at Santa's Parade with his newest conquest.

Goddammit! I was not furious about what they wrote because I *was* captivated, but I hated it when they posted stuff without any research and didn't even consider that someone's privacy could get compromised for their musings. She wasn't any ordinary, nameless girl I'd picked after a party. I wanted to know her. And if this continued, she'd never let me in in her life.

I didn't know how Rania would react to all this media exposure at her work. She didn't sound angry when I spoke to her today. But if I were in her shoes, I couldn't imagine facing people on Monday, either. No wonder she sounded anxious. I must do something to protect her from this bizarre situation.

There was one more picture of us during our dance with another caption.

Jingle Bells or Wedding Bells? Toronto's most elite bachelor in a festive mood—utterly bewitched.

What did she think when she saw those pictures? There was no grain of doubt that she looked extraordinarily beautiful, and I looked desperate and besotted, but knowing Rania, I was sure she must have been vexed. I made her laugh during the dance when I joked about men approaching her. The moment had been beautifully captured, and I had no shame in admitting that I loved this picture and had decided to enlarge it and place it somewhere in my apartment.

I had slept with so many women, but none had made my heart race the way she does when our eyes meet. No one had invaded my thoughts and had kept me awake all night the way she'd done to me since yesterday.

I was engrossed in my phone, gazing at her pictures individually, when a thudding sound broke my trance. A folded and crumpled gossip magazine was placed on the table.

I looked up, and my heart suddenly stopped beating. Time halted again, and there was no one in this universe—just me and her.

I got to my feet and offered my hand.

She put her bag down and took my hand. "I hope I'm not late," she said.

"I arrived a couple of minutes ago, too." *Liar! You've been waiting for eternity.*

She looked incredibly beautiful in her brown velvet skirt and pink crepe top, a silk scarf tied around her neck.

"You look…" *So fucking hot!* I paused and stared at her brazenly, searching for the right word: "magnificent." She looked down, blushing. "Your blouse matches your skin." She raised her eyes to mine, an unusual shyness in them.

She instantly pulled her hand. "Thank you." She took the seat. "I haven't eaten anything since morning. Can we order an appetizer first? What would you like to have?"

"You're the host. I'm here to be entertained by your hospitality." I smirked at her, relaxing back on the cozy cushions.

She picked up the menu and hid her face behind it. After a few minutes, she put the menu down and called the server. She ordered bruschetta made on Persian flatbread with their blended yogurt and lemonade.

We sat quietly for a moment, each waiting for the other to break the ice. I had no idea how fucking difficult it could be to talk to a girl when she was the one to whom I wanted to tell everything I felt about her. When I realized she might not say anything, I picked up the magazine.

"I'm sorry for all this," I began.

"This is insane, Adam." She looked agitated but super cute. "How can they print pictures like that? There is no such thing as privacy? And who the bloody hell took this picture?" She pointed to the one on the bench. "People have so much time to waste."

I smiled at her annoyance and kept my arms crossed over my chest.

"Will you stop looking at me and say something, please?"

I averted my gaze to study the paper. "How you manage to look beautiful in this, I just don't know. You—"

"Are you mocking me?" She gave me one of her sharp looks.

"Nope."

She picked the magazine. "Now listen to this." She shifted her position, sliding a bit closer to the table. "*It is disappointing for all the young women in Toronto that our city's sexiest and most eligible bachelor seems to have been taken off the market.* Duh!" She rolled her eyes. "Who writes like that? You are not a property for lease."

I laughed at her annoyance.

"*Though Adam Gibson has always insisted that he doesn't believe in relationships, a picture says a thousand words. If this isn't a relationship, then what do we call it?* Crap. All crap. Everyone knows about you. And this picture says nothing. You joked, and I laughed. It's as simple as that."

"Yup." I tried to curb my laugh.

"*The lucky lady, Rania Ahmed, is a graphic designer at Greenway Advertising.*" She put the magazine down. "Oh, for God's sake. I'm a public figure now." She lowered her voice. "You know… everywhere I went in the morning, people were just staring at me as if I had horns on my head. I couldn't even finish my morning run. And worst of all…I'm getting messages on my LinkedIn.

For God's sake!"

"I'm so sorry."

"Do they post about every single woman you hang out with?"

"I don't date, Rania," I objected, my tone suddenly serious. The media knew I hadn't approached a woman before.

She sat back, eyebrows knitted. "Then why do they call you a womanizer?"

I sighed and sat back, too. "Because…never mind. Finish your article."

"As if you haven't read it?" She grumbled.

"I haven't."

"Why not?"

"Because," I smiled, "I was busy looking at our picture."

She blinked at me for a moment. "You are too blunt."

"I can't lie to you."

We gazed at each other for endless beats when the server appeared and placed the cutlery and plates on the table.

She picked up the magazine to read. *"Although this is the first time Adam and Rania have been spotted together publicly, the pictures make it clear that they are more than just acquaintances."* She looked up. "No, we are not. See…a little bit of research is all they needed to do before publishing it. I don't know how this kind of crap even gets editorial approval."

"You're right."

She continued reading, *"Does it mean that this girl has tamed Adam Gibson—"* She slapped the magazine again on the table. "Tamed? They sound as if you're an animal." She looked up. "Doesn't this all bother you?"

I sighed heavily. "I can't control everything. And I don't care what they wrote about me. What concerns me is how you're feeling. Please tell me the truth." She fixed her eyes on the table as she picked up the napkin, her delicate fingers toying with it.

"I'm worried about Monday. This is so embarrassing." She

propped her head against her hand, her elbow on the table.

"Are you embarrassed because you were spotted with a womanizer?"

She blinked at me, stunned.

"Or because you had been turning down other men and, according to the media, finally ended up with me?"

She knitted her eyebrows. "What makes you think I push men away?"

"I was keeping count at the party, remember? I'm sure I can extrapolate from that. You turned me down, too."

"What else do you know about me?" She gave me a sharp look, leaning back.

We were interrupted by the server again, who now brought our appetizer.

"You said you can't lie to me." She took a sip of her lemonade. "Now tell me, what else do you know about me."

"Is this how you treat your guests?" I chuckled, trying to ease the tension in the air. But she remained silent, waiting for my response. "Okay! I'll tell you the truth. Obviously, I know where you live…" I paused for a moment, and she rolled her eyes. "I also know where you work and other official details. I know you don't drive, as you don't have a driver's license on your record. You graduated from UofT as a software engineer and later changed your field to graphics and joined Ben's company." I paused again. "Nothing more than that, except that your…umm…boyfriend happens to be Ben's son."

"Mike is *not* my boyfriend," she snapped. That was the best news I'd had all day.

"He isn't?"

"He is my best friend. We grew up together. He's always been there for me, and I'm grateful to God that He has blessed me with at least one sincere friend." I was trying my best to conceal my happiness and excitement, so I kept Mike as our common topic. It was much easier for me to tolerate that fucking hunky cop when I knew this girl had no feelings for him.

"It doesn't look like a mere friendship the way he looks at you," I pointed out.

"Oh, because when we were at school, we promised each other that if neither of us had found a suitable partner by twenty-five, we'd get married." She smiled, reminiscing about the past. "He is still holding his promise for me."

Holy shit! I was right. The guy was in love with her.

"Do you feel the same for him?"

She was quiet momentarily, toying with the straw, then continued without looking at me. "No, I don't feel like that about him or even anyone." She paused. "There will be no one," she mumbled. She must have assumed I hadn't heard her, but I did.

Suddenly, her declaration was reflected in her eyes as the shadows of the past tore through them. She must have suffered a broken heart. And I didn't know how to dig up that information. Was that the reason she left her home country and moved here?

I didn't want her to cry, so I changed the subject.

"Umm…there's one more thing I didn't tell you. My intelligence service also mentioned that you attend a dance school." I picked the bread. "There was no chance you could have tripped yesterday."

She looked away. We got interrupted again by the server, who showed up to take the main course order.

"Please have a look at the menu. I'm not sure what to order for you."

"Anything you want," I answered. "I've liked your choices so far."

"You should not trust a stranger like that. What if I poison you?" She peeked one eye out from behind the menu to look at me.

I sat back and sighed. "I'm already stung hard with your

beauty, Rania. How much more can you do to me?"

Her face turned beet red as she averted her gaze from me and looked up at the server to order—two platters of chicken kobideh.

When the server walked away, I asked, "You don't like it when someone compliments you?"

"I find them very cheesy." She sipped her lemonade and continued, "They all send the same message… lets-get-laid."

Her words jarred me. I wasn't expecting this kind of remark from her. I adjusted myself to a different position, but nothing changed the tension in the air.

"But that's not always the case, is it?"

"It always has been. What else do men want other than a sleeping partner? They certainly do not think from their heads."

I looked down at the food, avoiding her sharp eyes as if she had the power to dive into my soul and read my intentions.

"You think Mike is the same?"

"Mike is different. I trust him."

"And he loves you," I pointed out again.

"Yes, I know he loves me, but he also knows I don't believe in love." She looked down again and dipped her bread in yogurt. There were so many messages in everything she said.

"You read books. I assume you must have explored the romance genre, too."

Her jaw dropped in surprise. "You're stalking my online activities?"

"I saw you picking up your e-book reader while collecting your stuff outside my office."

"Oh, how observant of you, Mr. Gibson." She pouted. "But that was very rude of you to—"

"I was taken off guard," I interjected. She narrowed her gaze at me but stayed quiet. "I was shocked…umm…I never thought I'd be smitten. Your beauty made me speechless…and witless."

Shit! I was actually saying this to her. She looked away, shifting with discomfort.

Why the fuck I'm acting like a prick?

I had a strong gut feeling that someone had played with her emotions in the past. What woman doesn't want to hear praises about her beauty? But if I kept acting like a sleazeball and poured my heart out every second, she'd walk away. I must get a grip on myself and follow Ali's suggestions. Conventional approach! Be friends with her first. Making sexy remarks would only push her away from me. She was close to Mike because he didn't wear a fuck-me look. I couldn't expect a physical relationship from her unless I gained her trust. She wasn't like other women, who'd be readily available on a call. But that was not the only thing I wanted from her.

"I don't want to give you any false hopes, Adam. You should be very clear by now that I'm not the person you're looking for…" *Is she a fucking mind reader?* She paused for a moment, waiting for me to look at her, and continued when I met her eyes, open-mouthed. "I mean…I've read about you, and you should know that—"

"You're not a conquest, Rania." There was something about her that compelled my heart to open. "Please, don't ever think I see you that way."

If jaws could drop, hers would have touched the carpet. Her expression was asking so many questions, like *how-do-you-see-me?* Had I scared her with the truth? Was it too much information to dump on her? I must change the subject.

"You were saying you've read something about me? Shall I say you've been stalking me, too?"

"I only read what was on the Internet," she snapped. "You don't believe in God? I mean, I read you deny His existence and that you're an atheist."

"Yes." I knitted my eyebrows. Where did that come from?

"I don't think there is any God."

"But that doesn't mean He doesn't exist." I opened my mouth to argue, but she cut me. "You don't see His existence in everything around you?" She dipped the bread again in the yogurt. "You don't see changing weather, colours of the land, and shades in the water? You think no one is behind their individuality? He gave you fame, money, power, and honour, and instead of being thankful, you deny His existence?"

It felt like my childhood days, sitting in Sunday service where we were told that we must be thankful to God all the time.

"Thankful for what I've done myself?" I grunted. "I have all this because I worked hard for it."

"But, what about the blessings you got without even working hard? Don't you think you are obliged to be thankful for those?"

"Like what?"

"Like the senses He gave you. Your vision, so you can see His beautiful creations; your ears, so you can listen to all the good things in life; your speech, through which you succeeded in taking over this city; your sense of touch, through which you can feel. He gave you all this and much more without you asking Him. There are many people in this world who are deprived even of these blessings. Don't you think these bounties are enough for you to be thankful?"

We looked at each other for endless beats. I didn't know what to say in my defence.

"You are trying to convince me," I snorted.

"No." She sat back. "I'm not. But He is there."

"I don't believe in something I can't see."

"Ah!" She exclaimed. "If you can't see it, it doesn't mean it's not there. Darkness is the absence of light, but does that mean there is no darkness? What about magnetic waves? Or heat? I'm sure you've studied science."

I thought for a moment. "How do you recognize Him?"

She stared at me for a moment, unblinking, as if reading my soul and shuffling all the pages inside it.

"Caliph Ali, one of the prominent figures in our religion, once said, *I have recognized my God from the failure of my intentions.*" She smiled sadly. "Things don't always go how we plan."

I stared at her, speechless. My intentions did fail when it came to kissing her, claiming her. I didn't know if it was some fuckin' divine intervention in our case, but something had come in between us.

"You seem to carry a strong faith within you," I said.

"I wouldn't have survived if I didn't have faith." She looked down again, toying with her ring.

"So, you're thankful to Him for everything?"

"Yes, I try to be, at least!"

"And how do *you* thank Him?"

"I follow what's taught in my religion. I pray. But it doesn't mean He won't listen if you approach Him in any other way. He does!"

"And what about the things you're not blessed with? Is there a way to complain?" I couldn't believe I was discussing God on my first date.

"We are responsible for our own actions. We can't blame God if anything goes wrong. Ungrateful are always dissatisfied. When you are thankful, you are content. The problem is how thankful you are when you have nothing."

"So you believe being grateful is also a blessing?"

"Absolutely."

"Don't you think it's unfair to those who are grateful?" I took a bite of bread. "I mean…there are some people who have everything, and yet they are not grateful."

"You are one of them, Mr. Gibson," she snorted. "What are you complaining about?" How very astute!

"I respect your faith, Rania. It is very strong. Always hold onto it. You're fortunate that you have been guided."

"Yes, I know. Do you know God says when you take one step toward Him, He will take ten steps toward you? The light guides you then."

"How do you know when you see that light?"

She studied me momentarily like one reads a classic and annotates it. "You've already seen the light, Adam. You're a good soul. Do you know how much goodness and grace you're getting from your generous donations?"

"You still didn't tell me why you reject men." I changed the subject. I don't feel comfortable when people praise me for my donations. She didn't say anything, evidently ignoring my question. "I have an offer for you," I added. She looked up. "I notice you don't like men approaching you." She rested her fork on the table. "What if we make this true?" I tapped on the gossip magazine. "No one will dare once you're my official girlfriend."

"You mean fake dating?"

I tried to control my smile. "Is that what you read in your books?"

"It's a very practical trope in romance books." She narrowed her gaze at me. "You're a businessman. You won't do anything unless it profits you. What will you get in this?"

Before I could answer, our main course arrived. It looked very delicious. We started our meal quietly. I gave her time to think about my proposal. *What the fuck am I thinking?* Why would she agree to be my girlfriend? And this was not an appropriate way to ask a girl if she was interested. *Damn it! I've messed it up.* I must say something before she walked away. Ali would definitely reproach me for this.

"Rania, I'm not gonna lie. I am *very* attracted to you." She blinked at me. "Like *really* attracted! And it's not going to be fake at my end. But I also know you don't see me the same way." She averted her gaze again and focused on her food as she took a bite of chicken. "This is also my first time approaching a woman, and I don't even know if I'm following the proper protocols here. But I can feel that you aren't pushing me away because you don't like me. I see pain in your eyes." As soon as I mentioned the word *pain*, she coughed and choked on her food. I offered her water, but she still groped for air. I crawled to her side and rubbed her back.

There was something very peaceful about her presence. As if she calmed the storms inside me, filled the void inside me and gave me so much pleasure; I didn't know what I'd do if she agreed to my offer.

"I'm sorry. I guess something got stuck in my throat." She took a sip of water. She was breathing hard, her breasts moving with her heartbeat. *Oh hell!* She should not find me turning on right now. I crawled back to my seat. "You didn't answer my question," she continued. "What is it for you in this?"

"How about we eat first?" I slid the platter toward her, which she seemed to abandon. I picked up the fork to continue with my food. She still didn't take a bite. "Eat, Rania! Please, finish your meal." My tone was a bit harsh with concern.

"I want my answer first. Why would you want it when you clearly know I have nothing to offer? What do you want from me?"

"I want only you," I mumbled. "Nothing else."

"Want me for what?" Her eyes were almost watery, but she blinked away. "I cannot give you anything. No pleasure. Nothing. You are chasing a shadow." She put her fork down with a clatter and wiped her eyes with a napkin. "I'm a piece of dead meat. You get me? There is nothing in me."

The conviction in her voice made my heart stop. Why was she calling herself a dead meat? What had happened to her?

"I'm sorry," I said earnestly. "I don't have your answer. I don't know what made me say this but, the moment I saw you crossing the street and heading to the building, my world hasn't been the same." I put the fork down. "You are extraordinarily beautiful. If I have pursued you, I'm sure other men must have too. And I can't…" I sighed heavily. "I…"

It was too soon to say everything. My words were already making her uncomfortable. If I told her that I couldn't see her with any man, she'd certainly think I was a psycho. If I told her I couldn't share her with anyone, she'd take me as an obsessive maniac. I must say something.

"Like you said, men do not think from their heads," I mused. She chuckled at my words, wiping away a single tear. "Perhaps I'm not thinking from my head, either. I just want to clean up the mess I created. You said I don't do anything unless it profits me. Your presence is all I want." I dared to take her hand in mine. "I want to be in the world where you live."

Her hand suddenly felt cold as she pulled it away. "You don't know my world."

"Then let me in," I almost pled.

"What if there are monsters in my world?" Something about her words made my heart race. Was there a monster in her life?

"Then I'll protect you," I answered solemnly.

She twisted the ring on her finger. "And why are you being so generous?" Flickering a painful emotion in her eyes, she dove into my soul to search for an answer.

"I don't know." I closed my eyes, shaking my head. "I'm feeling charged to do all this. I can't say anything more." I opened my eyes and found her gaze fixed on me, agape.

"Charged by whom?"

"Maybe…God?"

"But you said you don't believe in Him."

I shrugged. "You leave me no choice."

"That's a very lame reason for believing in Him."

We both remained silent for a few minutes, trying to understand what just happened to us. Within a day, I felt like we had walked so far together. We have not shared any secrets, but I still felt a strong connection.

To avoid the awkward situation, I handed her a fork. "Please finish your food."

With that, we both finished our meals in silence. The food was not warm anymore, but it still tasted scrumptious.

"The kebab was excellent."

"Thanks. It is one of my favourites, too. Would you like to have some dessert?" She was trying to prove her hospitality. I nodded at her with a smile.

The server returned and took the order for a hot fudge sundae. We shared a few moments of silence until our dessert arrived.

We both gaped at the dessert.

"Oh my!"

"You think you'll finish it?" I checked the size of the bowl again.

"You must know women have a separate compartment for desserts in their stomachs." She flashed a mischievous smile. "And you will help me finish it." She took a big spoonful of ice cream from the bowl, with all the nuts and chocolate, and started to lick the spoon slowly. *Oh fuck! Is she tempting me on purpose?* No, she seemed utterly oblivious to my feelings.

"For the love of God, stop licking your spoon like that. It's turning me on." She was stunned for a moment, spoon in her mouth. Then, slowly, she took the spoon out of her mouth, caressing it with her tongue, and giggled sinfully.

"This is turning you on?" She knitted her eyebrows as she took more ice cream and repeated the process. This time, she also licked her upper lip.

Fuck! Stop it, girl, or else I'll suck your chocolate-coated lip right here.

"Don't provoke me, Rania. There is an animal inside every man."

"Ha! Who knows that better than me?" she snapped. "Some men are not even humans. They are only animals." With a grave look, she put her spoon down and closed her eyes, hiding her dread. I wanted to ask her what animal she'd encountered, but I must gain her trust first. I put my hand on hers to provide her comfort. She didn't recoil. "I'm sorry. I was just teasing you," she added, the pain still flashing in her onyx eyes.

"No, I'm sorry. I don't know how to keep my mouth shut."

"That's okay." She forced a smile. "I'm slowly understanding you now." She pulled her hand and swirled the spoon in the bowl, mixing all the layers of ice cream and fudge. "You don't know how to lie."

I took the bowl from her. "Like it or not. It was very erotic." I confessed again and dug my spoon into the ice cream. She giggled like a child, taking it as a joke. To lift her mood, I argued with her like a child myself. "Hey, you ate all the nuts from the top. That's not fair." She checked the ice cream innocently to see if I was telling the truth.

Taking another spoon, she continued, "They must think we will stay here forever." She giggled again. I was surprised by how ice cream changed her mood. Perhaps, next time, I should only invite her for dessert.

"I have a question," she said. "I read about your mother."

"That is not a question," I seethed.

As if she could sense my discomfort, she didn't ask.

"You know…grudge is a weight that sits really heavy on your soul."

I sucked in a breath. How did she know I had a grudge with my mother?

"I don't feel any weight," I said. Who was I lying to? It was heavy on my soul.

"Learn to forgive. We must learn that our parents are old now. We don't have much time left with them."

I looked away. "I like the way you believe. It makes everything sound like a fairytale."

The thought of my mother hurt me…always. There was a void in my heart that no one could ever fill.

"Where is she now?" She put her spoon down, giving her undivided attention. "Only if you want to tell me."

"There is nothing much to say. She left my father when I was six. My parents used to fight all the time. The only good thing in my childhood was my baby sister, Eva." I smiled at the thought of her. "She was two months old when mom left and took Eva with her. I missed Eva more than my mom." I didn't know why I was sharing all this with her. I haven't mentioned Eva to anyone before. "You say God exists, but where was He when I called Him to help me? Why didn't He hear a child's cry?"

She took a moment to answer. "Please remember that prayers are never abandoned. Sooner or later, they are always answered in much better ways than you could have imagined." Her words were comforting, but they did not hit my heart. We had different beliefs based on our pasts.

We continued our dessert.

"So, does your secret spying company hire people?" She changed the subject, a mischievous gleam in her eyes. "I have read enough detective books to become a detective now."

"Like a modern-day Sherlock Holmes?" I asked. "You know…you can be a good detective. When I look into your eyes, I say nothing but the truth."

"Then tell me why you were stalking me?"

"I wasn't stalking. I just wanted to learn about you before I could talk to you."

"You could have asked."

"Ha!" I sat back. "You think you'd have cooperated?"

She pouted her lips and took another spoon. "No. I wouldn't, but I also believe that it's not just about..." She waved her hand back and forth between us. "There is something on your mind. You want to ask me something. Right?"

I stared at her for a few seconds, wondering if she truly had the power to read minds.

"Someday, I will. But not today."

She didn't probe more. I wanted to tell her everything, my one-night experience with an enchantress, but I feared she'd never believe me.

"So, what kind of books do you read apart from mysteries?" I changed the subject.

"All kinds of fiction."

"Why fiction only?"

"Because it takes you to the world of imagination, where reality doesn't exist. It's like a journey to another world, far from cruel reality. Do you read?"

"I don't have the time or, in fact, the patience to read fiction. I live in the real world."

"Then your reality is more colourful than your imagination." She lifted her gaze dreamily—and enviously. "Dating so many pretty models and actresses, I'm sure it is colourful."

I laughed at her remarks, pointing at the newspaper she'd kept at the corner of the table.

"You see this? It says I've been spotted only with you. It says *you* are my girlfriend." My words suddenly shifted the air in the restaurant. "The women you're talking about, they were only bed partners. I never had anyone to date. To talk like this." She gaped in return. "I didn't break anyone's heart. It was a pure transaction. Pleasure or favour in exchange for money."

Aghast, she asked, "So you keep... I mean... umm... do you have something like... umm... mistresses?"

I gave a short laugh again. "No. I don't carry such baggage. I don't see any point in keeping one woman for a long time when you're spending money on them. You don't wear a single dress daily when you can afford a variety." My remark had certainly stunned her. It was too much information. She was going to run away screaming.

I was afraid she'd think I looked at her the same way. I must do or say something to make this better.

I took a small box out of the inner pocket of my jacket and placed it on the table.

"I have something for you." She leaned forward, glancing at the dark blue velvet box with Tiffany & Co. embossed on it, but she didn't touch it. She was clearly not expecting it.

"I can't take it, but thank you." She sat back again, pushing the box toward me.

"At least open it and see if you like it or not." I pushed the box.

"I'm sorry, Adam. I can't take it. I'm not used to these kinds of gestures. So please—"

"Then get used to it. You're my girlfriend."

"No, I'm not," she snapped. "I haven't agreed to your proposition." She pushed the box back, evidently showing her frustration.

"Don't argue like a child."

"A child is always eager to receive gifts." She threw daggers at me.

"No one has ever rejected me—"

"Then get used to it." She pulled her hand away.

We both managed to stay silent, the Persian music playing in the background. I was offended by her rejecting my gift. She was resentful of my dominance. She was one challenging woman. What woman wouldn't accept Tiffany? She hadn't even bothered to open it and see what it was. Even though I felt rejected, she made one more inroad into my heart. She was not like other women, running after money. This was all my fault. I was pushing my luck too hard. I should have gained her trust first before giving her gifts. It was our first date, and she hadn't agreed to accept me as her boyfriend. That was a first for me, too.

A girl rejecting me!

After the dessert was finished, the server brought the bill. I realized that we'd been in the restaurant for almost three hours. How had time passed so quickly?

She placed her hand on the bill to grab it, but I stopped her by holding her wrist.

"Now, at least don't argue on this one." I gripped her wrist with firm decisiveness, but she struggled hard to get it out of my grasp.

"Adam, please. We decided this dinner is on me, so stop acting like a male chauvinist." It seemed like the ice cream had lost its effect.

"If you pay for this, you accept my offer and my gift." I had no intention of letting her go unless I made her agree to my terms. I was just afraid she'd return the bill and walk out. This was the biggest gamble of my life.

"What kind of bargaining is that?" She looked around the restaurant and back at me with wide eyes. "Let go of my hand, Adam. You're creating a scene. People are looking at us," she hissed.

"I know there is no one here except us. The restaurant is almost closed. If you're worried about the damn server, I don't give a shit. Be a good girl and give me the bill. Don't test my patience." I didn't even bother to look around to confirm. "You will let me pay for this dinner, and you will accept my offer, along with the damn gift." She stared at me, stunned and intimidated.

As if taking it as a threat, she let the bill go. I released her hand. She sat back, creating distance between us. *Shit! I lost her.* She let me win this battle, but I achieved nothing.

I took my credit card out and waved the server over to collect the bill. We both sat silent during the payment. As soon as the server left, thanking me, she gathered her bag and got to her feet.

"Where are you going?" I gripped her arm firmly.

"The restaurant is almost closed. You plan to stay here forever?" *I wish.* I must be more cautious when speaking. She was constantly firing my words back at me. I must calm her down, but nothing came to mind. "You're forgetting something," she reminded me, glancing at the box we left on the table.

"It's not mine," I snapped.

She pulled her arm out of my grip, picked the box and placed it on my palm. "If you have money to waste, give it to someone who needs it and appreciates it. I'm neither needy nor greedy." She turned away, but I stopped her again.

"But you never bothered to open it. At least take a look—"

"Adam, I'm not from medieval times. I know what Tiffany sells."

"Oh, for fuck's sake! Stop being so hard on me."

"You don't need to do all this. You're making me feel cheap." Her argument shifted something inside me. I took her face in my hands. She closed her eyes at my touch. I wanted to kiss her desperately, but I knew I didn't have her consent.

"Don't ever say that again," I whispered. "Every girl likes gifts."

"I'm not like *every* girl," she objected, meeting my gaze. "I already told you." She was not rejecting out of her habit of keeping men at arm's length. This refusal showed her agony. "I don't know why you're wasting your time."

"You don't even know what you deserve. This gift is not even worthy of you. It is just my way of apologizing for the trouble I caused. If you don't want it, that's okay, but please don't think like that." I shoved the box back inside my jacket. *What kind of woman is she? Rejecting a twenty-five-thousand-dollar necklace?* I promised myself that this personalized piece of art would only adorn her beautiful neckline.

"It's late," she said. "I want to go home now." She turned around, heading to the coat rack. I followed her and helped her with her jacket.

As we stepped out, cold, hard wind awaited us. Taking out her phone, she made a call.

"Yeah, hi. Can you please send a cab to…"

What? I'm standing next to her, and she's calling a fucking cab at this hour?

I snatched the phone from her and ended the call.

"What the hell do you think you're doing?" I barked.

"Calling a cab?"

"Can't you find a better way to insult someone?" I gritted my teeth to control my anger.

"What's with you and public transportation?" she asked curiously. But when I opened the passenger door, she slipped inside quietly.

We stayed quiet all the way to her apartment. I parked the car in front of the building. She stepped out before I managed to open the door for her. She wrapped her arms around herself to avoid the cold wind. It had never been as hard to say something as at this moment, and I didn't want to go home, where only empty walls and furniture waited for me.

We looked at each other for a few minutes. I wanted to pull her close and kiss her, but I knew I didn't have consent. Still, I dared to take a step.

"I know my certain acts look crazy to you, but…" I looked away momentarily. "Someday, I want to tell you the reason why I'm doing this."

She looked past my shoulder. The cold wind blew at her face, a strand of hair blocking her one eye. I dared to move the hair lock away and tucked it behind her ear. She inhaled sharply at my touch and closed her eyes for a second as if she really wanted to feel my touch.

I kept my hand there, her warm face leaning against my palm. I took another step. "Someday… you will know why I'm chasing you like a maniac, but I hope you believe me."

She looked at me the way one looks at old objects—in a nostalgic way as if I was an heirloom that connected many memories for her.

"You can tell me now," she said softly.

I sucked in my breath and took another step. We were an inch apart. If I dipped, I could steal a kiss. "But I want to know you first. I want to know…"

She closed her eyes again, and as if she was mentally ready that I'd kiss her, I bent forward with the intention of kissing. But as I closed my eyes, I felt something very cold between us. It was not the wind—I was sure of that.

I snapped my eyes open to look around. Her face, which was warm against my touch a moment ago, was suddenly icy. It was the same cold I felt when I met that woman a few months ago. This cold seeped into my body, and I couldn't avoid the shiver that ran down my spine. I felt she'd sensed the same cold as she jerked and stepped back.

"We are not allowed to stop the car here at the driveway." She gestured at the car.

"Right." I put my hands in the jacket pocket. "Thank you." I forced a smile.

"You paid. I should say thank you." *Oh! She is still annoyed.*

"Thank you for choosing the restaurant. I really enjoyed the food and your company. But if it bothers you, you can pay next time." I grinned at her.

With a poker face, she answered, "There will be no next time, Mr. Gibson. Good night!" She turned around and disappeared inside without listening to my farewell words, taking all my hopes with her.

I knew I must work really, really hard.

CHAPTER 7
A BEAUTIFUL JOURNEY

RANIA

It was Monday morning. I was en route to Quebec City on Via Rail, thinking about the phone call I received from Ben yesterday.

As I dreaded and predicted, my father was interrogated at his workplace about the daughter of the UN Secretariat dating a rich Canadian Casanova. Ben told me Baba sounded really deranged.

Today, another picture of us from the restaurant on Saturday night was in the paper. I didn't understand why the media couldn't give us space to breathe. Maybe with Adam, this was just part of the package. He was always in the limelight, which meant I'd be in it, too. I had no clue what it was like to date the most influential man in Toronto. My father is a notorious man in the Middle East, but that never put his family at risk of losing their privacy. Baba made sure of that.

While Adam was an open book, staying close to him meant people would turn my pages, too. Ben warned me that I was giving Adam hope, and Baba was unhappy. I knew how hard he'd worked to attain his position in the Arab world, and my stupid actions were bringing him shame.

I was grateful I no longer needed to face my colleagues at work since I was attending conference by Adobe for graphic designers and illustrators in Quebec City. I could have flown, but since the conference would start Thursday, I used my paid holidays, which I hadn't consumed this year and requested Ben that I leave early by train and have some time on my own. Plus, it was a good way to avoid Adam and all the media drama happening in Toronto. I hoped the French Quebecois didn't follow this nonsense.

After what happened to me in the past, I never had a thrilling day. I have never felt excitement in the past five years, but going on this trip on my own excited me. It was the first time I was going to Quebec. Although November wasn't a good season for a holiday, I didn't mind bundling up and exploring the city. I had seen enough pictures and watched enough videos to stroll on the cobbled alleys. And the best part was that they had authentic German-style Christmas markets that had already started last weekend.

On Saturday night, after Adam dropped me at my place, I rushed into my apartment without saying goodbye to him. I was crying, missing my mother, wishing to share everything about Adam, when suddenly, he knocked at my door. I was so scared of finding him at my doorstep that I fell to my knees and couldn't stop crying. I was frightened about how much power he had to bypass the building security and approach my apartment. But the wall of formality and stiltedness was broken down when he crossed the threshold and entered my apartment. Whatever reservations I had with him were gone when I broke into tears in his arms that night. I cried about my mother, and he remained patient, not asking me for details. It was as if I was trying to seek closure, and he was there to mollify my wounds.

I had never cried in front of anyone, not even before Mike,

but with Adam, it seemed like he was there to heal me. He watched me pick the photo frame of my mother's picture—how I had held it tightly while he stayed in bed with me until I sobbed and eventually slept. I didn't know if he stayed longer, but when I woke up, I found flowers at my bedside with a note saying I looked pure and innocent while I slept. For the first time in five years, I hadn't had any nightmares. I had an uninterrupted sleep without my pills.

I had planned to call and thank him for the lovely flowers, but after Ben's call, the idea of giving Adam hope made me reconsider. I pretended to ignore his flowers and the message and moved on. My life was locked in a gilded cage of belief and culture. We were from two different worlds, and neither of us could be a part of the other.

And here I was, escaping from my forbidden fruit, travelling to a new city.

When the boarding started, I opened my cell phone and checked Adam's voicemail, which he had left the day before.

"Hi, Rania. This is Adam. I just called to see if you're doing okay." He paused again as if he was failing to find words. *"I don't know if I should say this or not, but I miss you. I'm in Montreal on business and will be back tonight. I was hoping you'd call, but I'm sure you must be busy. I look forward to seeing you tomorrow at work. Take care."*

Even after my rudeness, not calling him and thanking him for his kindness, he was still worried about me. After so many years, someone was looking after me. No one would believe I'd seen another side of Adam, which no one knew. The image of the playboy he had managed to keep all these years—I see it now that it's just for the show. He wasn't what the media said. *One who is not thankful to a person is not grateful to God.* The Prophet's quote buzzed in my head, and I decided to call him, thanking him during my journey.

I took out my breakfast from the bag—banana bread and tea—and looked out the window. It was seven in the morning. The train slowly started moving, and the city covered in glittery snow blurred like a carousel but was still waking up.

I pondered on Ben's warning—my father's message. After my mother's death, it was just his job that was keeping him active. Otherwise, he'd have decayed in depression. It had been five years since we'd spoken. What I had done was reprehensible.

By the time the train crossed the borders of GTA, I'd finished my breakfast. The next main stop was Peterborough. I started my book, glancing at the view in between, but eventually dozed off. I woke to the sound of commotion, realizing I'd slept till the next stop. It was densely covered with snow.

I looked outside to see which station it was, but I couldn't figure it out. Had I slept my entire journey?

A staff member of Asian descent announced they were shifting passengers bound for Quebec City to another compartment. I told her my seat had been reserved for the journey, but she convinced me that seats could be changed without notice. She assured me that my luggage would be moved.

I followed her quietly and ended up in a super glam compartment. I took in my surroundings, wondering if she had mistakenly led me to business class, but with a pleasant smile, she asked me to take a seat.

White leather couches with high-definition flat screens on the other side adorned the room. Rich and soothing perfume filled my senses. A small bar and dance floor awaited its patrons at one corner. The sleeper cabins were tastefully designed with comfortable beds and attached mini washrooms. *It's a moving hotel!* Though my journey was short, and perhaps I wouldn't need a cabin, stretching my legs sounded very enticing.

I verified my ticket, wondering if Ben had been generous when booking my journey, but it still showed economy class.

I took my seat, and the same girl appeared again, offering me fresh orange juice and fresh fruits, chilled to the perfect temperature.

The train moved again, but the strange part was that no one else was in the coach. Of course, it wasn't easy to afford all this, but something was odd and alarming. I should be excited if the staff made a mistake and I ended up here, but something didn't feel right. My chances of being struck by a lightning bolt were higher than winning a lottery, and this was no less than a lottery.

I resumed my reading. I was on a fictional joy ride. I didn't realize it was heavily snowing outside as if the blizzard was on its way.

After many minutes of reading, I put my e-reader down and closed my eyes to give them rest.

"Reading is good, but you shouldn't overstrain your eyes." It was a familiar voice.

I snapped my eyes open, finding Adam sitting opposite me. I rubbed my eyes again, wondering if I was daydreaming, but he smiled at me. His gaze was, as usual, very intense, and he kept stroking his lower lip with his index finger.

I looked around the coach to check my whereabouts, wondering if I was imagining this. "It's just the two of us, Rania. There is no one else." He still smirked at my expression. *What is he doing here?*

Perhaps dread and shock were evident on my face, so he added, "You're still on Via Rail, and you're still heading to Quebec City." I got to my feet slowly, gaping. "Don't worry. You're not abducted. Sit down." I took my seat.

I looked around again, checking if they had a button to call staff or help as they do on flights, but the dread was blurring my vision. But what would I call for? He was not harassing me. I didn't own the coach.

He studied my every action. I tried not to show my fear,

but my hands still trembled, thinking of all the things a psycho stalker could do. He managed to sneak into my apartment building. He managed to chase me on my journey. What else was he capable of?

Leaning forward, he took my hands, his gaze intensifying, turning into a darker shade of green, like a dense forest.

"Are you running away from me?"

A dark shadow flickered in his eyes. I had no freaking idea where we even were geographically, and he thought *I* was running?

I looked down at our entwined hands. I wonder if he was agitated that I never returned his call or texted him. Would he take it as an insult? What would he do?

"Rania?" He gently caressed my palm with his thumb as if wanting to read my lines. I didn't look up. "Am I frightening you?" His simple touch was turning my bones into liquid, making me mushy from the inside.

I just sat there, pretending to be numb. I wanted to say no, that I was a horrible person for not thanking him for that night, that I felt embarrassed about breaking down in front of him. Instead, I squeezed his hands tighter. He moved closer and knelt before me to meet my eyes.

"Are you running away from me?"

"Thank you for the flowers." I finally met his gaze. I couldn't find words to talk about my breakdown.

His shoulders relaxed. "I thought you didn't notice. I—"

"It was the first thing I saw in the morning. Thank you." He didn't know anything about me. I was neither pure nor innocent.

He got up and sat beside me—very close, reading my every expression.

Still feeling the heat of his passionate gaze, I mustered my courage to continue, "I'm not running. It's an official trip. I have a conference to attend." I slid closer to the window, creating distance between us. As if on cue, he moved back to his seat opposite me.

We sat in silence for a long time. The only sound we heard was the movement of the train. I felt his heated gaze, but I kept looking out the window. There was nothing other than the white landscape.

Everything that Ben told me about my father's job and Adam's lifestyle…it all started to toll, like a warning bell before the war. I knew I should stay away from him, that perhaps he had the power to hurt me, but I wasn't scared of him. He didn't harm me when I was in my most vulnerable state. Why would he harm me here?

Still, I was curious about what a man who ran such a vast empire was doing on a weekday.

"What are you doing here?"

He gave a slight lopsided grin. "Going to Quebec City."

"Do you have business there?"

Oh! That pompous grin! "By now, you should have guessed I'm chasing you." *Of course, you are!*

"Was there anything urgent?"

He leaned forward, elbows on his knees. "I wanted to see you."

"We would have planned for next week."

"I could not wait." His sincere answer moved something inside me. "You didn't mention you were going. I learned from your office that you aren't coming for a week."

"Am I supposed to share my schedule with Gibson Enterprises now?"

He released a heavy sigh and sat back. "It's just Adam here." The way he said it, with so much conviction, made me almost believe that he was just a boy falling in love with a girl. But I must not forget that tagging my name with his would put me on centre stage.

"How did you find me?"

"You weren't on any flights. You don't drive. There was no bus schedule today. So, the train was the only other option." *Stalker!* "By the time I found out where you were, your train was almost outside the border of GTA."

"You could have flown directly to Quebec City," I mumbled.

"I wanted to share this ride."

"How did you even get here?" I failed to control the curiosity in my voice.

The corners of his lips twitched in a smile. "You know, Rania, I can track you down. Why do you always ask?"

"No, of course. With your stalking nature, you'd know where I was, but how did you reach here?"

"My friend is in charge of operations for Via Rail. I asked him to stop the train for a while at the nearest station. You were in Kingston when you moved in here." Now I know how I got so lucky to move in here.

"But how did you reach Kingston?" *See, Rania! You* are *struck by a lightning bolt. Winning the lottery is never meant for you.* "It's a three-hour drive. Did you teleport?" I sounded very sarcastic, but the fact was, I was flabbergasted.

He pursed his lips, trying to suppress his smile. "Yes, you can call it a chopper." *Of course, he has a chopper. This man knows how to use his fucking money.*

He leaned forward again. "Why are you running?"

"I'm not running," I objected. "I told you I have a conference to attend."

"The conference starts Thursday. You'll reach Quebec by evening." I blinked at him, wondering what to say in my defence. "You're a very pathetic liar, Rania. So, stop lying. It shows on your face." He chuckled, reading my stunned expression. "I know you're running away from me. I don't know why I intimidate you. I don't know if it was yesterday's news or the flowers or my voicemail, but I'm certain you're avoiding me." He took my hands again. "This whole coach is booked for us, all the way through Quebec. We will be together till evening. There is no media, no restaurant server, and no one to take our pictures and post them on the Internet. It is just us."

Six more hours with him? In this coach? I couldn't breathe properly when he was around, and he expected me to stay with him all day.

"This train will stop at Ottawa for half an hour. If you're not comfortable by that time, I'll head off. But until then, I want to know what's troubling you. What is it that frightens you about me?" He paused for a second and continued. "I know you're judging me from my past habits, but trust me, it's not like what you think."

I saw the sincerity in his eyes. All his declarations diffused in my blood like a drug, but I had only one question in my mind.

"Why me?"

He took a deep breath, taking a moment to respond.

"One day, I will tell you why I chase you like a maniac." So, he acknowledged his craziness. "But not today because I know you won't believe me." He mentioned this over dinner, too. Did I remind him of someone? I wanted to know, but since he already said not today, it was pointless to ask. "I feel I've been living in the dark, and you're the only one who could bring me into the light. I know it's crazy for me to follow you down the train tracks. But I'm living the life of a moth that wants to stay close to the light, yet it knows it will flay soon. I know you have nothing to give me, and I'll end up burning, but I can't help it."

His sudden confessions almost brought tears to my eyes. He didn't admit he was in love with me, but what I saw in his eyes was beyond the feeling of love. I couldn't name it. How could I enlighten him when my soul was lost in darkness?

"Adam, please…"

"I will not go anywhere until you tell me why you're running from me."

I took a moment to reveal the truth. "Ben called me this morning." It was pointless hiding from him, as he would find out himself eventually. "He was not happy with the media attention."

"As far as I noticed, he was trying to push you to establish a relationship with me." *Oh god! He is smart.* "Why a sudden change of hearts?"

"He is sort of my guardian here. My father has given him responsibility for me. Baba is not happy about the news. I'm sure you know who he is. He has a very respectable job, and people gossiping about his daughter is not good for him." I averted my gaze to look outside. The snow was getting denser, and I had no idea how much time had passed.

"People should mind their own business," he snapped.

"Adam, you and I belong to different cultures," I argued, my voice clipped. "We don't have the liberty to be seen in public with boys. In our culture, a girl's virtue and image is an honour. Dating men, especially those who are always in the limelight, is not something I can afford. I can't make you understand, but all I can say is that this is creating trouble for my father at work."

"He can let you hang around with Mike since childhood, but this news is creating issues at his work. Ha!" He sat back, grunting with disapproval. "That's bigotry."

"Stop comparing yourself with Mike. He is my childhood friend. You are…." I paused. "Baba said he isn't stupid that he can't see how you looked at me when we were dancing." Adam shut his eyes momentarily at my words.

"Why don't you tell him we are just friends? Like you and Mike are."

"Are we friends? Really?" He looked away. "Anyone can see how you look at me."

"I can't help it."

"You're making it obvious, Adam. Even my father can see across seven seas what your intentions are."

"You think Mike doesn't look at you the same way?"

"With Mike, I don't end up on the front page of the newspapers every day. It's *you* who brings a spotlight on me."

He made a sour face and looked outside.

"So, if I were some ordinary guy, you'd have accepted my friendship?"

I remained quiet, not sure what to say in return. I never thought about it that way.

What if he was just Adam, with no wealthy and notable baggage attached to him? Would I have considered making him my friend? I didn't know. I was still aware of his feelings. We could never have a pure friendship when I knew we were both attracted to each other. But Baba wouldn't have known if I dated an ordinary man.

Reading him intently, I nodded. He scratched his temple, thinking. "So basically, my wealth is a problem for you. You won't accept me with this?"

"It's not about wealth, Adam. People know you. Anything you do becomes news. Please, keep me out of it. The media is always digging into your life. I don't want…" I zipped my lips, realizing what I was about to disclose.

"You don't want them to dig into your past?" He studied me curiously, but I looked outside. "What is it that you're hiding? Maybe I can help."

"It's not what you think."

"Then I want to know what it is."

I remained quiet, not willing to share anything. How could I trust him with my deepest, darkest secret? It was outlandish for anybody to believe.

"You can trust me," he said quietly.

I stared at him for endless beats, thinking what to say. It was too early to trust him. I didn't even know him. We met only two days ago. He and I both didn't know we existed.

"Like you said, it's too early. You won't believe me, either."

He seemed to think over it. "Friends, then?"

I couldn't help but smile at his persuasion, the way he offered me his hand again. "You are relentless."

He returned me a smile. "So I have been told."

As I took his hand, he sat next to me.

I tried to squeeze more toward the window, but he hadn't left me any space. Just then, his phone started ringing.

"Yes, Sylvain. Any news?"

"Mr. Gibson, I have sent all the details to Mr. Fraser, and they said they are interested in meeting you personally. I told them you are busy this week, but they—"

"Tell them I'm out of town. If they want to meet with me, I'll be available on Monday, but this week is not possible. I'm booked already." He glanced at me when he said *booked*. Although his phone wasn't on speaker, he was sitting so close to me that I could easily hear the other person on the line.

Is he postponing all his business meetings because of me? I wanted to ask, but then, he would say something that would make our situation more awkward. I picked up my e-reader and resumed my reading while he explained a few things to Sylvain. Still, during his conversation, I could feel his eyes on me.

"Yes, Mr. Gibson," said Sylvain. "I will schedule it for Monday. Thank you. Good day."

I didn't initiate our conversation because, in my book, I was at a point where the man was about to confess his feelings.

"I want to know what you're reading," Adam began, his voice conspiringly low. "What's the secret behind this secret smile?"

Was I smiling?

"Nothing." I shut the case. "I picked an advanced reader copy of some book and have to write a review about it."

Before he added something to it, my phone started ringing. I fished it out of my bag, noticing it was Ben calling.

"Pick it up," Adam ordered as he read Ben's name on Caller ID. "He's been calling me since morning. I wanna know what he wants to talk to you."

"Why do you want to know?" The call ended by then. Before I could say more, Ben called again.

"Put it on speaker."

"You're impossible," I grunted. "Hi, Ben. Good afternoon." I picked up the call.

"Hey, Rania, how is your train trip going so far?"

"Never better."

"Listen, do you know where Gibson is?"

"Why do you ask?" I glanced at Adam.

"Right. How would you know? You are travelling," Ben mumbled. "I spoke to his assistant, and she told me Mr. Gibson is out of town for the whole week. I was just wondering if he told you about his plans."

I glanced at Adam again, thinking about what to say, but he shrugged nonchalantly as if he didn't care what Ben thought.

"I'll let you know if I find out," I answered. "How is the moving going?"

"Ah yes, we can work from the new location next Monday. You carry on and enjoy the conference. I heard there are some fresh graduates attending as well. Try to meet them and see if any are a good fit for us. We need some bilingual people, too. I trust you."

"Thanks, Ben. I'll keep that in mind."

"I have emailed your hotel bookings and conference tickets. And one more thing." He paused for a moment. "Stay safe. He is a dangerous man, Rania. Keep your eyes and ears open. Your father is very concerned." *Right!*

"Oh, I know how concerned he is about his reputation. Don't

worry. Tell him I won't ruin it."

"But Gibson is a man with power. He possesses what he wants. I don't want you to end up being one of his possessions—"

"That will not happen, Ben."

"I'm sorry I shouldn't say this, but after what happened to Sarah, Ahmed has been like this." He didn't need to elaborate on how my father had changed after my mother's death. "But I just want to say I understand your situation, Rania. I also miss Sarah. If Ahmed is not moving on, you should." Had he called me to talk about my past?

"I am trying, Ben," I said, my voice slowly cracking. "Can we talk later, please?"

Perhaps he understood. "Sure." And I disconnected the line.

I tried to gulp down my tears, but somehow, they still managed to blur my vision. Without seeking my permission, Adam draped his arm around me, sensing that I needed comfort. Why was it that whenever he offered me his hand or comfort, I willingly took it? Why did my body always act greedily for his touch? We barely knew each other, but every time he was close to me, I felt protected and sheltered.

He was entering through the darkest passage of my heart without even knocking at the door. A tree of forbidden fruit, walking down close to tempt me.

"I will not ask about your past," he said. "If you think being with me will bring your past into your present, then I take all the responsibility to protect you from it. But please, don't ask me to stay away from you. I can't do that. If you think fame is causing trouble, we can keep our relationship private. I will use all my power to protect you, Rania. All I want is your trust. That's it." He gently rubbed his hand on my arm, comforting me. I never wanted to leave here. I already felt protected.

"Why are you doing this?"

"I don't know. Maybe God has appointed me for that?"

"You don't even believe in God," I chuckled.

He studied me intently. "You know, everyone is sent with a purpose. I guess this is my purpose." He gave me a soft smile. "Perhaps I'm beginning to believe He exists." His warmth melted me like snow under the sun.

We stayed in companionable silence as the train whirred at its constant speed, scenes shifting in blurry motion.

After a few minutes, he asked, "So, dangerous, eh?" He smirked. "You know…the more he talks, the more he pisses me off."

I let out a snort. "Please, don't sabotage his business deal with you."

"Of course not. I would never put you in a difficult situation. But what's his fuckin' problem? He's not your dad."

"As if you don't know?"

He shrugged as if he really didn't know.

"First," I counted on my finger. "Your reputation precedes you, Mr. Gibson."

He rolled his eyes.

"Secondly, I believe he sees my mother in me. That's what makes him more protective of me." Adam slid back a little bit, looking at me inquisitively. "Ben and my parents graduated from the same university. They all met in Scotland. Ben was the first man who proposed to my mother."

"Seriously? He was your mom's boyfriend?"

"Not a boyfriend. He was in love with her, but it was one-sided. My father joined a semester later. It was love at first meet-up for both. Since they both belonged to the same culture and religion, my father had the privilege of marrying my mother after their graduation." I recalled the time when Mom told me about this. "I think he doesn't treat me as Ahmed's daughter but as Sarah's daughter and feels responsible for taking care of me."

"That's interesting! So, your mom and dad had a love

marriage?"

"Yes, they did," I answered. "My grandfather was not happy with the idea, though, because my mother was Egyptian and my father was from Lebanon. My grandfather wanted her to marry an Egyptian and stay in the same country."

"Your parents told you their love story?"

"I was sixteen when my mother told me. Whenever she talked about Ben, I always saw sparkles in her eyes. It was a very strange affection."

"Did your mother ever love Ben?"

"I don't know—she never confessed that. All I know is Baba had the advantage of being a Muslim. But he loved her. All my childhood, I never saw them arguing or fighting. He is still in love with my mother as he never married again." I looked down, just noticing that his hand was caressing mine. "Whenever I saw them together, I believed that fairytales do exist. Love exists. We just need to find the right person." I paused. "Mom had very hard labour during my birth. Baba wanted a son, too, but he couldn't see my mother in pain again. So, he never demanded another child. I guess that's what love is."

Perhaps noticing the pain in my eyes, he changed the subject. "And what makes him think I'm dangerous? I mean Ben."

I cleared my throat. "Do you want me to show you the articles about your lifestyle?"

He grinned at me, and we both burst into laughter.

"Do you see danger?" He sounded serious.

I thought about it for a moment. "I see the danger. I won't lie. But not for me."

"Oh, don't go there again." He got to his feet and ran his fingers through his hair. "Nothing can make me change my mind for you."

"You're risking your reputation. I don't—"

He cut me in the middle by offering his hand. "Dance. You

owe me a dance."

His sweet smile made me follow his steps as he guided me to the dance floor. I just noticed now that he wore a dark grey suit tailored to perfection. His tie was already loosened when he came in.

The music—Shostakovich's Waltz No. 2 started playing itself. I didn't know how he did it, but I was impressed. My heart suddenly felt lighter, as if a heavy fog was lifted off my soul. We danced slowly in a muted silence, enjoying each other closeness. The lights kept changing above us, and I wondered if someone else was there.

As if reading my mind, he added, "There is no one here. I have promised to protect your privacy, and I'll keep my promise."

"So, you booked the whole coach just to—"

"I can keep this train moving for the rest of my life if you keep on dancing with me."

"You always surprise me," I said, feeling the heat of his gaze. His words were creating a haze around us.

"I wish I could tell you what you do to me," he mumbled. Perhaps he thought I didn't hear it, but his words filled the room with warmth.

"This is very lavish. You shouldn't have spent so much."

"Do you have any idea what this means to me?" He nodded at our hands. I looked away, purposely trying to avoid his evident feelings for me. "So, what did you do yesterday, apart from being reprimanded by your *guardian*?" He sounded sarcastic.

"I was babysitting." He knitted his eyebrows at my answer. "One of my neighbours has twin girls, around nine months old. They're adorable. I guess they are the best things in my life. I look forward to every Sunday afternoon." I smiled.

"You babysit every Sunday?"

"Almost. I give the parents some time out. Meanwhile, I play with the babies. But they are going on vacation for a few weeks.

I'll miss the little angels. I don't even realize how time flies with them." I smiled sadly. "I wonder if this is how parenting is. In a blink, your kids grow up from kindergarten to college."

As if he could sense my yearning, he didn't say anything.

We continued with our slow dance, and I didn't object when he placed his hand on my back and pulled me closer. I rested my head on his chest, feeling his warmth, his intoxicating cologne filling my senses. *What is happening to me?* My soul feels free when I am in his embrace. He said he was drawn to me, but he didn't know the feeling was mutual. I didn't know if I'd ever be able to express my feelings to him. But I must tell him that I was grateful for his comfort.

"Adam?" I paused for a moment, waiting for his response.

"Hmm?"

"Thank you for everything." The music still played behind us, the track switching to Schubert's Serenade. Classical music had never felt so calming before. "In case I didn't mention it earlier…I trust you." He eased his embrace to regard me, delight dancing in his eyes. "I hope we never break this trust."

"Never."

"You don't know anything about me. There are things I wish I could tell, but—"

"It's enough for now that you trust me. I want to know you better, but let's give each other some more time until we form a bond where you don't have to think before talking to me." I rested my head on his chest again.

After our blissful, magical moment, I excused myself to visit the restroom. He guided me even though the entire coach was at our disposal. We could move about however we pleased.

After my restroom visit, I looked up at the panoramic glass ceiling. It was dark already, though it wasn't even two. I was also hungry. Perhaps I'd grab something from Ottawa Station.

As if my stomach was audibly grumbling, Adam said, "Let's

eat something."

We sat by the bar, and Adam handed me the menu. There was a menu! Of course, there was. It was a business class. We ordered a hummus sandwich, fresh orange juice and a platter of fruits. The order came in no time.

"I'll be back," he said.

Just when Adam disappeared into the restroom, his phone started ringing. I peeked over the table, wondering if Ben was calling again, but the Caller ID said, 'Brian Moore.' The call kept on ringing until it went to voicemail.

"Do you want something else," Adam asked as he sat back.

"I'm good." I took a bite of the sandwich. "Your phone was ringing." He checked his phone, his expression darkening. "Everything okay?"

Just as he picked up his sandwich, the phone rang again. It was the same Caller ID.

"Attend your call. It could be important."

"Never mind." He rejected the call and continued eating.

I was now concerned about the way he was behaving, but we ate in silence. As long as I could remember, Brian Moore was Adam's stepfather.

After a few minutes, the phone rang again. "Pick it up, Adam." He didn't pay any attention and continued eating. I pressed the accept on his behalf and put the phone on speaker, gesturing for him to speak.

He rolled his eyes. "Yes, Mrs. Moore."

"Hi, Adam. How are you?" The woman called him by his first name, which meant this wasn't an official call. If it was Brian, then it could be his wife—Adam's mother.

"Why did you call?" I felt the tension in his voice.

"I read the news. I'm happy for you. The girl is pretty."

"Yes, she is," he replied in an undertone, glancing at me. *Oh, they are talking about me.* "Is that the only reason you called?" I noticed he had stopped eating. He closed his eyes, rubbing his forehead.

"It's nice that you finally found someone. It's obvious how you look at her, even in the pictures."

"Oh! So you can read my eyes, eh?"

"Adam, I'm your mother. Of course, I can read my son." *I was right!*

"Did you want anything else, Mrs. Moore?" Adam asked annoyingly. *How can he talk to his mother like that?*

"I called to invite you for a family holiday dinner on Saturday."

"We are not family, Mrs. Moore. You have a family, which you *chose* over us, and I suppose they will show up." He kept his eyes closed, but I could feel how stressed he was.

"You are my family, too, Adam. I was wondering if you could bring Rania with you—"

"We've already accepted an invitation elsewhere. I'm afraid we won't be able to come." *When did that happen?*

"You do this every year, Adam—"

"But I don't see why you call me every year when you know I won't come," he snapped.

"Adam, I—"

"I am busy, Mrs. Moore. I'll talk to you later. Bye." And he hung up the phone.

He remained quiet. Although he needed comfort, a reproach was much needed.

"Adam, were you talking to your mother?" He looked away. "Do you realize how you were acting? She was—"

"You don't know anything, Rania."

"No, I don't know. But I saw you spoke to her very rudely, and this is not the way to talk to her," I scolded him.

"What? You think I'm at fault?" His eyes widened at my reprimand.

"I don't know who's done what, but right now, you *are* at

fault. She called to invite you for the dinner, and you—"

"I haven't seen her in ages. I can't accept it now."

"Call her and apologize," I ordered, folding my arms over my chest.

"What? You expect me to call her and say sorry? For what?"

"For your behaviour, Adam. This is not the right way."

Leaving his seat, he shook his head in frustration. "I can't believe you're asking me this."

"Yes, you will do it. We have accepted each other as friends, so in friendship, you will listen to me."

"Are you threatening me?" I hadn't seen Adam acting so insolent.

"No, but you're wasting all your good deeds when you're not good to your mother. God will not like it."

"Oh, for fuck's sake. Don't lecture me about God now," he snapped. "I had only one relation, and that was my father. Then *your* God took my father from me, left me with nothing. And you say I should be grateful to Him?"

"But He gave you a good heart," I objected. "You feed and provide shelter to so many people. He is watching you. You have a very powerful soul. Nothing will be wasted. You will be rewarded in life, maybe through a stronger relationship. Or a more prosperous life."

"I have more than enough, Rania. And I worked bloody hard to earn it. Your God didn't shower it from Heavens."

His words made me realize that perhaps he wasn't angry at his mother but at God.

"But don't abandon what is left to you. Time doesn't wait for anyone. I can't believe you reject her every year. See, she still calls you. It is only because her love is unconditional."

"Oh yeah? Where was her love when I was only six, and she left me? She married a rich man, leaving my father and me in hard times. Where was love then?" He held back his anger, and

I realized he was restraining his tears, too. Holding him firmly from his shoulders, I guided him to sit again.

"Spit it out, Adam. Let it go."

He stayed silent for a few minutes, then finally began. "I haven't seen her in so many years, except occasionally at parties, but it has been a long time. She calls me every year, but I always refuse. It's very hard for me to confront her now, after so long. I can't do it. I don't know how I'd react. I don't know if I'd be able to talk to her or not. That frustration comes out in the form of rudeness every time I talk to her. I can never forget what she did to me, Rania. I needed her so much. We had no home, and when I used to sleep in shelters with strangers…" His voice trailed off. Pain flickered in his eyes. He had suffered so much in his childhood, and there was nothing I could do to change it.

"I understand your pain, Adam, but it's over now. You can't go back and fix it, but you can make the most of what you have now. Did you ever try asking her why she left you? You've heard only your father's side of the story."

"What excuse could there be to leave a child?"

"At least try to talk to her. It's obvious she wants to reconcile, and I know, deep inside, you want her in your life, too. You're dragging it for no reason. Life is too long to hate someone, but it is too short to love." I picked up his phone from the counter. "Now, you will call her and apologize and tell her you'll join her for dinner."

"But she has asked you to come also."

"I'll come with you. Now that we are friends, I'll ensure you talk to your mother and sort out all your differences." I smiled at him, handing him his phone. "Call her."

"I can't believe you're making me do this," he mumbled. "I didn't know you could be so controlling."

"It's persuasion," I grinned at him. "And I learned it from the expert."

He shook his head and dialled the number. She answered on the second ring. "Adam, you called back?" I heard the joy in her voice.

"I called to say…umm…I'm sorry for my behaviour…" He glanced at me with hesitation.

"Oh, Brian, my son has called me…" She called out to her husband. "That's all right, my dear. You've called me for the first time. That's what matters most."

"I also called to say that we will join you for the holiday dinner."

"You will?" Mrs. Moore's voice was filled with happiness.

"Yes, we both will come." His gaze softened as he watched me.

"Oh, Brian, he said he'd come for dinner. I'm so happy, Adam. I love you so much." He remained quiet, so I mouthed to say, *i-love-you-too-mother.* He rolled his eyes at me, and I glared back.

"I love you too…Mom." He averted his gaze.

"Oh, Brian! He said he loves me too." I felt a sense of achievement in her voice. It was a joy to hear.

"I'll see you on Saturday. Bye." He disconnected the line without listening to any goodbye from her side.

He got to his feet and headed to the bar. I picked up my orange juice and followed him. I sat opposite him, watching him make his drink—scotch on the rocks. Evidently, he was agitated about what I made him do, but I still said, "Thank you for listening."

He didn't answer as he downed his drink and made another one. It was time to change the subject.

"Do you mind if I ask you something personal?"

He nodded. I patted the seat next to me. He came over and sat beside me, giving me his undivided attention.

"This." I showed him my phone—the article about Friday's

party. "It says that was the first time you've been spotted dancing with someone."

"Yeah?" His voice sounded coarse.

"But you also pick up women at parties. It's not that you haven't danced before."

He returned a shy smile, his mood slowly changing. Was he blushing?

"You know…how you don't know a person on a flight, and yet you sit with them even if you don't have a choice."

I didn't believe he had ever flown in a commercial flight or economy class, but okay.

"They are mostly business associates or someone who accompanies me later to bed," he continued. "I have never approached a woman before. That's what surprised the media."

I was still curious. "So, the ladies you…umm…slept with. You never knew them?"

"No."

"What do you talk about then?"

He knitted his eyebrows as if I had asked him the formula of kinetic energy. "We fuck. That's it."

I coughed at his words. "You don't even inquire their names?"

He shrugged. "Do I have to? When I don't have to see her again?"

"Right." He sounded like a spoiled rich billionaire from the books who spends his evenings drinking, partying and then sleeping with a new woman every day. How cliché!

I knew it was too personal to ask these questions but now I was suddenly curious about how his brain functions in that department. When he had asked me out, poured out his heart at every turn, demanded my trust, stalked me on a train ride, I must know what he did to the women he'd met.

"And what happens when you don't like someone?"

He looked at me blankly as if he had no idea what I'd asked.

"I've never thought about liking or disliking. I never notice their faces, really. Even if I did, I don't remember. Their job has always been to fulfill my sexual needs."

His statement was so blatant that I choked on my juice, coughing again. I should have known how blunt he was—that he always spoke his mind. Placing a hand on my back, he rubbed it. "Are you okay?"

I nodded, trying to digest his words.

As if he could read my churning mind, he said, "Your mind is too loud." I snapped my gaze at him. "What else do you want to know?"

"Did you ever have a girlfriend?"

I knew he hadn't because the media said so, but I was still curious. Maybe a high school sweetheart?

"I have never taken interest in anyone until now."

I looked away at his words. I should stop inquiring more, but my curiosity got the better of me. The more I asked about him, the more he appeared as someone from a dirty romance novel.

"Umm…did you like anyone after your night?"

"I told you. I don't remember any. They were paid to please me. That's it."

"Have you ever tried pleasing any of them?"

"What does that even mean?"

"I mean…I've read a man enjoys giving a woman pleasure more than taking from her. Her moans are usually a turn-on for a man," I explained. "Have you ever thought of pleasing anyone?"

His eyes turned a darker shade of green again—the same forest that made me wander through it. His mind was arrested, thinking as he stroked his lips with his index finger.

"This is what you read?" He nodded at my e-reader kept by the window.

"No," I objected defensively. "But in some romance novels, a man wants to give pleasure rather than demand it."

"None of them ever asked for any pleasure."

I rolled my eyes. "No woman does. Duh! You have to figure it out on your own."

He put his glass down, his gaze suddenly inquisitive. "And how do I do that?"

I felt heat crawling up my face. I cooled myself down by taking another sip of orange juice. Where was this going? Now, I was supposed to tell him how to please a woman?

"I really want to know," he said innocently. "How do I know a woman wants pleasure from a man?"

"How do I know?"

"Like, you know what men usually like," he snorted as he nodded at my e-reader again.

"Oh, that!" I blinked at the device. "In books, they say the man senses it from a woman's body language, like a change in heart rate, or breathing style or body temperature."

He looked at me for endless beats—as one looks at an art piece in a museum.

Before he could add something, I asked again, "It's quite strange that even though you have slept with so many women, there is no mention of a girlfriend in any news."

"I'm a very private man, Rania," he said quietly. "If you've read about my lifestyle, then you'd know I don't do girlfriends."

"Not even a high school sweetheart?"

He smiled sadly. "I couldn't afford that time."

"Huh?"

"I haven't been rich all my life. I've seen what poverty is. I know what hunger is. When my mother left us, my father was in a very bad financial state. He could hardly afford meals for us. He used to drop me at the community center after school and then went back to work. I used to eat whatever people provided, used to wear their discarded clothes. You can't understand what hunger is unless you've experienced it. I was homeless for three years." His confession stunned me. Was this the reason for him providing shelter and food to the needy—because he had experienced such need in his childhood? I truly felt sorry for him. "Later on, in high school, I paid my own bills by working part-time. I couldn't even afford to go to prom." I felt so horrible and sad that I just stared at him in return. "It was either prom or my grad. We didn't have enough to attend both."

"I…" I didn't know what to say.

"Did you have a prom?"

"I did," I said cheerily, willing to change the subject. "I studied in an American school in Dubai."

"And I believe Mike was your date?"

I chuckled at his question. "Mike had already moved to Canada by then, but he flew back to be my date. Baba would never allow anyone else."

"Of course," he mumbled.

He remained quiet for a moment, and I sensed he was thinking about his teenage years. What a sad high school he had.

"So, are you an only child, or do you have siblings?" he asked.

"As if you don't know after all the research." He gave a short laugh. "But I had a very colourful childhood. Although I had no siblings, Mike was my family. We were both born and brought up in Beirut. When I was fifteen, my father got his UN job and moved to Dubai. Ben and Mike moved to Canada. I did my secondary schooling there. I moved here when I was twenty. You know the rest."

"Do you want to talk about your mother?"

Stale years and regrets whipped in front of my eyes. I blinked away the tears and left my seat.

As if sensing my hesitation, he took my hand. "I'm sorry. I shouldn't have asked." He gently walked me to the nearby couch and pulled me into his embrace. It was strange how willingly my body submitted to him…again. "I'll wait until you're willing to talk about it." With eyes cast down, I noticed a tiny mole on the back of his palm. "But you know that sharing your pain eases your burden. I'm no doctor, but if it helps, I'm always here to listen."

I let his words sink in as the sound of the train moving swiftly calmed me down. "I miss her. Every day. Every moment." He remained quiet and patient. "Sometimes I picture the whole scene in my mind where I'm calling her, telling her about my day, asking about a new recipe, or even just gossiping about something. She was like a friend to me."

"How old were you?"

"Eighteen."

He gave a heavy sigh. "You're lucky you get to spend your childhood with her. It's hard to grow up without a mother."

I sensed pain in his words, yet I didn't push him or inquire why he never visited or talked to his mother when they lived in the same city. If it were ever possible, I'd call my mom every day. But my heart was too heavy right now to ask him about his life.

The train slowly came to a halt. I knew we'd reached Ottawa, but this warmth was so calming that I didn't wish to leave it. This coach was booked for us, so I was sure no one would interrupt us. He asked me if I didn't want him, he'd walk out at this station. Perhaps he was thinking the same. But I kept my head on his chest, let his arm wrap around me until the moment passed and the train started again.

I didn't realize when I dozed off in his arms.

CHAPTER 8
MAISON CARTIER

ADAM

I WOKE UP AT THE SOUND OF COMMOTION. Rania sleepily stirred beside me.

Was I in heaven? Or perhaps this was how heaven was meant to be—waking up with the most beautiful woman beside you.

"Hey."

She blinked and looked around. "I can't believe I napped again."

"I'm not complaining," I grinned at her. Placing my palm on her face, I said, "Do you have any idea how beautiful you are?"

She rolled her eyes. "Have we reached?"

"Yes, we have."

She got to her feet. "And you're sitting like you have nothing else to do."

"I don't."

"Let me bring my trolley bag."

When we stepped out at the platform, she looked at me with mild surprise. "I see you didn't bring any clothes."

"Oh, it's already in my car." I checked the time. "Let's head out. I think it's here."

She blinked at me again, looking stunned. "Adam." I paused and turned around. "I have this reservation at a hotel." She showed me her phone. "I know if I had mentioned taking a cab, then you'd have made a whole deal about it, so I'm asking politely if you could give me the ride there."

"I'm glad you're beginning to know me now," I smirked. "Show it to my chauffeur when we sit."

"Of course, you'd have a chauffeur," she mumbled as we exited Gare du Palais.

As the car started, I gave the address to the driver.

"Your plan here was spontaneous," she began. "Did you manage to book anything?"

"No." I sat back. "I'm coming with you."

"What?" She snapped her head in my direction. "That's not possible."

"Why not?"

"Because," she glanced at the driver and lowered her voice, "it has a single bed."

"I'll sleep on the couch."

"There is no couch."

"Then I'll sleep on the floor."

"Oh, you are impossible." She huffed and looked out the window. "Where are we going?"

I inclined toward her and looked out from her window. "It isn't in the Old Quebec. Where the hell did you book?"

She pouted her lips with agitation but didn't answer. We let the car take us until it stopped outside an old, run-down building. "Nous sommes là, monsieur," the driver announced. *We are here, Sir.*

"Attends ici un moment," I instructed the driver. *Wait here for a while.*

I collected Rania's trolley bag from the trunk. She punched the code on the security keypad by the entrance and let us in.

"I assume there is no elevator?" I asked, looking around the dingy staircase going up, with moulded carpet and some strange smell I couldn't place. It didn't even have a foyer or reception.

"There are two floors. What do you expect?" She snapped. I could sense she wasn't much excited about her booking either. What did she even think?

On the first floor, she checked the doors. "Door 3." She pointed, punched another code, and let us in.

I looked around and whistled. It was a horrible, horrible room. A small bed that wouldn't fit a tall man of my height, wallpapers with their colours lost or chipping at most places, a table they might have picked from some garage sale with a coffee machine on it. I wouldn't dare to make coffee in that. And that was it. There was no nightstand, no TV, no dresser.

"Maison Cartier," I said amusingly.

She folded her arms and looked at me sharply. "You are welcome to check in elsewhere, monsieur."

"Did you already know they don't have an attached washroom?"

"Huh?" She looked around, clueless. "What the hell!" She opened the main door and peeked outside. "It never mentioned a communal washroom."

"This is what your company provides you?"

"No," she answered. "I have a booking in Chateau Frontenac starting Wednesday." She raised her chin with pride. "It's just a matter of two days. I came in early to use my holidays."

"And to avoid me," I added pointedly. "You seriously aren't considering staying here, are you?"

"Do I have a choice?"

"You do."

"Adam." She folded her arms again. "Old Quebec is out of my budget. You know, even a basic room is more than two hundred dollars per night. I'd rather spend that money on my food."

"But there is no space for me to sleep."

"You aren't even sleeping here. Get your own room."

"I can't imagine the daughter of the UN secretariat staying in a shady place like this."

She sighed and sat at the edge of the bed. "Adam, I have left that life a long time ago. I'm on my own now. I don't take money from my father."

I sat beside her. "Has he ever—"

"Yes. I have an account where he transfers money every month, but I don't use it. I don't want his money. That's not how it works."

Oh, she had too much pride. I couldn't even offer her to allow me to move her elsewhere, somewhere clean.

"Perhaps." I leaned in closer, wanting to say many things, when suddenly she shrieked and jumped up.

"Yikes!"

"What?"

"You have a spider on your arm," she screamed. I checked my left arm and jerked the spider off. "Aren't they supposed to hibernate during winter?" She ran around the room in panic, trying to escape it. "Oh, goodness! How many are there?"

I picked up the spider and tried to open the window. It didn't budge. "Help me open it."

"Oh, they gave the strict instruction not to open the window in winter."

"What?" I snapped at her. "Where do I throw it then?"

"In the corridor," she said, her face flushed.

"For fuck's sake." I headed out the door and dropped the spider on the moulded carpet. "Just FYI, you will freeze to death tonight because the radiator doesn't seem to work." I turned the knob on both sides, but nothing came to life. "Unless you plan to cuddle into me for warmth."

She huffed and puffed, sat on the bed but decided that perhaps another spider might surprise her, she got to her feet again.

"Call the concierge?" I suggested.

"There is no concierge," she mumbled.

"Right." I rolled my eyes. "I should have known."

"It didn't seem that bad on the website." She looked around again, hoping to find anything good about it, but there wasn't anything. Not even the location. "It says it's a boutique hotel."

I couldn't help but snort, but looking at her expression, I realized it was better to shut up.

"How about you forward me your booking, and I'll ask Ali to get you your refund?"

"But…"

I stepped forward and held her face in my palms. "Do you trust me?"

She blinked at me a few times. "I do," she whispered.

I wanted to kiss her right now, but something pulled me apart from her. I couldn't place it, but whenever I tried to close the gap between us, I felt someone around me. But there wasn't anyone here.

"Then come with me." I pulled back and collected her bag.

CHAPTER 9
THE CARRIAGE RIDE

RANIA

EMBARRASSMENT WAS AN UNDERSTATEMENT.

I had no right to object, argue, or even inquire where he was taking me. I was sure it would be better than what I left behind. I had no regrets.

Swallowing my pride, I looked out the window and noticed we were going uphill, back in the town. The ramparts along the left side passed in blurry movements. Wow! What a view! I could live here forever.

As the car entered the VIP valet of Chateau Frontenac, I felt like a princess whose carriage ride had brought her to a ball.

I have watched so many videos, seen so many pictures on the Internet of this hotel, but nothing compares to what you see with your naked eye. It was majestic!

Facing St. Lawrence River, on the upper side of the old town, the hotel had eighteen floors and more than six hundred guest rooms. I had read they had their own herb garden and cellar.

Too embarrassed to ask Adam if he already had bookings, I let him lead me out of the car and into the grand lobby through a revolving door.

For a moment, I froze in the lobby. Dark wood-panelled walls, coffered ceilings with beautiful ink-blue wainscots, huge immaculately clean marble tiles, and paintings of historic characters warmly welcomed us. Adam, perhaps noticing my awed expression, took my hand and led me to the front concierge.

"Bienvenue," said the woman at the reception, clad in a white blouse and black pencil skirt.

"Merci." Adam took out his wallet and placed a card at the reception desk. Even the people around me talked in French. I felt like I was in France.

The woman picked up the card, read it and flashed a smile at Adam.

"Bienvenue, Monsieur Gibson," she repeated. "We are always glad to see our Executive Gold Members."

"I requested for two rooms," he said.

"Yes, I believe I spoke to your assistant, Monsieur, but unfortunately, the hotel is booked entirely."

"What?" I interrupted, then noticing other heads in my direction, I lowered my voice. "There are more than six hundred rooms."

"Madame, Monsieur Prime Minister is here," she explained.

"Oh, right!" Adam said. "The G7 Summit. I completely forgot."

I cleared my throat, trying to clear the cotton ball stuck in it. The image of Maison Cartier still haunted me. Having the G7 Summit meant the leaders of seven countries, their staff, security, and other local ministers would all be residing here. I believe there weren't so many people to take over six hundred rooms, but perhaps, due to security reasons, they kept the hotel unavailable till the summit. It was pointless to argue with her because she wouldn't be available to help us.

"It will end this Wednesday," she added.

"So, there are no rooms left?" I asked.

"Oh, no, madame. We always keep a room for our gold members." She looked back at Adam. "Right now, we have only Grace of Monaco Suite available on the fifteenth floor."

"All right," Adam said as he took out his credit card.

I had gobbled through this hotel's website enough to know the room suites, and this one was like a chamber in a castle's tower. I didn't even know the per-night cost because they hadn't even mentioned it anywhere.

"Excuse me," I interrupted and grabbed Adam's arm to walk away from the reception. "Adam. We can't get that room."

"Why not?"

"You don't even know its price."

He raised his eyebrow as if I had asked him to walk naked in the lobby.

"If I am to split the cost here, I must know how much it is," I whispered.

He rolled his eyes and turned back to the reception. "Please, make the checkout for Saturday."

I waved at him to talk, but he ignored me.

"Merci, Monsieur Gibson," the woman said cheerily. "While we ensure the room is prepared, let us offer you some refreshments in La Bibliotheque."

She waved at the bellman, who appeared in a blink and instructed something to him in French.

"Par ici, Monsieur," the bellman said and led us to the other side of the lobby. We took the spiral stairs and entered Champlain—a classic landmark that offers an exquisite dining experience.

Tall, dark, wooden-framed windows overlooked the city on one side. The restaurant blended historic charm with the latest design, ornate woodwork, and a grand fireplace, highlighting its beauty. We crossed its gilded ceiling and navigated through the passage, the bar on my right, and into another private room. The restaurant was buzzing with people's chatter, clinks of glasses, men clad in tailored suits, and women wearing business casual clothing. I believe they were all part of the G7 Summit; perhaps some people from the media were also here.

As if the bellman could read my mind, he explained in his thick Quebecois accent, "The summit has kept the hotel very busy, but for our gold members, we offer services in La Bibliothèque and some reprieve from all this commotion."

Hundreds of books, enclosed in glass and dark wooden bookshelves, lined on one side, while tall windows overlooked the Dufferin Terrace and St. Lawrence River beyond. Beige armchairs and dark round tables complemented the room.

"Wow!" I exclaimed.

The bellman pulled the chair by the window for me first and then for Adam. "I will return later when your room is ready, Monsieur."

"A library." I looked around, fascinated. "I can live here."

In a blink, a server appeared and placed a platter of cheese and fruits.

"Bienvenue monsieur et madame," he said. "Je serai votre serveur aujourd'hui." *I'll be your server today.*

"Parlez vous Anglais?" I asked. That was the only thing I could speak in French. I tried so hard to learn in school but somehow never got the hang of it. I understood in pieces, though, but I couldn't speak at all.

"Of course, madame," the server said politely. "What would you like to have? We have some local champagnes from Île d'Orléans, and some vintage wines from Côte-de-Beaupré."

"Do you have any fresh fruit juices?" I asked.

"Orange juice?" he confirmed and turned to Adam. "And you, Monsieur?"

"I'll take from your white," Adam instructed. "Bring whatever you think is good."

The server nodded and left us.

I scooted the chair forward and looked around, ensuring no one was there. "Adam. You haven't told me the price of the room. I must know what I have signed up for."

Adam smiled shyly, broke the red grape from its stem and popped it into his mouth. "By now, you should learn I'm ignoring you on this topic."

"You can't do that. You can't pay for my stay here."

"I'm paying for mine, Rania." He sat back. "You are my guest. Just like I was in your Maison Cartier."

I narrowed my gaze at him. "You're mocking me."

"Oh, I cannot dare, Mademoiselle." Oh, again, this pompous grin.

I sat back and folded my arms over my chest. "I won't go in the room unless you tell me how much it costs."

"How about we make a deal?" He offered. "I know you did enough homework before coming here, so you must know the places to visit." I nodded. "You be my guide. In return, I offer you lodging."

"No guide is worthy enough to afford a place like this," I snorted.

"Mine is," he smirked. "Besides, it's only for two days. You do have your booking here from Wednesday." His words did make sense. "Otherwise, we can go back to your Maison Cartier."

I huffed at his mocking. "You knew…didn't you?"

"Knew what?"

"How the hotel was?"

"Don't insult it by calling it a hotel. It was merely a hostel."

"But you knew how it was?" He remained quiet. "And you chose to remain quiet."

He leaned forward. "If I had told you what a shady place you have booked, with no heater and no attached bath, would you have listened?"

I looked away, outside toward the river.

"You would have made a whole fuss about how you don't accept a penny from your father, so why would you accept my offer, blah blah."

The server appeared with a glass of orange juice for me and white wine for Adam. Perhaps, noticing our sour faces, he chose not to offer anything and left us.

"You promised to guard my privacy, and yet you bring me to a hotel, share a room. Do you think no one will find out?"

"No one will."

"This hotel must be flooded with media right now to cover the summit. You think no one will recognize you?"

"Rania," he said, "I have a team that works on these matters. I take the accountability for everything. I can't let you stay in that bloody room, nor do *I* wish to stay there."

"I'm not asking you to stay there," I objected. "You..." I exhaled heavily. It was pointless to argue with him. He would still stalk me in any case.

"Yes, say it," he challenged me. "Say what a crazy man I am."

So, you are!

But I looked away, seeking solace in books.

"And if it's troubling you, I'm asking you to be my guide. Show me the city."

"As if you haven't," I scoffed.

"I have not."

I narrowed my gaze at him. "You haven't visited Quebec City before?"

"No. I mean, yes. I have come here often for meetings and conferences but never had a chance to roam around. And come to think of it, how bizarre it sounds to walk alone."

"It's called solo travelling. I can't believe you haven't gone out." I looked around. "Not even Notre Dame?"

He looked out to the Dufferin Terrace—a dark shadow

crossing his face. "It gets very lonely." His gaze tracked the people walking in slushy snow on the terrace. "When you see people from up here, walking hand in hand, it's hard to find the courage to go out alone."

His words made me realize that money does not buy everything. Things like good company, an honest friend, or a passionate lover come to those who are blessed. He grew up alone, motherless. He had a lonely adolescent, had a very hard-working youth and now, when he had everything, he really had no one to share. When you are struggling, you don't realize or feel loneliness because you are too busy making both ends meet. But when you have everything, as he did, the luxury spent alone makes you feel lonelier than ever—as if wealth without a partner or a friend embodies forlornness.

I reached out to take his hand. "I am going to make you walk so much that your feet will hurt."

This made him chuckle as he squeezed my hand. "I wouldn't mind travelling to the ends of the earth as long as you're by my side."

In the past three days, he'd confessed in so many ways that he loved me but hadn't really said *I-love-you.* I wonder if he even knew what love was—considering what life he had led. And I didn't know how I'd react if he ever said it. What would I say if he demanded my love in return? I had nothing to offer him.

I stayed quiet and pulled away my hand. We drank and ate in silence, enjoying our blissful privacy while the restaurant outside was flooded with people.

After a few minutes, the bellman appeared again and informed us that our suite was ready. Without paying, which I believe added to Adam's tab, we followed the bellman.

Inside the elevator, Adam stayed close behind me. I recalled the time when we first met in the elevator. Though it had been only three days, I felt like I had known him for a very long time.

Perhaps he was in dire need of a friend. He was pursuing me relentlessly but wouldn't disclose why. But I knew it was not about just sleeping with me. He had no shortage of women, so wasting so much time on me was pointless.

We followed the bellman until he tapped the card on the door lock and let us into the Grace of Monaco Suite. As we entered the foyer, a mustard-coloured velvet armchair welcomed us, surrounded by photographs of the Princess herself. The suite smelled of wealth and luxury, like the perfume of a rich, aristocratic widow.

Adam tipped the bellman, and he nodded cheerily when he saw a hundred-dollar bill. My goodness! He had so much money to spare.

I turned left and entered a vast living room accentuated by a fireplace, a large flat-screen TV, a beige sofa, and a few comfy winged-back chairs spread across the room.

"Woah!" I looked out and gazed at the city. "I see Notre Dame from here." Adam, hands in his trouser pockets, just watched me. "You know…I have travelled a lot with my father in my childhood on his official trips. But I haven't experienced this kind of luxury." I caressed the pink fabric of the armchair. "He is an honest man, so he never used the UN's money to spend on our trips. He paid for our travels, but the UN paid only his bills."

Adam just smiled in return.

After checking the washroom, I crossed the foyer again and used the right door.

"They have two washrooms," I announced. "You take this one, and I'll take the other one."

"As you wish."

The bedroom was decorated with a king-size bed with an upholstered headboard, a desk by the window, a fireplace with another TV, and a velvet chaise. I looked out the window.

"A river view!" I exclaimed. "This is very lavish, Adam."

He sat on the bench at the foot of the bed and took off his shoes. "Please, don't start an argument again."

I sat opposite him on the chaise. "Okay then, let's finalize our sleeping arrangement. I'll sleep on the couch outside, and you sleep on the bed."

"Like I said, I am in no mood for an argument, Rania. You will take the bed, and I'll take the couch."

"I can't let you do it. You are paying for the room. You should take the bed."

He got to his feet and sat next to me. "How about we keep this topic for later and freshen up?" He tucked a strand of hair behind my ear. Suddenly, the privacy of a luxury suite made me conscious and uncomfortable. I'd be spending two nights with one of the most notorious men in the country, expecting I wouldn't stir a gossip. Was I delusional?

I looked away, feeling suddenly nervous. "You think no one will see us sharing a room? This could reach my father."

"I have given special instructions to the staff. That shall not happen." He tipped my chin to make me look at him. "You sound unsure?"

"I..." I didn't know what to say.

"I know your boundaries, Rania," he said quietly. "Unless you don't want it, I'll never cross it." I inhaled sharply at his words. "All I want is your trust."

"It's not about trust, Adam. Anyone from outside would think we have more than a friendship."

"It is more than a friendship from my side, and you know that."

I averted my gaze, purposely trying to ignore his feelings.

"But for you, I'll keep my emotions in check. I don't want to break whatever we have right now. This friendship we started over texting each other all Friday night."

I smiled at the memory—how we kept texting after I made

a fuss about leaving the party—the one he organized to see me.

"So, if we are friends, we split everything fifty-fifty."

He sat back, evidently annoyed by my suggestion.

"Whatever we eat, split the bill," I said. "And as your guide, I will pay for the museum tickets."

"I won't let that happen," he snapped.

"Why not? You pay the tour guide for service, and in return, they take charge of everything. That's how it works." I raised my chin defiantly. "You're paying for this room, so let me offer you full service."

Before he opened his mouth for another argument, a bell rang at the door.

I headed to the door and found the same bellman bringing our luggage cart. He dropped our trolley bag and left quickly.

"I have to attend a few calls," Adam said. "You can freshen up meanwhile, then we will go out."

"Okay." I opened my trolley bag and took my clothes out for a shower.

Adam disappeared into the bedroom with his trolley bag and closed the door behind him. I spent my sweet time showering, drying my hair and getting ready. Noticing Adam might take longer, I picked up a few magazines to go through local events around the city.

After almost half an hour, I sensed Adam settling next to me, watching me intently, rubbing his index finger on his lips, which he usually did when thinking. He had showered and changed into a white rib-knit sweater and a pair of jeans that looked deliciously sexy on his masculine build. I dragged my attention to the magazine, pretending I wasn't drooling at his beauty, though I was. *You're a pathetic liar.* His words rang in my mind, and it was embarrassing if he read my face now.

"You like Opera?"

"I've never attended one. Though I never understood what

they sing, but they fascinate me."

"Nobody understands what they sing. It doesn't matter what language it is."

"Have you attended?"

"Yeah, many times. Mostly in Vienna." His mind seemed elsewhere. "But, like I said, it gets very lonely. It was more like a business meetup than attending the show." *Wow! And he is complaining about it. Duh!*

I didn't know what to say. Was attending Opera alone so dull?

"It's tomorrow evening, and I checked their tickets online," I said cheerily. "They are sold out, so it's not possible. Perhaps we'll check something in Toronto and go there." I closed the magazine and was about to put it aside when he took the magazine from me, checking the show timings.

"We will go." He sounded serious, but I still let out a short laugh.

"Perhaps you didn't listen. It is sold out on the website."

I got to my feet to fetch the jacket when he took my hand. "You don't trust me? If I say I'll take you there, I will."

"And what kind of power and influence will you use in this case?"

He smirked and slowly rose from the couch. "Anything for you." He brushed my semi-wet hair from my forehead.

"You've got to be kidding me." I rolled my eyes. "I was just reading it. Nothing serious." He still grinned at me. "Adam, I know you can make anything possible with your wealth, but please don't make it so awkward. Even if you could make it possible, I don't want you to spend a rubbish amount of money to do it."

"I just want to see you happy," he said, caressing my cheek ever so softly. I didn't know when, where, and how I permitted him to make these small gestures that sent jolts all through my body. Small touches like tucking the hair, caressing my cheek, and holding hands seemed so trivial, yet they showed how much he cared. "If I don't spend it now, I'll spend it another day. The money and I come in a package. You might as well get used to it."

I blinked, not sure what to say.

"Shall we go?"

He studied me for a few seconds and looked away. "Sure."

CHAPTER 10
A TOURIST IN THE CITY

ADAM

WE EXITED THE LOBBY AND out onto Rue Saint-Louis when she exclaimed. "It's bloody cold." She took out her gloves to wear them.

"We can go back if you want," I suggested.

"No. I want to see the Christmas market today."

I followed her, crossing the Fountain Monument of Faith and then onto Rue Saint-Anne. The town was filled with a lively buzz as Christmas decorations and music created a festive atmosphere.

"This is magical," she exclaimed. Her eyes sparkled under holiday lights, which made me realize she loved this time of the year. She was not one of those people whose mood gets darker in winter days; this season thrilled her. The way her face lit up made me painfully want to kiss her in public, not caring who was watching us. But I kept my emotions in check.

She cut through the crowd, traipsing through Christmas stalls, stopping at each one of them to check the local artisans. She bought a few candles and soaps, some Christmas tree ornaments, while I just followed her like a fool who couldn't bring himself to tell her the reason for stalking her to Quebec. How would she react when she found out why I was here? She thought I was here because I was obsessed with her and wanted to spend more time with her. That was also true, but the actual reason was something else. Why did I make sure she stayed with me and not in some motel or any other room in this hotel—how could I find the courage to tell her?

After an hour, I realized she had no plans to leave the Christmas market. "Shall we go somewhere to eat?"

"I ate so much cheese." She rubbed her tummy. "I don't think I can have dinner." Noticing my expression, she said, "But we can go if you want to eat." She looked around. "They have good food here, too."

I cleared my throat and came closer to whisper in her ear. "I haven't eaten like this in a while."

"Like what?"

"Like this." I waved at other people. "Eating while walking."

She pursed her smile and snaked her arm with mine to walk me. "How about we try this time?"

"Oh, no. Not today. I'm not ready. Let's sit somewhere."

Perhaps noticing my hesitation, she didn't push it. "Okay, you pick wherever you want to eat."

"I don't know places other than the hotel. We can go back and eat in the restaurant—"

"And spend an enormous amount of money on a single dinner." She rolled her eyes. She thought for a moment. "Are you willing to walk?"

"It's fuckin' cold. Let me call my chauffeur." I pulled out the phone from my jacket pocket. She took the phone from me.

"We will walk," she ordered. "It's not that far."

She dragged me out of the market. We turned right onto Rue Pierre-Olivier-Chauveau, which went downhill to Côte de la Fabrique. Many times, we almost slipped into slush and managed to grab each other, but right before crossing the street, our fall seemed imminent.

"Ouch!" Rania shrieked. "I broke my ankle."

"I told you this isn't a good time to walk." I tried to pull her up. "You'll wet your clothes."

I tried to scoop her in my arms when she shrieked again. "Adam, no. What are you doing?" She looked around. "People are noticing."

"People are noticing you sitting on the street like a beggar. Let me help you."

Without listening to her fuss, I collected her and placed her on the bench behind us.

"Give me my phone. I'll call my chauffeur."

"Oof!" She folded her arms over her chest. "Can't you function without your chauffeur? The restaurant is right there." She pointed at the pub across the street. "We will eat and then walk back."

"You could have swelling."

"Right now, I feel nothing. It's frozen, actually."

I checked her boots. They weren't even snow boots. "Rania," I seethed. "You're wearing fall boots."

"They work fine in Toronto."

"But the weather here isn't like Toronto. It's minus twenty-five right now. You'll have a frostbite. Unless we get you new boots, you aren't leaving the hotel."

"You are so controlling," she grumbled and rushed to her feet. But she lost her footing, and I immediately grabbed her by the waist.

"Easy." Her hair fell over me as she grabbed my shoulders for support. I closed my eyes for a moment—the scene when I grabbed that girl in a place that didn't exist played vividly in my mind. It was the same fragrance—the feeling, the way my heart beat in this moment—I could never forget it.

"We will eat and return. I've heard they make excellent churros." I jerked my eyes open and gazed up at her, almost compelled to tell her about my experience. "What?"

I kept looking at her like a drunken fool. "Do you know if you had been in some Ancient Greek time, you'd have been some goddess of…"

She straightened at my words. "Let's eat now. I'm hungry."

She pulled my hand to make me leave the bench. She just mentioned she wasn't hungry after all the cheese she had eaten. She had always deflected the topic every time when I praised her.

We luckily found seats in an overcrowded pub and settled on sharing a traditional fish n' chips platter. I ordered a pint while Rania chose Jasmine tea.

"Is your ankle okay?"

"It's thawing," she said quietly. "The tea helps."

"If it's hurting too much, we can go back."

She shook her head and sipped her tea.

We ate our dinner quietly. Perhaps due to her ankle pain, she wasn't willing to talk much. After dinner, I called my chauffeur and headed back to the hotel. It took almost fifteen minutes to help her to the room.

She sat on the couch and bent to remove her shoes.

"Let me," I offered and gently removed her wet boots. "It's this one?" I touched her right ankle, and she flinched at my touch. "Lie down." I gathered a few cushions and lay her straight on the couch. "Let me bring an icepack."

"They have an icepack here?"

"The suites like these always have first aid supply." I checked the room refrigerator and brought the ice pack to her.

The first-aid kit had Ibuprofen, too. I fetched a glass of water and handed it to her.

"Take this. It will help." She took the glass without a fuss and downed her medicine.

She squirmed as I placed the icepack on her ankle, but I held her leg firmly. "It's not that bad, actually, if you ice it tonight."

"I better be fine by tomorrow," she mumbled.

"What's tomorrow?"

"Nothing," she shrugged. "I want to see the city. Then, starting Thursday, I have a conference for two days, so I won't have any time. And then, on Saturday, we are leaving."

"You know...we can stay here more if you want to." I looked up at her.

"We made a commitment, remember? You can't keep your mum waiting."

"I can ask her to reschedule," I suggested.

"And create gossip and show the entire world where we are."

After a few minutes of icing, I gently pulled her feet up and placed them on my lap.

"What are you doing?" She asked.

"A massage will help."

"A massage always helps," she answered shamelessly. "You will be my favourite person if you're a good masseur." She reached out to collect the body butter from the coffee table and handed it to me. "Be my guest."

I applied the butter to her feet. "Your feet are cold. You want me to fetch socks?"

"No, they'll be fine after the massage." She closed her eyes, focusing on my touch. Her feet started to get warm.

"Did anyone ever tell you how beautiful your feet are?"

"Have you noticed any woman's feet other than mine?" She grinned. I pursed my lips. She had a point.

She moaned slightly as I rubbed her heels.

"Am I hurting you? If I am, please tell me." I paused the massage for a moment. She opened her eyes instantly.

"No, not at all. It's so blissful." And she closed her eyes again. So, the sounds were of pleasure, not pain. *Her moans are usually a turn-on for a man.* I recalled her words. She was right. Her sound was turning me on like a horny teenager. Her body had gradually started warming up to my touch. Were her feet a starting point for turning her on?

Stop, you pervert! She is only enjoying the massage, nothing else.

I shook my head to blow out all the dirty thoughts clouding my mind. I noticed she had drifted away into the sweet slumber. *The painkiller worked.* She looked innocent and untouchable while sleeping. I shifted her feet and adjusted them on the couch, covering them with the blanket. I crawled on the floor, close to her head, and brushed away a few strands of hair from her face. I might never get another chance to see her so closely.

As I immersed my soul in her beauty, I recalled William Wordsworth's phrases:

I saw her upon nearer view,
A Spirit, yet a Woman too!
Her household motions light and free,
And steps of virgin liberty;
A countenance in which did meet
Sweet records, promises as sweet;
A creature not too bright or good
For human nature's daily food;
For transient sorrows, simple wiles,
Praise, blame, love, kisses, tears, and smiles.

I kissed her forehead gently, not wanting to wake her up. *You are the most beautiful woman I've ever seen.* I kissed her forehead again and left the room to let her sleep.

I DIDN'T KNOW HOW LONG I'D SLEPT, but when I woke up, I felt the urge to visit the washroom.

Just as I finished, I heard a scream, and I rushed back to the living room to find Rania on the floor, whimpering in her sleep:

it-hurts-please-have-mercy-on-me over and over. I knelt on the floor and shook her hard to wake her up.

"Rania, wake up. It's okay, dear. It's just a dream. I'm here. Wake up."

I shook her again to pull her out of her nightmare. She opened her eyes, filled with tears, and tried to catch her breath. I cupped her face in my hands, wiping her tears.

"It was only a dream. You're safe."

She blinked at me as if I were a ghost. I moved the hair out of her face.

"Are you okay?" Obviously, she was dreaming about someone hurting her, but I didn't know who.

Suddenly, she jumped to hug me tightly, crying as if I'd rescued her from a prison camp. It caught me off guard to see her trembling so badly. All I could do was hug her back and tell her I'd be by her side. She cried for a few minutes until she was out of tears, and the pain was released from her body.

When she settled down, I pulled her back to the couch. "Let me get you water."

She grabbed my hand firmly as I got up to leave.

"No, please, don't leave me. What if he comes here and hurts me?" She looked around in fear. *Who is she talking about?* It wasn't appropriate to ask right now, as she didn't look well to me. She was still terrified.

"No one can come here. You're safe with me." I tucked her hair back. "You had a bad dream. No one knows we are here. Let me put you to bed now. It's very late, and you need to sleep."

I scooped her in my arms and took her to the bed. Her eyes darted around everywhere as if sensing some danger, but she didn't say anything. Tucking under the blanket, she rested her head on the pillow.

"Please, don't leave me," she repeated.

I sat on the edge of the bed beside her. "I'm here. I'm not

going anywhere until you go back to sleep."

She gulped, looking up at the ceiling. "I can't sleep without my pills."

"You take them every day?"

"It gives me constant sleep. I don't wake up like I did today." She took my hand and tucked it under her face.

"Are these nightmares consistent?"

She nodded. "More than five years."

Goodness! "And when you take pills, you don't see them?"

"I do, but I resume my sleep. That night, when you stayed with me, I hadn't had my pill. But I didn't wake up, either. I had no nightmares. I don't know how it happened. It was my first night without a pill."

"In how long?"

"Around five years."

Shit! "That's a pretty long time, Rania. Don't you think it's harmful to your health? These will damage your brain cells."

"The doctor keeps changing it. Otherwise, I'll get immune to one formula, and it won't work."

"But still, it's not good for you."

"I don't desire a long life, either."

Her confession was jarring, eyes like a blank canvas, with no hope or desire for anything. Who had taken the dreams from her eyes? *Who did she dream of?* I wish I could ask her, but it was better not to push when she wasn't willing to share. I hoped that one day, when she trusted me completely, she would reveal all her secrets.

"Shall we try tonight again?" I moved back her hair. "See if my staying here helps?"

She sighed and rolled toward the other pillow. "I trust you," she said as she patted the pillow. "Please lie down with me." Her sudden appeal jolted me, showing me her fear and vulnerability. It wasn't an intimate invitation, but I couldn't name this feeling—how my heart was beating so erratically—that she might hear the excitement pulsing in my veins. I couldn't even tell her how happy I felt to earn her trust.

Resting our heads on the pillow, we faced each other.

"Thank you," she whispered, smiling sadly. "Thank you for everything." She held my hand tightly and tucked it under her cheek again.

Dealing with an emotional female was a first for me and a very overwhelming experience. It was still surprising she didn't argue about not taking pills. Would I be able to keep my promise? Would she allow me to guard her sleep at night? She was afraid she'd ruin her father's reputation, but what that man was doing was completely unjust. How could he leave his daughter alone in a strange country and expect her not to get involved in a relationship? Did he know his daughter was suffering from a painful past? Was he aware of her nightmares?

I wanted to ask her everything about her relationship with her father, about her mother's death, or if there was a man in her past. I couldn't believe anyone would hurt her, emotionally or physically. But someone was responsible for her condition.

"I never expected you'd see this side of me," she said quietly.

Now, I was curious. "Does Mike know?"

She shook her head. "No. We have never lived like this." She took a moment, perhaps thinking. "He is family. He is my refuge, but there are things even Mike doesn't know."

"Then he isn't your refuge."

She blinked at me.

"A refuge is where you feel safe, where you live carefree, knowing nothing will come to your harm. Knowing that person will safeguard everything around you. He will make sure you are never afraid, that you can sleep peacefully."

The way she looked at me, I felt like she was diving into my soul, just like that woman did after her mysterious dance.

"Then perhaps *you* are my refuge." She smiled sadly. "The one who safeguards my dreams."

I inhaled sharply at her words. I had been praised many times for my philanthropic work, remarked on my looks, and applauded for my business, but no one had spoken so highly of me—making me her refuge. I had not even done anything for her.

I would do anything to make her happy and protect her from her demons, even if I had to pass through hell for her. I had no idea what kind of feelings were developing inside me, but it was far from lust and greed. The feeling was sacred and pure, just like her. I don't deny the fact that I was physically attracted to her and wanted to claim her body, but more than that, I wanted to conquer her heart and soul and keep them safe with me forever.

With her divine beauty and enchantment before me, I closed my eyes and dived into sweet slumber.

CHAPTER 11
FLOWERS

RANIA

I OPENED MY EYES AT THE BREAK of dawn and noticed the first glimmer of daybreak through the blinds. Lost in our conversation, we'd forgotten to shut the blinds before sleeping.

The first thing I noticed was Adam sleeping next to me. I had held his hand under my face the whole night, and he hadn't complained, even for a moment. I wondered how two people, emotionally so close to each other, could have a sacred and chaste relationship based solely on trust and friendship. I always thought Mike was my best friend, but when I looked at Adam, I saw a man who was sincere and loyal to me. If it wasn't my refuge, then what was? His presence was so angelic that perhaps my demons were afraid to come near me. I never thought I'd ever find a man who would promise to protect me, even in my sleep, without harming me physically and emotionally.

I couldn't deny that I was attracted and captivated by his physical appearance. Was it too soon to fall for him? If he ever tried to come close to me, would I refuse, or was this something I was also craving? Was it okay to flow with his emotions, or was he just forbidden fruit for me?

Closing my eyes momentarily, I took a deep breath and slipped out of bed smoothly, not disturbing his sleep.

After my regular washroom trip, I decided to explore the hotel until Adam woke up. After changing my clothes, I collected my room key and handbag and descended to the main lobby. It was warm, panelled with beautiful dark wood, and many people milled around from business and political backgrounds. There was almost chaos at the front desk, and considering they were hosting such an international event, it was still quite in control.

I checked out a few stores beside the lavish lobby, which inspired me to buy something for Adam. He deserved gratitude, though no words or gift could repay what he had done for me.

I had no idea what to give to a man who had everything. After an hour of searching, I ended up in a souvenir shop and bought a silver photo frame. They offered an engraving service, so I requested for a message to be engraved onto the frame. I hoped Adam would like it. I also bought cufflinks for him with his initials engraved.

When I received the finished photo frame, it still looked incomplete. I inquired about their printing facilities so I could add a picture to enhance the frame and my feelings for him. I checked the time and realized Adam would be looking for me if he woke to find me gone. I thanked the store manager and headed toward the elevator.

When I entered the room, Adam had his phone in one hand and the other hand tangled in his mussed hair.

"Here she is. I'll talk to you later." He threw the phone on the couch and approached me. "Where the hell were you?" Worry was etched on his face.

"Is everything okay?"

"I woke up and couldn't find you. I searched everywhere in the hotel and asked people at the reception desk, but no one knew where you were." He looked utterly panicked.

"You could have called me." I tried to calm the tension between us.

"You left your damn phone on the table. There was no way I could find you. Where were you, Rania?" Despite his bitter tone, I sensed the worry in his voice.

"I went out for a walk—"

"Without a jacket?" His gaze dropped to my clothes.

"Umm..." I looked down, not sure what to say. "I just had a stroll in the lobby."

He took a step forward. "Are you hungry?"

I thought for a moment. "Yeah. I went to check the breakfast menu downstairs," I lied.

"Why didn't you wake me up?"

"You were sleeping."

"I thought you ran away." Shaking his head with agitation, he collapsed on the couch as if my absence had drained him. I put my bag down and sat next to him.

"Why would I run away?"

"I don't know," he mumbled. "I thought I might have done something wrong." His intense gaze melted me like the tiny snowflakes melting under the sun. I wanted to tell him I went to buy something for him to express my feelings, but I also wanted to surprise him with my gift.

I placed a hand on his shoulder for reassurance. "I'm not going to run away from you. What you did last night—I can't even express it. I don't know how you did it. I had no nightmares. I took no pills, yet I slept peacefully the whole night. You think I'd run away after that? No, I'm very selfish, and I want to sleep without nightmares."

"Don't ever leave again without informing me." Despite sounding like a demand, it was a plea. "I was so worried."

"I'm sorry. I'll take care next time." I looked around. "If you had looked carefully, all my stuff was there. Why would I run without my clothes?" I winked at him.

His gaze swept across the room, mild realization hitting him slowly. Perhaps, in his panic, he didn't bother looking around.

"Whom were you talking to when I came in?" I asked.

"Reception. I called everywhere. No one saw you leaving the hotel."

"That's because I never left. I wonder why they didn't see me in the lobby. Anyways…" I stood up from the couch. "Please, order something for breakfast. I'm starving." He blinked at my demand. "Or we could go down and have breakfast there. The restaurant smelled of French bread. My stomach was literally grumbling." I was only gone for an hour or so. There was nothing to fuss about.

"I'd love to feed you." He headed toward the desk to call reception. "Let me ask them."

"I'll change in the meantime." I smiled back at him and headed to the washroom.

I checked myself in the mirror, noticing I looked homeless and dishevelled—hair a mess and no makeup. No wonder the hotel management didn't recognize me.

Rummaging through my luggage, I took out a light blue cashmere sweater. I applied some makeup and made myself presentable.

When I entered the living room, Adam looked up from his laptop. He only blinked for a few seconds, evidently stunned.

"You look beautiful."

I smiled, heat slowly creeping up my cheeks. I wasn't prone to blushing, but his words had started affecting me. He had never shied away from sharing his thoughts and hearing them from his mouth so many times made me wonder if I was really this pretty or if he was the only one who found me beautiful.

He gently took my hand and led me to the corner dining table for two by the window. I looked out for a moment, ignoring his heated gaze and focused on the snow-covered dome of Notre Dame.

"Since I know how fond you are of French bread, I found out that there is a French bakery/ café at a few minutes' walk that also offers French patisserie."

I looked back at him and then noticed the table set for us.

Wow! He had rendered me speechless again, but I still had to say something. "This is too much." I studied the table—fresh baguettes with butter and jam, eclairs, fruit buns and whatnot filled the table. "But thank you." We took our seats.

As if he could read my face like an open book, he took my hand again and asked, "What's wrong?"

I pulled my hand away and looked out again. "I feel like I'm using you."

He pushed the platter of eclairs toward me. "Eat."

"Adam—"

"Please," he said firmly. "Let's not ruin our morning." He picked up a fruit bun and took a bite. "What's today's agenda besides Opera in the evening?"

I exhaled a heavy sigh and decided not to think too much about it when he didn't want to talk. But God knows I wasn't using him.

"Why am I not surprised that you managed to get hold of tickets?"

He gave me a shy smile. A few crumbs of bun settled on the side of his lips. I wanted to kiss them away, but I purposely ignored them.

"I promised you."

"I never asked for it, but thank you again."

"Can you please stop this nonsense of *thankyous* and *sorrys*? I thought our relationship was above all of those." I looked out again. "How would you feel if I kept thanking you for helping me confront my mother, or giving me company over dinner last night, dancing with me on the train, showing me the Christmas market—"

"Oof!" I exclaimed. "All right. I'm sorr—" I paused. "I get it."

"Good. Now eat." He offered me tea.

We ate for a while in companionable silence, enjoying each other's company. When I told him last night he was my refuge, I wasn't lying. He was. A refuge is also a person where you don't have to tell everything. They just understand your silence.

"Tell me," he began again. "Have you ever been to Paris?" I shook my head, so he continued. "Paris is the home of cheese and bread. Beautiful bakeries around every corner. When you go out for a morning walk, all you can smell is the fresh bread."

"I'm sure it must be tempting."

"It does, but I haven't really experienced sitting in the café."

I stared at him. "Why not?"

He looked out. "Like I said, it gets very lonely. I'd look stupid sitting and sipping coffee alone." I still stared at him. I had done this endless time—sitting in a café with a book and coffee but never felt so lonely.

"Perhaps you should take a book with you then," I suggested cheerily. "A book is a good company."

He chuckled and sipped his coffee. "You know I'm not a reader. How about I take you next time for my company?" He sounded serious, but I gave him no answer to hope.

When we finished our breakfast, we moved to the couch.

"Adam?"

He was busy on his phone, probably checking emails, but he looked up, attentive. "Yes?"

"I was wondering…the opera is around eight in the evening. I wanted to visit the Musée national des beaux-arts du Québec. It's not that far. I can take a cab. I just wanted to tell you so you don't end up calling half of the city to look for me."

"You don't want me to join you?" He asked, sounding

disappointed.

"It's a workday for you. I don't want to interrupt your schedule."

"I have no work when I'm with you. I'm completely yours."

I blinked at him. "They have a flower exhibition going on. I thought you might not be interested."

"It seems like *you* don't want me to come."

"Of course, I want you to come. I just thought you might find it boring."

He closed the distance between us. "I can never be bored if you're around." He gave me his sweet smile. "Let's leave in half an hour. I have to make some calls and answer a few emails first." He picked up his laptop and headed to the desk in the bedroom.

While watching a morning television show for half an hour, I didn't realize how much time had passed when I noticed Adam standing next to me, dressed in his casual attire. He was clad in black jeans and a sweater T-shirt, the same colour as my top. How he coordinated colour with me made me smile.

"You look nice." I stood up, brazenly checking him out from head to toe.

"The most beautiful girl in the world is complimenting me," he chuckled, "Wow! I am on cloud nine."

I giggled but turned serious when I sensed his intention. He closed the gap between us, and I realized my back had hit the wall.

"This laugh of yours," he said lazily, his voice heavy as he tucked the hair behind my ear. "You have no idea what it does to me."

We were both aware of this game of seduction—of this hide-and-seek our minds, bodies, and hearts were playing. I wanted to tell him and share everything about my past, but I was afraid to lose what we had. For the past five years, I have lived in the present state and never thought of the future. With Adam, I was slowly beginning to consider my future. But did I have a future with him? Had he thought this far, or was I the only one who was hopelessly falling for him?

The way he chased me, the amount of effort he put into throwing a party, the way he had pampered me until now—I may not tell him how much I treasured those acts, but I still couldn't see if we'd have anything beyond this.

Adam inched forward, so close that he could steal a kiss if he wanted to. But he just stayed there, studying me so closely as if I were some ancient tablet he wished to decode.

"What do we have between us, Rania?" He placed his palm on my cheek. I closed my eyes, my head leaning to his palm. His warmth was enough to turn my bones into liquid. "It isn't friendship." I slowly opened my eyes to meet his gaze. "I can't name this feeling—how my heart beats when I look at you." In books, this feeling is called love, but I didn't dare to say it. I didn't want to confuse his mind. Perhaps, with his free lifestyle, he wasn't open to having a serious relationship. "I want to say so many things, but..." he inhaled sharply, "Something clouds my mind, and I am unable to say it."

"You can say it now," I said quietly.

"I want to but..." he looked around as if sensing someone's presence, as if we had an audience. "I don't know what's happening around me."

I placed my palm on his shoulder and forced a smile. "Perhaps you need some time. We barely know each other. Perhaps you aren't open to any relationship."

"But I want you." He exhaled a heavy sigh. "I want you so bad, but I don't know what's stopping me."

I slowly pushed him away. "We should give each other some time." He nodded. "Shall we go?"

Quietly, Adam removed himself, and we headed down to the lobby.

The same car that dropped us off last night was waiting for us. As we drove, Adam made his work calls and checked emails, and it was again sending me on a guilt trip that he had to accommodate my wishes during his busy schedule. Although he assured me he wanted to accompany me, it still made me feel like a spoiled toddler who couldn't stop demanding.

During our ride, he confessed he wouldn't have concentrated on his work while I wandered alone. I should have kept my mouth shut about the art gallery and stayed in the hotel.

Due to the heavy snow, the drive was very slow and took almost thirty minutes to reach. A local boy in his early twenties greeted us and handed us our tickets and badges. It was blissfully warm inside, so we gave our jackets to the coat check. When I removed my woollen hat, my hair clip caught Adam's eye.

"Where did you get that?"

"It was my mother's. It's pretty, isn't it?" I touched the clip with pride.

"Yes, beautiful. It reminds me of…" His words trailed off as he studied the clip. "My mother. She used to wear something similar." Sad memories flashed in his eyes. It was obvious how much he had missed his mother all these years. I was glad I pushed him to talk to her and break the ice between them. At least he wasn't avoiding the subject.

"That is so sweet, Adam." I smiled cheerily at him. "You still remember?"

He nodded.

"I remember brushing her hair one day and putting on something similar. I was not even five at the time." He shifted his gaze from my hair to my eyes. "It's her birthday on Saturday, not a holiday dinner. She always uses the holidays as an excuse to invite me."

"That's wonderful. We should get something for her then."

"I don't know what I should give her. She must have everything. She married a rich man." He sounded bitter.

"Money doesn't buy everything. Why don't you give her a hair accessory like the one she used to have? It would let her know you still remember fixing her hair." The smile reached his beautiful green eyes as if I'd resolved a long-standing riddle for him.

"Will you help me choose it?"

"Of course I will. What are friends for?"

We headed to the exhibition on the Central Pavilion. The exhibit included art that showcased flowers from the Dutch Golden Age to the Impressionist Age to modern-day photographs, surrounded by glass walls and a rooftop garden, which was closed due to weather. The flowers from the paintings were displayed neatly alongside the artwork. Light flooded from every corner due to the transparent structure.

I have always loved visiting art galleries, but this one was quite unique. We were surrounded by arrays of beautiful colours, like a mini paradise inside a snow globe.

Adam followed me quietly as I studied their descriptions and took my sweet time to admire the respective art. He didn't seem much interested in the exhibit, so I didn't know why he wanted to tag along. The entire morning, I learned about exotic flowers, and Adam amused himself by taking my pictures from his phone.

"I'm surprised there is no one here today. People aren't into art these days, I suppose." I looked around. "Not even a school trip."

"That's because the place is booked for the two of us." I heard his voice behind me.

I turned around, staring at him, agape. Returning me a wry grin, he snapped another picture with his phone, capturing my baffled expression.

"Don't be so surprised. It's part of our pact, remember...

protecting your privacy." He grinned. "Oh, I like this bewildered Rania." He flashed his phone at me.

I was speechless for a moment.

"How can they do you such a big favour? Do people always do what you ask them to do?"

"It's not a favour. I believe if money can buy something, you should never ask for favours. It is very easy to return the money, but too hard to return favours. You can never justify them."

Yeah, easy for you, maybe.

"You paid to book this whole place? Why?"

"You didn't want us to be seen in public together. I promised you I'd take care of it."

"I thought it would be different here. You should have told me. We wouldn't have come here at all." It was disgraceful to make him spend so much money again. Of course, he'd never tell me how he managed to book this place in such a short time. "I don't feel good about this."

"Hey, come on." He put his arm around my shoulder, giving me a friendly squeeze. "Relax and enjoy yourself. By the way, I didn't know spending the day with art and flowers could be fun." His sweet smile was more colourful than the flowers. "Come on, we haven't seen the roses yet."

"What fun are you having?" I asked. "You're only taking my pictures."

"And that is fun for me. Just you and I and the poor speechless flowers. At least they won't gossip." His cheery voice suggested he wasn't bored after all. "You might not know it, but I haven't ever been to a place like this, except for school field trips or official events. Nothing like this, having time on my own." He turned me to face him, his expression serious. "Thank you for bringing an ordinary activity into my life in an extraordinary way."

"Hey!" I punched him lightly on his forearm. "Remember,

we are not to thank or apologize for everything?"

He gave me a shy smile.

"You have no idea what this all means to me. If these moments can be bought, I'm ready to spend all my wealth on them. But this is all possible because of you, Rania. You're my only friend. You're the only person with whom I'd want to share all these little pleasures." Closing his eyes momentarily, he continued. "And there will be no one else."

I don't know how these things mattered to him, but considering his past, it did make sense. I couldn't imagine how hard he had worked to achieve his current social status. He was no different than other men, yet his way of expressing his feelings to me was exceptional.

"Thank you." Heat crept on my face, making it warm. To avoid him seeing me like this, I turned around and entered the rose pavilion. It was a heavenly view.

Adam and I stood there for a moment, absorbing the beauty and serenity of the place. As I admired a few flowers, Adam snapped a few pictures of mine.

He leaned closer to read the lavender rose's description. "Commonly used for the expression of love at first sight." His comment caught my attention, and I joined him. "Interesting!" Gaze fixed on the lavender roses, he seemed lost in thought, rubbing his index finger on his lower lip.

"They are beautiful, aren't they?" I broke his trance. He blinked at me with a strange and unreadable expression, but I continued. "God has amazed humans with all the beautiful colours and fragrances of flowers. Humans have chosen a different message for each flower, but I see them as pure and angelic beauty. Any colour rose, for me, represents divinity and perfection. A human cannot achieve perfection. It is God's individuality which is perfect."

"I've never seen flowers like you do," he confessed. "I always thought they were just for weddings, funerals and parties. You have a very different way of looking at nature."

"That's because I appreciate everything in nature. God has created beauty for our eyes everywhere. It's up to us to acknowledge it or not. Have you ever been to a tulip festival?" Adam shook his head. "In the spring, we will go to one together." My honest offer cheered him up.

"I can't wait for the spring, then."

We finished our tour, stopping at the souvenir shop on our way out. I picked up some magnets and brooches with different flower designs, and then my attention was diverted to the masquerade masks displayed in the corner of the store. I picked up one bronze-coloured mask and tied it around my eyes. I checked myself in the mirror and was astounded to see how different I looked—unrecognizable. No wonder spies sneaked into the Carnival of Venice, and no one could recognize them until it was too late.

Suddenly, Adam was standing behind me, his reflection in the mirror flabbergasted. The colour drained from his face as if he'd seen a ghost.

"Hey! Is everything okay?" I took off the mask.

"You turned into someone else." He still looked shaken. "More beautiful than you already are."

I could sense this wasn't what he wanted to say. Maybe this mask reminded him of someone. "I remind you of someone, don't I?"

He inhaled sharply and looked at me quietly for a moment. "Never mind. Shall we go?"

I nodded and turned to the counter. The cashier—a blond girl with blue eyes whom anyone would mistake for the Aryan race, kept passing inviting looks to Adam. I wasn't sure if I was borderline jealous, but I didn't like how she gawked at him. I took the wallet out of my handbag, but Adam had already offered his credit card to the girl.

"Adam, please. Let me pay." I pushed his hand aside. "This is my stuff. So please, don't try to act like my boyfriend."

"He isn't your boyfriend?" The blondie interrupted, her eyes sparkling. I was right. She had a faint German accent, her puppy eyes blinking softly at Adam.

"Yes, I am. But my beautiful girlfriend keeps forgetting about it." Adam offered the blonde an impersonal smile.

"Adam. Don't create a scene here," I mumbled. "Let me pay, please."

"For fuck's sake! Why do you make things so difficult?" He seethed.

"You are a big-time mid-century sexist." I deliberately spoke loudly for the girl to hear. Startled, he glanced at the girl, whose mouth hung open. "I'm not buying anything." I deposited all the stuff on the counter. "Sorry for the trouble." I left the store without a backward glance.

I waited outside near the exit of the gallery and retrieved my jacket from the coat check. Adam joined me ten minutes later. I wonder what had taken him so long. *They must have exchanged numbers.* I pushed away my jealous thoughts, noticing the store bag in his hand. The boy at coat check brought Adam's jacket, too. Reading my evidently annoyed expression, Adam didn't say anything until we settled ourselves in the car.

As we drove, I looked out the window, pretending he didn't exist. It was humiliating how he assumed I could not afford such things. That he would offer his wallet every time I wanted something. He had already spent an enormous amount of money in less than a week. If he kept spending at this rate, he'd be a beggar in a month. He had earned all this wealth with struggle and devotion. I couldn't let him squander it.

"You're not going to talk?" I heard Adam's voice from the other side of the car. I didn't respond. He said something to the driver in French, which I totally ignored, but after a few minutes, the car stopped at a corner, and the driver stepped outside. I turned to Adam. "He is not going to drive unless you talk to me," he said with no hint of humour.

"Are you kidding me? The poor man will freeze to death." I tried to open the door from my side, but it was locked.

"He's a local. He's used to these temperatures. If you pity him so much, then talk to me. I'll call him back." He moved closer and placed the package on my lap. "You left this at the store."

I pushed the package away and ignored him. "It's not mine. You paid for it, so it's yours." I crossed my arms over my chest and looked outside at the poor driver. "Please call him inside."

"You have compassion for everyone. Why are you so cruel to me?" He whispered. I realized he was only an inch away from me.

Shifting closer to the window, I watched him curiously. "Cruel? That's what you think of me?"

"You won't take this package. You always refuse me whenever I—"

"Adam, I can't accept presents from you."

"But this is yours. You forgot it on the counter."

"You paid for it," I scowled. "It's not mine." *He is too much.*

"What difference does it make?"

"It makes a difference to me. Please, stop spending money on me. I feel disgraced." Hiding my face in my hands, I rested my elbows on my knees.

"Don't talk about yourself like that in front of me. If that's the case…" He paused, so I opened my eyes to see what he was doing. He took the receipt out of his pocket. "Pay for it then. Or let's go back to the store, and I'll return it, and then, you pay yourself." He opened my palm and placed the receipt on it. "I never intended to crush your pride." His sudden change in attitude, having all the sweetness in the world, melted my heart.

We were arguing over fifty-two dollars only. "The poor man is freezing outside," he added. "Have some mercy on him. Do you want to pay me now or return to that blondie?"

The way he mentioned the girl made me laugh. He waved to the chauffeur, who returned and started the car, and we were back on the road. I took out the exact amount of money and placed it on his palm. He pulled a pen from his pocket and handed it to me.

"Write something on it. It is our first. I want to keep it forever." His sincerity matched his eyes. I didn't argue, as it was his money, so I wrote on the fifty-dollar bill:

For our first argument...

I signed my name and added the date. He took the bill, grinned from ear to ear, and put the money in his wallet.

"Happy now?"

I nodded cheerily.

Our car stopped at the corner of Rue Saint-Jean in the old town. I followed Adam to a local Italian restaurant. It was the main street, with lots of local businesses, not crowded due to a weekday. The aroma of food made my stomach grumble. We sat by the window to enjoy the Christmas decor and the soft snowfall. I could barely see the cobbled street.

Our server brought warm garlic bread right away and asked if we'd like to start with drinks and appetizers. Adam ordered fresh orange juice for me and red wine for himself, with roasted peppers and mozzarella bites as an appetizer for us to share. I looked around the restaurant and figured out that the absence of other people was once again due to his enormous spending.

"How do you manage to book places all to yourself so quickly?" This had bothered me ever since we'd met—the train, the art gallery and now the restaurant.

He returned me a lop-sided grin.

"It's not just for me. It's for us." He sat back. "You're very innocent, Rania. You have no idea how money works in this world. Let's not talk about it. Enjoy your lunch."

"I want to know about opera. You can't be—"

"I'm not a fool. The artists can't perform if only two people are in the audience." He had a valid point. "But…we will have a private box, so you don't need to worry."

On that, a blonde waitress stepped in to take the orders for our main course. She kept checking out Adam like the store blonde did as if I didn't exist at this table. *Either he has a thing for blondes, or they all like a man like Adam.* She was clad in a very short black skirt—almost scandalous—over her long, slender legs, with a button-down white blouse, showing the perfect amount of cleavage. I wonder if she'd change her clothes before going out.

I hid my face behind the menu, laughing at the woman ogling Adam, batting her ridiculously long eyelashes as if he were a lord from the Regency Era and she a prospect bride. Perhaps Adam was not only exceedingly rich but also notorious enough to grab every female's attention. Perhaps all these girls did read business magazines or stalked him on the Internet.

I ordered baked shrimp scampi, and Adam ordered chicken cacciatore. He was aware of the girl throwing sexy glances at him. I tried to stifle my laugh when I returned the menu. As soon as she left us, I snorted, covering my hands over my mouth.

"What's so funny?" His innocent question made me laugh harder.

"You don't know what just happened?" He shook his head, clueless. "Oh, come on, Adam. That girl was completely checking you out." He blushed at my remark like a schoolgirl but didn't say anything. "Didn't you notice the way she gave you a show of the right amount of her body parts? And she was batting her eyelashes." I started laughing again. Adam felt like laughing with me, but he pressed his lips together. "Oh, God! You look so cute when you blush. Let me call that hottie and see your expression again." I looked toward the kitchen area.

"Don't be stupid." He turned my face to look at him.

"I just can't believe Adam Gibson can blush over a girl checking him out. Ha!" Adam sat back and folded his arms over his chest. "Now, I should take a picture of that."

I couldn't stop laughing. Though his nostrils flared, I knew he was enjoying this moment, too. I dabbed my watery eyes with the napkin.

"So, what did that store girl say to you when I left?"

"That little girl?" he asked with surprise.

"I'm sure she was not that little. She must be past puberty."

He chuckled at my blunt remark. "You want to know what she said?" I waited for him to continue. "She said, 'your girlfriend has too much ego.'"

"What? Just that? And you took more than ten minutes to listen to that?"

"You were keeping track?" Adam raised one of his eyebrows in surprise. He wanted to know if I was jealous or curious. I was both, in fact, but I wouldn't tell him. "She said I should have let you pay and said you're very beautiful, and I'm lucky to have you."

"She was checking *you* out, you fool." I tried the appetizer, realizing he might not tell me what they discussed. He was undoubtedly handsome, and since he looked rich from every angle, it was enough to grab a girl's attention. I shouldn't interrogate him like a girlfriend.

"She was checking *you* out. She wasn't into men." He chuckled behind his wine glass. *What? Is he serious?* "She wanted to know if I could help her find a girl like you, as I did for myself, so I told her that God has made only one person like that, and she is luckily just for me." I gaped at him, but the way he spoke told me he wasn't lying. "She also told me that she was watching you when you entered the store and how you tied the mask over your eyes, which blew her away. She fell in love with you." I put my hands on my mouth to hide my astonishment. He took a sip of wine, his eyes locked on me. "You're very naive, Rania. You can't read people's eyes. You don't know what the other person is feeling for you. It's good sometimes, as it is easier to ignore the assholes, but it's also dangerous. You can't read the other person's intentions." I looked down at my glass. "Anyway, she gave me her number to give you in case you need a friend someday, but I assured her that would not happen."

He handed me a piece of paper, smirking. His sincerity made me smile again. I took her name and number.

"I can't believe it."

"She's lucky she was a girl. I can't imagine how I'd have reacted if she were male." His expression turned darker.

"Why? What would you have done?" *Oh, please, Adam. Don't tell me you'd get jealous.*

"Don't ask me, and never provoke me, either."

A heavy awkwardness settled between us. I was glad that our main courses arrived, and we ate in silence.

By the time we reached our room, the sun had already set. We relaxed on separate couches when Adam broke the silence.

"Have you decided what to wear tonight?" When I didn't answer, he continued. "Women mostly wear evening dresses for opera."

"I thought I could wear anything."

"You can. But I hope you don't feel underdressed."

"I don't have an evening dress with me. I just came with some casuals and two dresses for official events."

"I know that," replied Adam, taking off his socks. We still had a few hours before the show, so I decided to change and hit the nearest store to shop, but I promised myself I would not take him with me. Otherwise, he would take control of everything and not let me pay.

When I reached the bedroom, I noticed some boxes and bags from Holt Renfrew on the bed. Since I hadn't ordered anything from there, I assumed they were Adam's, so I didn't bother to open them. Adam followed me, noticing the boxes as well.

"Oh, they delivered already. That was quick," he said, sitting at the corner of the bed. "Won't you open them?"

"What is this?" I asked, taking out a top from my trolley bag.

"It's for you." *For me? Is he crazy?* There were four boxes.

"I didn't order anything." Ignoring the boxes, I continued digging in my luggage for a matching skirt.

"You don't take care of yourself much, so I thought I'd take the charge." He got to his feet and handed me one of the boxes. I opened it and found an elegant full-length lace dress with the label Burberry Prorsum on it.

"I can't accept this." I put the dress down on the bed.

"Don't you like it?"

"Who wouldn't? But this is too much. Why do you keep on—"

"It's a dress for this evening. It's not a big deal." He shrugged. "Try it on, and if you don't like it, we'll go and get something else."

"It couldn't be better, Adam. Is this your choice?" I studied the lace pattern—so pretty and intricate.

"No, the fashion advisor at the store picked it up," he answered. "I told her what I wanted, and that's it."

"Thanks for all the effort, but…"

"Don't make it such a big deal. Now, try it on and let me know if it's okay." He collected the dress and handed it to me.

"I've never worn anything like it. It's perfect." I caressed the soft lace.

He placed his hand on my cheek. "Not more than you."

Within a blink, he was so close that if he dipped a bit, we'd steal a kiss. I wanted to live in this moment, but the shadow of my past lurked in the room. I shouldn't let him fall for me.

I stepped back. "Is this all for me?" I glanced at the other boxes with surprise.

He nodded with a forced smile. "Get ready."

"But we have a lot of time."

"I have a few people to meet at the venue." He quietly disappeared into the washroom.

I sat on the corner of the bed, gaping at the boxes, deciding which one to open first. The sound of the shower running meant he'd be in there for a while. I started with the shoebox and was baffled to find sparkling Jimmy Choo pumps. They fit me perfectly. How did the fashion advisor know my size? *Did Adam tell her everything?* My feet looked prettier in the designer's shoes. The dress itself was extraordinary. It was more than I ever desired.

Adam was creating a fairytale, and I was losing myself in it.

I opened the third box and found a Chanel scarf that matched the dress. I felt the scarf's silkiness against my cheek. A pair of stockings was also paired with the scarf. He had thought of every detail, making me feel very special. I opened the last box and found a silver Hermes evening clutch that perfectly complimented the dress and shoes. The box also had matching earrings and hair accessories. I couldn't wait to try everything on for tonight. I checked the dress in the mirror. It was adorably sweet of him to consider my reservations and pick something modest.

Although none of the items had a price tag, I could tell they were worth more than ten grand. It would take me a lifetime to return this much money.

Just as I removed the tag to head to another washroom, Adam stepped out with only a towel wrapped around his waist.

Oh my!

He looked so deliciously sexy, like a Greek god, that made me want to eat him as a post-lunch dessert. He ambled toward the closet, his body covered with droplets like diamonds glistening, and I just sat there, agape, wondering how he would taste if I licked him or ran my hand over his broad chest. It had been a lifetime since I had been intimate with anyone or felt like this. I had almost forgotten this feeling—this pleasure of being a woman, and after so long, Adam had evoked these feelings in me.

Without noticing my awed expression, he walked past me in a very seductive and provocative manner, as if showing off and teasing me what I was missing out. Now I understood what all women felt in his presence.

God help me!

I bit my lower lip, bridling my desire. The sight of him was titillating. In a relationship between a man and a woman, a very fine line divides friendship from intimacy. I was standing on that line. If I moved, I'd fall on the other side. I had never felt so seductively attracted to any man, and somewhere down in my body, it tickled...pleasurably.

Control the woman inside you, Rania. He is a bloody mind reader.

He removed the clothes from the closet and disappeared into the washroom again. I sat there, reeling his body in my mind. Before I could go and change, he appeared again in black trousers and a white button-down dress shirt, showered in a very sexy fragrance that screamed wealth and luxury.

Oh, Gibson! You look so much better without clothes.

I was still shamelessly staring at him when I realized how awful I looked. No matter how hard I tried, I could never match his charm and grace. He looked at me through the mirror, buttoning his shirt.

I blinked away. "Everything is perfect, Adam. Thank you."

"I'm glad you liked it. I'll thank Olivia personally, the fashion advisor." He returned to the washroom, still talking, leaving the door open. "She picked all the stuff."

"How did she know my size?" I asked, raising my voice.

"I told her." He stepped out of the washroom and sat at the other corner of the bed. "I saw your shoe size from your boots, and I took some liberty to go through your belongings."

"It was a perfect guess. Thank you." He looked happy that I hadn't made a fuss about his presents. It wasn't a good time to discuss it. I didn't want to ruin the moment. Perhaps, after the show, I'd ask him if I could pay him back in installments. Yet, I had to say what was bothering me. "I'm not used to all this."

"Then get used to it." With a scowl, he left the bed and began searching for something in his night duffel. "We have to leave in an hour. You should get ready now."

Gathering my belongings, I headed back to the washroom.

CHAPTER 12
OPERA

ADAM

IT WAS A RELIEF THAT RANIA accepted the things without creating a fuss.

Giving a quick call to Oliva, thanking her for all she had done in such a short time, I waited eagerly like a child for his Christmas present. I was impatient to see Rania in the pink dress, recalling how much pink suited her when we had dinner at the Persian restaurant last Saturday. The colour matched her skin when she blushed.

I made some official calls, but she still wasn't ready. Should I knock on the door and ask if she needed any assistance?

I had never felt so bonded with anyone, and it hadn't been even a week. *What is she doing to you, Gibson?* With her, I relived whatever I had missed in my youth. She was giving me a simple life again—as simple as a blink of an eye but as pleasing as a bed of roses.

I never knew spending a day with flowers could be so exhilarating. I loved capturing those moments, how she mocked me over the server's flirting, how my heart melted with her laugh. She had such an infectious smile that one could not help but smile in return.

I thought about the mask she wore. I was so stunned that I couldn't even tell her that she looked exactly like that woman I met nine months earlier, who danced with invisible people. Would she ever believe me if I told her my spiritual experience? It was hard to explain. That place had never existed. I had been there several times since, and no spiral structure stood there.

Pushing my crazy thoughts aside, I pulled on my socks and shoes. Then I heard the door opening.

I looked up as she emerged in the living room. I looked away instantly, unable to absorb her stunning beauty. She must maintain a safe distance from me; otherwise, I wouldn't be able to control myself.

"How is it?" she asked.

I returned my gaze to her, drinking her riveting beauty. This feeling of stealing your breath away or snatching the rug under your feet—it just pissed me off that I had no control over my body. I was getting hard.

I cleared my throat and loosened my tie to breathe. "Is it okay if we cancel our plan?"

She knitted her eyebrows and closed the distance between us. She studied my face for a moment and touched my forehead. "Are you okay? Did you catch a cold?"

I looked up.

"You can't go like that." I shook my head, unable to understand my own struggles. Confused, she checked herself from feet to the waist.

"Is something wrong with the dress? The fit seems to be good."

"I don't want…" I ran my fingers through the hair. "I don't want other men to see you and fantasize about you."

"Pfftt…" She rolled her eyes.

"You have no idea how beautiful you look right now." *And*

sexy! My voice showed unmistakable seduction, which I was sure she could sense. *And the fuckin' lace. I just want to rip it off of her.*

"Oh, come on. Tell me something new."

Perhaps I have praised her beauty so many times that it had lost its importance, but she had no idea how she looked tonight.

"I am no caveman, but right now, I want to keep you locked here so no one can approach you. I don't want any man's eye to set on you."

She blinked at me for a moment. "You do sound like a caveman, and it doesn't suit you." She turned to check herself in the full-length mirror. "It's a beautiful dress, indeed. I feel like a princess."

"You are a princess."

She turned around and placed her hand on my shoulder. "Thank you." She smoothed the lapel of my jacket. "The princess is worth more than ten grand right now, isn't she?"

"You have no idea how much you're worth." I drank her beauty, enough to make me heady. "Pink is your colour." She blushed at my words—oh, how much I loved this shade of her.

"You look handsome yourself, Mr. Gibson." She fixed my tie. The way she looked at me with her soft gaze made me wonder if she was as attracted to me as I was to her. She had told me there was nothing inside her, but I sensed something else.

I stepped closer, so many wild questions running rampant in my head. She must have read my intention as her expression turned serious. As I closed the distance, I didn't realize her back had hit the mirror. There was no one to stop us now. My body craved her touch, and I was also getting the same signals from her. As I inched closer, she closed her eyes, her body radiating heat for the invitation, her breath shallow.

Suddenly, I felt heaviness around me, the same heavy air I'd felt in the afternoon. I sensed a shadow in the mirror behind her, but when I looked through it, there was nothing. I looked around. I swear I could sense someone's presence, but I also knew no one else was in the room. She wasn't warm anymore. Dread coated her face. She must have sensed I was about to kiss her. Why was she afraid to kiss?

Placing my palm on her cold face, I kissed her forehead and turned away. Her stiff body relaxed as she opened her eyes, noticing the distance between us—a distance that needed more time and trust to end.

"Let's go," I whispered, pretending like nothing happened.

As I collected my jacket, she disappeared into the bedroom but returned in a few seconds with a paper bag in her hand.

"This is for you." She handed me the package with a lovely smile.

"For me? It's not my birthday." I took the bag from her and peeked inside it.

"It wasn't my birthday, either," she scowled and waved at her dress.

"Thank you." I took the armchair, and she sat beside me on another one.

"Though nothing can reciprocate what favours you've done for me, I hope you like it."

"I wasn't doing you any favours. I told you, I'm a very selfish man. I was only doing it for myself." I took out the small package from the bag. "But thank you. Can I open it now?" She nodded with a smile. I opened the package neatly, like a little boy eager to open his Christmas present. A box with sterling silver cufflinks with engraved initials on them skipped my heartbeat.

"They're lovely. Thank you." I changed my cufflinks to a new one. "When did you buy them?"

"This morning, when you were busy calling the whole city looking for me."

Another box was inside the paper bag, so I opened it curiously. It was a beautiful silver tabletop photo frame with crystal stones on the sides and two engraved messages on the top and bottom.

For our good time
I am lucky to have found you

What surprised me was the picture of our first dance together, with us looking into each other's eyes with a passionate smile. It melted my heart and almost brought tears to my eyes. I turned my head away, not willing to share my emotions. I closed my eyes briefly to calm myself, then looked back at her. I had never acted on my emotions. What was happening to me?

"Thank you so much. I don't have words to express it." I took a deep breath. "No one has given me a present, just for me, since my sixth birthday." She stood up and sat at the arm of the chair, placing her hand on my shoulder. "My mother used to bring gifts for me on birthdays. My father was never the present type. After Mom left, Dad used to take me to McDonalds for the Happy Meal, and a free toy was my birthday gift. At that time, a good meal was a better present than a toy." I put my hand over hers. "You are giving me all the childhood treasures I missed all those years. Thank you."

Perhaps noticing my watery eyes, she ran her fingers through my hair and kissed my forehead. I closed my eyes, inhaling her sweet scent as she engulfed me in a warm, friendly hug. I wanted to stay like this forever, shrouded in her presence, and I would never desire anything ever again. We stayed there motionless for a few minutes without uttering a word.

A text message alert on her phone disturbed our privacy. She took the phone out of her clutch bag and read the message, her face wrought with concern. She handed me the phone. The message was from her boss.

Ben: I just learned that Adam Gibson is also in Quebec City. Did he get in touch with you?

What's his fucking problem? Noticing her tense face, I responded to the message on her behalf.

> *Rania: Yes, he did. We agreed to dine out together.*
> *Ben: Find out why he is in Quebec. If he is chasing you, please do not agitate him. A man like him can't stand rejection.*
> *Rania: Don't worry. Your business is safe.*
> *Ben: Be safe, my child. I worry for you.*

Rania snorted as she read the text.

"The bastard pretends to be your father," I scowled.

"He worries for me."

I rolled my eyes. "Worry, my ass. Let's go."

On our way to the opera, I made a few calls while she looked out the window, contemplating. *Is she thinking about my attempt to kiss her?* Did shc pull away because she read everything through my eyes? I had no idea what happened to me at that moment. It felt like the angels and demons of emotions were at war, and the angel won as I read her frightened face. I never even believed in this theory, but with Rania, I was beginning to think that there was more than our eyes could see. I couldn't describe the heavy feeling I had at that moment. It was as if I felt someone else there.

We reached the theatre an hour earlier. As we threaded through the crowd, I stopped by to meet some known faces. Rania seemed pretty comfortable despite being in public. We met the local MP and his wife. A lot of men turned their heads to check her out, but I kept my hand on the small of her back to let all the fuckers know that she was beyond their reach. As long as I breathed, I would not let anybody near her. I itched to gouge their eyes out. She was indeed turning me into a caveman.

We settled in our box and checked our program. The opera was Othello, and Rania read everything carefully before focusing on the performance. She was completely engrossed in the show for two hours, and I in her.

Tears rolled down her cheeks when Othello confronted his wife, Desdemona, and accused her of adultery with Cassio. Desdemona attempted to persuade her husband of her innocence, but he refused to believe her and ultimately killed her. Rania gasped at the horrific scene, stood up and left the box.

I ran after her and found her leaning against the door. She breathed hard, but as she noticed my presence, she wiped her tears away.

"I want to leave." Her request moved something inside me.

"Hey...what happened?" I cupped her face.

"Why couldn't he trust his wife? She loved him," she cried. "She left her father, her wealth, everything for that man. And what did he do to her? Accused her of adultery and killed her."

"Shh..." I pulled her into my arms.

"Why can't a man trust a woman's love? Why does a woman need to pay a price to prove her love and show her loyalty?"

"Relax. It's just a play."

She pulled away and headed to the exit. I didn't understand why she was taking the opera so seriously. Was it something related to her past? Why would anyone accuse her?

I followed her to the exit, and we headed to the car before the show was over.

She remained quiet until we reached our suite. Taking off her winter coat, she rushed to the bathroom. I waited patiently for her but couldn't hear any movement or sound. After thirty minutes, when she didn't come out, I knocked gently at the door.

"Rania, are you okay?" I knocked again, but I didn't hear anything from inside.

Was it appropriate to try the door? My ensuite bathroom didn't have a lock. I wonder if this one had.

"Rania," I called out again. "I'm opening the door, okay?"

I hope it wasn't locked from the inside. I twisted the handle and found it unlocked. I didn't want to invade her privacy, but I wanted to ensure she was all right. She didn't look well when we left the Opera.

She stood in front of the vanity mirror in her night clothes, a towel draping over her shoulder. I didn't even hear the shower running. And didn't she shower before leaving in the evening?

Utterly lost into oblivion, she didn't notice my presence in the mirror. Eyes staring at nowhere, she'd even forgotten to blink. Water dripped off her hair, wetting the floor mat. I looked around the washroom and felt the presence of something else besides us—the same presence I had always felt in our privacy. It felt heavy—very heavy, as if I was carrying the weight of a thousand tons.

I tapped on her shoulder gently. She flinched at my touch as if I scared the hell out of her.

"Hey, are you okay?" She stared at me blankly and then at the door. Perhaps she wondered how I got in, so I explained. "I knocked several times. You weren't responding. I was worried." Still expressionless, she was not convinced by my explanation. "By the way, if you don't know, these doors don't have a lock. I'm not a ghost who can sneak through locked doors." I winked at her, trying my best to cheer her up. Her eyes widened at my words.

"Who are you, then?" Her question startled me. "You show up everywhere I go, like *they* do. If you're not a ghost, then who are you?" *What is she talking about?* "You're not my shadow. You're not one of *them*. Then, who are you?"

"What are you talking about?" She didn't say anything. She just walked out of the washroom like a ghost. I wanted to bring her back to this moment, so I grabbed her by the arm. "Your hair is completely wet. Let me dry it." I pulled her back to the vanity and started the hairdryer.

Parting the locks with my fingers, I began drying them. Staring straight ahead, she remained completely still, her gaze fixed on me through the reflection. I had never seen this look, this sharp blankness in her eyes. There was something definitely wrong.

I focused on her hair, drying a few strands at a time, but every time I glanced at her in the mirror, she had the same empty expression. She had beautiful hair, and it was a great pleasure to touch it. I never knew a woman's hair could be so soft, like silk threads. I only remember my mother's hair when I used to ask her if she'd let me brush it. But touching a woman's hair, a woman who is a charmer, a seductress, a beautiful goddess—I never imagined a moment like this.

Lifting her hair up, I noticed a burn scar just below her neck, on the back of her right shoulder. It looked like a cigarette burn. Were there more like this?

I removed the towel and dragged her top a little down, finding more scars from cuts and burns on her back. She was still frozen, oblivious to my horrifying discovery.

"What the fuck is this? Who has done this to you?" Turning off the hairdryer, I repeated my question to draw her attention and turned her to face me. "I want to know the name of the bastard who tortured you. Talk to me." I shook her hard to pull her out of her trance.

She fell to her knees, howling like an injured animal, her head bowing down to the floor mat. Her whole body was trembling. I sat down with her, lifting her face gently.

She continued screaming, and I let her, despite knowing the other hotel guests might hear. I wanted her to let out all her fears. Terror gripped her body, and all I could do was wrap my arms around her in a tight embrace. Whimpering and snivelling in pain for more than ten minutes, she finally gathered herself until she had no energy left to shed more tears.

"Please don't ask me about my past, Adam," she sniffed, resting her head on my arm. "It's very painful to go back in time. I want to forget everything."

I nodded, holding her face in my hands to reassure her. Her screams had said everything. I wouldn't push her to revisit her past.

Wiping her tears with my thumb, I kissed her forehead. I lifted her from the floor mat and led her toward the bed to tuck her in. She was utterly exhausted. I settled her under the comforter and turned off the bedside lamp.

As I headed to lie down on the chaise, she grabbed my hand. "Please don't go."

"I'm not going anywhere." I sat beside her and caressed her forehead like a child needing a mother's touch. "I'll stay here in the room with you. You can go to sleep."

Eyes reddening with tears, she watched me momentarily and then rolled again like yesterday to make room for me. She took my hand and tucked it under her cheek.

After a few minutes of silence, she asked, "Who are you, Adam?" I blinked at her, clueless about what to say. "Are you an angel or a fine spirit?"

I scoffed. "I am no angel."

"You can't be a Djinn, either." Her words startled me. "Please, tell me who you are."

"They're all fairytales—these angels and demons."

She studied me for a moment. "I believe them, and I think you're an angel in the guise of a man."

"I'm a normal human being," I chuckled. "What made you think I'm an angel?"

"Humans don't possess angelic qualities," she answered, her voice dropping a few decibels. "Neither do Djinn. I haven't seen anyone like you."

Like the butter melting under heat, she melted me with her

words, tempting me to kiss her passionately, to do something only humans could do, but I bridled my emotions.

"I have broken many hearts. I haven't been a good son." I caressed her face with my other hand. "And if we talk about levels of sins, I have crossed almost all of them. Don't think so highly of me. I'm almost like a Satan."

"No, you can't be Satan," she objected softly. "He was created from the smokeless fire. The difference between Satan and a human is the flesh and fire. You don't possess any fiery quality."

I knitted my eyebrows. "Interesting. Tell me more?"

"I thought you said you don't believe in God's existence," she said. "Why would you believe in Satan?"

"Honestly speaking, God has not done much to me in the past to justify His existence, but yes, I know for sure Satan exists. I guess all humans are partially demons. Don't you think?"

"We have a different belief, but I'm sure you won't be interested in knowing."

"No. Tell me more." I wanted to know what she thought. I wanted to know how her mind worked. And I also wanted to divert her attention from the past incident.

"When God created Adam in heaven, He asked all His angels and other creatures to bow to the newly created flesh. All creatures obeyed God except Satan. He was gifted with a will, unlike angels, and he possessed all the characteristics we humans possess—envy, disbelief, arrogance, stubbornness, and false pride."

"He wasn't an angel?"

"No, in the Islamic version, Satan is a Djinn, a demon. Before God created mankind, Satan dwelled on the earth, along with the angels, and imitated the angels' actions and behaviours. At that time, he was one of the most devout worshippers of God. Satan was extremely knowledgeable, which made him very proud. He considered himself one of the best of God's creations."

"Why did he refuse to bow to Adam?" I never imagined discussing it with a woman in bed with me.

"Pride. Pride took everything from him. He thought he was more divine and powerful than Adam, so he refused to obey God, though it was His command. God never wanted the angels to worship humans. But since Satan was a proud Djinn and disobeyed God, he was thrown out of heaven and was designated as the King of Hell." She paused for a moment, her gaze softening. "You are certainly not a Satan."

"I'm not an angel, either," I scoffed. "I do possess will. That makes me either human or Satan."

"But you're not obeying your will, Adam. You're doing everything against it. Here with me, helping me cope with my nightmares, following me here, providing me with a room—you're following what God asked you to do."

I inhaled sharply at her words. I didn't believe it. "I am here because I want to be with you."

"Then why do you want to protect me from my nightmare?"

"Because." I thought for a moment. "Because it's the right thing to go."

She chuckled softly. "Exactly. And the right thing is God's way."

I didn't know what to say in return. She had her own theory of believing things that didn't exist, and I didn't want to spoil it. And she had this beautiful way of telling a story—no matter how bizarre it sounded—you were still compelled to listen. Her knowledge about the concept of Satan and angels could draw anyone into the conversation. I wanted to learn more from her, though I didn't believe in all this. It was like a bedtime story; the more she told me, the more I wanted to hear.

"How do you know all this?"

"It is part of my belief. It's in the Holy Quran. Even the Bible explains this concept of angels and demons. Haven't you read it?"

"What makes you think I'm a Christian?"

"I thought so…"

"I told you I don't believe in God."

"You still don't," she said.

Taking a deep breath, I looked back into her eyes. "I don't know. Sometimes…" I paused for a moment. I didn't know what to say, so I changed the topic. "So, are there any differences between Djinn and humans besides their appearance?" I wanted to distract her mind from previous trauma, so it was better to keep her mind in a place where she was very invested.

"Humans are made of clay. God collected seven different kinds of clay from the earth to create Adam. Clay supports and gives life, whereas fire destroys and burns." When she talked, she looked like an angel, perhaps with a halo I couldn't see. "But like Satan, humans also carry pride, envy and arrogance, which sometimes work as a fire. There is a very thin line between humans and Djinn. Though they're invisible to humans, they do exist."

"So, there is only one Djinn, I mean Satan?"

"No. They are more than the human population. They have a world within our world, but we can't see them unless they want to be seen. There are males and females. There are good and bad ones, as well. You know what the interesting part is? Each human has been assigned an angel and a Djinn. We don't see them, but they are always there. Angels are here to guard us, protect us whereas the Djinn's job is to draw us into worldly sins. He creates a temptation for us. We recognize it when our soul is not strong enough to protect our body, and our demon takes it over, and that's how we sin."

"It's a convenient way to blame someone for your actions," I scoffed as I looked up at the ceiling. "Aren't we the ones involved?"

"No, and yes. We are physically involved. God created

humans with goodness. If our soul is not strong enough to believe in Him, our demon empowers our body by manipulating our soul. It is our duty to protect ourselves from our demon."

"So, what happened to Satan when he was thrown out of heaven?" *Do I really have to believe all this?*

"Due to his pride, he did not ask for forgiveness. He only asked for respite from his punishment till the Day of Resurrection. So, God delayed his punishment till that day. Once Satan knew he was safe from destruction, he rebelled and declared war on Adam and his descendants. He was determined to make disobedience attractive to humans and to tempt them to commit immoral acts and go against everything pleasing to God so they'd share his fate on the Day of Judgment. Just like the forbidden fruit, he made sin more tempting to humans than the deeds considered good. On the other hand, God gave him powers, knowing that the humans He created can love, forgive and repent. He has faith in His creation, that no matter how much Satan tries to magnetize a human to sin, a person always has an open door for repentance."

"So, you're saying that no matter how sinful you are, if you ask for forgiveness, you'll be forgiven?"

"Yes, that's what God's nature is," she said with a soft smile, her voice sweet and tender. "You just need to seek the light and find the right path."

The way she explained sins and rewards in such a simple way, I never imagined I'd listen to all so patiently. I was right about her. She had something magnetic that was pulling me toward her. Perhaps it was the light in her that attracted me.

From what she just said about Djinn or demons, my theory was: if I don't see something with my own eyes, I don't believe it. But the way she explained everything, it was hard not to. I'd never have found the light in my life. I'd never have asked for forgiveness from my mother. For the very first time, I thanked

God, although knowing He didn't exist, for the blessing He had bestowed on me. I felt as if I'd been rewarded in exchange for an unknown deed. What good have I done in my life to get Rania's faith and companionship? She was a friend, a listener, a saviour, a guide—and one day, I'd want her to be my lover. How effortlessly she made me agree to see my mother, even after so many years. She was making me face my own demons that haunted me for years.

"Do *you* believe in Djinn?" I asked. "Aren't they more like a mythical creature?"

She gave me a short laugh. "Believe me. They are as real as you and me."

"Right." I rolled my eyes. "Just like angels. And you cannot see both."

"Depends," she said thoughtfully.

"Depends on?"

"How you believe it."

"How can I believe it when I can't see it?"

She watched me for endless beats, her eyes slowly washing with exhaustion, but she didn't answer my question.

"How about we eat dinner?" I suggested.

"I'm not hungry."

I wanted to ask so many questions, but if she wouldn't open up to me, I wouldn't dare.

"You don't take care of yourself properly. Someone has to… and I want to be that person."

She gave me a soft smile. Hope and pain danced together in her sad eyes. I dared to slide closer and cupped her face in my hands. She closed her eyes at my touch. I couldn't resist kissing her innocent face. I wanted to tell her so much—what I felt and how much I had longed for her, but her vulnerability stopped me every time.

Planting a deep kiss on her forehead, I moved my lips slowly to her eyes. Her heart was beating loudly and audibly with my touch. There was no fear on her face that I saw earlier when we left for the play. I gave soft baby kisses to both of her eyes and felt her body heating up for me. I wanted to divest us both from all the fabrics, to feel her heat. But I'd take it slow.

All the feelings thrashing inside were entirely new to me. I never knew my heart could beat so fast for a woman. I have fucked so many women in my life, but this was something else, something beyond my understanding. *I want this forever!*

Taking my sweet time on my journey to discover her beautiful face through my lips, from eyes to cheeks, and then to her nose, I constantly checked her expression. Her fragrance was driving me crazy. Her eyes were still closed, but her body was so warm that it was almost painful not to feel it. I itched to run down my hands on her skin, but I had learned my limits.

I kept exploring her face with my lips, kissing every corner of her skin gently, but she didn't pull away. She sucked in a breath when I touched her warm lips with my thumb. As soon as I decided to kiss her lips, I noticed a teardrop rolling down from her right eye. At that very instant, her body suddenly turned cold. Very cold, as if she could see my corrupt intentions even with her eyes closed. I sensed the same heaviness in the air again. Something was around us, something hollow like we were sucked into a vacuum. And something was pushing me away.

I looked around, but there was no one. *Damn it! What's going on?*

She might have sensed my hesitation and slowly opened her eyes. Was it the dread of being kissed spilling from her eyes? There was no passion, no affection in her gaze when she looked at me. They were empty.

A wave of awkwardness washed between us. In all these passionate moments, I didn't realize I was putting our friendship and trust at stake. If she didn't want me as her partner, I'd also lose a friend. I'd lose her trust if I kept acting like a desperate. She might run away and never look back. Right now, she trusted me enough to allow me to sleep by her side, as she knew I'd never hurt her. If I kept on showing my feelings through my body, there was a chance I might lose her one day. I should have known from my first try that she was not ready to advance in our relationship.

"You must rest," I said quietly. I was about to pull away, but she tucked my hand under her face again.

She watched me for a few seconds as if wanting to say something, but weariness from previous events had worn her out.

I knew she had felt the same thing during our almost kiss. What was stopping her from taking another step? It was as if someone was trying to invade our private moment and destroy it, and I had a feeling she knew. Her eyes said so many things the way she looked at me, but I could do nothing to remedy it.

Slowly, she closed her eyes, my hand under her face. Her scars were creating millions of questions in my mind. When I investigated her background, I didn't find out if she was visiting a therapist. If she couldn't share her past with me, she could at least discuss it with a doctor. How would she take it if I asked her to do that?

If she didn't want to rehash her past, I would never push her.

CHAPTER 13
BEWITCHED

RANIA

I WOKE UP TO THE SOUND of water running. It must be Adam taking a shower.

I left the bed and headed to the washroom to change for the day. I was surprised to find the towel on the floor. Why would I do such a thing?

When I came out, Adam was already dressed in a dark green sweater that matched his eyes. He was on the call in the bedroom and didn't know I was watching him from the living room.

"Make sure he isn't out of your sight," he ordered someone on the phone. "Yes, it's under control here." He paused to listen to the person on the line. He typed something on the laptop, his other hand holding the phone to his ear.

I knew he wanted to kiss me last night, but I didn't know how he sensed my fear. He never questioned, never demanded, but he was always there. It was surprising that my body did not refuse him when he began exploring my face with his sensual lips, as if this was what I craved. I had never allowed anyone to be that close to me in the last five years, yet when he touched me, a current passed inside me, tearing all my nerves into bits and pieces and forcing me to surrender to him.

Who are you, Adam? An angel? A guardian? What should I call you?

When we started our friendship, I thought he'd take advantage of our solitude and might seduce me, but he proved me wrong every time. Whenever I had the slightest grain of doubt about him, he proved that all men are not the same. He showed I could trust him with anything—my nightmares, my past, my demons. After all the time I'd spent with him, I realized *I* was taking advantage of him, profiting from his trust and loyalty. It was *I* who was getting everything, and he wasn't getting anything in return.

Sometimes, life puts us in a situation where we get two right paths. The two sides of the coin are displayed together. My life stood at such a crossroad. One path was the ordinary life that I had, with nightmares, but it also safeguarded my father's reputation. The other path led me to Adam, revealing me to the light, but the intensity of that light burned everything around it except me. I was getting all the warmth from the light that healed my soul. Should I be selfish, or should I spend my whole life asking for an apology from my father?

I fear what will happen when Adam learns the truth about me. He'd always taken me to be an innocent person with a painful past. I wish I could tell him that, along with all my nightmares, I had also encountered demons. I wish I could tell him how tormented my soul was, and now that he was in my life, he was secretly picking up all the charred and broken pieces. I wanted him to be part of me, but I knew if he got to know more about me, he would torture himself and spoil his notable reputation. My burned pieces would burn him, too. I wish I could tell him I'm not the girl he always sees.

Adam hung up the phone and noticed me watching him.

"Good morning," he said in a cheery tone.

"I will once you start your conference tomorrow," he answered. "Though I wish you'd also skip it, and we just spend our days like this." He sat back, giving me his adorable boyish grin.

"Mr. Gibson." I leaned forward. "Some people have their bosses to answer."

"How about you work with me?" He asked. I blinked at him, incredulous. "I won't question you at all."

"You're joking, right?"

"No." He leisurely spread jam and butter on the baguette.

"And what position are you thinking to offer?"

"We will find something," he said quietly. He couldn't be serious. "You can start as my travel companion and advisor."

Of course, he was joking.

I scoffed and looked outside. "That's not even a thing."

"All your travel expenses will be covered. All you need to do is find destinations to visit anywhere on this planet for a week every month."

I stared at him blankly. "And what do I do for the rest of the month?"

"Find good local spots to spend our weekends," he grinned. "You will have more time to read as well. Think seriously."

I just watched him with utter bafflement. Even if it was a joke, he looked so serious that anyone could buy this nonsense. He wanted me to become a rich, spoiled, desperate housewife.

"How about I stick to what I'm good at," I suggested.

"Trust me…you're the best companion I've ever had."

This made me smile. "Thank you for your offer, but I'd like to stay in this field and attend my conference tomorrow."

"Don't ever think I was bluffing. I am serious." He paused for a moment. "What's today's plan?"

"It's very windy outside, so roaming around town doesn't sound like a good idea."

"Better to stay in the room then," he smirked.

"No. I plan to visit a monastery."

He returned a sour face. "What's there to see?"

"They were the first hospital established by nuns in all of North America." I scooted my chair forward and lowered my voice in a conspiring tone. "They say some nuns performed exorcism there. It was their first case."

Adam studied me for a few seconds. "I'm curious why you're into these things."

"What things?"

"This stuff which isn't possible or doesn't even make sense."

"How can you say so?"

"Because." He paused momentarily. "It's not possible. You can't know if it's true because you can't see them." I opened my mouth to say something, but he raised his hand to shush me. "No. Don't give me that bullshit logic that you cannot see heat and wind, and yet you feel it. Heat and wind are scientifically proven. These ghosts and supernatural stuff—science cannot even prove it."

"Science doesn't even prove God's existence," I objected.

"There's your point," he said. "He does not exist."

I sat back, wondering what to say to a person who believes only in what he sees. Arguing with him was pointless.

"You're welcome not to join me."

"I didn't say that," he said. "Of course, I will come. Who knows what trouble you'd put yourself into."

"Excuse me?" I scoffed. "What do you mean?"

"Nothing." He rolled his eyes. "Let's finish breakfast and then leave. It's getting too stuffy here."

He was right. It was getting too crowded with time and too noisy with so many people in line.

It was a five-minute walk to St. Augustine Monastery. I had already emailed them to inquire about the English-guided tour.

The tour guide welcomed us and let us in. We explored

the nuns' cells, the cloister, and the indoor corridors, which displayed artifacts from New France. The guide also explained how the girls came here and how one used to become a nun in the seventeenth century. I still wondered why Adam decided to join. There was nothing for him here.

When the guide finished her process of explaining about becoming a nun and stepped into another room, Adam held my arm to stop me. "You don't plan to take any inspiration from all of this, right?"

I giggled at him. "Don't be ridiculous."

We explored the old hospital area and how nuns cured the sick.

"I have heard they performed exorcism once."

"Yes," replied the guide in her Quebecois accent. "Hallé worked as a servant in Beaupre. She had an obsessed lover, Daniel Vuil, who used some black magic on her. They were on the same ship that brought them to Quebec. Hallé was then brought to Catherine de Saint-Augustin, who, at the time, was revered as the holiest woman in New France. Mother Catherine tried to heal Hallé but provoked the demons instead. She's mentioned in her diary how demons threatened her from time to time—sometimes they surprised her by appearing as an angel or disturbed in her prayers."

"And how did she explain what the demons look like?" Adam asked.

I turned to him, baffled. How had he gotten invested in such a topic? I thought he didn't believe in all this.

"They sometimes appeared as normal people, asking for confession. Sometimes, she saw nothing but sensed her bed moving during the night or her holy water misplaced."

"Did she feel something heavy around her?" he inquired. I was again taken by surprise that he had managed to listen to the guide.

The guide thought for a moment. "She mentioned in her book that she felt the presence, but later on, Mother Catherine concluded that the man who cast a spell on Hallé was a wizard. Since he could not take Hallé's rejection, he opted for diabolical art. Bishop Laval, at that time, was convinced that he had converted Vuil to Catholicism during their journey, and what Vuil did here was unacceptable. It was considered a punishable offence by death."

"What happened to Mother Catherine and Hallé then?" I asked.

"Hallé recovered and went back to her work. But Mother Catherine suffered dark days till her last breath. She knew something was wrong, but since she was the head healer, no one could cure her."

I noticed Adam looking around skeptically as if searching for ghosts. It made me wonder if he had sensed something before.

"This is the last room of our tour," the guide announced. "You are free to roam around, though. The chapel is open for another hour." We exchanged goodbyes, and she left us in the hall surrounded by beds and medical paraphernalia.

"I'm surprised you showed interest in it," I said cheerily.

Adam didn't say anything, but he took a step and pulled me into his arms.

"Do you believe in black magic, Rania?" I looked up at him with surprise. Before I could respond, he said, "Until now, I have never believed in magic, but with you, I'm starting to believe that you have indeed cast a spell on me. I wonder if you practice witchcraft, too."

I scoffed and rolled my eyes, wanting to pull away, but his grip was so firm that there was no room for air to pass between us.

"Why do you say so?"

"Don't you see I am under your spell?" he asked. "You have

bewitched me. I am beginning to believe that there are things beyond my mind that I could fathom or that my eyes could see. For example." He snaked his arm through the back of my neck and pulled me closer. "I want to corrupt you, and be corrupted by you, but every time I come closer, I sense someone's presence. As if he knows my intention."

I inhaled sharply at his words. "He who?"

"Whoever is around you," he whispered. "I have a feeling you know who it is."

I looked away. "It's all in your head, Adam."

"Then who comes between us?" he asked, holding my chin to face me. "What is there that frightens you?"

"I'm not frightened," I objected.

"Yeah?" He studied my lips. "Are you sure?"

My heart beat so loudly in the quiet, monastic hall that I was sure he could hear it. Perhaps the ghost of Mother Catherine could also listen to it.

He dipped closer, grazing his cheek with mine. The warm touch and scruff from his stubble were melting me like a tallow candle from this monastery. I knew he was testing how far I could go. My insides were turning into warm liquid, and I burned with a desire to seek out his lips myself, not caring how brazen I sounded.

His lips roved from my forehead to my eyes, to my cheek—like an episode continued from last night. My mind and body were waging war between lust and chastity, and I wanted to lose in the world Adam was offering me. But once again, the ghosts from my past lurked behind the doors and windows. They haunted me, pulling me away from this fantasy.

Adam exhaled a heavy sigh. "That is exactly what I was talking about."

"I'm sorry," I whispered. A tear dropped from my eye.

Adam pulled away and wiped it off my cheek. "Let me help

you, Rania."

Oh, how nice it was to hear it, but I wasn't sure if his help could be useful.

"Someday…" I gulped and looked out the window, into the snow-covered courtyard. "I will tell you everything." I turned my gaze back at him. "But first, I want to make sure you'd believe me."

"Try me now," he offered.

I shook my head and pulled away. "You won't believe it." Before he could ask again, I cut him, "Please, not now."

I left the hall, and Adam followed me quietly until we reached the souvenir shop. I picked a few magnets and headed to the cash register.

"Bonjour," said the man cheerily. He looked around my age. His name was Eugene on the name tag. "Did you enjoy your tour?"

"It was very informative," I answered.

"We offer spa services," he glanced at Adam behind me. "We offer massage services for couples too. We have a head massage, Thai yoga massage and—"

"Do you offer reflexology?" I asked.

"Oui." He bent and retrieved a flyer from the drawer. "You can check the rates and give us a call to book."

"I was wondering if you have anything available now?"

He checked the time and said, "I can book you for a foot massage after thirty minutes."

"That would be lovely," I grinned.

"You are the therapist?" Adam inquired.

"Oui," Eugene cheered.

"Do you have a masseuse here?" Adam scowled.

"Not at the moment, Monsieur," Eugene answered, sounding hesitant.

"We can wait in the restaurant meanwhile," I suggested to

Adam.

"That's a long wait," Adam snapped. Grabbing my hand, he pulled me out of the store.

"That was very rude of you." I glared, folding my arms over my chest.

"And what were you doing? Taking a massage from him?" His anger reflected mine. *What's wrong with him?*

"Oh, come on. Just because he is male—"

"But I do mind," he seethed, leaning closer. "Do you get me? I *do* mind if another man touches you." I blinked at him, speechless. *Is he serious?* "Do you know what sounds you make when you're given a foot massage? Extremely pleasurable and highly erotic!" I blinked again, agape.

Oh my God! This is so embarrassing.

Flushed, I walked to the exit. Was he getting possessive about me? If not, then what should I call it? All my life, I had been running away from this feeling, from a possessive man—the feeling that swallows all other feelings like love, trust, and companionship.

I started to shiver, unsure if it was cold or my past holding up a mirror to me once again.

Adam grabbed my arm and stopped me. "I'm sorry for my behaviour." So, he finally admitted his mistake. "When I gave you a massage the other night, you made sounds only a man can understand. The feeling I got at that moment—I don't want another man to experience it." He threaded his gloved fingers through mine. "I don't want to sound like a caveman, but I never thought I could ever feel jealousy. I can't share you with anyone."

He possesses what he wants. I don't want you to end up being one of his possessions. Ben's words churned in my mind with all the mixed feelings I had for Adam.

He had shown me care and kindness. He had surprised me in various ways I'd never dreamed about. Yet, his sudden change in attitude had rung an alarm in my head. I guess Ben was right. I should be more cautious. It was just a foot massage by a stranger, and he was frenzied about it. What if I told him about my past? How deranged would he act? Where was the trust he had been asking for?

Adam called his chauffeur, and we headed back to the hotel.

CHAPTER 14
PARADOXICAL

ADAM

THERE WAS NOTHING IN THIS WORLD that I could not buy—luxury, comfort, even peace of mind—but I could not slow down the ticking time. I wanted to hold onto this time and never let it go.

I don't know what was happening to me, but it frightened me to return to my old life and spend my days and nights without her. What should I do to convince her to live with me? She wasn't one of those women who would be okay with having a living-in relationship outside of marriage. Her culture and religion wouldn't allow it. And the way she spoke of her father, I knew she never wanted to displease him.

We returned to our hotel and sat down on the couch.

"Goodness, it's hailing now," Rania said as she looked out the window. "I was thinking we could go for tobogganing."

"And freeze us to death," I mumbled. When I noticed her sad face, I said, "I promise I'll bring you back here. How about we come in the summer? It would be nice to walk without bundling so much?"

This brought a charming smile to her face. "Are you hungry?"

"I am. Always."

"Wanna have hot chocolate?" She got to her feet. "The one I got from the Christmas market?"

It had been many years since I had hot chocolate, but the way she offered it, I could never refuse her.

"Let's watch a movie," she suggested as she poured milk in two mugs she brought from the Christmas market the other day.

"I believe you want to watch a rom-com?"

"I find them very cheesy. Just fictional nonsense."

"You think romance is nonsense?" I asked.

"A guy meets a girl in some bizarre scenario, and they find each other attractive. Not to mention, they are both always good-looking, have perfect bodies and promising careers." She emptied the sachets of hot chocolate into the warm milk.

I chuckled at her remark.

"They don't make stories like they could meet in a gym, both trying to combat obesity. But no…both have perfect bodies, and in the entire movie, you wouldn't see anyone hitting the gym."

It was funny how she created her own story.

She started the microwave. "Or they could show a scenario where a man is jobless, and the girl is struggling to make both ends meet. Why all these romcoms never show people's true financial crises?"

"That sounds like a horror movie to me then," I snorted.

She joined my laugh. "And that's not all. The moment they meet, they start dating with a kiss and end with wild sex in the bedroom. That's what all romance movies are about. You can't call them love stories. There is no slow burn. It's pure lust, one of the deadly sins." She took out the mugs and stirred the milk. "Do you believe in romance?"

I stared at her for a moment, unsure what to say. "I haven't experienced it, but I'd like to believe it exists."

"Love is a very strong emotion. Perhaps it only exists in

books." She stood there, looking down at hot chocolate. "Love is taking care of each other's needs. Respecting each other. Trusting each other. Things like…the girl is tired so he cooks for her—that's love. The boy wants to relax so she gives him space to enjoy his games—that's love. Not jumping into each other for sex. It's just lust, then."

"Isn't lust another form of love?"

"Love is not a sin. Lust is." She handed me the mug and sat next to me.

"So, is it not romantic when people in love surprise their partners with hearts and flowers? You think it's lust?" She had my undivided attention now.

"I don't know." She looked at the TV screen absently. "I told you earlier, I don't believe in it." She blew on the hot chocolate and sipped it gingerly. "And aren't all endings the same? If a guy offers hearts and flowers, he expects the girl's naked body in his bed."

I blinked at her.

"Sadly, it is the truth. So where is love, then? It all starts with lust, doesn't it?" Her response took me off-guard.

"But sex is another form of sharing and expressing love," I objected.

"So, when you had sex with the women in your past, were you in love with all of them?" Her question rendered me speechless.

"I'm not saying sex is equivalent to love, but in the end, when two people are passionate about each other, they'd certainly opt for sex. It's how our human bodies have been made since the very beginning of time." She looked away at my words. "I agree sex is a part of lust, but it is also a part of sharing each other, physically and emotionally."

"If you're emotionally attached to someone, would you physically want to attach to her too?"

"Of course, I'd want to. I would want to make her feel,

through my body, how I feel about her." Oh, how I wish to show her right now.

"That happens only once or twice. Then men get used to the same body, and there is no passion, no surprise." She looked down into her mug. Something painful passed through her eyes, like a dark memory that still hurt her.

"Are you afraid of sex, or are you afraid to fall in love?"

I heard the sharp inhalation of her breath. She stood up. "I need to warm my drink."

I grabbed her hand. "I'm asking you something, Rania. Which scares you more? Love or sex?" I moved her back to the couch. She kept her gaze down, watching the steam rise up the drink. She didn't need to warm it.

Noticing how I was reading every expression on her face, she closed her eyes for a moment.

"Both!" she answered, her voice trembling. "Love breaks the heart and tortures the soul, whereas sex bruises the body. It's painful both ways." A strange darkness passed through her eyes. Her words reminded me of the scars I noticed the other night.

I tucked a few strands of hair behind her ear, her eyes welling up, but she forced herself not to show it. She was indeed hiding pain, and I couldn't stop asking her this time.

"Who has done this to you? Who has made you so…bitter?" Noticing her gaze still fixed on the mug, I took it from her and placed it on the coffee table. "What happened to you in the past? You can trust me."

She didn't blink.

"I want to remove all the scars and bruises if only you ever give me a chance."

Ignoring my words again, she collected her mug. "This is rather cold now. Would you like yours warmed up, too?"

It was quite obvious she didn't want to discuss her past. I exhaled a heavy sigh and handed my mug to her.

"Decide the movie, please," she called out.

"Any suggestion?"

"Home Alone?"

I turned on the TV and looked for the list of movies available. Luckily, the Home Alone Series was there.

I watched her admirably as she warmed the milk in the microwave. This small domestic gesture was already warming me from the inside. Without a glass of whiskey, it made me heady—if it wasn't magic, what was it?

She returned, holding two mugs. "Be careful, Adam. It's very hot," she said cheerfully. She handed me one mug and then sat beside me, warming her hands with it.

"Thanks." I decided not to discuss her past again, so it was time to change the subject. "I haven't had this since…my mom left." I took a sip, and it took me back in time, reeling in my mind the vivid memory of my mother in our tiny kitchen.

Rania remained quiet and played the movie.

At one point, she handed me her mug, grabbed the plush throw, and wrapped it around both of us. She was utterly lost in the movie and didn't realize how close she was to me. I felt her warmth next to me, and it was driving me crazy.

Control yourself, Adam!

She laughed like a child when the boy in the movie devised a plan for thieves. I sat there like a fool, hopelessly getting more addicted to her laughter. After we finished our hot chocolate, she cuddled back into the throw, folding her arms. Sensing her feeling cold, I wrapped my arm around her, and surprisingly, she didn't object.

"Do you want me to stoke the fire?" I asked.

"This is better." She snuggled into my arm very chastely while her eyes were glued to the screen. Her laughter close to my heart made me want to kiss her in mad desperation, but I tried to keep my hands to myself.

Perhaps sensing me watching her, she looked up. "What are you looking at?"

"You are very beautiful."

She scoffed and turned to the TV.

"I'd like to paint you on canvas one day." This made her turn again.

"You paint?"

"Sometimes," I said quietly. Though painting made me happy, it also made me sad, made me realize that I was lonely. "I do it at home, in my spare time. I haven't ever painted a real person. It's either landscapes or objects. But I wonder if I'd be able to capture your beauty."

She blinked at me.

I studied her face carefully, the contours of the cheek, her rosy lips, her beautiful black eyes. "Only God can create such divine beauty. Humans are far from this talent, I believe."

"You don't even believe in God."

"I still don't, but whoever has created you is a perfectionist."

She blinked again and turned back to resume the movie.

I didn't realize the first movie had finished and the next had started. I sensed she had stopped responding to it. I turned my head to find her sleeping on my arm.

I thought about this morning's incident at the monastery. What I did was not ethical, but I wanted to test if my mind was truly playing tricks or if what I sensed was even plausible.

I purposely pulled her close to kiss her, and my speculation began to make sense. She was afraid to kiss me—or any man. Witnessing her scars and nightmare episodes, I could tell she had a brutal past. She was scared to trust any man—afraid I'd hurt her someday. But what I could not understand was this heavy yet invisible presence around me. Surely, she wasn't stalked by a ghost of a man who'd hurt her after his death.

I couldn't believe I was even fanning the flames to this

preposterous possibility.

As I spent more time with her, she was becoming a folded mystery, wrapped in a hard shell that could only be broken with trust and time. If she felt comfortable sleeping in my arms, then I was sure one day I'd find the passage to that mysterious door, which she called a hideous past.

I was beginning to brew a story that perhaps she was under some curse, and once I kissed her, her spell would be broken. Sharing her bed, I had even begun to think like her—like a fairytale.

I was about to close my eyes and join her when Rania's phone rang somewhere in the room.

She jerked and bolted upright. "What happened?"

"Your phone is ringing."

She blinked, and realization washed over her face that her phone was ringing somewhere in the room. She looked around to check where the sound was coming from. She moved a few cushions and finally found her phone buried under them.

"Ben," she exclaimed as she picked up the call. "Yes, I know. I got the confirmation. The check-in opened at three." Her expression darkened at something. I waved her to put it on speaker, but she turned around instead. "I know," she whispered, but I could still hear it. "Tell Baba I'm a grown woman now." She ended the call but stayed like this for a moment, her back to me.

"Is everything okay?"

I heard her exhaling a heavy sigh as she turned around. "My room is ready."

It took me a moment to fathom what she was talking about. Her booking in the same hotel started today. Eventually, she'd need to move in there. But how could I tell her that I wasn't letting her go? I didn't want to sound like a caveman, and I couldn't even tell her what dangers she could expect there.

"Do you wish to go?"

She sat down on the armchair. "Ben knows you're in the same hotel. He doesn't know where I am, but if he caught wind of it—"

"Why do you care what he thinks?"

"Adam," she paused. "He tells everything to my father. Baba would never approve of this arrangement." She waved around the room.

I sat next to her. "Then I'm afraid you'd need to accommodate me in your room."

She scoffed and rolled her eyes. "Don't be silly."

"I'm serious."

Perhaps she read the intensity in my eyes. "Why?"

"I'd love to tell you why, but this is not the right time." I sat back. "Also, your nightmares won't let you sleep." She remained quiet, thinking over. "How about you do a check-in to show Ben where you are? You don't need to pack everything and move to the other floor."

The way her eyes moved everywhere, I was certain her mind was processing the option.

"Let me change, and I'll go to the reception to get the room key."

"We can go out for dinner then," I offered.

She nodded, smiled and disappeared into the washroom.

Her phone pinged again with a message alert. I took the liberty to look through it.

Ben: Have you met Gibson yet?

I replied on her behalf. I was sure she'd get mad, but that man needed to stop.

Rania: It's the G7 Summit in Quebec. He mentioned he had meetups scheduled with some ministers.

Ben: He is staying in the same hotel. He might invite you to his room.

Ben: Greet enough not to give him false hope, but don't be too friendly to aggravate Ahmed.

Rania: Do you honestly want me to date him or want me to say no to him strictly?

Ben took time to respond, perhaps processing what he needed to say.

Ben: I don't want you to blow up our professional agreement.

I wanted to smash the phone or punch the bastard.

Rania: If he had committed, he'd not sever his agreement. I won't do anything to vex Baba.

Rania: I'll update you tomorrow after the conference. I'm on a break, Ben, so let me enjoy my holidays.

Ben: Sorry, my love. Yes. I forgot since you never took off. I should let you go now. Take care.

Never took any break? Really?

Just then, Rania came out of the washroom. She was dressed in a black velvet shift dress with velvet leggings. Her dress matched her eyes, and now I could relate when, in books, they say: she took my breath away. She really did.

"What's wrong?" She asked. She noticed her phone in my hand. "What were you doing?"

"Please, don't get mad," I said slowly, my heart racketing against my chest. "I saw Ben's message, and I couldn't help it."

She took the phone from me and read our conversation. After a few seconds, she looked up, but didn't say anything.

"I'm sorry," I said. "But your boss is extremely annoying."

A smile escaped her lips. "Indeed."

I breathed a sigh of relief that she didn't look angry. "My offer is still open. You can resign today."

"Don't be silly." She turned and collected her bag from the couch. "Let's go for check-in."

When we entered the elevator, I asked, "You're not angry with me, right?"

"I'd have written the same."

"Why have you never taken off?"

She blinked to digest my question. It took her a second to realize we were still discussing the text messages. "I never really needed one," she shrugged.

"I thought you travelled with Mike."

"Only over long weekends, but I never needed to take my time off."

"Everyone needs a time off." When she didn't say anything, I asked, "Don't you visit your father on your paid holidays?"

"When was the last time *you* took a break?" She asked. It was obvious she didn't want to talk about her father.

I thought for a second. "I travel a lot for work. But when I'm done with meetings, I spend a quiet time in my hotel rooms."

"Why do you never explore the city on your own?"

"I don't understand the concept of solo travelling." I closed the gap between us. "That's why I asked you to be my travel companion."

The door opened and broke our trance. Rania blushed as one family waited outside the elevator for us to vacate.

She reached the reception and asked for her reservation. When they handed her the room key, she joined me, and we left the hotel.

AROUND THREE IN THE MORNING, I woke up to fetch water and found Rania missing. I assumed she must have taken a washroom trip, but I heard no sound of water running. I had a feeling that we could have that episode repeated when I found her staring at nowhere, but when I opened the washroom door, I saw no one. The lights in the living room were turned off, so I didn't bother peeping inside it. But strangely, a blast of cold air left me disconcerted. I checked the thermostat in the foyer and read the temperature inside the suite. It was normal.

Where was the cold air coming from? *And where is Rania?* I called out her name but heard nothing back. I went back into the bedroom and noticed her phone by the bedside. If she had gone out, she'd have taken her phone.

I tiptoed into the living room, shrouded in darkness, just to ensure she wouldn't wake up if she decided to sleep on the couch. But when I switched on the lights, terror sprouted like weeds in my veins.

Rania was standing on the small balcony, its glass door opened ajar. Ice-cold air drafted through the window, making the entire room an Arctic Tundra. I was so horrified that it took me seconds to fathom the situation. If she took one more step, she'd fall off from the fifteenth floor. What was more strange was that the thermostat showed the regular temperature. How the hell was it possible?

"What the hell are you doing outside?" I yelled and pulled her inside the room, shutting the door behind us. She stood like a marble statue, unresponsive. "How long were you out there? Are you fucking crazy? You'd have gotten frostbite." I rubbed her arms quickly to warm her, but her eyes were two dark holes. It was the same emptiness as when I dried her hair last night. What threw me off, though, was that when I touched her hands, her body temperature was normal, warmer than mine. I touched her face, and that was warm, too, as if she hadn't been outside at all.

Am I dreaming? But this was too real for a dream. I touched her bare feet, and they were also not cold. This temperature could freeze a person within seconds, and it took me over ten minutes to search the suite.

She stared blankly at the wall, and I followed her gaze, but I could not work out what she was looking at. Like a programmed robot, she walked mutely toward the bed, and I followed.

"Rania, will you please tell me what you were doing on the balcony?" Still, there was no response. She crawled under the duvet and closed her eyes.

What was that?

I lay back down on my side of the bed. She was sleeping peacefully as if she never woke up at all. Day by day, she was becoming more of a mystery to me. There was something she was hiding from me. I had no choice but to wait for her to reveal all her secrets. My only fear was: what if she was trying to kill herself? Perhaps a trauma wasn't letting her live with happiness. She must see a doctor.

When my heart returned to its regular beat, and I was about to fall into slumber, I realized this suite had no balcony.

Fuck!

What did I experience?

It took me back in time when I met that girl in a place that never existed. It was the second time I had travelled to a place that was impossible. If I asked her, there was no way I could prove it to her.

Sleep vanished from my head like a ghost.

I didn't remember how long I'd stayed in bed and stared at the ceiling.

CHAPTER 15
THE SUMMIT

RANIA

I OPENED MY EYES AND found Adam's sweet face. How he had always been there to pick me from my torment had never ceased to amaze me.

I slowly turned to check the time, not to wake Adam, but jolted upright when I realized I had forgotten to set my alarm. The summit would start at nine, and I had less than an hour to prepare.

I tiptoed out of the bed. It was still abnormal for me to accept his offer last night. I was supposed to be in my own room, yet I chose to stay with Adam for my own benefit. I was sick and tired of my nightmares. Adam had given me hope that I might see days without suffering—that maybe one day I'd get rid of it. It was selfish of me to make him believe that I agreed because he desired, but he didn't know I was using his presence to avoid my demons. How his presence was creating the absence of my nightmare was still incomprehensible.

Pushing these thoughts out of my mind, I headed quietly to the washroom. I didn't even bother to take a shower, as the noise may wake up Adam. Ready in no time, I checked the conference information on my phone. It was at Québec City Convention Centre—fifteen minutes drive from Fairmont.

On my way, I decided to send him a text message so he wouldn't worry about me again.

Rania: Thank you for understanding—in every way.

I sent one more message.

Rania: I have left to attend the summit. See you in the evening.

When I reached the Québec City Convention Centre, I checked my cell, but there was no message from him yet. *Still sleeping!* Disappointed, I sent him another message.

Rania: The summit is about to start. In case you're worried, I behaved like a good girl and had my breakfast. I'll also make sure I take my lunch on time.

I wasn't expecting so many people to attend the conference, but it was a global event beyond my imagination. I was glad I had dressed formally and professionally.

At the entrance, we were asked to show our invitations and the security team handed out our badges. People from social media companies, telecoms, and other technology-oriented businesses milled about the hall. They offered hands-on training in new technologies in Adobe and other creative products used for digital marketing and publishing. I hoped to learn a great deal about the latest publishing products that would be extremely helpful to incorporate at Greenway.

The summit started with a small speech from the digital media head. The person's name was Ethan Murray. His accent was English—tall and handsome, in his late thirties, seeming to climb high on the corporate level. Everyone seemed to know him. I was fortunate that Ben had arranged my seating in the first row. I was excited to learn everything today.

"Good morning, ladies and gentlemen. I welcome you all to Adobe Digital Marketing Conference 2012." Mr. Murray's eyes drank the crowd. "The Conference offers an unmatched networking opportunity with your industry peers to learn how others track current digital marketing challenges." He sipped his coffee. He was dressed perfectly in a black suit and a light gray shirt, and three hundred faces were turned to him. "We offer more than seventy breakout sessions, featuring many real-world customer success stories based on solutions from the Adobe Digital Marketing Suite. Many sessions will feature in-depth case studies, highlighting best practices from technology experts. Each session will emphasize specific takeaways for attendees to implement immediately. It includes seven different tracks: Digital Analytics, Targeting and Optimization, Web Experience Management, Digital Advertising, Social Marketing, Marketing Innovations, and Tech Labs." As Mr. Murray continued with his speech, he focused on each person in turn. His words were accurate, he didn't bother exchanging pleasantries with the crowd, or talk about some metaphor in this context.

My phone chimed suddenly, breaking everyone's trance. I turned beet red when Mr. Murray settled his gaze on me, eyebrows knitted with agitation. I completely forgot to put it on 'silent,' and its bloody sound echoed through the hall.

This is so embarrassing.

It was Adam calling. Mr. Murray continued his speech. I wasn't paying attention anymore and waited for my call to transfer to voicemail. I typed a message.

Rania: I'm at the summit.

Adam: Sorry. I didn't realize.

Rania: I forgot to turn my phone on silent. It was so embarrassing.

Adam: Oh, dear. Apologies. I'll see you in the evening.

Within a few seconds, I received another message.

Adam: I miss you already.

This made me smile, but I pursed my lips when I noticed Mr. Murray was scowling at me. Perhaps he was one of those people who demanded undivided attention when they addressed.

Rania: Don't you have work to do?

Adam: I took a week off. You know that.

Rania: Have you checked their indoor pools? I'm sure you'll find entertainment there.

Adam: Since when did you see the pool?

Rania: There is something called the Internet.

Adam: My entertainment is you nowadays. Anyway, I have an interview with CBC Quebec within an hour. I'll be free by lunch. Shall I pick you?

Interview with CBC? The media knows he is here. It was pointless to ask him.

Rania: Sorry. Training all day. I don't think it's possible. See you in the evening.

"You seem to be distracted this morning." I heard a familiar voice coming from the next seat. I didn't realize that in all these text messages, the speech had ended, and Murray was seated next to me. Some other men from social media companies were making short speeches after him. "Ethan Murray." He extended his hand, and I took it, smiling.

"Rania Ahmed."

"Rania…that's a pretty name. Where are you from?"

"I am from Toronto. I work for Greenway Advertising."

I was a bit intrigued by the way he talked. Was it the British accent or his grace and charisma that charmed me?

"So, what training do you plan to take today?"

"Creative Suite," I answered. "And I'm very glad to be part of it. Your speech was very informative."

"You barely paid any attention." He nodded disapprovingly at my phone. I pursed my lips in embarrassment and cursed my phone. Reading my expression, he continued. "What exactly is your job?"

"I work with the digital media and printing department. Basically, catalogue designing and publishing. They are mostly e-catalogues, designed for different operating systems and smartphones."

"Interesting. Where did you graduate from?"

"University of Toronto. But digital media was not my field. I studied software engineering, but playing with colour was always my passion, so I took some courses and chose this field." I smiled genuinely, feeling good about my choice.

"That's impressive. Have you planned further study in this field?"

"Yes, Mr. Murray. I plan to do a master's in digital media and graphics, but probably not until next year."

"Please, call me Ethan," he said, his eyes turning a darker shade of gray. "I don't like to be addressed so formally by a beautiful woman like you." I smiled back at him, not sure what to say. Luckily, Murray got distracted by his colleagues and removed himself from our chat to join them. I headed to the training room, where the session had already started. I stayed there until lunchtime, learning many new things about the latest tools.

Many people from Toronto were present, creating a more comfortable environment for communication and learning, as we shared similar interests. In between presentations, we discussed our favourite places in the city. By the time we headed for lunch, I was starving. As soon as I stepped out of the training room, Murray greeted me.

"Good to find you here. I was looking for you." He blocked my way. I glanced at the other trainees. "You guys carry on with your lunch. Miss Ahmed will join you back for training in an hour." They looked at me dubiously and left. "Please join me for lunch, Miss Ahmed. I want you to meet some people. Come." I followed him quietly.

We exited the conference hall and entered an exquisite restaurant within the convention centre. Murray introduced me to his two colleagues, who worked in the same department at Adobe. They launched into a technology-oriented discussion regarding Creative Cloud and its advanced features. I listened to their discussion quietly while sipping orange juice. I had no idea why Murray had invited me to lunch, where my presence was not even noticed. After a short discussion, the other men excused themselves, and I was left alone with Murray at a table for four.

"So, what would you like to have, Rania?" he asked, his gaze fixed on the menu.

"I'd like Caesar salad and minestrone soup, please," I asked the server, who was ready to take our order.

"That's it? That is your lunch?" Mr. Murray inquired curiously and put the menu card down on the table.

"Yes, please."

"I'll have mustard salmon with cobb salad, please." Murray handed both the menu cards to the server, who departed instantly. "Thank you for joining me for lunch." He adjusted his thick-rimmed black glasses over his deep gray eyes. "I always enjoy feeding beautiful women."

"Thank you for inviting me, Mr. Murray. I was not expecting, umm—"

"Expect the unexpected," he interrupted me. "Where are you originally from?"

"Lebanon." I tried to maintain a calm façade, but his gaze was making me nervous. *Why am I even here?* We remained silent for a moment until the server reappeared with my soup, salad, and meal for Murray.

"You don't talk much?"

"It's not like that."

"So, do I intimidate you?"

I blinked at him, not sure what to say. "I do talk, but we hardly know each other."

"Yes. Good point. That's why I invited you to lunch. We should get to know each other." His words were very confident like he had this all planned. But fate showed some mercy on me, and I heard my phone vibrating in my bag.

"Excuse me." I took out the phone, never so elated before to receive a call from Adam. "Hi. It's so good to hear your voice." That was undoubtedly the truth.

"Really?" He sounded pleased. "Then I'm glad I called. How's your training going?"

"It's good. It's a learning experience." Murray's gaze was still probing me through his thick-rimmed glasses. "How about you? How was your interview?"

"It went well. Boring at the start, though…you know, general business questions. They were interested in us also."

"Really? What did they ask?"

"I'll tell you when we meet. You had lunch?"

"I'm having it right now." I put a forkful of salad in my mouth.

"Please, carry on. I was wondering if we could hang out and see a movie tonight?"

"That sounds interesting. I'll call you when I'm free." I smiled over the phone.

"Take care."

I put the phone back in my bag. "Sorry about that."

"Boyfriend?" He adjusted his glasses, examining me like a specimen under a microscope.

"Yeah. How did you know?"

"You were blushing like a rose. It was obvious." I looked out the window to deflect his remarks, but his eyes were still on me.

"You are very beautiful, Miss Ahmed. Has your boyfriend told you that?" I gaped at his blunt remark.

I adjusted my scarf and focused on the salad. "Yes, he keeps reminding me."

"Charles Kingsley once said: *Never lose an opportunity of seeing anything beautiful, for beauty is God's handwriting.*" He regarded me with satanic greed. *What a sleaze!* I looked away. Noticing my uneasiness, he wisely changed the subject. "Have you ever been to San Francisco?" I shook my head. "It's a beautiful city, with amazing weather all year round. You should visit it. Be my guest." He took a bite from his plate.

"Well, thank you."

"There is another conference in New York around New Year's. Do you have an invitation for that?" Giving him a quizzical look, I wondered exactly where this was going. "You are a bright young woman. These kinds of summits and conferences will accelerate your career. May I have your email so I can send you an invite? I'll send you two invitations. You can bring your department head or whoever is interested in coming."

"That's very kind of you, Mr. Murray, but I already have an invitation. My boss has mentioned it, but in case it's not the same one…" I took out a pen and scribbled my email address on a paper napkin. "I'd love to attend another conference like this. Thank you very much." Now, we were talking like professionals.

"Have you ever thought about living in California?"

"No. Why?"

"I'd like to offer you a job in my department. We take good care of our employees, Miss Ahmed. I saw your work today, and I must say I'm very impressed. You are very skillful and technical, and your choice of colours and perception in digital publishing is unique. The two people you just met, I wanted them to meet you so we could discuss things further." I didn't even meet those people. I just sat like a spectator.

He took a sip from his glass and continued.

"Consider yourself very lucky, Miss Ahmed. This kind of career opportunity comes once in a lifetime." Speechless and baffled, I had no idea how to react. Ethan Murray was offering me a job at Adobe. It was certainly a big boost in my career. I had never imagined working in Silicon Valley. People dream about this kind of job, and I was being offered with my soup and salad in a fancy restaurant.

"It's an honour, Mr. Murray. I—"

"Think about it. I'm not asking for an answer now. We can discuss it tomorrow or perhaps over the phone next week."

"Sure, Mr. Murray. But—"

"I have good experience in digging out gems." He paused for a moment, then continued. "So…what does your boyfriend do?"

I blinked for a second, surprised at how swiftly he changed the subject. "He is a businessman."

"What kind of business?"

"Umm…he builds…houses…communities and…" I wasn't sure what else to add.

"Rich man. What's his name?" I didn't know if I was supposed to disclose his name or not, but since I had already said so much, there was no escape.

"Adam Gibson." I couldn't believe I was confessing to having a boyfriend.

"The man behind Gibson Enterprises?" He took off his glasses, shock masking his face.

"You know him?" I asked curiously.

"Who doesn't know the most eligible bachelor in Toronto? I am originally from there, by the way. Though it has been ten years since I moved to Silicon Valley, I keep track of my city's news. He is the talk of the town every time he makes a move." He took a sip and continued. "In fact, I read last week about his recent affair and…" He put his glasses back on as if meeting me for the first time. "Are you the same girl who hit the news last week?" I nodded but was also surprised that a man like him followed some stupid gossip in an entertainment magazine. The world seemed so small right now. I wanted to hide somewhere. "I must say he is a lucky man."

"I'm lucky to have him."

After a minimal pause, he continued. "Please, let me know soon about your decision."

"Do you want my resume, Mr. Murray? Or any letters of recommendation?"

With a flirtatious smile, he lowered his head to look at me from his gray eyes, his glasses resting on his nose. "Do you know *personal beauty is a greater recommendation than any letter of reference?* I didn't say it. Aristotle did." Unblinking, he indulged himself pleasurably in his drink. *What the hell!* "What are your plans for tonight? Are you joining us for skiing? Everyone is going."

"No, I have other plans."

"Your boyfriend is here in Quebec?"

"Yes."

"I'd like to meet him, then." He smiled with a hint of sharpness in his eyes.

"Sure." I looked down to check the time on my watch. "Thank you for the lunch, Mr. Murray, and for your offer. I'll let you know soon. My training is starting in ten minutes, so I need to go..." I stood up, and he joined me.

"Bring your man for skiing tonight. It's going to be fun."

"Let me ask him, and I'll let you know. Thanks for the invitation, though. Good day."

"Take care." He fixed his glasses and followed me.

Was it just me who felt he was walking deliberately close to me?

"Your fragrance is very charming, Miss Ahmed. I like floral

perfumes on beautiful ladies. It is a great blend of feminism with flowers."

I felt a wave of danger in his message, so without looking back at him, I scurried to enter the main hallway. Our badges were checked again as we headed in.

Fortunately, our ways parted, and I felt myself breathing normally as I joined the others at the training session. I still couldn't believe my luck that I had been offered such a huge opportunity. Though I had not decided about it, I was dying to share my excitement with Adam. With the hands-on training on the recent versions of Creative Suite, I was so engrossed that I didn't realize how much time had passed.

After two hours, Mr. Murray peeked in with an announcement. "We are serving tea and coffee outside."

We all halted our work and headed out, along with our trainer, Mr. Godfrey, a pure Californian in his early forties. Ethan Murray and Richard Godfrey got pulled into a conversation with other trainees, including me. I noticed how some female trainees were getting too cozy with Murray, perhaps seeking his favour. He had the charm and charisma to draw the crowd.

I managed to remove myself from the discussion and poured myself some tea. As soon as I touched the milk pot, a masculine hand covered mine.

"Allow me." I turned to find Ethan Murray behind me. His charming smile made me smile back at him. I released the milk pot, and he added the milk to my tea.

"Thank you." I picked up the sugar.

"One tea for me, please," he added.

Picking up another empty cup, I prepared tea for him. He guided me to sit at a round table away from everyone else. I ignored the girls who were rubbing themselves to Murray like kittens a minute ago. They were watching me curiously, talking to each other as if they were gossiping.

"How is your training so far?" he asked.

"It's very informative. There is a lot to do with the tools."

"All the trainees will get the latest versions so you can learn more on your own machines."

"That's better still." I took a sip. "Were you involved in the development and enhancement of the latest version?"

"Yes, in bits and pieces. But primarily in documenting it in the web world. Most of my time is spent on integration research and writing product tutorials."

"I have seen your books."

"You have a chance to read them?"

"Ah, no! Technology books are not my forte."

"Let me guess," he mused. "You are a fantasy reader." I pursed my lips. "You like unreal things."

"They are less tormenting than reality," I mumbled behind my cup of tea.

"Very astute." We didn't speak further.

After the tea break, I rejoined the training session. I concentrated completely for the next three hours until Adam called, reminding me the day was over.

Adam waited outside in the lobby, so I picked up my bag and hurried to the washroom to check if I was presentable for my newly created fake boyfriend. When I left the washroom, Ethan Murray was waiting for me.

"Are you leaving?"

"Yes."

"Your boyfriend is here?" He asked with sarcasm.

I knew he wanted to meet Adam, perhaps to make connections with a notorious man like him, so he followed me. Adam was sitting on a black leather sofa, dressed gracefully in his casual clothes. He stood up when he saw me coming toward him. I had never been so delighted to see him waiting for me.

Dropping my bag on the floor, I hugged him tightly. He

paused for a second, and I was certain he must be wondering what I was doing since I'd never acted this way before. He held me closer in his warm, scented embrace.

"I missed you," I confessed, inhaling his sweet, comforting scent as he gently rubbed my back.

"I missed you too…" He paused for a moment and continued. "You look tense."

How does he know me so well?

He knew I was covering up. He studied my face when I pulled away.

"I'm just tired. It was a long day. Take me away." It felt really good in his arms. I felt protected. I hugged him again to embrace the blessing that was holding me warmly. Was this feeling called home?

"Ahem, ahem." I heard someone clearing his throat. I turned to find Ethan Murray waiting for us. Adam's expression changed as soon as they made eye contact.

"Mr. Gibson," Mr. Murray addressed sharply.

"Mr. Murray," Adam nodded. It seemed like they already knew each other. Why did Murray not mention it?

"I had the pleasure of meeting your girlfriend today—and such a beautiful lady."

Adam pulled me closer, glaring at Murray. I could sense he was trying to control his temper, so I decided to interrupt.

"Do you two know each other?" I looked back and forth between them.

"I told you, Miss Ahmed. Who doesn't know Mr. Gibson?" Murray offered his cheeky grin when he noticed Adam's grim posture.

"Let's go." Ignoring Murray, Adam collected my bag, wrapped his arm around my shoulders and dragged me away.

"She isn't your type, Gibson?" Murray remarked behind us, making Adam freeze in his tracks.

Adam turned around and faced Murray. "Stay away from her," he seethed.

"Will someone tell me what's going on?" I asked Adam, who seemed more furious. "Adam?"

Ethan Murray adjusted his glasses, regarding me with a jagged smile. Adam dragged me out of the lobby. Our car was waiting outside. I slipped inside, and he joined me. Noticing his grim face, I remained quiet all the way back to our hotel, but I also wanted to know what was behind his exchange with Murray. Obviously, there was some history there.

Ten minutes later, we were seated on the couch. Adam was rubbing his lower lip, evidently showing his agitation. There was definitely something churning in his mind. He went to the bar and made himself a drink, still angry but putting up a calm façade. He returned with a glass of whiskey and sat beside me on the couch.

"How do you know Ethan Murray?"

"I should ask you that." I crossed my legs and faced him.

"Answer me first, Rania. How do you know him?" His eyes were fixed on the wall.

"I met him this morning. He is a digital media head with Adobe. He opened the conference with a speech, and afterwards, he introduced himself."

"There were three hundred people there. What made him introduce himself?" Adam's sudden question startled me.

"I…umm…I don't know." I shrugged.

"What else did he talk about?" He still stared at the wall. *Why isn't he looking at me?*

"He invited me for…lunch…" I answered with hesitation, twisting the ring on my finger. He whipped his head toward me with a disapproving look.

"You lied to me?"

"I didn't lie," I objected. "He introduced me to other

colleagues, and we had lunch. He offered me a job in Silicon Valley."

"And you accepted it?" He rose from the couch. "After all… who can refuse the charming Ethan Murray?"

"I just don't understand what you're implying."

He turned, squatting down before me, still holding his drink.

"What else did he say?" He leaned closer, placing one hand under my ear and caressing my cheek with his thumb. "Did he tell you how beautiful you are? Did he tell you that you entranced him? Tell me. Did you like him complimenting you?"

"What are you talking about?" I jerked his hand off my face. He was not in his right mind—something was bothering him terribly. If I told Adam what he just asked was true, I had no idea how he'd react. So, I lied.

"No, Adam. It was strictly professional. He didn't say anything like that to me." Taking his drink, I pulled him up to sit next to me. "What is it that you're holding back? Please, tell me."

"Did you accept his job offer?"

"No, I haven't said anything."

"Are you going to accept it?"

"I don't know. His offer was good and—"

"And you will think about it. Right?" He looked down at the floor. "After all, it would be a big boost in your career."

"I haven't decided anything. I have to finish my time in Canada until I get my citizenship, and—"

"Is that the only reason you're staying here?" he asked. "If you had citizenship, would you have considered his offer?"

"Adam! Stop talking in riddles and tell me what this is about!"

"I'm sure he must have invited you to the next conference in New York," he mumbled, pressing his lips.

"How do you know?"

"He intends to fuck you, Rania, that's why," he snapped, his eyes bloodshot. "He wants to use your body so he can torture my soul. Will you let that happen?"

"What nonsense. Don't you know me by now?"

"I know you, but I also know him. He is a fucking charmer. How he lures women with his sweet talk. Before you know it, you'll be in bed with him."

"Please, stop it," I scowled. "How can you say something like that?"

"Because I know." He raised his voice. "He fucked my sister when she was only sixteen."

I stared at him, horrified. I gave myself a minute to absorb his words.

"I hadn't seen Eva in so many years," he explained. "One night, she called me from a house of some private midwife and told me she was all alone after an abortion because some fucker made her pregnant and left her by herself. It took her three months to recover from the trauma. She was only sixteen, damn it." I hadn't seen Adam ever losing his patience before. "She hadn't even finished high school yet. She informed our mother that she and I had reconciled and spent a summer to bond, but the fact was I used to take her to psychiatric treatment, and after three months of therapy, she was able to face her family." He paused for a moment. "Mom still doesn't know about it. It's a secret between Eva and I." He was on the verge of breaking. "You're the only person I've ever told. I'm telling you because I see the same danger coming to you. The way he looked at you…he was fucking you with his eyes. He is the true version of Satan, and the worst part is, I *can* see him." I put my hands on my mouth, shocked at his revelations.

He continued bombarding me with the rest.

"Eva never really found the courage to return to high school, so we worked on her credits privately. She finally got settled in university and started her academic career. Mom never found out about her abortion. Once I knew she was fine, I didn't see her anymore. Meanwhile, I registered a complaint against Murray. He was doing his doctoral program. The university suspended him for six months, and he flew to California, where he started his career once again. He tried contacting Eva and blackmailed her. The fucking prick had videos of them having sex. I had to pay him a handsome amount to hand over everything to me, but I know he still has the originals. Who would sexually use and abuse a sixteen-year-old girl and then blackmail her with the videos? Isn't he a walking Satan?"

I still had my hands over my mouth, horrified by every word.

"Have you wondered how you got a front seat at the conference when there were giants of technology attending? You think Ben did that?" His question jolted me. I didn't think about it earlier. And how did he know I sat afront? "He wanted you in the first row. He's been chasing you since he found out I have someone in my life. His luck is fucking awesome that you are in the same field. He sent an invitation through Ben and asked if you could attend this conference so he could meet you in a new city and seek you out."

"How do you know all this?"

"I have assigned someone to look after you," he said quietly, staring at the wall. "You can call it stalking or whatever you want, but since I first saw you, I felt like I was supposed to protect you. Don't ask me why I'm doing it. It's not in my hands." He turned to me. "Anyway, that person told me about Ethan's intentions Monday morning when you boarded the train. I was told that Murray has been watching your every move. I had no other choice than to join you. If I had told you right away, you wouldn't have believed me because there was no trust relationship between us then. You didn't even know him. I had to spend time with you on the train to gain your trust." He sighed heavily. "I brought you here with me because Murray arranged your accommodation in the room next to his." Raking his finger through his hair, he continued. "I've already seen my sister traumatized. I can't see you like that."

I took a moment to absorb all of it. After a few minutes, I placed my hand over his. "Do you trust me, Adam?"

"More than anyone."

"Then, do you think I'll get seduced by his words?"

"He knows how to play. He *fucks* through his words."

"He is only playing a mind game with you. Let him do it. You know I don't get easily carried away by men."

"That's one of the things I love most about you," he chuckled, and the room brightened up. "Even though you pushed me away, I knew at least you would not let him play with you." His lopsided grin changed the very air of the room.

"Let's go." I stood up, pulling his hand. "You were taking me to a movie, remember?" His eyes sparkled at my offer, and it was enthralling to cheer him up as he'd always done to me.

I had no idea what he had gone through all those years ago and how suddenly seeing me with Murray would torture him. He cared about me greatly, and I'd ensure the trust remained between us. I'd never let Murray cast his spell on me with his filthy mind. Adam had given me enough insight into his personality to deal with him tomorrow.

While Adam finished his drink, I headed to the room to dress casually for our movie night. I didn't care if someone caught us in the theatre or posted a picture on any social media website. I just wanted Adam to have a good time. He had saved his sister without telling his mother and taking no credit for himself. He had made all this effort to follow me to protect me from Murray. He deserved a happy memory. I wanted to make him forget about our discussion.

My heart had raised him to the highest level of respect and trust. I could never feel about anyone the way I do for this man.

CHAPTER 16
A TRUE COMPANIONSHIP

ADAM

Rania was my sun, who emanated light, making a warm haven. She was too powerful to absorb any negative energy around her. With her strong will, I was certain she wouldn't let Murray pollute her mind. Was it her past that made her so protective of herself, or had she always been so different? Her scars showed me a hint of her past, but I'd never bring it up until she trusted me enough to share her pain as I did today. I had nothing to hide from her now, my soul feeling lighter, soaring high in the sky as if it had been released from a death trap.

I downed my whiskey when she returned, clad in jeans and a beige sequined top.

"Is there anything that doesn't look good on you?"

Blushing, she smiled shyly. *Ah! What do I do with this pink shade?*

"You need to get your eyes tested, Mister." She laughed at me and headed to the door. When we got in the car, she checked her phone, and her expression changed. She turned it off and shoved it into her jacket pocket.

"So, which movie are we watching?"

"I assumed you're fond of animation," I asked.

"You'll watch it with me?"

"I can go to the ends of the earth with you. I have told you this several times." Heat radiated from her body as I slid close to her. "But if you want, we can go somewhere private. You know...cinemas are a public place, and I'm afraid I didn't book a private show."

"Don't worry," she giggled. "I don't think anyone would even notice us."

We reached the Cineplex within ten minutes and waited in line to buy tickets. As per the plan, we agreed to watch an animation. A few couples noticed us in the popcorn queue, but we ignored everyone and stayed in our own capsule.

Two hours later, we left the show with laughter following us. We got in the car and drove back to the hotel for dinner.

"Let's stop here," Rania announced, looking outside. We were in the lower quarters, facing the St. Lawrence River. The chauffeur stopped the vehicle at Bd Champlain, just at the crook of Petite Champlain. Rania stepped out without waiting for my input.

"Have you gone mad?" I asked. "It's freezing outside." It was minus eighteen degrees Celsius, and with a river at such a close distance, it was fucking cold.

Rania ignored my warning and started traipsing through the crowd. I followed her while she took pictures of several Christmas trees, yet struggling to amble uphill on the steep and slushy cobbled path. How many Christmas trees would she capture on her phone?

She stopped by a few souvenir shops and tried a few silly hats. I didn't want to spoil this moment, which made me realize that I hadn't been to a theatre for ten years. I had missed all this fun and got so absorbed in my work that I didn't know what life offered beyond corporate clients and board meetings. All I did now was follow her like a fool and capture every moment of her every act on my phone.

We took a break at a pizza and wings take-out restaurant furnished with only four bar stools in the corner. We were actually dating like a typical teenage couple who couldn't afford a fancy restaurant but would rather spend the money on a movie. It was my worst pizza, but with her company, everything was worth it.

"Tell me something from your childhood," she asked. "Something no one knows."

I thought for a moment. "I was once involved in shoplifting."

"No way!"

"It's true, but luckily, I never got caught."

"What did you steal?"

"A tie. For my grad ceremony."

She stared at me horridly, but perhaps sensing the dreary air, she said, "I was a mafia at school."

"Huh?" Now, I gaped at her.

"Or you can call me a bully. Ask Mike. As my father would put it, a menace."

"You don't look a mischief type."

"The boys in my school were nasty. Someone had to discipline them." She shrugged. "But my parents never got any complaints from the school. I was my teachers' favourite because I was a very bright student."

"I wish I had seen you causing trouble."

"Oh, just wait and watch." She winked, sipping from the drink.

After our extremely unhealthy yet blissful dinner, we leisurely strolled on the snow-covered streets, hand in hand, as if we had no other obligations. It was so peaceful to walk with her that I wished to do it every day for the rest of my life. She was slowly making me addicted to her. *What happens when this is all over?* Even the mere thought scared me.

We entered an ice cream parlour where Rania took around fifteen minutes to try different flavours. She savoured each flavour, eyes closed, before trying the next. The boy behind the counter waited patiently, but by looking at Rania, it didn't look like she'd decide the flavour in this century. After quite some time, my patience ran out.

"You're taking too much time to decide," I seethed. "Do you even plan to buy one?" The number of spoons she'd had, I don't think she'd even consider getting one. To my surprise, she ordered the largest choco-vanilla soft cone I'd ever seen and didn't pick any flavours she tried. "What was the point of trying all the flavours when you were going to pick this?"

"You are so gullible, Gibson," she laughed and tapped my cheek as if I were a child. "That's how you get ice cream. You taste all other flavours while already knowing what you want to get." She sounded so serious that I almost believed this nonsense.

"Are you sure you can eat all this?" I checked the cone incredulously. "You will catch a cold."

"Aren't you going to share with me?" She asked, and I couldn't help but accept her offer.

She took the couch while I sat in the armchair opposite her. I studied the place, noticing how one group of college boys were looking at Rania while she was obliviously engaged in licking her cone. The boys whispered something to each other, leering at her. I wanted to gouge their eyes, but as I looked at Rania, I gaped.

It was the most erotic thing I had ever seen. She was giving a show to the horny boys. I had to stop her.

"Care to share?"

She looked up, staring at me as if I had horns on my head.

"Are you going to eat all of it?"

"I thought you'd never ask," she giggled and stood from her seat and sat on the armrest of my chair. "It's heavenly."

She handed me the cone, putting one arm over my shoulder

for support. It was a wrong idea to ask for ice cream. How could I tell her that I had never licked a cone like this since childhood and I'd be a fool to ask for a spoon? I managed somehow, but the boys were still passing nasty glances in our direction, snickering at some joke they shared.

"Do you know females have a special relationship with chocolate and ice cream?" She took the cone from me and started licking the chocolate side of it. "They activate the hormones of happiness. Usually, girls crave chocolate and ice creams during their menstrual cycle to combat the depression that comes with it." *What?* "Yes, in case you're wondering why I asked for this, I wanted to come out of this shit hole." After a few seconds, she burst into laughter at my horrid look. "What are you looking at? You haven't seen a girl on her cycle?" She patted my shoulder, which forced me to look away.

Is she high? Could anyone be drugged on sugar doses? She'd never talked to me like that.

She handed me the cone, expecting me to lick it again. I wondered if the boys heard us. They were seated very close.

"Hey! What are you looking at, you suckers?" She shouted, drawing everyone's attention. "You understand English, right?"

The boys looked everywhere but here, almost blushing at the uninvited attention.

"Haven't seen a hot, sexy man licking a cone?" I gasped at her words and dropped the cone. The boy behind the cash counter laughed hysterically. Rania got to her feet and approached the boys. "Now, see what you've done. Stop drooling over him. He is not licking your popsicle, you sleazeballs. He is not one of you." With that, she headed to the counter to fetch napkins.

She began picking up the broken pieces of the cone. I was so aghast that I just stared at her.

The boys scurried out of the store, embarrassed. When I noticed Rania wiping my shoes, I grabbed her hand.

"Let me clean it. It's gonna melt in your shoes, otherwise," she said. "You'll have to learn how to do justice to ice cream, Mr. Gibson." She looked up with a childlike smile. "The boys scared you?" I still stared at her, blown away, but when I didn't say anything, she explained, "They were gay." She pursed her lips, trying to stifle her laughter. "Now we are even."

"What? No. They were looking at you."

"Are you kidding me?" She stood up with the dirty napkins in her hand. "Where in the world boys come to ice cream shops? Didn't you notice their outfits or how they were checking you out?" I blinked at her. "Their pink hats?"

"Anyone can visit the ice cream shop," I objected defensively.

"No. Boys do not, and I'm not being sexist, but it's a girl thing. Straight men do not have that appetite for desserts." She threw the napkins away and sanitized her hands. "Didn't you know they followed you to the shop?" She fixed my scarf. "My sexy man is a head-turner."

As she left the shop, I glanced back at the store boy, who threw a flying kiss in my direction. *Oh, for fuck's sake!*

My sexy man...Her words buzzed in my ears. It was intoxicating how she claimed me.

I heard her voice behind me, holding the door open. "He is not available, Mousier!"

The boy immediately straightened like a newly sharpened pencil yet blushed like a schoolgirl. The ice cream had indeed drugged her.

"You are so unpredictable," I mumbled.

"Oh, you've no idea what you've got yourself into." She nudged me slightly, winking at me. "You have a lot to see. Just wait and watch." With that, she trotted ahead, again leaving me baffled. I could now imagine what mischief she talked about in her school days. She'd already shown me.

"Shall I call the car?" I took out the phone from my pocket, but she snatched it from me and shoved it into her pocket.

"Can't you see the hotel from here?"

"You can see this hotel from every spot of Old Quebec," I seethed. "I'm not signing up for your adventures."

Still, she offered me her arm. "What about going to the ends of the earth with me?"

"Yeah, only if we survive this cold. I take my words back."

She dragged me. "Don't worry. I won't let you freeze to death."

"It's two kilometres walk—almost twenty minutes."

"You're complaining as if you don't work out."

"Not in this shit cold," I grumbled.

"So what?" She pulled my hand, and we started our stroll carefully on the wet and slimy path. "Loosen up, Gibson. This isn't your official trip. Normal people walk, regardless if it's raining or snowing."

After a few minutes, I realized that with her warmth, I wouldn't freeze after all. Her touch was keeping me warm, even in this harsh weather. The sun always emits warmth, no matter how cold it is.

We almost slipped a couple of times on black ice, but we managed to support each other and laughed along the way.

I was on a magical journey, learning how normal people live, free from worries about meetings and business deals. Walking with her, hand in hand, in the falling snow was priceless, more valuable than a ride in any luxury car or chopper.

She stopped momentarily to look up at the snow-filled sky and embraced the snowflakes falling over her face. She didn't blink, even for a second, though some flakes dissolved in her eyes. Tears sneaked through the corners of her eyes, but she kept her gaze glued to the sky. I felt the time freezing. Everything moved in slow motion, like in a movie.

When she looked back at me, it was so strange that, for

a moment, I thought she had forgotten who I was. But then, she stepped forward and wrapped her arms around my neck. I wanted to stay in this moment, so I pulled her close and drowned myself in her warmth while we stayed in this white winter land.

It was the best snowfall of my life.

After a few minutes, she pulled away and meandered through the crowd. I sucked in a breath, reeling what just happened.

WE FINALLY REACHED THE HOTEL LOBBY around ten, our coats coated with snow. People passed us disapproving looks as if two muggers had won a lottery and decided to stay in this lavish hotel. We ran to the elevator, catching our breaths.

The room was comfortably warm. Rania divested her jacket and fell on the couch.

"Oh God, I'm so tired." She checked her watch. "And I have training tomorrow." As I bent to remove her shoes, she stopped me. "What are you doing?"

"Your boots are filled with snow. You'll catch a cold."

"I can do it myself. Please!"

"Did you listen to me at the ice cream shop?" I grunted and removed her shoes before she could complain.

She left the couch and went to the washroom. I removed my accessories, recalling that she had put my phone inside her jacket. Since we both had the same phone brands and colours, I mistakenly checked her phone and found an unread message.

> *Ethan: No matter what wonders my eyes have seen, nothing amazes me more than when I look at you. Ethan (P.S. Looking forward to seeing you tomorrow)*

Pervert! I wonder if he picked up the words from a greeting card, hoping he'd get into her panties. The message was sent around seven when we left for the movie. That was when she checked her phone in the car, and her expression darkened. She was displeased with this message since I'd already warned her about Murray. I controlled my anger. She assured me she would handle him, so I had to trust her judgment. She hid the message purposely so as not to ruin our evening.

I brought both phones into the bedroom when I realized she was using the ensuite washroom. I used this time to change in the room. I had changed into my lower and just removed my shirt when she stepped out of the washroom. After a quick glance at my bare-chested body, she crawled into the bed. I quickly pulled on my T-shirt, shut off the lamps and slipped into bed. She picked up the phone I had placed on her pillow and began setting the alarm. I shifted to face her, propping my head on my hand on the pillow.

"Thanks for the wonderful evening," I said sincerely.

She looked at me from the phone. "We set the rules for no *thanks* and *sorrys*. Remember?"

But she must know how I feel. "Every time we do something together, I think it's the best time I've ever had, and then the next time is even better."

"I had fun too, though the pizza sucked big time." She placed her hand on her tummy. "I think my stomach is upset."

"The amount of ice cream you had…"

"Hey! Don't blame the ice cream. You dropped all of it."

"And how many flavours did you already try?"

"Pfftt. That doesn't even count. I think it's the pizza. How is your stomach?"

"Can't say about my stomach, but I had the most erotic dessert of my life."

"Erotic?" She giggled. "Sure, it was erotic for those boys." Regarding her beautiful face, I marvelled at her beauty. "There's something else." *How does she know I've something on my mind?*

Dazzled, I riveted every inch of her face. "You are very

beautiful." That was all I could say.

"That's not what you wanted to say."

"If you know, why are you asking?"

"I want you to say it."

"I read the message on your phone. I picked it up by mistake."

"I know. I saw that. Never mind." She put her phone away on the nightstand.

"Will you still go tomorrow?"

"Why shouldn't I? He can't make me do anything against my will. The position he is in, I doubt he'd mess with his career." She snuggled down under the covers and continued. "One complaint is enough, Adam."

"You certainly know how to handle assholes."

She giggled, turned to me and took my hand to tuck under her face. It had become our norm, and I had started to love it.

After a few seconds, she asked again. "There is something else."

"Can I share a secret with you?"

She waited.

"The other night, I found you on the balcony. The living room was freezing."

"Huh?" She blinked.

"What is going on, Rania? I feel like I'm going crazy. I'm not delusional."

"What balcony?"

"The one in the living room." She opened her mouth to say something, but I cut in. "I know. There is no balcony, but I saw you there."

She knitted her eyebrows. "You must have dreamt it."

"No. It wasn't a dream," I said quietly. "I woke up in the middle of the night and couldn't find you. Then, I saw those curtains were parted, and you were standing outside, watching the sky blankly. I pulled you in right away."

"But…"

"I know there is no balcony, but I'm not crazy." She must consider the urgency in my voice. "Tell me what's going on?"

She remained quiet for endless beats, perhaps analyzing what to say. I had a feeling she knew the answer, but I was disappointed when she said, "Sometimes, dreams are too real, and we cannot separate them from reality."

I thought for a moment. "You told me every human is born with its angel and Djinn. Do they carry our memory, too?"

"They are with you always. They see what you see."

"Is it possible that my Djinn saw the balcony?"

She blinked. "They see what *you* see, Adam. Not the other way around."

I sighed heavily, wondering how to make her believe. So, I decided to change the subject. "Are there others besides that are tied to us?"

"They are," she pondered. "Some live in the sky, some reside on earth. They come with different superpowers, with varied job descriptions. Why are you so curious about them?"

Because you are shaking the world around me.

Because I am experiencing things and places that my mind cannot accept.

Because I know there is someone between us—someone invisible, and you won't tell me.

Because I am losing my mind.

But I said none of it.

"*You* made me curious. That night, you asked me who I was—an angel or a Djinn in disguise. I had no knowledge of either of them, so I dug up on the Internet." I couldn't tell her that after my interview today, I spent the entire afternoon researching this topic, about my paranormal experience of the balcony. But nothing made sense to me.

"I don't know everything."

"But you know enough to explain it to me," I objected. "So, do you really think they exist? I mean, the Djinn?"

"Of course they do," she answered immediately as she was certain of it, as if she had seen them. "But you don't believe, do you?"

"I believe what I see."

Her eyes were like the night sky, tempting me to wander through the dark.

She sighed and turned to look up. "You will feel it, Adam… one day you will."

We didn't speak after that, but I kept reading her until we both closed our eyes and fell asleep.

CHAPTER 17
PARANORMAL

ADAM

FINALLY, THE LONG DAY ENDED, and it was time to pick up Rania. I knew she had been busy all day, so I didn't bother texting her, but I was curious whether she had talked to Ethan Murray.

I kept myself engaged, visiting some promising properties around Old Quebec to figure out the business prospects with local builders. I didn't realize I'd miss her company so badly. She was making me addicted to her, and I was enjoying this addiction more than anything else in the world. I had never wanted anything as much as I wanted to see her smiling, sitting next to me, and doing silly things like she did yesterday at the ice cream parlour. She was unpredictable yet mesmerizing in her way. She had always taken me by surprise. She enjoyed life's pleasures, but I'd seen her nightmares, too.

I looked up at the sky, wondering if God truly existed and if He was watching me. I'd pass a message to Him. *Please take away all her pain. She deserves better than nightmares.*

When I arrived at the lobby, I noticed people streaming out of the conference hall. I waited for ten minutes, then called her. After no response, I headed to security.

They informed me that she'd already left during lunch break and even handed back her badge.

I called her again, but her cell phone was switched off. I called our hotel, and they informed me that she had already returned.

When I entered the suite, it felt eerily quiet. Noticing her jacket and handbag on one of the chairs, I sneaked into her bag and checked her phone, along with the room access card. It was indeed switched off.

I looked around the living room and then to the bedroom, but she was nowhere. With a feeling of *déjà vu*, I parted the drapes, hoping to find a balcony again, but there was only a window there. I sat on the chaise, wondering what was happening to me lately.

In the acute silence of the suite, I heard strange sounds, like people whispering behind the washroom door. No light emanated from beneath the door, but the voices were certainly originating from there. I leaned to the door, trying hard to listen, but the whispers were so soft I could barely hear them. With mild reluctance, I turned the doorknob. Though it was pitch dark, I saw a shadow moving. I switched on the light and found Rania standing in front of the mirror.

Clad only in a towel, she was covered from her breasts to halfway down her thighs. Water droplets dripped from her wet hair as if she'd just stepped out of the shower. *What is she doing in the dark?* She didn't move when I entered, nor did she notice my presence.

Frozen like an ice sculpture, she faced the mirror. Her eyes had the same emptiness I'd noticed during the other night. There was no sound now, no whispers. As if in a trance, it seemed like time had stopped on her. I stood behind her, studying her eyes through the mirror, but she still didn't notice me. She was somewhere else; otherwise, she'd have created a fuss upon my presence and seeing her like this.

The air felt like a vacuum, making it hard for me to breathe. It felt too heavy, yet too hollow—the same feeling I had yesterday when I tried to kiss her as if there was an invisible presence in the room. The look in her eyes sent a shiver down my spine. I moved aside her hair gently and checked the marks on her back and shoulders. There were more than I imagined.

I waved my hand before her eyes, but she didn't blink. It seemed like she wasn't even breathing, but if she weren't, she wouldn't be standing here. I turned her to face me, cupped her face and called her name. There was no response. Her body was as cold as ice, so I dared to give her warmth with my touch.

As soon as I placed my lips on her forehead, she inhaled sharply, like a drowning person emerging out of the water. Her eyes were still like two deep, dark stones. Repeating what I did the other night, I touched her lips with my thumb. That time, her body was warm, and it started to get cold when I explored her face through my lips. This time, it was the opposite. She was cold, but when I touched her, I heard her breathing, her body beginning to warm. She didn't move, but her breath said everything. *She wants my touch, her body wants my touch, and I want it, too.*

Caressing her face with my lips, I inhaled her fragrance. Her skin felt soft and velvety, like a rose petal under my lips. The sun was close to me, and I wanted to burn in the light and be engulfed in her warmth.

As I reached her lips, a loud noise from the bedroom jarred me as if someone had turned on the television. I scurried out, wondering if it was the room service and found Rania in this state. But in the bedroom, the television was off, and no one was there. I had no clue where the sound came from. I rushed back to the washroom, but the door was closed. I opened it without knocking and found Rania dressed in her jeans and navy-blue top, brushing her hair.

What the fuck?

"You should knock before coming in," she frowned. "We still have some boundaries, Adam. Don't try to cross them." She glared through the mirror. With my feet frozen, I gaped at her. *How can she change clothes in less than a minute?* My heart started beating out of control, my mind frantically trying to make sense of what was going on. I leaned against the doorframe, feeling disoriented. She turned around. "Are you all right?" With a concerned look, she touched my face. "You look pale." I looked into her eyes. She pretended as if nothing happened. "Were you running?" She grabbed my hand and pulled me out of the doorway, guiding me to the bed. "Your heart is beating very loudly. Even I can hear it." She picked up a water bottle from the nightstand and handed it to me. When I reached for it, my hands were shaking. She noticed my trembling fingers and held them tightly. "Adam? Talk to me. Do you want me to call the doctor? Why are you shaking?"

I stared at her, unable to form words. How could she be standing frozen, wearing nothing but a towel, and seconds later, completely dressed and turning my mind upside down?

I gathered all my energy to ask. "Where were you?"

"I was in the washroom. You just saw me there."

"I went to pick you up at the conference. You weren't answering your phone. The security guard told me you left early."

"Oh, yeah. That!" She rolled her eyes. "That sleaze—Murray—drained out all my energy. I left early because I couldn't stand him. Then, my phone battery ran out. I came in for a nap. I woke up half an hour ago and took a shower. I was coming out when you opened the door without knocking."

"When did you dry your hair?" I touched her hair, puzzled.

"Ten minutes ago. Why do you ask?" She had no recollection of the event.

"When I came in..." My voice trailed off. "Your hair was wet, and now..." I ran my fingers through her hair. "Did you dry your hair before I came?"

"Why are you asking all these weird questions?" She giggled, making me feel stupid. "Yes, I blow-dried it before you came in. But why do you ask? What's with my hair?"

I studied her face again, but she seemed so collected as if nothing happened.

"When I entered the washroom, you were in a towel, with water dripping from your hair. And you were standing like..."

"Stop daydreaming, Adam. Do you think I'd stand there and let you watch me in just a towel? What kind of fantasies are you conjuring in your mind?" She asked playfully.

"It's not fantasy," I urged. "I saw your body. You have scars on your back and shoulder, right?"

Her face turned white as a ghost as she looked down at the floor. "How do you know?"

"Because I saw them. I saw them the other night, too, before we had the Satan discussion. But I didn't bring it up. I thought you didn't like to discuss your past."

She raised her gaze at me, clueless. "I don't know what you're talking about."

"When I came in, I found you in the washroom, standing in darkness." There was no point in hiding my experience. "I heard whispering and saw shadows, but when I turned on the light, it was only you, wrapped in a towel, staring nowhere." I took a deep breath to collect myself. "You were cold, not even breathing, but you started to breathe when I kissed you on the forehead. And then, I heard noises coming from the room, but no one was there. When I returned, you had already changed." I shut my eyes briefly but felt her hand touching my forehead as if she were checking for a fever.

"Adam, I have no idea what you're talking about. You have

been dreaming lately. Last night, you mentioned a balcony, and now…" She placed her palm on my forehead again. "Are you okay?"

"Do you have scars or not?" My sudden question startled her. She nodded but didn't say anything in her defence. "How would I know if I had not seen your body?"

"How come I don't remember you noticing my scars? Could it be your sixth sense? A state of premonition?" Confusion masked her face.

"I don't believe in all that. It was real. You inquired about the previous night when you couldn't recall how you made it from the bathroom to bed. That was real, and so is this."

She placed a hand on my shoulder. "Adam, do you think *I* need to see the doctor? Is it a memory loss issue?"

"I don't know who needs to see the doctor, you or me." I exhaled a sigh. "We have different stories of the same events."

We remained quiet for a few minutes, letting our hearts settle.

I checked my watch. "We have a flight to catch. Time to pack up and go home."

After we finished packing, Rania stopped by the door to look around.

"Have you forgotten something?"

"No." Her gaze swept over the entire suite. "We created a memory here." She stepped out of the room, leaving me speechless. *How can she say complex things so easily?*

I looked back at the room just the way she did. It was a strange feeling. I wonder if I could ever recreate those moments.

During our flight to Toronto, I handed her a Tiffany's box.

"I bought this yesterday for Mom. Tell me what you think." Her face brightened as she opened the box.

"It's beautiful."

"Do you think she'll like it? Or shall we get something else?" I asked, checking the hair clip.

"It's perfect. This will make her cry with happiness. But you know, Adam? It's not the gift. Your presence is what matters to her. Even if you go empty-handed, she'll love you just the same." Her words boosted my spirits.

We reached her apartment building around midnight. Either it was not as cold as Quebec, or our bodies had acclimated in the last few days.

"Thank you for the wonderful time," I confessed, holding her hands as if taking a vow. "I had the best days of my life." She smiled shyly and looked down at the concrete.

"I should thank you for everything—the train, the flight, the hotel, the opera and saving me from Murray. I had no idea he was staying next to me."

"You never told me if you saw him today." I almost forgot to ask her. When I'm with her, nothing else is on my mind.

She blew a breath. "He is so sneaky. Ouff!" She shook her head.

"What did he say?"

"He was trying to prove you don't deserve me."

"I don't," I said quietly.

She studied me for a few seconds. "It's up to me to decide." She smiled with a mysterious sparkle in her eyes. "He was curious about us. I made him believe…" She paused, her cheeks reddening. "I made him believe that we are in a relationship. And he kept warning me about you." We laughed together at her words. "I wish you could have seen his expression."

"I believe you."

We stood there for a while, her hands in mine, wondering who'd be the first to say goodbye.

Were we addicted to each other? I was sure about myself,

but I couldn't tell how she felt about me.

She glanced at the entrance and pulled her hands.

"I should go now," she said. I stayed quiet. *Does she want me to come with her to protect her from nightmares?*

I knew if I came inside tonight, I'd never be able to control the demon inside me.

"Good night," she said, turning toward the entrance. Dumbstruck, I watched her leave but couldn't say anything.

I planned to meet her the next day for dinner, but that seemed an eternity from now. I didn't want to go home and stay alone. I had become so addicted to her presence that I didn't want a moment without her. How could I tell her that I wanted to stay here or beg her to come with me?

As if she could read my thoughts, she paused by the door and turned around. Something beautiful sparked in her eyes. She'd never looked at me like this before. As if everything was frozen in time, my heart stopped beating momentarily.

Unexpectedly, she ran toward me and pulled me into a hug. A million sparks travelled inside me, thawing my cold heart. The sun had finally seeped into my soul.

Burrowing her face into my neck, she whispered, "Thank you for everything, Adam." The warmth from her lips burned my entire body in a fraction of a second. Tonight, I realized money couldn't buy everything. Money wouldn't let me hold onto this moment. It would slip from my hands like desert sand.

She pulled away and, without meeting my gaze, turned and disappeared behind the tinted glass doors.

And I craved my sun more than ever.

CHAPTER 18
SOMETHING NEW

RANIA

It was the first time in five years I'd slept alone without a nightmare when Adam was not around. But I had a strange dream. I'd been lost in the dark woods, and Adam had rescued me from the darkness.

I knew Adam was not a man who believed in relationships. He hardly believed in God, yet my heart couldn't help but slowly fall under his spell.

I flung out of bed and plugged my phone into the charger. There were a few unread messages.

The first one was from Ethan Murray. I rolled my eyes in frustration as I read it.

Ethan: You have cast a spell on this poor man with your angelic beauty.

I deleted his cheesy message without even thinking. The second message was from Mike, which made me smile.

Mike: Dad told me you'd be back on Saturday. Let's hang out. A movie or bowling? I'm off duty tonight, and all yours. XOXO!

Adam also sent a message around four in the morning, the

same time I woke up from my dream.

Adam: I wanted to stay with you for your nightmares, but if I had stayed, I'd have let my demon win. I was trying to protect you from it.

I inhaled sharply as I checked the time again. Perhaps he hadn't slept at all. I wondered what he was thinking about me.

A thousand questions ran through my mind. It was better to respond to the message than to live in confusion. I'd call Mike after breakfast, and as for Adam, I thought for a moment.

Rania: Your soul defeated your demon last night. I didn't have any nightmares. It was your soul that met mine in the dream. Thank you.

As soon as I headed to the washroom, I heard my phone ringing. It was Adam.

"Good morning." His sweet voice stirred every nerve fibre.

"Good morning or afternoon, whatever," I giggled. "How are you?"

"Missing you." His voice was heavy from sleep, and I sensed he was still in bed. "You dreamt about me?" My text must have woken him.

"Yes. No nightmares, surprisingly."

"What did you dream of?"

"I was lost in the woods, and you came from nowhere and led me out of them." He exhaled a heavy sigh but didn't say anything. "Adam? Are you there?"

"Yes, I am."

"What is it, then?"

"I dreamed the same thing and woke up in the middle of the night and texted you without thinking."

I let his words sink in. I didn't remember who hung up first, but neither of us said anything, not even goodbye.

After my breakfast, I called Mike to return his message.

"Bonjour, Mademoiselle," he mused.

"How are you, Mike?"

"I am on a duty," he said dryly. "How was Quebec? I heard you stayed at Chateau Frontenac." He whistled. "I want to know about every minute you spent there." Mike had always wanted to visit Old Quebec, and we'd always planned to see it together, but somehow, one of us had always been occupied. And he loved gossiping like old ladies of the Regency Era. "We must meet. It's been a while." Yes, it had been a while. He was in Calgary for three months, and the day he returned was the day I met Adam for the first time. With Adam around all the time, I never got a chance to talk to my best friend properly. But he was asking about tonight. And if I didn't join Adam, he wouldn't see his mother.

"Tonight is not possible. Sorry. I'm already—"

"Dating Gibson?" he interrupted. Noticing my silence, he continued, "You like him." His blunt statement startled me. I remained quiet, not sure what to say. Or was I too afraid to admit it? "Shall I take this silence as a 'yes?'"

"It's not what you think, Mike. We are just friends."

"So *just-a-friend* would stalk you all the way to Quebec?" *Shit. How does he know?* "Just because I stay quiet doesn't mean I don't know anything." He sighed. "You remember Kevin? We took photography lessons together?"

"The Russian guy with nerd glasses?"

"Yes. Apparently, he was at the conference you attended. He was covering the event." *Oh!* "He saw you running into a man and hugging him in the lobby..." I remained quiet. "Kevin obviously knew it was Gibson. But he mentioned another man, and Adam had an argument with him. Who was he?"

"He is Ethan Murray. He conducted the conference." Mike whistled. "But he is a sleaze, Mike. He spared no moment to hit on me."

"He isn't the first man," Mike mumbled.

"Yes, but he radiated such negative energy."

"Rania," Mike said. "Every man is negative to you. Have you given anybody a chance..." he cleared his throat and lowered his voice, "other than Adam?"

I gulped at his words. I didn't know what to say. Was it true that I had never considered any man other than Adam? Not even Mike?

"Does Ben know about their argument?"

"You are my best friend. And I know my father. He is a blabber and would gossip to your father. I know where to stay quiet."

"Thank you. You are a true friend."

"Yes, and I love you too." His spontaneous remark made me giggle. "So, did your Richie-Rich boyfriend meet you in Quebec, or did you both travel together?" Oh, how much I missed gossiping with Mike.

"We are just friends," I objected again. I could tell he must have rolled his eyes.

"Who is he then? A stalker? A secret agent? What was he doing there?"

"He had some property business in Quebec."

"Right. He only had business when you were there. You are now even lying to me."

I sighed. "All right." I thought for a moment how to put it. "Adam found out that Ethan Murray had something planned."

"What does Murray have to do with you?"

"Not with me, with Adam. They had some old grudge, and Ethan wanted to hurt Adam through me."

"And how did Adam find out about his intentions?"

I remained silent.

"He is stalking you?" Mike asked. "Tell me he is stalking you."

"It's his way of looking after me," I said quietly.

"Come on, Rania. What's wrong with you? The man is evidently obsessed with you. And where are you dating him tonight? I must know your whereabouts."

"It's not a date," I objected. "He is taking me to his parents' house."

"What?" he snapped. "Things have gone so serious that you're now meeting his family? Isn't it too soon? You hardly know him."

"It's hard to explain. Can we talk about it some other time?"

"No, baby! We need to talk about it right now," he insisted. "He chased you to another city, and now he's taking you to meet his parents. Has he proposed or what?"

"Good, God. Where are you going? And of all the women in the world, why would he propose to me?" I scoffed. "As if he had a shortage of women."

"Because, among all the women in the world, he has chosen you to meet his parents," he grumbled. "Why is he taking you there?"

"He is not taking me. *I* am taking him. He hadn't spoken to his mother in years, and she called him in my presence. He refused, but I insisted he should meet her. I'm only accompanying him to make sure he behaves well."

"Ha!" He snorted. "Since when have you started teaching manners?"

"Don't be ridiculous. He is a good man. Sometimes, he loses his temper. That's all."

"Okay." It didn't look like he was buying it. "I trust you, girl. But you know how the paparazzi chase him like vultures." Mike was right. What if someone spread the news that I was going to his family home? This would indeed reach my father. Should I ask Adam to keep it private? But how could he? Anyone could see us there. "I hope that doesn't happen," he added. "Good luck teaching him manners. I'll dig into this Murray guy and let you know. You take care, okay?"

I should have considered the consequences of tonight. I just hoped my father wouldn't learn. But it was too late to refuse Adam now.

CHAPTER 19
AN UNSPOKEN TRUTH

ADAM

Rania: What time are we going for dinner?

I received her text message while I was driving. I was almost there and forgot to tell her.

Adam: I'm on my way already. Sorry. I forgot to text you.

After thirty seconds, my phone beeped again.

Rania: Then you'll wait. I'll let the security know. I'm just starting to get ready. The front door is unlocked, so make yourself at home.

When I reached her front door, I let myself in silently and looked around the living area. A large picture hung on the wall above the couch—a black and white photo of Rania blowing a dandelion head. Her image had been captured beautifully, as if she was unaware of the camera. Her eyes were smiling innocently, her beautiful lips pursing to blow, her skin so soft and fragile, creating a halo around her as if she was some angel I had seen in medieval paintings. I leaned closer to the frame to study the photographer's name embossed on the bottom right. *Mike Dynham.*

If he took this picture, he must have the original. I wonder why I didn't notice it when I was here last week. Was I too lost in her?

I gawked around the living area again, noticing another painting of shooting stars in the starry night over a desert. It looked magical. The inscription said: "Inspired by Arabian Nights." She must have purchased it from a museum or an art gallery.

I pulled the dining chair to sit and waited for her. She stepped out of her room without even noticing me and checked herself in the full-length mirror by the entrance closet. She fixed her makeup, put lipstick on her smooth lips, and adjusted her top. She was humming very low and was clueless that I was watching her. I had no idea how I would keep my eyes off her tonight. She radiated and glowed in the white lace top and skirt. *Yes, the fucking lace!*

I couldn't resist.

"Sing louder, beautiful. I can't hear you," I called out from the dining area.

She whipped her head. "When did you come?"

I approached her without blinking away. Perhaps noticing our proximity or the intentions in my eyes, she stepped back, but I still moved closer. She stepped back again till her back was against the mirror.

I placed my hand on the mirror, right above her head, touching her face with my other hand. She closed her eyes, inhaling sharply. *Do I intimidate her?* Her divine beauty would absolutely drive me crazy someday. Arrested in her intoxicating fragrance that had always made me heady, I knew it wasn't the right time to lose my senses. I didn't need a drink—her beauty was potent enough to turn my world upside down.

A few strands of hair were stuck behind her pearl earring, so I untangled them, tucking them behind her ear. She opened her eyes, relief on her face. I studied her, riveted, drinking in every feature. *So beautiful!*

"I never believed angels existed, but when I look at you, I imagine you must have fallen from the sky."

She giggled and shook her head.

"You have a halo. Your beauty is unparalleled. You know how to cast a spell on me."

"I could be a witch, too," she mused. She fixed my collar. "You must beware, Mr. Gibson."

I didn't say anything because she looked so beautiful tonight that no words were enough to reflect my emotions. We stared into each other eyes, perhaps both trying to dive into each other's soul, but I couldn't read her thoughts. Could she read mine? Could she see how much I ached for her touch? That I had never desired a woman this much before. That no one had ever made my heart stop and beat wildly simultaneously.

"We are running late," she said quietly. "Let me fetch my purse."

I pulled away and let her pass. Whenever I'd tried to show her my soul, she had looked away. I was certain she was aware of my feelings, but she never willed to return them. Was it her past or her father's judgement that forbade her from growing feelings for me?

We remained quiet the entire drive to Moore's estate. She seemed nervous about meeting my mother, but didn't mention it.

It was a very unexpected, mild evening in December in Toronto, and neither of us wore winter jackets. I parked the car in front of Moore's estate. I was surprised that there were no guests. We were late, though. We stood by the door for a minute. She waited for me to ring the bell, but I hesitated.

"It seems unreal. I don't know what to say to her," I confessed.

She placed her hands firmly over mine. "Don't worry. I'm with you." Her smile boosted my courage. I rang the doorbell, and Mrs. Moore opened it.

We stepped inside together. Eyes welling up, Mrs. Moore covered her mouth with her hands. I had no idea what to do, so I glanced at Rania. She gestured, asking me to hug Mrs. Moore. I did, and Mrs. Moore broke into tears, holding my jacket tightly, not concerned about anyone else. Confused, I darted a glance at Rania again, her eyes welling up too. Do all women react the same way when they are emotional? Rania mouthed something, and like an obedient lover, I followed her.

"Happy Birthday…" I checked Rania again. "…Mom."

Mrs. Moore looked up. "What did you say?"

Inhaling sharply, I looked toward Rania again, who mouthed the word. "Mom," I repeated. Amid her tears, Mrs. Moore smiled and started peppering kisses on my cheeks.

"Oh, my baby, I love you so much. I've missed you so much." She wouldn't stop kissing me. I managed to look at Rania, who flashed me a warm smile. *So, this is natural.* Feeling awkward, I stood frozen, my mother kissing me like a crazy woman. Finally, she stopped and managed to look at me. She looked old. It had been many years.

I noticed Rania mouthing words to me again, so I repeated after her. "Happy Birthday." I handed over the gift. "Umm…This is for you." *Could this be more embarrassing?*

"For me? You remembered, Adam?" She gaped. "Can I open it?" I nodded. She took the box out of the bag and opened it. "Adam, you still remember?" She hugged me again, spilling a fresh set of tears.

"All right, my love. Enough of it." I heard a man's voice behind her, and he took my mother in his arms. "You're making my wife cry and smile at the same time." Embracing her warmly, he caressed her arm.

"Hello, Mr. Moore." I offered my hand for a handshake.

"Welcome home. It is really good to see you here, Adam. And who is this beautiful lady?" Mr. Moore gestured at Rania.

Rania offered her hand for a handshake. "Rania. Pleasure meeting you, Mr. Moore."

"Call me Brian, please." He kissed her knuckles instead. "Hey, love, you don't notice anyone besides your son?" Mr. Moore asked his wife.

"I'm sorry, Rania. How are you?" Mrs. Moore pulled Rania into a motherly hug. "Thank you so much for bringing him home. It would never have been possible without you. You have completed my family. I owe you for life."

Rania slid back, smiling shyly at my mother. "Please don't mention it. I didn't do anything special, but I'll make sure he behaves like a good boy tonight." She winked at Mrs. Moore, making her laugh. "And oh, Happy Birthday, Mrs. Moore. That's for you." Rania handed my mother a small box. *That was very thoughtful of her.*

"Oh, thank you, beautiful. This is the best birthday of my life." She hugged Rania again and kissed her on the forehead. "Call me Grace."

"Are we going to stand in the foyer forever, or will you invite your son and his girlfriend to come in?" Mr. Moore asked.

We all stepped into the grand house when I noticed Eva in the hallway, standing silently, tears rolling down her cheeks. *Not again!*

"Eva," I said, but she stayed frozen against the wall. I looked at Rania once again. I didn't know why I kept looking to her for guidance. As she nudged me towards Eva, I hugged my sister. "Eva."

She cried in my arms. *I will never understand women.*

Brian appeared again for the rescue. "Come on, Eva, don't get started like your mother. It's time to be happy that your brother is home. I can't handle two crying women in a row." Addressing Rania, he continued, "I'm glad you're not next."

After collecting herself, Eva gave Rania a sisterly hug and

greeted her.

"I'm so happy," Eva shrieked, "Adam finally found a girl. I don't know what you've done, that he is here with you, but whatever you're doing, please don't stop it." Confused and speechless, Rania glanced in my direction. "Please keep on loving him like this. You two are perfect for each other."

Noticing Rania's uneasiness, I decided to chip in. "Eva? Will you let us in?"

"I'm sorry, Rania. Please, come in," Eva said apologetically. With this tear-jerking drama and my overly hyper sister blabbing, Mrs. Moore guided us to the formal sitting room. Rania looked quite uncomfortable. Everyone thought we were in a romantic relationship, and we were not in a state to defend ourselves right now.

"I'll get us drinks. It's time to celebrate." With that, Mrs. Moore disappeared into the kitchen.

"So, Rania…where did you meet my brother?" Eva began like a curious, nosy neighbour. "How did he ask you out? I'm sure it was love at first sight for him. I wanna know everything." She bombarded Rania with her stupid questions. After all these years, she hadn't matured at all. Rania, turning beet red at her absurdity, looked at me for rescue.

As soon as I opened my mouth, Mrs. Moore returned. "Eva, stop asking so many questions," she reprimanded.

Eva totally ignored her. "Please, tell me, Rania," she insisted. "I want to know everything." She scooted closer, lowering her voice. "Tell me, how is he in bed? I hope he shows some patience there." From her glaring at me to smiling sweetly at Rania in a blink, it was astonishing how quickly Eva switched her emotional gears.

I rolled my eyes, frowning, unsure how to shut up my sister. Rania was silent, but the blush on her cheeks told a different story.

"Eva. Don't start again," I grumbled. Eva neither noticed my glare nor my patronizing. "If you want to know, I'll tell you. I met her outside my office a week ago, okay?" I had no idea baby sisters could be this annoying.

"And what did you feel the first time you saw her?" she asked dreamingly.

"I was…" I searched for the word. "She is beautiful, so…"

"Aww…that is so so so romantic," she squealed, her gaze softening as if she was watching a rom-com. "And how did you ask her out?"

Mr. and Mrs. Moore exchanged a glance and decided not to reproach their spoiled daughter this time.

"We are just friends, Eva," Rania interrupted. Eva studied both of us. "I'm not his girlfriend."

"Yeah, right!" Eva rolled her eyes. "The newspaper…?"

"The media wants spice to fill their pages," I said.

"So, no sex?" she asked loudly this time.

"Enough, Eva," Mrs. Moore scolded. "Help me in the kitchen. Now." She took Eva out of the room.

Still a chatterbox, Eva kept on talking. "I can't believe she's not his girlfriend. Why are they hiding? It's so obvious…" Her voice faded as they walked away. We were silent for a moment, and then Brian changed the subject.

"Rania, what do you do?"

"I work for an advertising company, designing and publishing electronic catalogues," Rania answered.

"That's pretty impressive," remarked Brian.

"Toast for the family." Mrs. Moore and Eva returned to the room with a tray full of champagne glasses. Eva placed the tray on the glass coffee table and offered everyone the toast. "And orange juice for you, Rania." She offered her a glass. "Mom told me Adam instructed about your…"

"Eva," Mrs. Moore warned in a sharp tone.

"But I find it very sweet," Eva ignored Mrs. Moore, "that he takes care of everything. Isn't it romantic?"

"Have you been reading too many romance novels lately?" I asked.

"Ha!" Eva sat back. "Very funny, brother!"

"Rania, does your family also live in Toronto?" Mrs. Moore interrupted our sibling banter.

"No. My father is in Dubai. And I don't have any siblings," Rania replied nervously. If they asked her about her mother, it would make her more anxious.

Knowing she didn't like to discuss her family, I changed the subject quickly. "How are your studies going, Eva?" I switched to my sister.

"Oh, good, good. My master's is finishing this year. I plan to apply for a PhD once I finish my research paper."

"Where are you studying?" Rania asked, curious.

"UofT. Medieval Studies," Eva answered, pride glinting in her eyes.

"Great." She formed her lips into a thin line, stifling her smile. "You remind me of a professor I read about recently, from the same university, in Italian Studies."

"O.M.G.! Are you talking about that Dante specialist?" Eva shrieked.

As if they both registered it together, they burst into laughter. The rest of us watched them with confusion.

"You know, Eva, I actually went to that department to look for him," Rania added, gossiping like a schoolgirl.

"Are you kidding me?" Excited like a lottery winner, Eva continued, "I'm literally studying there because of him. I seriously want that professor in my life." Both women high-fived.

"Who are you talking about?" Noticing my grim expression, they both laughed harder.

Eva shifted to sit on the coffee table before us. "Okay, Adam.

I have a question for you." Her eyes sparkled. "Imagine your sister and your girlfriend in love with the same man—a man who is very charismatic and alarmingly sexy, who has a very powerful personality. But you know he is a terrible sinner. Whom would you protect? Me or her?" Though she sounded playful, her question caught me off-guard. Were they talking about Ethan Murray?

I gaped at Rania, who was looking down, trying to control her laughter.

"Come on, Eva." Rania patted Eva on her knee. "Stop teasing your brother. Look at his face." Both the girls laughed again.

"Eva?" Mrs. Moore interrupted.

"Oh, Mom, please," ignoring Mrs. Moore, Eva arrested me with her curious gaze. "I need an answer from Adam. Come on, Adam. Tell me, who would you protect?" *Is she fucking serious?*

Aghast, I stared at both, back and forth. This was news to me. My sister and the girl who I cared about most were besotted by the same man. And they both were taking it so lightly?

Flustered, I rose from the couch. "Rania, can I talk to you in private?"

Eva laughed again, but reading my stern expression, Rania didn't join her.

"Come on, Eva. Stop teasing him. He is serious." Rania grabbed my hand, urging me to sit. "Sit down. Eva is joking. We are talking about a fictional character—a book boyfriend." She put her hand on mine gently. "You don't need to answer her."

"Husband," Eva corrected. "He is book husband."

"Ah, I wish," Rania said dreamingly.

I cleared my throat.

"Duh! He is so dramatic," Eva snorted. "How do you deal with him?"

Rania glanced at me. "I'm getting used to it."

"Have you checked the professors? Urgh! It just ruined my

fantasy."

"I know," Rania conceded. "I attended a conference at AGO, where all the professors were guests. So disappointing."

"They are grandfathers," Eva complained.

"Why can't they have young PhDs in academia like books?" Rania added.

"So, there is no man?" I interrupted.

"No, Adam. There is no one." Rania reassured with her secret smile. "We're talking about a book."

"And you say this is only friendship?" Eva rolled her eyes.

"All right, kids. Dinner is ready," Mrs. Moore broke in.

During dinner, Rania and Eva discussed books and what they called 'book boyfriends.' The rest of us enjoyed their conversation but didn't participate. It was the first time I had seen Rania talking so much. Otherwise, she was mostly a quiet person when it came to strangers. This made me realize I had never asked her if she had any friends besides Mike. Why hadn't I ever asked her about her favourite book or character? I had seen her reading so many times, but it never occurred to me that I could get closer to her if I talked to her about books.

I felt like a total fool at the table.

I looked around and noticed that Mrs. Moore's other family members, Brian's two sons, were missing. "Is it just us tonight?" I asked Brian. "I thought your sons would join."

"Scott has moved to Calgary and Nathan is in California for work. He'll be back by Christmas, though."

The conversation flowed swiftly while we ate. After dinner, we headed back to the formal sitting room. Rania and Eva continued their book fantasies, and I just stared at her like a love-sick puppy and wondered how pretty she looked, how her eyes sparkled when she expressed her literary emotions.

Mrs. Moore sat beside me. "You remind me of your father," she almost whispered. "The way you look at her. It's just like

Richard."

I turned to her, not sure why she brought him up. "So, you still remember the poor man?"

She looked down at her lap, trying to find words. "He was the first man in my life, Adam. How could I forget him?"

Our conversation drew everyone's attention.

"Dad, why don't you come and help me with the dessert?" Eva got to her feet, and Brian followed her. Rania was also leaving with them, but I grabbed her hand.

"We're leaving. Let's go." I joined her.

"No, we are not," Rania scowled as she pushed me back down on the coffee table, facing Mrs. Moore. "You are going to listen to her without any argument, and don't you dare act like a jerk." Mrs. Moore looked up at Rania and then at me.

"You can't be serious," I snapped. "I don't want to listen to her."

"Yes, you will. Enough of your nonsense, Adam," she reprimanded as if I was a child. "I will not let you hurt your mother and yourself like this. At least listen to what she says, and then you can leave whenever you want." I'd never realized she possessed the power to control me, but I sat there, helpless. She took my hands and placed them in my mother's lap, over her hands. Tears fell from my mother's eyes, and she gave a rueful smile to Rania, hope dancing in her eyes. "Don't worry, Grace. I'm here, and your boy will listen to you."

Mrs. Moore took a moment to begin. "All my life, Adam, I've wanted to tell you why I left you and your father, but you never gave me a chance." She lifted my chin so I could look her in the eye. I tried to move, but Rania's hand on my shoulder ground me like a lamppost. I never imagined listening to my mother like this. *I am still not ready.*

Mrs. Moore took a deep breath and continued. "We loved each other from high school. Richard was very romantic, but he lacked practicality. I was young and didn't realize that romance wasn't enough to run a household. When you have a family, you must take things seriously, putting your romantic fantasies aside. I got married at the age of twenty. Richard was only a year older than me and had not even graduated from university. We started our lives by doing basic labour jobs, and after some months, Richard won a lottery—just enough to start his business."

She paused for a moment.

"When you were born, we were in a good financial state. I didn't know that sometimes, easy money is also easily taken away. He thought he could get lucky the next time. His gambling habit was becoming an everyday norm. He used to lose, but he used to win, too. Winning made him greedy, and in a few years, we lost everything. I started working again, and Brian was my new boss. Brian became my friend, my confidante." Stealing a glance at Rania, she looked down at our hands, unwilling to meet my gaze.

"Richard became an alcoholic to avoid his frustrations and used to come home angry every night after losing money in the casinos. He also started stealing my hard-earned money that I kept for your college. When you were five, I was expecting Eva." She exhaled a heavy sigh. "Things got worse. Richard was never there for me. I often wondered what happened to our love but never found any answer." A tear ran down her cheek. "He was searching for shortcuts, and when it didn't work out the way he wanted, he got more frustrated with life. Brian supported me emotionally when I needed a companion. I wouldn't have survived if Brian hadn't helped me out. His wife died while giving birth to Nathan and left him with two sons to raise on his own. I started working as the babysitter, and he paid me well." The world around me began to spin at her words.

"Richard wasn't even there when Eva was born. Brian looked after me during Eva's birth. He even took care of you. You remember me leaving you, but you don't remember your father fighting with me, do you?"

She was wrong. I did remember their fights.

"One night, Richard was so angry that he accused me of adultery, that Eva was not his baby." I inhaled sharply at her words. "That was the end of our relationship. I left that night with Eva." She gave a sad smile. "I know you must have wondered why I took Eva and not you. Richard never accepted Eva as his daughter. You were his son. If I had taken you with me, he'd have fought for your custody. I wanted Richard to show responsibility, so I left you with him." Wiping her tears, she continued. "Brian gave me immense love, but in all those years, not a day has passed when I haven't thought about you."

Time seemed to freeze around me as I tried to grasp the truth.

"After a few months of my marriage with Brian, Richard confronted me and begged me to accept his apology. That I should return to him, but it was too late. I wanted to be true to Brian. He helped me when I needed someone most. He was my best friend, my mentor." She held my face in her hands, so warm and tender. "I never wanted to leave Richard. I never wanted to leave you, Adam. I have ached for you my whole life. Please don't hate me."

I shut my eyes. It was almost impossible to process her words. All these years, I hated her for leaving my father, and I never gave her a chance to tell her side of the story. I never knew my father was such a coward that he couldn't come clean and tell me the truth.

"I'd have lived with Richard without money if he hadn't accused me of sin. He didn't trust me. Everything is pointless when there is no trust in a relationship. But I never wanted you to hate Richard. He loved you. He lived for you, Adam."

Rania embraced Mrs. Moore warmly, and she burst into tears on Rania's shoulder. Brian and Eva watched us from the kitchen but didn't meddle.

I sat there motionless, no words forming in my mouth. What should I say after all this?

As if Rania could read my mind, she said, "Are you okay, Adam?" She placed her comforting hand on my shoulder. "Let me know when you want to leave." Failing to articulate my chaotic thoughts, I remained quiet, unable to meet her gaze. Luckily, Brian entered the room just at the right time.

"My love has cried enough for tonight. Let me cheer her up." He pulled Mrs. Moore in his arms, making her smile and blush like a newlywed bride. *This man has truly loved my mother.* She wouldn't have survived without Brian's love and trust. He took her into another room, but before leaving, he addressed Rania. "Hey, beautiful, would you like some music?"

Taking my hand, Rania got to her feet, making me rise too. The music room was elegantly furnished with a grand piano taking center stage, complemented by a collection of guitars and violins adorning the walls.

Brian sat down on the piano bench, Mrs. Moore joining him. He turned to me, "This is your mother's favourite song. Though I'm a poor singer, she listens to me every time and applauds as if I wrote it." He looked back at my mother. "Happy Birthday, my love." He gave her a passionate kiss, not caring for the spectacle. "But tonight, I dedicate this song to this beautiful lady." He gestured at Rania, who blinked at Brian with surprise. "Who made this family dinner possible, who made my Grace happy tonight." He beckoned Rania to stand by his side. He took her hand and kissed her knuckles. She blushed, acutely aware of the attention. "Thank you for completing us." Rania didn't meet my eyes and quietly moved to the corner, leaning against the wall.

Brian began singing *'Since I Fell for You'* beautifully on the piano, looking at his wife with absolute love. They didn't care about anyone's presence, as if the outside world didn't exist.

The song reminded me of the dinner at the restaurant back in February before I encountered that enchantress.

Rania watched them with longing. *Is this her fantasy? To have an eloquent partner?*

When the song ended, Rania was the first to clap cheerily. Eva, meanwhile, returned with a tray of ice cream cups. Rania beamed at her, and when she noticed me looking at her, she passed a secret smile—the secret only we shared—our last ice cream experience. I could never have ice cream again without thinking about her.

When we all sat back in the sitting room, Eva asked Rania, "Can I call you someday to catch up for lunch?" I wondered how she could talk with so much ice cream stuffed in her mouth.

"Yes, sure," Rania replied enthusiastically.

"I'm going to a club this Friday with some friends. Will you join me?"

"Rania doesn't go to clubs," I interrupted. Everyone looked at me quizzically, including Rania.

"Thank you, Eva. Of course, I will come." Rania glared at me.

"Cool. We won't tell your dramatic boyfriend where we're going." The girls gave each other high fives.

"You know I can find you anywhere," I mumbled. She knew I wasn't bluffing.

"Do you stalk her?" Eva punched my arm. Rania pressed her lips in a thin line, trying to stifle her laugh, but it was enough for Eva to consider me a stalker. "Oh my God! I can't believe my brother is a stalker. How do you cope with him?"

"I'm used to it now," she said while holding my gaze. "It's hard to change him."

"Do you hear, Mom?" Eva squealed. "You gave birth to a stalker."

I glared at my annoying sister while everyone laughed. When I met her last time, she was coping with her trauma. We barely talked. And now, looking at her, I wonder if Rania's company had changed everything.

Eva and Rania dove back again to their bookish talk, this time picking Hollywood celebrities and matching them with a book character. Eva had kept Rania so busy that I barely talked to her this evening.

Eva left to fetch something but returned with a board game quickly.

"Since we are all here for the first time, let's play a game together. Mom, Dad, you both are in. And you too, Mr. Stalker. The game suits your personality." She put the Clue game down on the table and opened the box.

We picked our characters, and Eva briefly introduced us to the rules. Rania played like a pro.

"Concentrate on the game." Eva snapped her fingers before my eyes to break my trance. "Stop staring at her. You haven't found a single clue, Mr. Stalker." *Why is my sister so irritating tonight?* Leaning towards Rania, she whispered audibly. "Is he this intense in bed?" Rania remained quiet, maintaining her poker face.

"You are extremely annoying tonight," I scowled. She was embarrassing Rania.

"And you're too overbearing, Mr. Stalker. Stop giving her those devouring looks."

Though Eva sounded serious, it made Rania laugh. Perhaps she enjoyed the sibling's bantering.

I sat back. "Unbelievable!"

"Eva," Mrs. Moore reproached.

"But look at him, Mom. He stalks her, and she is okay with it."

"I have no choice, Eva," Rania objected. "He wouldn't change."

"Do you want me to change?" I asked Rania.

She watched me for a few beats and slowly smiled. "Too much obsession isn't healthy." At least she acknowledged my obsession.

"Friendship, my ass!" Eva mumbled.

We continued our game, but I failed to concentrate at all. There were so many things I wanted to say to Rania, but Eva's constant blabbering made it impossible.

Brian and I indulged in a glass of whiskey during the game while the ladies had another round of ice cream. I wonder how much sweetness a woman could consume.

Since I hadn't focused earlier, I didn't realize Rania had won and proved me the killer, holding all the cards of my character, weapon, and room. Eva cheered at Rania's victory as if she'd won herself. I couldn't recall how many drinks I had, but when I went for the next round, Rania held my hand, giving me a look as if it was time to stop.

I put the decanter down. Eva, obviously, would not miss this opportunity to provide her opinion.

"Seriously?" She snorted. "Mr. Stalker obeys?" She nudged Rania on her arm. "At least there's someone to control him."

Rania blushed at her words but looked at me for help. I checked the time. It was almost midnight, and we had been here for five hours.

"Oh my!" Mrs. Moore exclaimed. "It's midnight. Time passed so quickly." Smiling at Rania, she continued, "Now I know why my son feels so drawn to you. We all are." *Why is everyone embarrassing her tonight?*

There was no doubt she had charmed everyone, but I could tell this attention made her uneasy.

"It's very late," I announced, leaving my seat. "We should be going." Everyone joined to see us at the door.

"Why don't you stay here tonight, Rania?" Eva offered. "Let him go. I can drop you home in the morning. We'll gossip about books."

Eva knew I wouldn't allow it, but she purposely said this to tease me. Also, with Rania's nightmares, I couldn't trust anyone.

"She has work tomorrow." I took Rania's arm.

"Tomorrow is Sunday, Mr. Stalker," Eva complained. "Just confess you are a controlling man."

"Are you this annoying all the time, or is today a special occasion?" I scowled at Eva.

Rania giggled as we headed to the main door.

Mrs. Moore kissed Rania on her forehead. "God bless you, child. I didn't know my son had the talent to find such a gem. Stay with him always." She held Rania's hands firmly. "And thank you for bringing him here." Rania hugged her back without saying anything. "This night wouldn't have been possible without you."

We exchanged farewells and stepped out of the house.

It had gotten a bit cold since we came in. I held Rania's hand and opened the car's back door, patiently waiting for us in the driveway. We both slipped into the back seat.

"Hello, Miss Ahmed. How are you?" Ali greeted us from the driver's seat.

"Hey, Ali. When did you come?" Rania asked.

"Just a few minutes ago. Hello, Mr. Gibson," he repeated with a curt nod.

"It's Saturday night. Doesn't your boss give you time off?" she asked Ali. Poor Ali glanced at me through the rearview mirror but said nothing.

"I didn't want to drive," I said. I had too many drinks.

"But he has a life too. We could have called a cab—"

I put my fingers on her lips to silence her. "Ssh."

As the car started moving, Ali politely asked Rania if she wanted to listen to music. He turned on the local radio station, and Rania requested he increase the volume.

Gazing out the window, she immersed herself in the music. During one of the songs, she closed her eyes and rested her head on my shoulder. Sensing her vulnerability, I wrapped an arm around her.

After a while, the radio station played *'Iris.'*

I focused on the lyrics that reciprocated my emotions. I wanted to confess everything, and I didn't want to go home tonight. Something very strong was slowly growing between us, but I didn't know what to call this connection. We remained quiet the entire ride.

When we reached her building, I noticed she had fallen asleep.

CHAPTER 20
ACCEPTANCE

RANIA

"Rania, wake up." I heard Adam's voice as I opened my eyes and found his beautiful face. "Wake up, princess. We have reached."

"Did I fall asleep?" I gaped, still dazed.

Gracing me with his sweet smile, he helped me out of the car. I had no idea if he was coming with me or just dropping me at the door. I stayed quiet and went with the flow. I knew he had quite a few drinks, and it was inappropriate for him to accompany me.

I headed to my apartment, but he followed me. It didn't seem like he even intended to leave. He took my hand when I entered my living room and pushed me down on the sofa. He sat on the ottoman, facing me, arresting me with his intense gaze.

I sensed he wanted to say something but was struggling with the words. Taking both my hands in his, he brought them to his lips. He didn't kiss them, but his lips rested on my knuckles as he closed his eyes, utterly quiet. I stayed still, not sure what to say. As he opened his eyes, I noticed them clouding with tears. *Is he crying?* His tears fell softly like morning dew on my knuckles as he sobbed, making me speechless.

Finally, he kissed my hands, placing them on his eyes like a sacred book to soothe him. He repeated the motion several times, kissing my knuckles and rubbing them over his eyes. He had locked my hands so firmly in his that I could not even free them to wipe his tears, but he managed to wipe them with my hands. When he finally collected himself, he looked up.

"Thank you for everything." Kissing my knuckles again, he rubbed them over his eyes like a blind man rubbing a holy relic to bring his sight back. "I didn't know I was blessed. And if it isn't God that sent me to you, then who is? I know He exists, and He has sent you to guide me." He touched my hands with his warm lips, his voice muffled. "I was living in the dark. The light you showed me today…" He kissed my hands again. "I'd have spent the rest of my life hating her. I didn't know I was hurting her so much. Thank you for protecting me from the sin I've been committing since childhood."

Oh! He is talking about Grace.

"You bring everything good into my life. You must know that you're living in me now, as a part of me. I am as much as you are. No more. No less. I begin with you, and I end at you. Please don't ever leave me." He placed his head down on my lap, hiding his face, his voice turning into sweet whispers. "Thank you for plucking out all the thorns from my life. Thank you for giving me what I've been missing." He paused for a moment. "You are an answer to all my silent prayers."

If this wasn't the declaration of love, then what was? My heart ached, and I feared I'd lose myself to him. He kept his head in my lap, his cheek pressed against my hand.

Pulling out one hand, I raked my fingers through his hair to comfort him. I knew I was giving him hope, that I should ask him to leave. But what kind of friend would I be if I left him at his vulnerable point? He had bared his soul to me.

He took my hand and threaded his fingers with mine.

"I don't want to stay alone tonight." He sat straight, his voice pleading. "Can I sleep here?" His eyes were glassed and dazed with alcohol. And yet, I could not find the strength to deny him. He wanted a friend to seek comfort. I nodded with a smile. "Thank you." He stood up. "Let me fetch my bag from the car," he said as he left the apartment immediately.

Did he come prepared? It wasn't the first time he'd spent the night with me, but somehow, today, it seemed odd. Perhaps it was I, who had always been an emotional one.

I headed to the washroom to change my clothes. It had been a tiring evening, but I was happy that Adam met his mother. They were all so loving—and the sibling's banter was hilarious. I had always missed the pleasure of arguing with a sibling.

When I returned to the living room, clad in my nightclothes, I found Adam gazing at the shooting star painting behind the dining table.

Sensing my presence, he asked. "Have you read this *Arabian Nights*?"

"Several times."

"What is it about?"

"It's a compilation of stories of one thousand and one night, based on old Arabic and Persian folk tales."

"Interesting," he said, still studying the painting. "Do you have it?"

"I've been reading them since my childhood. Different authors have translated the stories in different ways. It is always interesting to read different interpretations."

"And what's the premise?" *Why is he still lost in the picture?*

"It's about King Shehryar, who holds a grudge against all the women in his kingdom. Having been betrayed by his wife, he promises himself to hate women for the rest of his life." Though he was studying the painting, I knew I had his undivided attention. "So, out of spite, he marries every night, a new virgin from his kingdom, and executes her at sunrise. He keeps on doing it until all the virgins in his kingdom are dead. His vizier has a wise daughter named Scheherazade, who asks her father if she can marry King Shehryar and stop him from committing this sin." The room fell into a hushed silence. "The vizier warns her that if she fails, the king will also hang her by sunrise. Yet, she remains rooted to this idea, and they get married. When King Shehryar enters her chamber, she starts with a story." Adam turned around, looking quite amused. "The entire night, the king listens to the story intently and is captivated by his new wife. Mind you, she is a very good storyteller. When the sun rises, her story is incomplete, so the king has no choice but to suspend her execution until the next night until she finishes her story." Adam looked at me like a child listening to a fairytale for the first time. "So every night, Scheherazade continues with a story but doesn't finish it before sunrise, so Shehryar keeps on deferring her death order. They are completely fictitious and magical stories within stories, blended together. She doesn't stop for one thousand and one nights. That's all it is about." I blew a breath.

"Can you read it to me tonight?" He pled. "I'd like to hear it."

"It's too long, Adam. It doesn't end in one night."

"Then I'll be King Shehryar and listen to my Scheherazade for one thousand and one nights." He took a step, his intention evident. "How about that?"

"You can't be serious?"

"I'm damn serious." Noticing him taking another step, I took a step back. "I want to hear the stories." *Has he ever heard no for an answer?*

"I can give you a hard copy. You can read it yourself."

"I want to hear it from your beautiful mouth." He moved closer with a drunken stupor. "The way you've started the story, I'll only listen to it from you and no one else."

I kept retreating until my back hit the wall. He surrounded me with his intoxicating presence. As he touched my face with his right hand, I suddenly felt weak in my knees. What was in his touch that my body had always betrayed my mind? He placed his other hand under my ear and caressed my cheek with his thumb.

With just a mere touch, he set my body on fire—as if this body had only longed for this forbidden fruit to sate its appetite. All these years, I'd avoided this feeling. Yet, he had touched every fibre of me without touching me. *How does he do that?*

"You make everything sound so magical. I want to experience the same magic with you in these stories. Will you read it to me?" There was no lust in his eyes—just a mere request.

"I'll get the book." I withdrew from his intense gaze and headed to fetch the book. He followed me to the bedroom, standing behind me to study my bookshelf. "I have a hard copy and one on my e-reader. Which one do you want me to read?"

"I think it might be better to read from your e-reader. I'll hold it for you, and we can switch off the lights and read it in the dark, right?" *Oh my! What does he intend to do besides listening?*

His sudden request made me nervous, but I pretended to stay calm. I should trust him. He wouldn't do anything against my will.

Adam excused himself to change his clothes while I browsed my e-reader to search for the book. He returned in a few minutes, joining me on the bed after turning off all the lights and lamps. We were in complete darkness—just the light from my book reader glowed. He tucked both of us under the duvet, put his arm around me and snuggled me in his embrace. I felt a comforting warmth as he wrapped his arms around me. His musky, masculine fragrance diffused in my blood like a drug, engaging all my senses. His back rested on the headboard, and my head and back rested against his chest. I could hear his heart beating through my back, but I hoped he wasn't listening to my heart, which was pounding like a drum from this closeness. At least, reading this way, he would not see my face, and his intense gaze wouldn't throw me off track.

He caressed my arms softly, causing goosebumps all over my body. I felt a jolt of electricity, even though our skins were separated by wobbly fabric that provided no protection against his stimulating heat. It was as helpless as me, as his touch took me to the world of fantasy—a world where no past haunted me, where Adam and I were floating in a paradise of pleasure—a paradise that had this forbidden fruit.

I imagined crossing to the other side of the line, where he waited for me to savour it. I longed to touch him, feel him, to engrave this fruit on every inch of my body. His teeth grazed my neck, his hands running down to the small of my back as he separated the poor fabric from my skin. He touched me everywhere, without touching me at all. I was on the cusp of losing control when I heard his voice bursting my bubble.

"Rania?" *Shit. Shit. Shit. What was I thinking?*

"Huh?"

"You have something on your mind." *Was I dreaming?*

"I really liked Eva. I'm glad she recovered from what happened to her." I derailed the topic. *Where the fuck was I?*

"Hmm. She is more annoying now," Adam almost whispered. I didn't realize his face was so close until he spoke. His voice burned my nape and dug deep into my nerves, splitting them apart.

"If you get tired, let me know. I'll stop," I added, opening the book on the reader. *And I'm losing control.*

"Hmm." He sounded sleepy. I didn't know why he wanted to listen to the story when we both had a long day. Ignoring his pounding heartbeat, I began the story.

"In the name of God, the Compassionate, the Merciful! Praise be to God, the Lord of the two worlds, and blessing and peace upon

the Prince of the Prophets, our lord and master Muhammad, whom God…."

I read the first story of how Shehryar and Scheherazade were introduced to each other, confirming with Adam occasionally whether he was listening to me. It was already past three when I ended the fifth story, but Adam didn't intend to sleep.

I kept on reading—his warmth slowly drugging me. I didn't realize when sleep blissfully succumbed me into dreams.

WHEN I WOKE UP, it was almost ten a.m. Adam had already left for work, though I never understood why he worked on weekends.

Feeling too lazy to leave the bed, I grabbed my phone from the nightstand beside my book reader. Adam had left two messages.

> *Adam: Scheherazade slept and left her Sultan hanging right at the beginning of a story about an ensorcelled prince.*

This made me smile.

> *Adam: I bet my Scheherazade is a better storyteller. What fool would read from the book if he had you?*

Something warm had started to grow inside me with his words. I knew he had always been very expressive at showing his emotions, but sometimes, his poetic manners left me speechless. I would want to make him feel the way he deserved, but no matter how hard I tried, I failed to form words like him. I knew it wasn't just an innocent friendship that bound us together. It was more than that, and we were both afraid to admit it.

I stepped into the living room and was taken aback when I found Adam working in the kitchen. He gave me his million-dollar smile.

"Good morning, my Scheherazade."

"Good morning, my Sultan," I exclaimed. "I thought you'd have left."

He gave me his lopsided grin that had always twisted my insides. "How could I leave my Scheherazade?" I giggled at his words. "You slept well?"

"Yes, I did. Thanks to you. No nightmares."

He planted a kiss on my forehead. Though it was friendly, it showed so much affection. "Are you okay with scrambled eggs? That's the only thing I know how to make."

"My oh my, His Majesty is making breakfast. I am honoured." I sat down on the bar stool. "Need any help?"

Watching him make tea, toast bread, and beat the eggs was more entertaining than any morning show. If the media caught the wind that Adam Gibson was cooking in my kitchen, I would make headlines in all Canadian media.

"The last time I made breakfast was for my father. I never cooked anything after he died." He pretended to be casual, but his eyes showed longing. I watched him quietly, riveting how his muscles moved when he picked up the kettle. The sound of pots and pans clattering had never felt so good before.

He placed a platter before me. "Bon appetite!" He came around with his platter and sat next to me.

We ate quietly, enjoying the comforting silence between us. Perhaps this was the true companionship when someone wasn't expected to say something.

"Mom called," he said quietly. I was glad he hadn't used her name. "She asked me to especially thank you for the gift."

"That's sweet of her." I took a sip of tea. "You must know they all love you."

"Yes," he nodded. "I wouldn't have known if you hadn't come with me. I guess my father felt too guilty to tell me the truth." He picked up the fork but didn't eat. "Though he never said Mom left him for Brian, I assumed she did. I had no idea my anger was hurting my mother so much."

We finished our breakfast in silence.

After a few minutes, when he noticed my empty platter, he swivelled my barstool and scooted it toward him. My heart thudded loudly, suddenly conscious about how he looked at me.

"You know things about me no one else knows. I have no friend beside you, Rania." I knew he was telling the truth. His life had always been about board meetings and corporate parties. "This… what we have between us… is a two-way street." I blinked at him. "I have walked as much as you let me, but when I see you…" Struggling to decipher a hidden code on my face, he studied me like an ancient tablet. "Your road is blocked."

I looked down into my lap, not sure what to say. I knew he wanted me to reciprocate his feelings, which I was too afraid to do. How could I tell him everything? He would never believe me. I would even lose what we have now.

He continued, "I want to clear away all the stones from your road, but when I try to, you add more."

"Didn't I tell you the first time we met that I can't offer you anything?" I asked quietly. "I was clear about that, Adam, but you still accepted it. So why change of hearts?"

"I'm not forcing you into anything." Closing his eyes momentarily, he exhales a heavy sigh. "But…" he looked everywhere as if searching for words, "trust me enough to share what's stopping you."

"I trust you, Adam," I said. "When I'll open my heart, believe me, you'll be the first to enter."

Relief washed his face. "And you know I would never go against your will." I nodded. He took a deep breath and continued. "If I ask you to…" He looked away, seeming to have difficulty speaking. "…to move in with me, would you accept?"

I blinked, speechless. *Does he know what he is asking?* Why would he want me to move in with him? We were not in an intimate relationship. Or had I given him false hope?

"I don't know how you've been living alone for five years,

relying on those pills. You didn't get a roommate because you didn't want to let anyone know about your nightmares. I can't leave you alone, Rania. It kills me." I looked away, but he held my chin to look him in the eye. "I'm not asking you to give up this apartment. You can always return if you don't feel safe with me, but…"

"It's not appropriate," I objected. "Letting you sleep next to me is already straying me from my values. But after all those years of living with nightmares, I'm too selfish to let you go because I know you're the only one who can guard me against my nightmares." I shook my head. "I don't know how this miracle is happening, but I also know I'm using you for my benefit. I'm tired of these nightmares. I know you want me to move in for *me* and not for yourself, but I can't do this to you.

"Every time you touch me, I feel how you feel about me. I know it is not just friendship, Adam, and I cannot give you any more than this. I'm sorry." I held his hand firmly. "There are no stones in my way. I'm tied with ropes that no one can unwind." It seemed like my words froze him. "I want you to know that if I ever manage to untie my ropes, I will travel on your road and no one else's. That is the only promise I can give you."

His gaze tracked me when I stood and walked around the counter to clean up. I could sense his disappointment, but there was nothing else I could offer.

His phone rang, and he strode into the room to attend the call, closing the door behind him.

I looked around my kitchen, noticing how much mess Adam had created from one breakfast. He had used almost all pans available.

After tidying the kitchen, I sat on the couch to watch TV. I assumed he must have a few calls, so I didn't bother going into the room, though I had to shower.

When I checked the time, it was around one in the afternoon. I decided to prepare lunch and offer my prayers.

When I quietly slid into the room, Adam was sprawled on my bed like a child, the laptop lid still open. Drinking his sexiness for a few minutes, I headed to the washroom.

When I came out, he was still sleeping, totally unaware of anything around him. I knew he barely had any sleep, so I didn't bother waking him.

Laying my prayer mat on the floor by the side of the bed, I began my prayers.

CHAPTER 21
CELESTIAL

ADAM

When I opened my eyes, I realized I had taken an unplanned nap.

I checked my watch; it was around mid-afternoon. I turned to the other side and noticed Rania deeply immersed in her prayers. She was covered from head to toe, with only her face, hands, and feet showing. She seemed so focused that it felt like she was talking directly to God.

The way her lips moved with utter concentration, this calmness and contentment on her face—she looked no less than an angel. The light radiating from her was so intense that I feared I'd incinerate if I dared to come close.

I recalled our discussion before my nap. She was afraid of stepping forward, and I had vowed to untangle the ropes she was talking about. I wonder if it was wise to talk to Mike about it. I was sure he knew. What happened that she and her father weren't on speaking terms?

Even though she had cultural boundaries that prevented her from stepping toward me, I failed to understand what was stopping *me*. Whenever I tried to get close to her, something came between us. I couldn't see it, but deep down, I knew there was something. I was not a person who believed in ghosts or supernatural events, but what was happening was beyond my understanding.

What she did for me last night, I was indebted to her for life. If only she allowed me to help her, I would lay all my wealth at her feet. She had restored chapters of my life which were burned and destroyed in my childhood. I could never pay this debt, but I promised to stay by her side to cope with her nightmares. If my presence had made them ward off, I would stay with her every night.

But how long will you be able to keep her in your life, Adam? You are only living in the present. What about the future? Is there a future? Her light may not be only for you. You may need to let her go someday.

She moved her head back and forth and cupped her hands in supplication. I wondered what she was asking from God. If I ever prayed, I'd pray for her, ask Him to end her pain and set her soul free from her terrible past. Though I didn't know the details, those scars were enough to give me an insight into what she'd been through.

When she finished her prayers, she offered me a smile. "You slept well?"

"You look beautiful in your hijab." I propped my head on my hand. "I don't believe in angels, but if I were an artist commissioned to paint one, I'd paint you." She chuckled and shook her head as she removed her hijab. "This purity and divinity—and this halo around you."

"Adam!" She rolled her eyes. "Have you been reading religious scriptures?"

I sat up. "You are making me think like a medieval monk." I glanced up at the art on the wall above her prayer spot. It was something written in Arabic enclosed in a bronze frame. "You keep religious scriptures too."

She followed my gaze. "Oh, that." She smiled. "These are verses from the Quran, an important part of prayer. It's called *Fateha*, meaning 'the Opening.'"

"You prayed this?"

"This and other things."

"And what does it say?" I asked curiously.

Surprise stained her pretty cheeks. "You really want to know?"

"I want to know what you were saying to God," I said.

"We praise God in this and ask for His forgiveness and that He shows us the right path."

"Do you think He always listens to you?" My question caught her attention.

"It doesn't matter where you pray—this mat or in a cave. He listens to everyone. But as humans, we are impatient. We want to achieve things sooner." She took my hand. "When Grace was with your father, she might have wished for a happy life with him, but what God gave her was much more than that. If you see Grace and Brian together, don't you think they were meant for each other? Some wishes are not answered in a way we want, but God gives us something better."

I raised her hand and kissed her knuckles. "If you were in the Middle Ages, you could have been an excellent priest."

She giggled. "Too bad I am not a man."

"Sometimes, I envy how you have such a strong faith. How can someone possibly be—"

"That's what I'm saying, Adam. We don't know what God has planned for us. Sometimes, leaving your fate in His hands is better than holding onto your reins."

"Do you pray for yourself?" I asked. "Have you ever asked Him to end your nightmares?"

She stayed quiet for a moment, then smiled sadly. "I don't remember asking Him to end my nightmares, but when I see you, I think He's already answered my prayer." She left the room, leaving me speechless.

I sat there, wondering for many minutes what kind of responsibility she had burdened on me. If she considered me her blessing, I'd ensure I wouldn't become a curse. But what about her other pleas? Was I the answer to her dark past or those scars?

When I followed her, I found her in the kitchen, setting plates on the countertop.

"Lunchtime, Your Majesty." She gestured to me to sit on the bar stool.

"Wow!" The club sandwich with a green salad and fresh orange juice awaited us. "Were you making this while I slept?"

"And cleaning."

"It already looked clean to me." I looked around.

"Oh, you don't know, but I'm a clean freak," she mused.

I took a bite of a sandwich. It was delicious. "Not only you're beautiful, you possess culinary skills."

"With this sandwich?" She snorted. "Come on, Adam. This is leftover chicken."

"It's one of my best meals."

She shook her head. "You have a habit of exaggerating everything. An angel in one minute and now a chef. Ha!"

"And a killer!" I pointed out.

"A killer?"

I sat back. "Let me count the victims." I took a moment. "Apart from this heartbroken and awestruck Adam Gibson, seventeen men at the party last week were deprived of the privilege of dancing with you. Then we have Mike, of course, and my family—Brian, Grace and Eva. The MP we met at the Opera." She rolled her eyes. "Oh, and the souvenir shop girl."

"Oh, come on!"

"And Ali," I added.

"He is like a brother."

"Right." I pouted at her. "He greets you before he even notices me when he sees us together. As if I don't exist when you're around."

"He's only being nice to me."

"Oh, sure, whatever. So where were we…" I grinned at her. "Your skills…as I can see, you cook well. So I have decided to bother you every day and eat here." She opened her mouth to say something, but I cut in. "And you are an amazing storyteller." She looked down at her glass shyly, avoiding my gaze. "When you were reading, I travelled back in time and became King Shehryar, and you were my Scheherazade, telling me all the magical stories."

"Then it is not my skill. The author's skill created an imaginary world for you."

"I beg to differ. I don't think it would be the same if I read it myself. It wasn't me who created the imaginary world. I stepped into *your* world—how you created the magic around us. I felt like a part of those stories." Taking a bite, I continued, "And not only you're a good narrator, but you have also robbed me of ever reading on my own."

She narrowed her eyes, her arms folded over her chest. "Anything else?"

"Yeah," I chewed for a moment. She had already finished her lunch. "You can make any man a caveman, a stalker. You make a man chase after you."

She laughed heartily as she stood to fetch more juice from the refrigerator. Looking inside it, she said, "I'm a good runner. It is truly hard to chase me."

"You do know I can find you anywhere."

"Right. Your intelligence service," she mused as she poured juice into her glass. "But the catch doesn't require intelligence, Mr. Gibson. It requires stamina."

She placed the glass on the counter and grinned at me

mischievously. I immediately read her message. She wanted to test my ability to run after her. Noticing me slowly leaving my seat, she ran to the living room. I rushed after her, making her shriek with excitement.

"You don't know this, Miss Ahmed, but I work out daily." She ran behind one couch, making me follow her. "You have picked the wrong man, my dear. You can't run far." She laughed and shrieked like a child, running everywhere, behind the dining table, and then to the bedroom. I chased after her like a fool as she hopped onto the bed to escape from the other side. I shut the door, restricting all her escape options and took a long stride before she jumped off the bed. I managed to get hold of her hand and pushed her to the mattress. She laughed and screamed with excitement as I pinned her hands to the mattress, locking her wrists.

When her heart slowed down, she registered my intention. The chase, her laughter, it had only fuelled my pheromones.

For a second, her eyes settled on my lips. Could she read what was going on in my head? Did she know how desperate I was to kiss her?

We held each other's gazes, perhaps both of us wondering what to do next. I wanted to try my luck, test those dangerous waters she had warned me not to tread. As soon as I brought my mouth close to kiss her, she closed her eyes. I was merely a breath away when I noticed she had trouble breathing. She snapped her eyes open and whipped her head towards the door. I followed her gaze, wondering what she had seen that I couldn't see. From the deathlike pallor on her face, I could bet on my life she saw someone. I could feel someone's presence—the same heavy air I had always felt whenever I had tried to come close to her.

"Let me go," she pled. "Adam, please."

I rolled away, releasing my grip, wondering what happened to the girl who was laughing a few minutes ago. She sat up immediately, her back ramrod straight, but her eyes were locked on the wall beside the door.

Something was amiss. The more I try to solve this mystery, the harder it gets. Perhaps some asshole from her past had hurt her so much that her body was conditioned to reject intimate encounters. If that was the case, why did I feel a presence? Whenever we shared these moments, she got frightened, as if someone had restrained her emotions.

She panted, her gaze still glued to the wall. When I tapped on her shoulder, she yelped and shrunk back.

"Hey!" I tried to comfort her. "What happened?"

The terror that consumed her nightmare had now surfaced back. She flung off the bed and charged out of the room. I followed her as she fetched water and leaned against the counter, her breath faltering.

I sat on the couch, watching her take some time to get her bearings. She didn't meet my gaze but instead distracted her mind by clearing the plates from the counter. She tidied up the kitchen again, fetched the mop and started mopping. Didn't she mention she cleaned when I napped?

The silence broke when my phone chimed.

"Yes, Ali. Yes…what?" I stood immediately. "Who did it? Yes, I am here." I headed to the door. "I'm coming down. Do you have security? Unbelievable…" I hung up and rushed down to meet Ali in the lobby. He was waiting for me with the newspaper in his hand.

"Who do you think leaked the news?" Ali asked.

The front page was bombed with pictures of Rania and me standing outside Moore's estate.

"Bastards!"

Another picture of us standing outside her apartment was taken last night. The article clearly mentioned that I followed her to her apartment and spent the night. There was no way of coming out clean from this. Our relationship had become national news. How would she face her father? I didn't care what they wrote about me, but I didn't want them to ruin her reputation.

"Call the lawyer," I ordered. "This is unbelievable. And make sure no one gets inside. I want twenty-four-seven security around her."

I returned to her apartment and sat on the couch, slamming the paper on the ottoman. Rania picked it.

"Someone has leaked the news of our visit to my parents last night. It is also on the Internet." Her face turned white as a ghost as her eyes raked through the images. "The media know I stayed here with you last night. Some photographers are still downstairs, waiting to snap us together for their entertainment magazines."

Rania covered her mouth with her hands. I didn't know what to say.

"Fuck it!" I got to my feet, raking fingers in my hair. "I should have arranged security outside Moore's estate."

"I'm sorry if my company is spoiling your reputation..."

"You are sorry? Goddammit, *I* am sorry. It's not about my reputation. It's about *you*. I promised to protect your privacy. This news could easily reach your father, and then he'd ask you to stay away from me, which I can't afford." She inhaled sharply. "I don't know for what bloody reason you're hiding your past from me, but I'm damn sure those vultures are going to dig out everything." I paced back and forth. She sat down quietly. "I can't protect you when I don't know what I'm protecting. I've tried asking you many times, but you keep pushing me away." I sat down and held her hands. "They're not here for me, Rania. They're here for you. So please, if there's anything you haven't told me, tell me now." She looked at me blankly, and I realized she had no plans to share. Her phone rang, and she dropped my hands to answer it.

"Hello...Baba? How are you?" There was silence. "No, Baba... there is nothing like that...he is only a friend...just like Mike...I swear, Baba...I promise..."

She looked at the phone, a tear rolling down her cheek. Her father must have hung up on her. I wrapped my arm around for comfort. She burst into tears. He must have said something that hurt her. She wasn't this upset last week when our news leaked.

"This is the first time I've heard his voice in five years," she said, her head resting on my chest, trying to catch her breath between sobs. "He didn't even ask how I am. All he had to ask was..." She cried again. I tightened my hug. "I've brought shame to him, Adam. I don't deserve any goodness."

I brushed her hair away, cupping her face in my palms. "Hey, look at me." She looked up. "Don't ever say that. You deserve everything good in life."

"My father hates me."

"No one can ever hate his child. Why would he hate you?"

"Because I killed his wife," she snapped. "I killed my mother, Adam." I blinked at her. "I took away the love of his life."

What was she saying?

"He hasn't spoken to me since Mom's death. We lived like strangers under the same roof for three months. He didn't even say goodbye to me when I came to Toronto. And now...after so many years, I hear his voice. He never missed me. If Mom doesn't exist, then I don't exist. I'm just a dark, lost shadow now, living under a curse."

I had no idea what to say to all that. She could never kill her mother.

"I know you couldn't kill anyone, Rania. But I want to know what happened."

Taking a deep breath, she closed her eyes in pain. "Mom and I were in the car. I was driving. Baba was never happy with my habit of speeding. We had an accident with a truck, and…" Tears clouded her eyes. "I bloody killed her. Why didn't I die instead?"

I pulled her to my chest and let her cry for a few minutes.

"I'm so sorry to hear it, but it was an accident. Why do you blame yourself?"

"Because I was driving. I was speeding."

So she knew how to drive, but her confidence broke after her mother's death. I wondered how severe was the accident that took a life. How badly was she hurt?

As if she could read my mind, she continued. "I was in a coma for three days. When I woke up, I heard from my aunt that my mom's funeral was over. I didn't even get a chance to pray by her side." She took a deep breath. It was painful for her to go through this again. "I was in hospital for ten more days. Baba didn't visit once. I consoled myself that he was grieving and that he didn't want to inflict his pain on me, but that was not true. He didn't want to see *me*." She looked down at her fingers.

"We lived under one roof without any communication. One night, he came home drunk and spewed everything he had on his mind. He blamed me for killing his wife. He told me how much he hated me, that he didn't want to see me ever again because I reminded him that his love was no more."

I rubbed her arm to soothe her pain, but nothing could ever heal this wound. I could feel her pain—this sense of abandonment when your parent disowns you, but I had Rania to make me reconcile with my mother. Who did she have?

Her father already disapproved of the idea of us together. How could I help her in this case? Why couldn't her father see her pain? She had also lost her mother. She also needed a shoulder to cry on. And when she finally had someone in her life, all he could do was exercise his parental power and shatter her world again. Was it the only reason she could not let me enter her life? That the guilt of losing her mother, the shame of defaming her father wouldn't allow her to walk in my direction.

"I can't hurt him more, Adam. I have taken everything from him. His job is all that's left. I don't want to ruin his reputation."

In other words, she was unable to continue our friendship. I promised to protect her privacy, but I failed. It was a sign that I must leave her alone. *No. How will I live?* I would never leave unless she asked me to.

I didn't say anything but gently threaded my fingers through her hair.

"No one knows what happened between Baba and I," she said quietly.

"Does Mike know?"

"No. Mike knows about my mom's death, obviously, but not what Baba told me that night. It is too bitter to share."

"Thanks for trusting me," I said. "Can I ask something?" I waited for her nod. "What does your father expect from you?"

"That I remain deprived of his approval and spend my life in guilt."

I held her chin up to look at me. "I won't let you feel this way. I don't care what he thinks, but if you think your guilt will let me walk out of here, it's not going to happen." I held onto her gaze. "I'm not going anywhere, Rania. Whether your father approves of it or not."

She studied me for endless beats as if trying to read my soul. But I had already shown her my soul. She knew what was in my head. She knew I wouldn't leave her.

She didn't argue and rested her head back on my chest. A moment of silence and comfort passed between us.

"Adam?"

"Hmm?"

"If one day… I tell you some things about me. Will you believe me?"

"I will always believe you. You should know that."

She looked down at my collar, trying to find words. "Even if…even if it sounds unreal…would you still believe it?"

I studied her face, trying to read her expression and work out what she was trying to tell me.

"I am eagerly waiting for that day, my dear."

She closed her eyes as I kissed her forehead.

"Someday…" I said, "I will also tell you things that sound implausible."

She looked at me quizzically and nodded, her soft gaze assuring me.

We sat in a comforting silence as the time churned lazily. I had wanted to ask something since we returned but didn't know how to articulate it.

"There is something else."

She looked up and nodded.

"Give me two weeks of your life," I begged. "Please."

She knitted her eyebrows, clearly not understanding my plea.

"I want two weeks of your life." She still looked clueless. "The time we spent in Quebec made me realize that I have not seen this city like this. I want to roam around through your eyes. Would you show it to me?" She blinked at me. "Last night, when you were asleep, I saw the photo album you and Mike made. You two have created so many memories together, and it made me envious. You've visited so many places in and around the city. I don't have any memories of anyone. Would you make a memory with me?"

"This is your city, Adam. You've always lived here."

"It's true that I have lived here, but I haven't experienced it—the way you and Mike had. I want to see museums, art galleries, tourist attractions, everything. I want to relive the life I missed. And I want to relive it with you."

She took a few seconds to process my words. "So, you haven't seen anything?"

"I went to the science center during grade school, if that counts. But other than that, I never did things alone, just for fun. I've never even walked down Niagara Falls Street." Her jaw dropped, totally disbelieving. "I've seen it from the top floors of hotels when I attended meetings and conferences. But not close enough. When we strolled through the cobbled alleys of Old Quebec, I realized how these little things create treasured moments. I want to build memories for myself." I took a deep breath. "I know it sounds totally weird to you, but can you take off from work for two weeks until Christmas?"

She still watched me, agape.

Slowly, a small smile sneaked from the corner of her lips. "Adam Gibson. Are you hiring me as your guide?"

"I'm serious, Rania," I frowned. "I'm tired of living an artificial life with meetings, conferences and public appearances. I'm tired of being scrutinized: what I wear, what I do, what I eat, where I go. I just want to live a normal life. And I feel normal when I'm with you."

"So you don't think you'd be scrutinized when you're roaming around in public places with me?"

"I don't care, as long as it doesn't bother you." Before she could say something, I added, "And no, I don't care what your father thinks. His tantrums won't stop me from meeting you." I grabbed her shoulders. "He has already vented, Rania. He isn't talking to you at all. What more can you do? What worse can happen? He can't be angrier than this."

Her gaze was glued to the newspaper. It was evident she was trying to process my words.

"I know you care for his approval, but living in guilt for five years is a lot. You're being punished for a crime you haven't even committed." She exhaled a tired sigh at my words. "What worse will happen if we spend two more weeks together?"

I waited for her response, but she remained silent.

"I know it's not easy, but I just hope you start trusting me."

"I trust you, Adam," she answered immediately. "Baba didn't argue then because, in Quebec, I was gone for work. Here…"

"Here, you're taking a break. Besides, he is on another continent. What can he do from there?"

"You want me to be rebellious?" She gave a sad smile.

"No, my dear. I'm asking you to live for yourself. For once, stop caring what others think."

"He is not 'other', Adam. He is my father."

"But no one treats his daughter like he treats you," I objected. "Just two weeks. Please."

"He won't like it," she repeated. "But I have already told him we are friends. There is nothing between us."

Right! She knew we were not. Who were we lying to?

"What can I do if he has difficulty digesting this meagre truth?" She shrugged. "My heart is clear."

"That's my girl." I flashed a smile. "So, two weeks then?"

"Let me talk to Ben about taking the time off."

"I already asked him," I mumbled.

"What?"

"He said you haven't taken any vacation for the past few years, so he didn't see any problem."

She folded her arms over her chest. "Don't tell me you used your influence."

I raised my hands in defence. "I asked him nicely. And he approved."

"Good, God!" She rolled her eyes. "You and your controlling habits. But I have some conditions. If you agree, then we will make it happen." I nodded. I would sign away my life if she agreed. No condition could stop me. "No spending money lavishly. No reserving places just for us. They are public places, so we will visit them as they are. Just like normal people. Okay?"

"Agreed. Anything else?"

"Since I am not on your payroll, we will buy our own tickets and our own meals. And I expect you not to argue."

"Why not?"

"Because we are not dating, Mr. Gibson. So be a gentleman and agree to my terms."

"Gentlemen don't let their ladies pay," I mumbled.

"Okay, then be a dirty friend. I want to be equal in this."

I rolled my eyes. "Okay, agreed. Next?"

"We will travel the way *I* travel. If you want to see the city from my point of view, then you must travel with me on public transport. No expensive cars and chopper rides. Okay?"

"Are you crazy? You expect me to ride on subways and buses? Why would I do that? I have a car."

"Okay, then split this condition. Any place within Toronto, we will use public transport. Anything outside the city, you can bring your grand cars, whatever." She was so hard to convince sometimes. Why did I always let her win? But did I have a choice?

"All right."

"Okay, so where do you want to start?" Her eyes sparkled with excitement.

"Anywhere. I'll follow you even to the—"

"Yes, yes, to the ends of the earth with me. I know." She rolled her eyes. "For now, we stick to the city only."

"I'm serious. I can go anywhere with you."

"We will see when the time comes for that," she mused. "Will you be able to take off from your business for two weeks?"

"I have worked a lot, Rania. I'm tired of running. I need to rest."

"Cool. So be ready for surprises." She grinned at me.

My phone chimed with a reminder. "Shit."

"What happened?"

"I totally forgot. I have dinner to attend at the mayor's house tonight." I caught her smirking. "What?"

"Nothing. I am picturing how the CEO of Gibson Enterprises will look like, travelling in a subway, hanging around in museums and other public places—the person who meets mayors and ministers and endorses high-end brands. He will be encountering a totally different life."

"It's because you're making me do things I never imagined."

It was almost five in the evening, and I had no choice but to go home and get dressed for the party.

"How about we go to dinner together? I'll pick you up in an hour."

"No way. My Adam is not the CEO of an empire, so he'd never expect me to accompany him to official meetings. The Adam I know is my friend, who still needs training on how to do justice to ice cream," she says, adjusting the collar of my T-shirt. *My Adam! So very sexy.* "You go and transform yourself into a CEO now, and I'll text you about the plan tomorrow."

"You are throwing me out of your house, eh?"

"Of course. This CEO is invited to a lavish party." She points to my chest. "And he needs to go there because he's already committed."

"I really wish you'd come, though. I'm going to be bored to death. All they talk about is politics." I wrinkled my nose in disgust, and she giggled at me.

Fetching my jacket from the closet, I kissed her on the forehead and left for the boring dinner.

CHAPTER 22
CONFRONTATION

RANIA

MY GOODNESS!

How effortlessly he convinced me—I couldn't believe I agreed. The photographers had already lined up outside my building to confirm if he'd stayed with me last night. So much was already at stake, and now I'd agreed to risk my privacy for him again. *What is wrong with me?*

Never in my wildest dreams did I imagine spending days and nights with someone I wasn't even married to, who wasn't even my boyfriend or lover.

So much had changed this past week. I had met someone who made me feel worthy of who I was, who gave me his undivided attention, who'd managed to pick up broken pieces of my past and was somehow slowly mending it. He had offered me his invaluable companionship, respected my boundaries, helped me cope with my nightmares, and all he wanted in return was to recreate those days we lived in Quebec.

How strange was it that when he wasn't around, his thoughts kept me busy. I knew I was under his spell, and I could do nothing to stop my heart from falling for him.

My phone buzzed and made me smile when I noticed Mike

calling.

"Hey, buddy?"

"What's going on outside your building?"

"Oh! Where are you?"

"That's not the point. Are you in your apartment?" he asked with concern.

"Yes, why?"

"I'm coming up." He hung up.

Within a few minutes, I heard a knock at my door. I let Mike in. He looked around to search for something as if my house was a crime scene and he a detective to solve a case. He was dressed in casual clothes. It had been long since I had seen him without his uniform.

"Where is that Richie Rich?"

I rolled my eyes. "His name is Adam."

"Whatever! Where is he?" He finally managed to turn to me, looking agitated.

"He is not here."

"Things have gone so far with you two, and I learn about your life from a bloody newspaper? Is this how you treat your best friend?" Stepping closer, he grabbed my arm. "What's wrong with you, Rania? What is he doing for you that I never did? Where did I fail?"

He ended my nightmares which no one ever could.

"It's not what you think, Mike." I shrugged him off.

"So…you like the royal treatment, eh? You should have told me that. I'd have treated you like a queen if you ever gave me a chance—"

"Stop it, Mike. Just stop it." This was the first time I'd yelled at him. "How can you have such a low opinion of me? You think I'm with him for his money? After all our years of friendship, you think I'm some gold digger?"

"No, baby, I'm not saying that." His voice dropped a few

decibels. "Please, I'm sorry. But with everything I'm seeing and hearing, tell me, what should I think?"

"You trust that gossip in the newspapers?"

He looked away, taking a seat on the couch.

"I have never loved anyone except you, Rania," he confessed... again. "The place you have in my heart, no one else can fill it. I know you'll never be mine, but Gibson isn't worthy of you. I've seen your life fall apart in the past. I just can't let your heart and soul crumble again." There was nothing but sincerity in his voice. "He's only in this for pleasure. He's not a man of hearts and flowers. Why can't you see it?"

I sat beside him. "I can't explain it to you, even if I try. I don't think you'll be able to understand."

"Are you sleeping with him?" His question jarred me. I shook my head in disbelief that he could even ask me that. But should I blame him? A stranger, an acclaimed playboy, who spent nights in my room, it was natural to think that way. But doesn't he know me?

"Why are you so quiet?"

"I don't know what to say," I answered. "But if it makes you feel better, he hasn't touched me once."

He read my face as if trying to read the truth. "Then what do you guys do all the time? Sorry to be so personal, but I can't help worrying about you."

I placed my hands on his. "You don't need to worry. We just talk. That's it!"

"He comes here to talk?" He chortled. "Since when have you started counselling?"

"Come on, Mike. What's the problem with being friends? He doesn't have any friends."

"The whole city knows him, and you say he has no friends?" He raised his eyebrow.

"That's his professional life. Just because the whole city

knows him doesn't mean he's surrounded by friends. I told you before, there is nothing between us but friendship."

"How can you let a man stay with you overnight? You don't even have a guest bedroom here. In all these years, you've never let me cross that boundary."

"Please, Mike." I was at a loss for words. "I don't know how to explain." He would never understand my nightmare problem.

"You are in love with him." He wasn't asking. It was a statement. I stared at him in return. I had nothing to say in my defence. He could easily read the truth on my face. He nodded at his own words. "I see."

If hurt and disappointment had a voice, this was how it sounded.

"What a lucky man," he snorted. "But if he ever does anything to hurt you or break your heart, I swear I'll be the first one to kill him. You mark my words." Though it was a warning, it was still comforting that he cared. "Does he know?"

I shook my head. I had confessed to myself just now. How would Adam know?

"And knowing you, I know you'd never tell him how you feel." He rubbed my arm. "Don't ever give your heart to someone who doesn't know the meaning of love. I know he likes you, but I don't see anything beyond that."

I closed my eyes and buried my face in my hands. "I can't help it, Mike. I don't know how I let my heart slip."

He pulled me into his embrace. "Love is a dangerous street to walk on."

"I didn't realize when I started getting addicted to him. When he is not around…I feel incomplete. He brings life to me." A fresh set of tears made their way. When all my tears were spent, he wiped my cheeks with his thumb. "I'm sorry, I don't know how I…"

"Hey, I'm your best friend, okay? If you don't share it with me, then who else?" I giggled at his words. "Has he expressed his feelings?"

"He has said things…" I fidgeted with my fingers. I didn't know how to form Adam's feelings into a sentence. It was hard to surmise. "He hasn't said he loves me, but he declared last night that he feels incomplete without me. I fill the spot, whatever was missing in him."

"How poetic!" Mike mused.

"I know he is attracted to me."

"Everyone knows that," he mumbled.

"I'm also attracted to him, but every time I try to take a step forward, my past pulls me back."

"Have you told him about—"

"No, I haven't. He has learned much about me already. I'm afraid he'll run away if I tell him other things."

"But you need to tell him before things get worse," Mike warned. "You have no idea what you're getting yourself into. Paparazzi are standing outside your building, trying to determine if Adam has a steady relationship." He blew a breath. "You had no idea who he was before, right?"

"I didn't know he was this famous," I shrugged. "I don't read business magazines."

"Yeah!" He rolled his eyes. "Only if you could raise your head from your fiction fog." I smacked my lips into a thin line. I had nothing to say in my defence. "Isn't it better you come clean and tell him everything? What if the media decides to dig deeper?"

I know Mike was right. So far, Adam had shared everything from his past with me, but I had not told him anything about mine, except for my mother's death. I was too afraid to lose him.

"What about Uncle Bari? Dad told me he was not happy with all this. He is being questioned at his work."

I took a deep breath, not sure what to say. "I told Baba that Adam is just my friend, and since he is rich and famous, the press writes down everything associated with him."

"Uncle Bari spoke to you? For real?" Mike asked in surprise.

I nodded. "There is nothing to worry about concerning your record. I've done a background check in the systems, and there's nothing. I'm sure Adam has done the same, but still, you never know how far the press might go. They know about your father and his position."

"Yes, I know. Adam showed me the paper."

"So where is he now? He left before the paparazzi showed up?"

"No, he left a while before you came. He had a dinner at the mayor's house."

"How fancy!" He grinned. "So, it's just us then?" His smile had always melted my heart. "You know, girl, it has been almost four months since I've eaten anything cooked by you. The training lunches and dinners sucked big time. And you know how Dad cooks. So tonight, you're cooking for me, baby." He sprawled lazily on the couch and placed his feet on the ottoman. "Is your stalker gonna come tonight?" Before I could say something, he cut in. "Of course, he will. Why am I even asking?"

I laughed at his agitation. How would these two men ever get along?

"What do you want me to make?"

"Umm…how about lasagna? It's been a really long time."

"Okay, let me check if I have the ingredients. Otherwise, you'll have to go for the grocery."

Mike had no plans to move. He had already picked up the remote and browsed through channels. It had been a long time since I had hosted him.

He started his commentary about a new crime investigation series and how different it was from real-life scenarios. While he continued his rant, I found everything I had to prepare lasagna. A box of cooked ground chicken was already in the freezer. I thawed it in the microwave and boiled lasagna sheets. Mike's commentary kept me busy while I arranged the lasagna on the baking dish and put it into the oven.

As I took my seat on the couch, my home phone rang. It was only meant to attend calls from the security downstairs.

"Yes?" Mike answered. "Can you send the parcel upstairs?" He waited. "Okay, thank you." He hung up. "You have a delivery." *For me?* I didn't order anything lately.

After a few minutes, we heard a knock at the door. Mike received a manila envelope addressed to me. He placed it on the counter.

"Open it," I asked. "I don't remember ordering anything." He tore the envelope and pulled out an entertainment magazine.

I took the magazine from him, baffled to see Adam and me on the main page.

"What the fuck?" he exclaimed.

Everything from the past week was there, like a rolling film on paper. Photos from the opera, walking on the streets of Old Quebec, pictures in the hotel lobby, at the entrance to Moore's estate, and then Adam entering my building with me. It was as if someone had all the time in the world to stalk us for the past week. I didn't even dare to read what they had written, but I knew it was all garbage.

Noticing my horrified expression, Mike snatched the magazine from me. "You stayed with him in the same room in Quebec too?" *What?*

I felt the earth shaking under me. Noticing my body trembling, Mike held my arm and pulled out the bar stool.

Baba! What will he think? Oh my God!

"It seems like someone is stalking you," Mike grumbled. "Watching your every move. Does Gibson know about all this?"

I didn't know if he knew. Just then, my phone pinged with a message. Perhaps Adam must have seen the magazine.

Adam: I'm so bored here. I told you to come with me. They are rambling about the House of Commons.

Adam: I don't feel like eating here. Miss your food. I'm coming home to eat.

Home? Did he call my apartment his home?

Oh shit! He was on his way. And Mike thought it was just us. I quickly replied.

Rania: Dinner is already cooked. I have a guest.

Within seconds, I received Adam's call.

"You didn't tell me you were inviting people for dinner," Adam said.

"It wasn't planned. Dinner is almost ready. I'm setting the table now."

"Who's there?" His voice showed concern and authority.

"No strangers. Come over and see for yourself."

"Hey, the garlic bread is ready," Mike called from the kitchen.

"It's Mike," Adam huffed.

"Who else?"

"How long have you and Mike been alone?"

"Adam." I rolled my eyes. "Bring some sodas and orange juice. I'll see you in a while." I disconnected the line.

"Hey, we're out of sodas," Mike complained, searching through the refrigerator. "Let me get something to drink. It's unfair to eat this heavenly lasagna without a pop."

"Adam is on his way. I've asked him to get drinks for us," I said.

He whipped his head at me. "You called Richie Rich?" He asked. "Wasn't he already attending dinner?"

"He got bored."

"Or maybe his stalking agency informed him that *I* am here. And he didn't want to leave you alone."

"Oh, come on, he isn't that bad."

Mike raised his eyebrow. "But you agree he is a stalker. An obsessive one."

I laughed at his words while I set up the plates on the table. "The stalker will stop at the store to get us drinks."

He whistled. "Richie Rich is finally getting domestic, eh?"

After ten minutes, Mike took out the lasagna from the oven and set it on the table. Adam had already texted that he was almost there. I heard a knock at the door.

Adam looked too adorable, holding a box of Coke cans in one arm and a bottle of orange juice in the other.

"Hey, I missed you," he said. "The dinner was so boring. I had to flee." I took the juice bottle from him. "You drink this one, right?" *So observant!*

Welcoming him like a dutiful wife, I fixed the collar of his jacket. "Someone is looking really handsome in Armani." He studied me momentarily, then heard a commotion at the table. I was sure Mike was looking at us.

It was hard not to ogle him. He looked so deliciously sexy and edible in his black suit that I could replace him with the lasagna. *Stop reading trashy romance novels, Rania. You have a dirty imagination now.*

Adam noticed the magazine on the counter. "What the hell is this?" he barked.

"I got this by mail just a while ago," I answered.

Adam turned around and noticed Mike already shooting daggers at him.

"Can you explain what this is about, Gibson?" No manners of exchanging pleasantries. Adam remained speechless. I didn't see that coming, either. "Can you tell me why you'd put my friend's life in the limelight?" He knew the backlash this could cause if Baba saw it. "Someone has been stalking her for a week. Her every movement is being captured, and you don't see that coming? Are you blind or what?" I hadn't seen Mike this enraged.

"Mike, please," I interjected.

"You stay out of this, Rania. Let me talk to him man to man." Adam just stared at the magazine, speechless.

"I'm sorry, let me make a call." Adam turned to leave the counter.

"You are not running away, Mister," Mike pressed. He was acting like a cop.

"Listen, Mike, let me find out who's behind all this." I had never seen Adam sounding so unsure and nervous.

"Better talk here," Mike ordered like a cop. "Put your phone on speaker. I want to know what's going on." I could see how he was at work.

Adam made a call. "Did you see *Entertainment Weekly* today?" Adam asked, anger raging in his eyes.

"Yes, Mr. Gibson," a male voice answered from the other side. "I just learned that Ethan Murray hired a private photographer to follow Miss Rania since she reached Quebec." Adam's fist balled with anger. *Bloody hell! Only he was missing.*

"How sure are you?" Adam seethed.

"I stole the photographer's laptop. He had the pictures. And…" The man paused.

"And…?"

My heart skipped a beat.

"And there were many pictures just of her. Close-ups."

"I want to see those files," Adam ordered. "Send me copies immediately."

"Yes, Mr. Gibson. Right away."

Adam ended the call.

"This is bullshit," Mike shouted at him. "I'm going to find out how this happened, and don't you poke your nose in it." He poked into Adam's chest.

"Listen, Mike. I am as concerned as you are. But—"

"No buts, Gibson. If Ethan Murray—whoever that asshole

is—finds out that you've hired an agent to go after him, do you think we'll ever be able to find out his true motive?"

"Mike." I placed my hand on his arm. "I know you worry about me, but he can't go against my will. He won't risk his job."

"Oh, cut out this crap about will, Rania," Mike snapped. "A man is watching your every move. We have no bloody clue how he's planning to use the information. Are you getting what I'm trying to say here?"

Mike's sudden look sent chills through my spine. I bit my lip in fear. Mike was warning me of the risks, how someone could use it against me. As if he could read my mind, he didn't add details about my past.

"I'll try to find out what this man wants. But this must remain discreet." He turned to Adam. "Ask your agent to stay low. I'll look into it."

"He's dead. I will kill that bastard," Adam groaned.

"Calm down," I said. "Don't overreact. You—"

Adam interrupted me. "Overreact? Do you have any fucking idea what he's doing?" His eyes blazed like a scorching sun. "And now your best friend blames me for everything."

"I'm not blaming you," Mike objected. "But let me handle it, okay? I'm working with the law, so don't get involved."

Adam ignored Mike's words. "I can't leave her, Mike."

"I know that. I'm not asking you to leave her. All I'm saying is that stalking is considered a harassment crime." Mike turned to me. "Rania, has Murray ever tried to harass you physically?" I shook my head. "Has he tried to approach you? I mean, through excessive phone calls or emails? Or left something at your door? Anything like that?" I shook my head again. "So basically, all he's doing is taking pictures of you secretly, and we can't prove it unless we either find that photographer and get him to testify or get Ethan's laptop." Mike's words made sense. "It's not a criminal harassment case yet. He was smart enough to only give the press the pictures with Adam in them. We can't do anything about that because Adam is already notable. The media have gossiped about Adam's life, not yours."

Turning his attention to Adam, Mike continued, "Adam, I know you care about her, but I want you to stay out of this. Your interference will only create more problems." He looked back at me and continued, "Under the criminal code, we can only charge him if he trespasses on your property at night, assaults you, sends you threatening notices or tries to intimidate you. So far, he hasn't done anything illegal that we can prove. So let me watch him, and I'll update you guys, okay?"

This was too much to take in a day. I was glad I agreed to take a break. I couldn't face people at work.

"Now come to the table, please," Mike announced. "Lasagna doesn't taste good if it's cold, and my beautiful friend has put lots of effort into making it for us."

We sat down on the table for four. No one initiated the conversation while we filled our plates. From Adam's pursed lips, his frustration was palpable. I wasn't sure if he trusted Mike.

Finally, my best friend broke the heavy silence. "Mmm..." Mike said as he chewed. "Where are your hands?"

"Huh?" I stared at him incredulously as he took my hand and kissed my knuckles.

"Never miss an opportunity to kiss a woman who cooks for you." He planted another kiss. "You're the best cook on this planet. God! I love this dish." He took another bite like a famished beast. Adam remained silent, fuming. Mike was too busy to notice. "I'll take the leftovers for lunch tomorrow."

Adam observed us quietly. Perhaps he wondered if Mike and I were a family—that how conveniently he asked me to cook and then take leftovers afterward. Did he feel like an outsider?

"Don't you like it, Gibson?" Mike asked.

Adam studied me momentarily. I knew this look—it had

always made me a nervous wreck. I drank orange juice to avoid him.

"I know she's a wonderful cook. She made me lunch today, but I have other ways to thank and praise her. I'll do it my way once you leave." I choked on his blatant words. Adam rubbed my back and asked me to look up at the ceiling. Did he have any idea what he just said in front of my best friend? What was Mike going to think of me?

Mike didn't remark, but the way he pouted his lips, I knew he'd call me later and inquire. He changed the topic and shared a story about a woman who accused her man of having relationships with other women. Mike's stories lightened up the atmosphere, making it easier for all of us to breathe.

At some jokes, Adam's lips curved at the corners, bringing his beautiful smile to his face, his tension draining. I was so glad of Mike's presence.

"Have you ever thought of becoming a professional chef, Rania?" Adam asked out of nowhere. I scanned his expression, wondering if he was joking. "I'd like to finance something in the food business. How about I launch a fancy restaurant, and you be the head chef? Hire your own staff, train the people the way you cook. What do you say?"

I blinked at his unexpected question, not sure what to say. *Is he kidding me?*

"That sounds awesome. I'll be the first customer," Mike cheered. "You should try what she prepares in Ramadan to volunteer at mosques. It's free food for thirty days."

"Is that so?" Adam's eyes sparkled.

I felt like hiding my face. Now I understood why Adam had always shied away when we discussed his philanthropic work. You don't do all this to flaunt. It's between me and my creator.

"People who don't even fast come to eat her food," Mike went on.

"I cook for pleasure." I looked at them back and forth. "Never thought of it as a profession. I have no degree—"

"You have got flavour in your hands, baby. What they say…" Mike snapped his fingers, "The way to man's heart is through his stomach—this fits for her food."

I almost choked again.

"I agree with you, Adam," Mike continued. "She should pursue this as a career. She is wasting this talent. Stop working with Dad. This is *real* business. People won't stop eating until the world ends."

Adam watched me intently, waiting for my response.

"Are you guys serious?"

"I'm always serious with you, Rania. What makes you think I was joking?" Adam's heated gaze turned my stomach into knots. *There is no biological connection between the eyes and the stomach. How does he do it? Damn it!*

"I never thought about it. But thanks for appreciating my dinner to that level."

"Did Ben call you to confirm for the holidays?" Adam changed the topic suddenly.

"No." I glanced nervously at Mike and then back to Adam.

"What holidays?" Mike chipped in.

"Rania and I are taking off for two weeks," Adam said.

Mike studied me, searching for the truth in my eyes. "Are you guys going somewhere?"

"Yes and no." Adam smiled as he took my hand and continued. "Rania has promised to give me two weeks of her life. We're not going out of town, just spending time with each other, to get to know each other better. Right, babes?" *Babes? Is he doing this purposely for Mike's benefit?* Mike's mouth hung open. "There's so much going on, we decided to escape and relax."

No, that was not the reason. He wanted to see the city. I tried to argue, but my tongue seemed to roll inside my mouth.

I forced a smile and nodded at Mike. I was sure he'd pull my leg later.

When Mike took his last bite, he asked, "Do you have anything for dessert?" I shook my head. "Then let's go for ice cream." His offer was very tempting, and I didn't know why I looked at Adam for approval.

"You already had lots of ice cream last night with Eva." *So, is that a yes or no?* "Plus, there is paparazzi outside."

I glanced back to Mike, who mouthed, *control freak*. I pursed my lips to stifle my laughter. Adam had no idea how much Mike and I gossiped.

"Someone has calorie issues," Mike mumbled, leaning back in the chair. His phone rang, and he answered it. "Yes? Okay… hmm… alright… I'm on my way." He ended the call, huffing. "Duty calls, my love." He left his seat. "I have to go, but you still owe me dessert. I'll stop by one evening, and we'll go out." Ignoring Adam's watchful gaze, he kissed my forehead.

"Wait. Let me pack the lasagna for you." I headed to the kitchen, carrying the dish. Mike followed me.

"You didn't tell me you were going on vacation with him," Mike grumbled, his voice barely audible. "He is a total control freak. How can you stand him?"

Studying his grim expression, I fetched a storage box from the cabinet. "He's a nice guy."

"Hell yeah! Maybe he is, but don't let him control you, Rania. He's acting like your master or something."

I laughed at Mike. "Oh God! You are making it erotic."

"I still don't believe he hasn't touched you. He literally eats and drinks you." He passed his fingers through his hair. "If he ever hurts you, would you let me know?"

"I will never hurt her, Mike," Adam interrupted. He was standing at the entrance to the kitchen with his arms crossed, leaning against the wall. *Shit! How long has he been listening?*

"And I will never control her." Standing calm and composed, he studied us with speculation.

Mike collected the storage container.

"You better not. I'll be watching you, Gibson." Giving his signature detective look, Mike headed to the door. Adam's displeasure was evident on his face. There was someone to challenge him, after all.

I followed Mike to see him off. He hugged me and whispered again to prompt him of any danger.

I shut the door and headed back to the dining room to clear the table. Adam joined me and helped me clean the table. After loading all the dishes into the dishwasher, I was about to leave the kitchen when Adam blocked my way. He studied me in a strange way. Mike's words buzzed in my head. Adam was indeed drinking me with his eyes.

I tried to ignore it, but he cupped my face in his palms, caressing my cheek with his thumb. I felt weak in my knees. Why did my body always betray me?

His green eyes burned like fire, ripping my existence apart, peeling off my clothes, tearing through my flesh and bones directly to my soul. He caressed my lips with the pad of his thumb, sending hot threads of desire along every nerve.

"You know, you are like a fire." He flicked his index finger gently on my face. My eyes closed at his touch. "Open your eyes, Rania, I'm talking to you." His voice was like a whisper, but heavy on my ears, breaking down the barriers, revealing the real woman in me. I forced myself to meet his gaze.

"You are a fire," he repeated. "I feel your warmth and compassion when I'm close to you. But when I touch you…" He paused momentarily, touching my trembling lips with hunger, then continued, "I burn." *What kind of confession is that?* "You're making me change my beliefs on worship. I am worshipping a fire. I enjoy the comfort, take the warmth. I obey this fire but can't feel it because whenever I try to…I burn deeply, and no one can see the scars. It's so strange, isn't it?" His lips curved into a small smile. "You told me that only Djinn are made of fire. Though I don't know if they exist, I know you're not one of them. Who are you, then? Why do I burn?"

I looked away. "I don't know what you're talking about."

"You know bloody well what I'm talking about."

"I think the *Arabian Nights* is messing with your head." I tried to leave again, but his grip was so firm that I couldn't move. He rested his forehead on my shoulder. I was sure he could hear my heart pumping so hard.

"A sweet, intoxicating fire." He took a deep breath. He whispered into my neck, making my whole nervous system shut down. His eyes were heavily lidded with passion. I had never seen this side of him.

"I know you feel what I feel. Your body responds to my touch, but your soul…" He nuzzled my neck, passing currents through my body. "I know you feel it, Rania, but I also know something else is blocking us. Something I can't see. I feel the heaviness between us every time I come close to you, as if some invisible force is pushing me away from you." He took my hand and threaded his fingers through mine. "I have a feeling you know what it is. Why won't you trust me?"

"I do trust you, Adam." I gulped at his words.

"Not the way it should be."

If I ever had any doubts about not being in love with him, he dispelled them. I was melting under his touch like a pool of burning desire. He had miraculously turned on all the hidden switches in my body. Not only had he found the passage to my heart, he had also sneaked his way to my soul. His way of expressing emotions was different, but I could tell that he was talking about soulmates. Were we soulmates? I didn't think God created a soulmate for me.

"You should go home." I put my hand on his shoulder, pushing him away, but I didn't have the courage to look into his eyes.

"My home is where you are." Something twisted inside my heart.

"I mean your place. We need to get up early if you want to see the museum. I have some work, too. Laundry and then—"

"Are you kicking me out?" I was about to protest, but he cut me off. "You can do all that while I'm here." I looked away. "Do you really want me to leave?"

I fell on my knees, hiding my face in my hands. The burden of his feelings was impossible to carry. He was holding my heart in his hand, and there was nothing I could do about it.

Nothing.

Embracing me, he gently passed his fingers through my hair, soothing me with his tender touch.

"I'm not going anywhere. Like it or not. Accept it or not, but I will be your shadow, Rania. A shadow that doesn't disappear in the dark." He kissed my hair softly.

As if I had no weight, he carried me like a ragdoll and took me to the room. He laid me on the bed and tucked me under the warm duvet.

"Can we stop pretending about our feelings?" he asked. I inhaled sharply at his words. "I don't know what to name this feeling, but what I feel for you is very strong." What if he'd never know he was in love? But if he did, would I be able to accept it? He knew nothing about me. He had no idea what path I had walked. "And I'll wait for you when you open your heart to me."

He left the bed and headed to the washroom. I heard the shower running, how comfortable he'd made himself here. I wondered if he was truly the right person to trust—that he wouldn't run away after hearing all the truth. And even if he did, what was next? There could never be an *us*. We belonged to different cultures and values. Even if he believed my secrets, he could not be my soulmate. It was impossible.

Adam appeared again in his pyjamas and T-shirt. His presence was marked everywhere in my apartment. Anybody would think he is living with me here. Should I tell him that he lives in my heart, too? Would he accept me the way I was—this broken, scarred and cursed girl?

Sprawling on the bed, he made himself comfortable and browsed his phone. He didn't initiate the conversation, and I was grateful for it. I left the bed and prepared myself for the prayers.

When I finished, Adam was watching me.

"Can you ask your God to help me too?"

I smiled at him. "He is your God, too. Why do you want me to ask when you can ask yourself?"

"Because you are celestial when you pray. I see you talk to Him directly, and I'm damn sure He is listening to you."

"I am an angel, then a priest, then fire, and now I am celestial?"

"Yes! You amaze me every time."

"Why don't you ask Him yourself?"

"Why would He listen to a sinner?" he asked, his expression sour.

"One of Prophet's Caliphs, Ali, once said, *the sin which makes you sad and repentant is more liked by God, than the good deed, which turns you arrogant.*" He blinked at me. "Don't think so highly of me. I am nothing like that." Folding my prayer mat, I removed my hijab, and sat on the other side of the bed. He rolled over to face me.

"Do you think using public transport is a wise idea?" His sudden change of subject grabbed my attention. "I mean, with all the pictures and the news."

"You're right," I sighed. "I'll have to compromise on your luxury cars then." I winked at him, and that made him smile.

He patted my pillow. "Grab your reader and lie down. I have

one thousand nights left to share."

"Aren't you too obsessed about it?" I fetched my reader from my nightstand drawer.

"Your execution is suspended, Scheherazade. I can't hang you till you finish your magical stories." He was truly obsessed with the story.

"Ah! My sultan is inquisitive," I exclaimed.

He regarded me for a moment, then changed the subject quickly. "Are there any side effects to suddenly quitting your meds?"

"I'm good without it." I put my hand over his. "As long as my shadow is with me, I have no worries." On my words, Adam pulled me toward him and settled me in the same position we were in last night.

Tucking his head behind my shoulder, he breathed in. "You *are* truly celestial. Your fragrance is divine. And it's not just a perfume. It's your fragrance. Every time I breathe you in, I travel to another world." He inhaled again. He rubbed my arms with his warm hands very gently, his raw voice sending encoded messages to my soul. It was truly a miracle that I wasn't melting here. "Thank you for Mom. It's nice to talk to her now. It's good to know that someone loves you unconditionally." He took my hand, entwining his fingers with mine, and brought them to his lips. "Thank you for completing me." He kissed my hand again. "And thank you for being…mine." My heart started to skip once more, and I was dead sure it could easily be heard. He melted me with his words…every time. The air in the room seemed to suck away, my breath shallow.

Focus!

Focus!

Focus!

Don't dwell in that world again, where his words take you.

"Don't you think we should sleep?" I changed the subject.

"The earlier we reach the museum, the better it is."

"Can I say something?" His hand gently rubbed my arm. I nodded. "Your place gives me a homely feeling." I turned around to look at him, surprised at his words. "It's like…" he paused. "When you return after a long day, this is the home you want to be." Now, that took me by surprise. What did I have that wasn't in his lavish home? I sat straight to study him. "You know, sometimes money doesn't buy everything."

"But it is better to cry in a Ferrari than on a bike." I rolled my eyes. He laughed at my response.

"I'd rather cry in someone's embrace," he said thoughtfully. "You know I have all the luxuries at my place, all the amenities—you name it, and I have it. I have invested a lot of time and money to build that place, but somehow, I don't feel complete when I go there, like the feeling I get when I'm here. What do you think is missing?"

His innocent question made me smile. "I haven't seen your place, Adam, but I believe it is your heart that you forgot to put there. I guess you're placing your heart here. That's why you feel like it's home."

In his utter silence, I noticed something flickering in his eyes, something churning in the back of his mind. I didn't know if he understood my point, but he didn't argue and watched me.

"My heart is where *you* are. Wherever you go, it will go with you." I held my breath

Was this called a declaration of love? No, we couldn't fall in love with each other.

It is impossible.

I wish I could freeze this moment and live in my fantasy, where no past stabbed me to death, where I could feel Adam's touch connecting to the real woman in me—a woman who was brutally murdered in the past.

"So, the sultan doesn't like his palace now?" I folded my arms, amused. "He finds this peasant's house comfy?"

He chuckled. "The sultan has decided to abandon his palace and move in with this peasant."

I blinked at him. "What?"

"You heard me."

I took a few seconds to process his words. "How can the sultan live outside of his palace?"

He knitted his eyebrows. "You're mocking me, aren't you?"

"Yes, because what you're saying is absurd."

"I should be where my Scheherazade is. So I better bring my stuff." I wasn't sure if he was joking. I couldn't let him move in with me. It was such a huge step. We were not even in a relationship. He crawled into my mind conveniently and read my expressions. "Can I?"

I combated our awkward moment by opening my book reader to continue from where I left off last night. *"Know then, O my lord, that whom my sire was King of this city…"*

I carried on with stories within stories, not sure when I closed my eyes and dived into a deep sleep.

CHAPTER 23
THE CONFESSION

ADAM

TWO WEEKS PASSED IN A BLINK.

I didn't realize how time had slipped from my hands. Rania fulfilled her promise and gave me the most treasured two weeks of my existence. For the first time in my life, I understood the true meaning of companionship. We visited all the tourist attractions, including fulfilling my desire to walk down the streets of Niagara Falls. From museums to art galleries, from theatres to concerts, from crazy malls to long walks under holiday décor, we did everything one could imagine. She had no idea what she'd given me—a gift of memories to keep in my heart forever.

Mike apparently got rid of the stalking photographer, or maybe Ethan was worried we'd trace the pictures back to him. There were no more pictures of us in magazines and newspapers. Also, I paid the local papers a good amount not to print anything about her, even if they had found out. We visited a new place every day. Sometimes, Rania cooked food and invited Mike to eat with us.

I hardly ever visited my place. Rania never agreed to my request to move in with her, but she also never asked me to leave. Every night after dinner, she read me *Arabian Nights*, which made me time travel with her into past centuries until she finished the book the day before our vacation time was up. In those two weeks, I got a chance to visit her dance classes. When she danced, it was not her body that moved with joy. It was her heart that danced.

Our friendship flourished with each passing day, but in all those days of companionship, I couldn't find her heart. I was starting to develop a fairy tale fantasy that she was captured in some spell, and once I'd kissed her, the spell would be broken. I knew her body felt my touch, but whenever I had tried to come close to her with the intention of kissing her, she had frozen, as if her soul had been pulled out of her body, making her a piece of dead meat.

I could not point out what was between us, but I knew someone was always present in our private moments.

For the past two weeks, I tried every possible way to dig her past out of her, but I failed. She had locked her heart in a hard shell and thrown the key away.

There were also more strange incidents in the middle of the night. Several times, I woke up to find her in the dark closet or washroom. From the other side of the door, it sounded like she was speaking to someone in a strange language, but when I came in, she was staring blankly as she had in the hotel room. Every time that happened, I had asked her about it in the morning, but all she'd said was that I was either dreaming or hallucinating.

I wanted to know about the scars that marred her skin and wounded her soul. She had made me promise never to bring them up, as she didn't want to walk down that horrible path.

We also argued about her attending the summit in New York. I needed to attend a conference in Toronto on the exact dates, and I was worried she'd face Murray without me. I was uncomfortable with the idea, but it was about her career. I had no right to stop her.

During our vacation, my mother called us and invited us to a Christmas Eve party that she'd organized in the grand party hall of the Ritz Carlton. Mom had been looking forward to this party and expected all her children to attend.

I decided I'd give Rania the necklace I wanted to give her on our first date before going to the party. I would confess my feelings and leave it up to her to write my fate.

Today was the evening of the 23rd of December, the day before the party, and I was stuck in a press conference in Halifax. I wanted Rania to come with me, but she preferred not to get involved in my business obligations. This conference was expected to continue for a few more hours, but I would make it by morning to attend the party in the evening with her.

The night felt endless without her. The meeting seemed nowhere close to end as the men sat in the boardroom, discussing green homes and their advantages in saving energy. I tried hard to concentrate, but my heart was stuck back in that one-bedroom apartment. A few times, Ali noticed my mind drifting away, so he answered on my behalf.

If I didn't tell Rania how I felt about her, my life would never move forward. But I'd also like to tell her about the woman I met at a place that never existed. I didn't know where my life was taking me, but imagining it without her was inconceivable. My eyes searched for her when she wasn't around. My body craved her when she was not there. I didn't know what this feeling was.

This feeling is love. You are in love, Adam Gibson.

Ali's cell rang, breaking my train of thought and forcing me to pay attention to the questions coming from the media. He walked out to take a call and then reappeared after a few minutes, but instead of sitting, he bent to whisper.

"Come out, Adam, there's an emergency." Sensing an alarm in his voice, I stepped out of the conference hall after excusing myself. "There is a fire on the sixteenth floor of Archeries condominiums, building number two."

I felt the ground moving under me. "That's Rania's floor. It's not her apartment, is it?"

"The one next door," Ali said. "The fire department is already there, but…"

"But what?" My heart skipped, making it difficult to breathe.

"We have news of two casualties." He paused, gulping for a second. "Both are dead at the scene. I'm trying to call Rania, but her phone is off."

I lost my balance. Ali supported me and helped me sit on a nearby couch.

"I'm pretty sure, Adam, there's nothing to worry about. Let's pray she is safe. I have asked Frank to update me every few minutes." The world around me still spun like a carousel, making everything hazy. "I've sent him Rania's picture in case he can locate her. They have evacuated the entire building. There's no one left inside."

"We are leaving," I ordered.

Ali called for the private aircraft. He returned to the conference hall, probably making an excuse for my absence. I closed my eyes and covered my face with my hands, resting my elbows on my knees.

Please, Rania, tell me you are okay!

There was no way she could leave me like this. We were meant for each other. She didn't even know about my feelings.

I looked up and didn't know who I was addressing, but I knew He was listening.

If you exist, you will keep her safe for me.

I felt Ali's hand on my shoulder for comfort. I had never cried in public, but my existence was crumbling around me.

People noticed me falling apart, but I didn't care. All my memories of her rolled through my mind like a movie. I still felt her innocent face. Her fragrance still lingered. I could hear her laughter.

I looked up at Ali. "She can't go away like this, Ali. She can't leave me."

"Don't worry, Adam. I have a strong feeling she's all right."

"Then why isn't she picking up the phone? Call Mike. Ask him to find out."

"I did. He and Ben are not in the city. But I informed them because Ben owns the apartment." Ali had tried everything.

During the two-hour flight, I kept trying to call her, hoping she would pick up, even though I knew her phone might have been burned in the fire. There was still no news from Frank. The two bodies that were recovered were unidentifiable without DNA testing. The journey seemed endless. My money, my power, my riches—they all failed to keep her safe.

By the time I reached Toronto, it was past midnight. I rushed immediately to Rania's building, where the fire had consumed my life. It was crowded with media, fire trucks and police cars billeting outside, but among those strange faces, I couldn't see her. I kept screaming her name, but there was such a stampede that no one heard me. Freezing rain poured from the winter sky, but the fire had such a hold that the rain wasn't affecting it. Everyone was soaked, running around like crazy, searching for their loved ones. My life seemed to come to an end, like the Day of Resurrection had already arrived, and there was no escape.

I was surrounded by reporters and photographers.

"Mr. Gibson, when did you get this news?"

"Mr. Gibson, we heard your girlfriend is in the building?"

"Mr. Gibson, have you been able to find your girlfriend?"

"Mr. Gibson, have you identified the burned victims?"

"Please, back off." Ali pushed everyone away from me. "Mr. Gibson can't talk to anyone right now. Please let us find her and pray that she is all right."

After thirty minutes of searching the crowd, Ali asked me if I wanted to visit the hospital. *No, I can never do that.* I had a firm belief that God had saved her for me. I'd never admit that she was no more. But Ali convinced me that they had looked for her everywhere.

When I approached my car, I noticed someone standing under a barren tree. My heart slipped away. It was Rania wrapped in her bed sheet—which I slept on last night—water dripping down her body. She was trembling with cold in the freezing rain without a coat. It took me off-guard that no one had seen her before.

Rushing to her, I pulled her into my arms, kissing every inch of her face, not caring how she would react.

"Rania…" There was nothing more endearing than holding her in my arms. "Thank God, you're okay. You have no idea what I've been through. I almost died." Peppering kisses everywhere on her face, I savoured her physical presence. "I was so frightened. I can't imagine my life without you." She stood mute and unresponsive. "I promise I'll never leave you alone again. Oh, Rania, you've no idea how much I love you." She didn't even pay attention to my confession.

In my happiness and excitement, I forgot to ask how she was.

"Are you okay?" I cupped her face in my hands.

As if she just registered my voice, she started crying, shaking helplessly.

"I lost everything, Adam. I have nothing left. My home, my possessions, my memories, everything is burned into ashes." She trembled with pain.

"No, my love. You'll get everything back. I promise. I can't thank God enough that He saved you."

"I am homeless, Adam. I have no shelter now." Agony reflected in her dark eyes. I heard Ali calling for medical help. "The picture of my parents has been burned, too. That was the only memento I had of them together."

Laying her head on my chest, she vented out all her pain in a fresh set of tears.

I hadn't thought about it like that. All I cared about was that she was alive. I hadn't considered what she had lost. The paramedics appeared immediately, and the medical assistant informed them that Rania was traumatized and was in danger of developing a high fever if she was not taken care of properly. Instantly, the paramedics took her inside the warm ambulance, but she was shaking so violently that she was unable to respond.

"We need to get her wet clothes and this sheet off," the medical officer advised me.

As soon as he touched Rania to remove her sheet, she snapped, pulling away, resisting the medical officer. Her blank eyes searched me for help. I knew she'd never let a stranger remove her clothes, but the wet, cold clothes could worsen her condition.

"Mr. Gibson, we need to take her wet clothes off," he said. "Please, ask her to cooperate with us."

"Can't you see she's shaken?"

"Okay," the assistant sighed. "We'll step out. Please, help her change." He handed me a couple of blankets, and they left us alone in the ambulance.

After making sure the ambulance was vacant and securely shut, I began, "Rania, you need to listen to the doctor and take off these soaking clothes. I'll turn my back, and you can undress and wrap yourself in the blanket. Here." I took off my jacket and handed it to her. She was shivering too hard to hold anything. "You can wear this under the blanket if you feel uncomfortable."

Unable to find any strength, she couldn't even lift her hand.

"Let me help you then," I offered. "Just look at me, please. Let me help you." Her silence wasn't conceding, but it wasn't defying me either. I started helping her, first removing the drenched sheet.

Underneath the wet sheet, she was wearing her nightclothes. I knew how modest she was, but she was so worn out that she didn't even have enough energy to argue. I locked my eyes with hers to tell her I would not look at her body.

Lifting her arms, I pulled off her T-shirt, then drew her closer, snaking my arms behind her to unhook her bra. I covered her nude body with my warm jacket, buttoned up to her neck.

With an unblinking firm gaze, I pulled down her pyjama trousers, and she stepped out of the wet clothing, holding my hand firmly. I wrapped her in the blanket. She was wearing her bedroom slippers, which were also dripping. I took off her slippers and replaced them with my socks.

Laying her down on the paramedic's stretcher, I called the medical officer. He checked her vitals, and a combination of ibuprofen and diphenhydramine citrate, along with a heavy dose of sedative to calm down her fever and pain, was injected. With a prescription, he advised her to sleep well.

Since she was too weak to walk, I collected her in my arms and carried her to the car. The photographers attacked us again, snapping pictures of our misery.

"Mr. Gibson, do you know the reason for the fire?"

"Mr. Gibson, is she the daughter of the UN secretariat you've been dating these past weeks?"

"Mr. Gibson, can you tell us how your girlfriend feels right now?"

"Mr. Gibson, we heard your girlfriend's apartment is completely burned down. Is this true?"

Ignoring the insolent questions, I made my way out of the crowd. Ali kept pushing the reporters and photographers away. Settling down in the back of the car, Rania rested her head in my lap all the way home.

It took almost twenty minutes to reach my apartment. The

medicine had taken its effect since she wasn't shivering anymore.

In the elevator, she was very quiet, looking down at her feet covered with my socks. I had no idea what she was thinking. It was very traumatic for her to lose everything, but I vowed to give it back to her. After all, her home was my haven, too.

When I opened the door of my apartment, she smiled. "Is this your place?"

"Yes. Since you're here, you may call it home now."

"It's beautiful…it's…out of this world…" She gawked around, her eyes shining bright. "I thought homes like these only existed in magazines and commercials." Her mood seemed to lift now that she was somewhere safe. "Oh my…" Kneeling on the floor, she touched the white flooring. "Holy shit! Who installs marble flooring in Canada? And it's heated…" Her curious eyes searched mine for an answer.

"I'm not a fan of wood flooring," I mumbled. "I know most Canadians don't use it because it's so cold in winter, but I always used to admire marble floors in warm countries. So, I installed radiant heat. Now get up. You need to rest."

I offered her my hand and helped her stand. She looked around the foyer, admiring everything as if she were in some magical kingdom. I must not forget that a sleeping med was already injected into her system. She could doze off anytime.

We stepped into the large living area, her eyes sparkling with the lights and colours of the living room.

"Who designed all this?" Her face was carved with wonder.

"If you're asking from an architectural point of view, I designed this building, including the floor plan of this place, but I got some interior designers to decorate it."

"It's beautiful, Adam. It seems like one of those places on HGTV million-dollar listings."

"Well…" I rubbed the back of my neck. "It actually is. They were after me to film it." She wandered around until she found her favourite place, the kitchen.

"What a kitchen!" She covered her mouth with surprise. "Look at the countertop."

She spread her hands over the quartz countertop to feel it on her fingers. The excitement in her eyes suggested she hadn't seen anything like this.

"Look at the gas grill. Eight burners? Wow!" She amused herself over the appliances as if I'd brought a history buff to an ancient ruin. "It is like a dream kitchen. I can spend all day."

"Really?" Her remark surprised me. "It's yours, anyway."

As soon as I said the words, her expression changed. "No. I am homeless." Tears started rolling down from her eyes again, and she hid her face with her hands.

"I promise I'll bring your home back."

"I don't know if the insurance…ah…none of my stuff was insured."

"Don't worry about the insurance. I promise everything will be okay. You are here, alive, and I don't think we should ask for anything more than that. I still don't know how to thank God for listening to me." I pulled her hands away from her face and wiped her tears. "I'll give your home back, just the way it was. You have my word."

Walking her out of the kitchen, I led her to the bedroom.

She stopped looking around the apartment, her excitement abandoned. Her loss had hit her again. Settling her on my bed, I took some clothes from the chest of drawers.

"Here." I placed a flannel shirt and pyjamas beside her. "You can't sleep in this jacket. Please, change. Make yourself comfortable and try to feel at home. I'll be out here, okay?"

Planting a soft kiss on her forehead, I left the room.

Meanwhile, I used the spare washroom. As soon as I came out, my phone buzzed.

"Yes?" I picked up the unknown number.

"Where's Rania?" I heard a familiar voice.

"Mike?"

"Where is she? I've been calling her for two hours."

"She's a bit shaky. She's lost everything. I guess her phone was in her apartment. I don't know how she managed to escape out of that death trap."

"Can I talk to her?"

"She is resting. When I found her, she was soaked and freezing. She has a fever, but the medics treated it."

"Where were you when it happened?"

"I was in Halifax. It took me two hours to get there." I sighed. "I don't want to imagine what she was doing alone under a tree, all soaked with the rain for two hours."

"Jesus! I feel bad I wasn't there. When you talk to her, please tell her I called. Tell her I tried my best to come down tonight, but all the flights are booked because of Christmas. I'll be back by the 25th in the afternoon."

"Sure. Let's hope she rests well tonight."

"Adam, do you suspect anyone behind the fire?" Mike asked, concerned.

"What do you mean?"

"I just learned that the fire started in Tammy's apartment, Rania's next-door neighbour. She hasn't been home for two weeks, and they say someone left the portable heater turned on in the kids' room. I spoke to Tammy a few minutes ago, and she says she doesn't have a portable heater." My heart sank at Mike's words. Was Rania's life in danger? "I know it sounds strange, but tell me, do you have any enemies?" His question startled me.

"Why would anyone want to harm her?"

"They don't necessarily want to harm her. Everyone knows about you two. Maybe someone is trying to harm *you* through her." He gave me a moment to absorb his words. "I suspected Ethan Murray, but he hasn't been in Toronto. Is there anyone else you think might be after you?"

"No." The world around me started to spin. The thought of someone burning Rania because of me was killing me.

"I'm going to investigate it personally. I have asked for CCTV tapes for the whole building for the past two days. Somehow, I have a feeling this was deliberate. They did it while you were away." I couldn't breathe. "I'll call in the morning once she's awake."

Mike hung up. With my nerves on high alert, I rushed back to the bedroom and opened the door without knocking. Rania was sleeping, looking wan and pale.

Sitting beside her, I held her hand firmly, but she didn't move or respond to my touch.

I won't let anyone harm you. I promise.

CHAPTER 24
AN ENCHANTED KINGDOM

RANIA

I OPENED MY EYES AND NOTICED Adam sitting at my side, holding my hand firmly. He kissed me on the forehead when I blinked at him.

"Good morning. How are you feeling?" He watched me lovingly, brushing the hair off my face.

I looked around to register my surroundings. I recalled Adam bringing me to his place, but I didn't remember sleeping in this bed. I clearly remembered Adam removing my clothes in the ambulance and wrapping me in the blanket, his eyes not flickering even for a second. The pain he'd endured was evidently marked on his face, fearing I had died in the fire. My pain seemed to wither in the face of his agony. It looked like he hadn't slept for a single minute.

"I feel heavy," I groaned. "My head is spinning."

"Do you want to sleep more?"

"No. What's the time?" I looked around again.

"It's noon. Would you like something to eat?"

"No, I…" Realizing I was in his clothes, braless, I pulled up the blanket.

"I'll wait outside if you want to change. There are some clothes for you in the closet." He pointed to a white double door.

The spacious bedroom was furnished elegantly, featuring a massive bed with a custom white leather-cushioned headboard, larger than any king-size bed I had seen. Everything in the room was white. It looked like a cozy, serene place to relax. I couldn't understand why he would leave such a nice room to sleep on that queen-size bed with me. The thought that the place where Adam liked to stay no longer existed brought the pain back.

I dragged myself off the bed, still groggy, and found the door to the bathroom. The luxurious bathroom, with its exquisite white French vanity, quartz counter, and high-end faucets, was something out of a magazine. The soaker tub was too tempting to ignore. The glass shower column was colossal, with a rain shower exuding luxury. I had only seen this kind of bathroom on TV shows.

My personal products—even the toothbrush and toothpaste I used were kept here. He seemed to have remembered everything as if he'd memorized me.

After washing my face and brushing my teeth, I headed to the walk-in closet. I was amazed at its size. The right side was filled with Adam's expensive suits. The other side had feminine clothes. *There are some clothes for you in the closet.* Some clothes? I felt the fabric, admiring the taste of whoever chose it. I couldn't believe Adam arranged all this while I was sleeping. All clothes were tagged with Holt Renfrew. There was not a single item that wasn't designer.

I pulled out a drawer to find numerous silk and woollen scarves. In the next drawer, expensive undergarments of every colour were laid. I picked up one bra and checked its size. *He even knows my size!* Interestingly, none of the clothes had price tags, as though they'd been deliberately removed. If Mike saw this, he'd call Adam borderline obsessive.

A knock at the door interrupted my thoughts.

"Are you in there, Rania?" Adam asked.

"Umm…yes."

"Is everything okay? Can I come in?" He slowly peeked his head inside. "You haven't changed yet? Is there something else you need?"

"Adam, this is…" I clutched one scarf to my chest. "Is this—"

"It is for you." He smiled softly. I opened my mouth to say something, but he raised his hand to shush me. "No need to make a fuss about it." I pursed my lips. "If anything doesn't fit, we can exchange it." Of course, this wasn't clearance stuff with no exchange, no refund policy.

"I can't take all this. This is too much…"

Moving closer, he rested his hand on my shoulder. "None of these matters. What matters is that you're safe. This is nothing." He waved his hand. "Please don't argue about it."

The way he asked made me speechless. Before I could say anything, he pulled me into a tight hug, dissolving me in his soul, giving me no space to retreat. He still looked shaky and distraught from last night.

"You didn't sleep?" I asked with my face buried in his T-shirt.

He held my face in his hands. "I couldn't. I thought I lost you, and I died every second when I couldn't know where you were." He rested his forehead against mine. "I didn't know how to plea and beg God to send you back to me, but He still heard me. He heeded my silent prayer." His eyes were glassy. "You must teach me how you communicate with Him. I don't want to be at a loss of words next time if I ever needed His help." I never knew I mattered so much to him. "How did you escape the fire?"

"I don't know," I answered, wracking my memory. "I woke up to hear the fire alarm. At first, I thought I was dreaming, but when I saw the fire outside my bedroom, I couldn't believe it. My mind was blank. All I could do was wrap myself in the sheet.

I still don't remember how I got out of the building." He shut his eyes at my words, his fingers flickering with distress. "When the fire trapped me, I thought I'd lost everything, and this was the end. I never valued my life until I saw death. I thought I'd never be able to…" *tell you how much I love you, Adam. I realized it when death stood at my doorstep, and I had not even shared my feelings with you.* "I thought I would never see you again." I still didn't have the courage to tell him the truth.

He hugged me tightly again. "I promise I won't let anything happen to you." His feelings, as if he'd also experienced the trauma with me, were evident in his touch. "I want you to relax now. I'll see you outside."

He kissed my forehead with quivering lips and left the closet. I recalled the moment when he found me under the tree. I wonder if my exhausted and traumatized imagination made me hear him confessing his love. If he indeed said it, he hadn't mentioned it again.

Flushing all these wild thoughts out of my mind, I realized Adam must be waiting for me at breakfast. I was sure he hadn't eaten anything today.

I searched for loungewear, which one uses daily, but everything was ridiculously luxurious. I finally picked up a pair of jeans and an ivory-coloured DKNY blouse. The Chantelle undergarments fit me perfectly; it was like I shopped for them myself. I looked like a pricey mannequin dressed to adorn some high-end boutique in Milan. He was making me feel worthy.

I entered back to the room and sat at the beautiful white French antique dresser, with very few items on display. What surprised me was my perfume and makeup. He even knew the shade and brand of the lipstick I used daily. It was the same hairbrush as if I'd teleported with my stuff to his place.

How long had he been noticing and memorizing this?

I stepped out of the room, barefoot, to look for Adam. A

long wainscoted passage, with multiple white doors on each side, awaited. As if wandering the enchanted castle from *Beauty and the Beast*, where Belle was lost and completely captivated, I walked gingerly, ignoring all the closed doors, till I found stairs at the corner of the passage. *This is a double-storey apartment?* Or was it a house? I clearly remembered entering through an elevator.

Down the very wide and heated marble stairs, Adam was talking on the phone in his living room, pacing back and forth on a thick, deep blue-and-white striped rug.

"She's doing okay, Mom… no, I can't ask her. I don't think she's well enough to attend the party. I'll stay with her…okay, I'll let you know." Noticing my presence, he ended the call. "You look…beautiful." His gaze made me acutely aware of his intentions.

I shyly glanced at my feet but offered a smile in response. "Thanks to you. Anyone would look nice in this blouse."

I passed my hands over my waist to feel the soft fabric. He chuckled in return, shaking his head.

"Come. Let's have something to eat." He took my hand and led me to the kitchen, where I met an Asian lady working.

"Hello, Miss Rania. How are you doing this morning?" *Do I know you?* I looked at her quizzically and then at Adam.

"She's my housekeeper, Julianne," Adam whispered.

"I'm good. Thank you, Julianne." I sat down on the barstool next to Adam. Julianne was in her early forties. *So she is the one who keeps this place so organized and tidy.* Everything was so neat and pristine here that I felt I shouldn't touch anything.

"Mr. Gibson mentioned you like pumpkin bread. I have baked some for you. Would you like to try it?"

She placed the warm bread in front of me. I smiled and tasted the bread. It was delicious. When Adam and I met for the first time, he hadn't had breakfast. And he was taken aback when I offered him one. If Julianne was such a nice cook, why was he on an empty stomach that morning?

"Penny for your thoughts?" Adam asked.

Two platters of Spanish omelette with fresh fruits were served. She already knew I take tea. I shouldn't be surprised after the closet episode.

I blinked at him, wondering if I should ask him, but decided to keep it to myself. Perhaps he lied that morning to talk to me.

"Thank you for everything. You have managed to keep the stuff I use every day." I didn't know how to formulate the words.

The corner of his lips twitched to give a shy, boyish grin. "When I tell you you're very precious to me, you must believe me." His words stirred something inside me. He pulled my seat closer. "When I tell you I exist because you exist, you must believe me." I held my breath. Was he confessing his love?

"Thank you." I looked down.

"And you should credit me for spending time in your closet. I got to know a lot about you from there." He winked. "You are engraved here." He tapped his temple. "How you eat, what you eat, what you wear, everything. I might sound like a psycho stalker." I rolled my eyes. "And if you want to call it an obsession, that's fine with me, too. I tried to find out everything about you." He took a deep breath, closing his eyes for a moment. "The only thing I couldn't find is your heart. But someday, I will."

Why did his words make me uncomfortable, as if my heart wasn't ready to accept that any man would selflessly and unconditionally offer me his heart? I feared that this would all fade away one day, and I'd be back to living in my darkness.

I turned to the breakfast. "You were talking to Grace when I came down?"

He frowned at my change of subject. "Yes. She wanted to know how you are." He took a bite of his toast.

"That's very sweet of her. I'll thank her when I see her

tonight."

"We're going?" Utterly surprised, he put his fork down.

"We're not going?" I repeated, equally surprised.

"No, I mean… I thought… you might not feel like—"

"Adam, I'm fine," I reassured him. "Grace has planned this evening for quite a long time. She wants all her kids to be there. If I don't go, you won't either. So, we'll go together."

"I'll let her know." He gave me a satisfactory smile. We continued our breakfast until he broke the silence again. "Oh, by the way, Mike called. He wanted to know how you are. He'll be flying back on Christmas morning."

"Why is he coming back? I thought they decided to stay with Uncle Joe till New Year's."

"That's what people do when they care," he mumbled. "Also, the apartment was under Ben's name, so he has to return to make his insurance claim."

"How did you get to know about the fire?"

"My company built it. I must ensure the fire had nothing to do with the construction."

"You built that building?" Why was I surprised again? He had built half of the city. "I didn't know that."

"That's because you don't take any interest in what I do." He teased.

"I have no interest in your money, Adam. You know that very well."

"But you must know what I do for a living, so you can stop complaining and arguing with me when I get you something," he grumbled.

"I'm not interested. I didn't accept your friendship for your money, so—"

"I know, Rania. All I want is for you to stop making a fuss when I give you something. Whatever's mine is yours." *What kind of confession is that?* Why would I take his money?

"Adam! This is your hard-earned money. Don't spend so recklessly."

"But it makes me happy to give you something. Why don't you understand it?"

"I don't need it."

"You don't know how important you are in my life? Do you want me to go through it again?" He frowned. "You've been taking care of me since we met. You helped me confront my own demons, pulled out all the thorns from my life. Buying clothes is nothing. And if it bothers you, consider it a minor way of showing I care. Okay?" There was no point in arguing with him. He had always won. Spending money was his way of showing care.

After breakfast, Adam asked, "Do you want to take a tour?" He waved around.

"Oh, I'd love to see my Sultan's kingdom."

He smiled shyly as he took my hand and started with the main level. Now that I wasn't in trauma and the sun had filled the place so brightly, I could see everything that I didn't last night.

Everything in the living room was perfect—the art, the décor, the furniture. I didn't know they could make such high ceilings in an apartment. The room was tastefully furnished with pastel blue suede couches that complemented the deep blue-and-white-striped rug I had noticed earlier. A huge baroque-style mirror was placed above the antique console table to add a classic feel. The place wasn't entirely modern but a mixture of old and new charm.

From the tall windows, Lake Ontario gave the feeling of living by the lakeside in a country cottage, with a grey sheet of silk spread across the water. I expected his place to be decorated in dark colours, usually mentioned for the heroes in romance novels, but Adam's place was warm and welcoming.

He slid the antique barn door, which led us to the dining

room. The table was dark mahogany, with room for twelve people. It held a beautiful centrepiece that caught my attention. The honey-coloured walls blended perfectly.

"Do you shop at Versailles?" I asked foolishly. "This centrepiece and that antique mirror."

"A few items were imported," he said casually, making me feel more stupid. "But it wasn't Versailles. I think it was some German monastery."

My mouth hung open at his words, but he ignored me and took me to the terrace, patio, or garden—whatever it was. It was a huge space with beautiful patio furniture, a fire pit, not to mention a state-of-the-art barbeque grill, and a vast swimming pool, which was enclosed in a glass dome. Despite feeling cold outside at this temperature, the sight and Adam's enthusiasm warmed me. The view from his terrace was majestic. I could see the entire city laid out.

"It's beautiful. And I can't believe you have a pool on your terrace." Pride danced in his beautiful green eyes.

"I haven't shown my place to anyone. You are the first one to come here."

"Really? I'm honoured, then. So how high are we?"

"The building has thirty-five floors. You can see we are on top." He looked at the view proudly.

"Are there others living here, too, in this building?"

"Oh yes, each floor has ten apartments. It's a residential building."

"And you own the building?" I asked. He nodded. *Of course!* Why was I surprised again? "And this is the space of ten apartments?" He returned a shy smile. *Holy Shit!* I did a quick calculation. How much money would he receive monthly from this building alone if all the apartments were rented?

He grabbed my hand and led me to a spiral staircase. "Come. Let me show you something."

I was taken off-guard when I reached the rooftop. A helipad? Though he mentioned that the place was filmed for HGTV, I guess that didn't matter if the cameras captured it. From his sparkling eyes to the pride in his words, I could tell I was the first person he was giving this tour.

As if he could read my mind, he said, "A few months ago, one channel approached to film this place. My designer suggested it. He was the one to show it around." So, he wasn't even there when they filmed it. He turned around to gesture at the chopper. "Meet my baby. I'll take you for a ride someday."

"Wow! Your baby is…" I chuckled. "What should I say? Huge?"

I placed one foot on another as cold wind tried to knock me off.

"Shit! I brought you out without shoes." He grabbed my hand, but rather than travelling back down the spiral steps, he took another door, which led us to an indoor passage. We both stopped to catch our breaths as an elevator brought us back to the apartment.

"Your place is wonderful," I said. "It's like having your castle in the clouds, just like Jack and the Beanstalk."

He laughed at my words. He showed me the rest of the main level.

Besides the gigantic living room, warm dining room and ultra-modern kitchen, a huge study took my breath away.

"My favourite room. I spend most of the time here," he said proudly as he entered. Talking about the home décor of Versailles, this room brought me back in time to the eighteenth-century English manor. The wood panels, the dark furniture, and the books lining the wall—it was a library out of a calendar.

"Wow!" I looked around. "You never told me you're a reader."

"Not the ones you read." He pointed out. "They are mostly architecture and design books." He stepped closer. "I know it isn't inviting for you. I'd need to add your reading list here."

"It is already pretty." I looked away from his heated gaze while studying the design papers scattered about the table.

Behind the chair, the floor-to-ceiling windows opened to the city skyline as dark clouds started gathering. I stepped away from the table and was again caught off-guard when I noticed an enlarged, framed copy of the picture of our first dance together on the opposite wall. I blinked at him with surprise. I wasn't expecting to see it here. He could see it every time he'd sit on the chair.

"I told you. This is my favourite room. Now you know why." He smirked. "When you're not around, I talk to you." He nodded at the frame. Fire and passion ignited in his eyes, burning me from the inside. At this very moment, I truly felt he was drinking me in.

"And when has it happened?" I rolled my eyes with a smile. "Since we have met, you've always been with me." I moved to the other side of the room and opened a sliding door, where I found a vast game room with a pool table in the center. "Why am I not surprised that this place doesn't have a game room."

"It was just part of the design. I think you need to have a good partner. I play with Ali when I work late on my designs."

"Are there more surprises in this castle?" I grinned at him with amusement. "Like a dungeon or something?"

"Castle?" He laughed, shaking his head. "Come on, I'll show you the rest."

He slid open a glass door from the study, leading to the pool I saw earlier from the terrace. I marvelled at the number of Mosaic stones inlaid around it. A hot tub at the corner was already inviting me. He pressed a button, and in a blink, the glass dome opened to the sky. My mouth hung open at the ingenious engineering.

"If you were someone else, I'd say such a show-off, but…" I

looked around. "This is heaven. You don't need to take a break to a warmer climate in winter when you have this."

He smiled innocently. I wished to capture this moment, the twinkle in his eyes, as he proudly showed me his home. I noticed a canvas placed on the other side of the pool. I approached to look at it closely, but a sheet covered it. Noticing my curiosity, Adam removed the sheet. I gaped at him, completely astounded to see an oil painting of my face.

"Like I said…you are here." He tapped his temple again. "You are etched in my memory, Rania. I can sketch you whenever I want." His raw voice sent my body to the crest of desire. He leaned closer and placed his hand on my cheek. "But someday, I'd like you to pose for me so I make sure I'm not missing any fragment of the beauty God has blessed you with." I blinked at his words several times, unsure what to say in return, though I was pretty sure he was not expecting anything back from me. He knew he had left me speechless.

I could sense he wanted to kiss me, but I stepped back. "What are other surprises?"

When we returned to the living room, he opened another door. It was a theatre with a massive collection of movies, an immense projection screen, and multiple black leather recliners. The walls were painted deep purple.

"You have this, and we stood in line for hours to go into the theatres?" I folded my arms, pantomiming annoyance. "Why?"

"Would you have agreed if I had asked you to come here and watch a movie in this room?" he asked. *Oh, he knows me so bloody well.* I pursed my lips to hide my smile.

We headed upstairs and back to the long, wainscoted corridor. The passage was artfully decorated with modern art. Whoever designed his place must have an exceptional taste. The first room on the right was the state-of-the-art gym.

"So that's the secret of your handsome body." I winked at

Adam.

"You find me handsome?" He looked surprised as if he didn't know how handsome he was. Like he never read gossip magazines? He closed the distance between us. "Do you find me attractive?" His eyes were so intense; it was a miracle I wasn't melting. I tried to avoid, but he held me with his heated gaze.

"How about the other rooms?" I changed the topic. The moment I'd let myself lose in his passion would be the end of us. He didn't know what he was signing up for, and I didn't want to give him false hopes. If he found the truth, he wouldn't even look back at me. And I didn't want to lose what we had. It was too precious to lose over my hideous past.

Closing his eyes momentarily, he rakes his fingers through his hair. "Come."

The guest bedroom was on the other side of the gym, beautifully decorated in beiges and browns. Another door, next to the guest bedroom, was a guest washroom, done all in gray and black. I had never seen a washroom like this. *Who puts a Jacuzzi in the guest washroom?* The opposite door was a state-of-the-art laundry room with an overly priced washer and dryer as if he spent all his day in the laundry room.

"Oh my god, I can marry this laundry room!"

"And here I thought women swoon over diamonds and designer stuff."

"This is designer," I objected, passing my hand over the deep red washer.

He let out a small laugh. "You never cease to surprise me."

I blinked at him as he led us to the last room I had already seen.

"I must say, your castle is enchanting, My Sultan." I gave him a little curtsy. "Is that all, or is there more for my amusement?" I sat at the corner of the bed, spreading my hand on the soft white sheet as I crossed my legs. "Aren't there any more surprises, Sire?"

He studied me briefly, his gaze darkening as he strode lazily towards me.

"The sultan has endless ways to amuse his queen in his chamber, only if she lets him." He sat so close to me that I could smell his cologne.

I didn't know why I was luring him into this conversation, but last night, when I realized I would not have another moment to spend with him, I vowed that if I survived, I'd share my feelings. I knew this was wrong, but for a moment, I wanted to forget about my past and live this moment—this moment of amorous passion.

"Oh, really?" I tugged his T-shirt. "I can't wait to be amused, then."

He noticed me licking my lips, his eyes turning into a deep shade of emerald. I rolled over to the headboard, and he stalked me like a beast, his eyes fixed on me as he crawled on the bed.

"The sultan wants to apologize in advance for his intentions and uncouth thoughts for his queen."

"You don't say," I mocked.

"The queen is expected to obey her sultan; else she will spend her days in dungeons."

And here I thought he didn't read fantasy.

I leaned against the headboard until no more space was left to move back further. He was almost a breath away. I felt my heart wedging in my throat. Was it wise to lure him?

I gave a nervous laugh. "Can I expect the sultan's mercy?"

"The sultan will lay the entire world at her feet only if his queen trusts and surrenders to him." He gently pulled my scarf away, throwing it on the other side of the bed. "Is my queen ready to surrender now?" He flicked his index finger over my lips, burning me deep in the core. I shouldn't have provoked him. I knew it would lead to this.

"Does my sultan promise to be gentle?" I forced a smile,

trying to drag the conversation. I could read his intentions like an open book. He takes my hand and kisses me on the knuckles.

"He will be as gentle as a dove." Lowering his head, he nestled his face into my neck. "But the sultan does not wish to send his queen to the dungeon."

Did he sense I might chicken out? After all the time we had spent together, he knew my limit. Was he testing me to see how far I could go?

He placed his palm on my cheek and gently rubbed his thumb against it. As simple as it sounded, his touch scorned me from the end of my hair to my toes.

"This sultan will abdicate his throne if the queen is willing to surrender to his desires." He planted a soft kiss on my collarbone. "The queen will not only have his heart but his kingdom too." What was he trying to say? He knew I didn't fancy his wealth. Was he asking for my trust to share the truth of my past?

I was so raptured by his touch and the sensation his words created in me that I didn't want this moment to end. I could sense his arousal, yet the sincerity in his eyes showed me immense love. It wasn't lust. It was pure love.

But if he loved me, why wouldn't he say it?

As if he could sense my hesitation, he sighed. "I have waited for this moment for so long." He looked around the room. "This is all empty, barren and colourless without you." He took my hand and locked his fingers with mine. "I want you to feel me, Rania." He whispered in my neck, planting phantom kisses under my ear. "I know you want me as much as I do. Just let go of everything and feel the passion between us." His lips travelled slowly to the other side of my neck.

His touch was making me so weak, my brain muddled with sensations I had not felt in years. I was losing my ability to think. The only sensation I could feel was his lips against my skin and how I wished I could let him explore my entire body through his lips.

As if he could read my thoughts, he pulled away momentarily and looked deeply into my eyes. "Let your soul meet mine. I promise I won't leave you in darkness."

He knew my soul was rotting. Or was it just a metaphor? But if it was, he could have just kissed me. Why was he seeking my permission? Why talk so deeply about our souls?

His lips grazed lazily over my neck, his heart thudding loudly in his chest as if it was his first time. He had shared a bed with many women, and yet I could sense his hesitation like a virgin adolescent.

As if on cue, he said, "I have never felt like this before." *Neither have I!*

We acted like a young couple, trying these dangerous waters for the first time. The air sucked up, and we floated in a vacuum state of passion, savouring this blissful moment like it was our last night on earth. I wanted to live in this fantasy world where I could run into his arms, where there was no pain or scars, where no memories of a haunted past resided, where the fear of losing him didn't exist. I burned to make love to him, but the dark secrets, like a veil, floated between us—translucent but an obstacle, nonetheless.

As soon as he put his lips on mine, his phone chimed loudly in his front pocket, breaking the steamy moment between us. He pulled away and took the call.

"Yes?" He frowned, a thousand emotions skidding through his eyes. "Yes, this is Adam Gibson…yes…Hello, Mr. Bari…" *Shit! It's my dad?* "She is fine. Yes… no burns…yeah, we should all thank God, nothing happened to her…yeah, the whole floor caught fire…almost ten people are burned, and two of them died…it is indeed very tragic." He took a deep breath. "She is my guest, Mr. Bari." Baba must have made a fuss about me staying with Adam. "I will take care of her. You don't need to…"

I pulled my knees up to my chest and hid my face. Why did Adam tell my father I was staying with him? He already had a low opinion of me.

"I've taken a vow to protect your daughter. I cannot think of harming her at all." He paused. "No, she is resting. Good day."

He hung up the phone, sounding annoyed. Though my face was hidden, I knew he was looking at me. I could feel his gaze. The moment we were in before was gone. I shouldn't have instigated it in the first place. Why did I even start this game of seduction with him when I knew how he felt about me? It wasn't fair to play with his feelings and mine.

Sensing the shift of motion on the bed, I lifted my head to notice him leaving. Within a minute, he returned with a box and sat beside me.

"Keep this since you lost your phone." He placed the new iPhone box in my hand. "It's the same number."

"Adam. I…"

"No arguments, Rania." He flung off the bed, heading to the closet. "In case you are wondering, all your contacts have been retrieved. You can turn the phone on now." He disappeared into the walk-in closet.

I opened the box and turned on the phone. There were many text messages from Mike, wanting to know how I was doing, if I was okay, and how I managed to escape the fire. I didn't feel like talking to anyone right now. I couldn't believe Baba called Adam to ask about me. *Does that mean he cares?* But why didn't he speak to me?

"Have you decided what to wear this evening?" Adam called out. I never thought about it. I had planned to wear the dress he'd bought me for the opera, but since I didn't have that anymore, I'd have to think about it.

It was already two in the afternoon, and since it was Christmas Eve, the stores would probably be closing within a couple of hours. I followed his voice and entered the closet, discovering his sweet smile.

"You know what you are going to wear tonight?" How could he be so nice to me when my father ruined our moment? He pulled out one dress. "What do you think about this?" It was a beautiful black lace shimmery gown.

I'd noticed he liked lace in women's clothes. I wondered if he had picked this dress.

Noticing my blank face, he said, "Natalia, my fashion advisor, arranged a few evening dresses. You have more. Try them on and let me know if you find anything suitable. Otherwise, we'll go to the mall immediately before it closes." *Suitable?* This closet was worth more than a hundred thousand dollars, and he asked me if I could find anything *suitable* to wear. It was the entire designer store.

"This is already too—"

"Sshhh..." He placed his finger on my lips. "You're still in the sultan's harem, and this is how he shows he cares." He smirked at me seductively. *So the moment is not lost after all.* "I'd love to see you in this one without making a fuss about it." He regarded my lips, his intention evident. "You are very beautiful, Rania, but tonight, I want you to look how *I* see you. Would you dress up tonight, only for me?" I drowned in his eyes, filled with a burning desire and perpetual passion. I had not dressed up for anyone before. "You might not know it, but almost three hundred people are coming to the party. I'm bringing a woman with me for the very first time. It will be our first public appearance as a couple." I nodded. He smiled again at my acceptance and took a few steps back. "I have called someone to pamper you before you get ready. They'll be coming shortly. We'll leave around six." *People, to pamper me? What does that mean?* "Enjoy."

He left me alone in the closet. *Is this some kind of test for me?* How does one doll up for a man?

We would eventually return to this room after the party. What would happen then? Would he continue where he'd left off?

There was no point in looking through the clothes when he'd already picked one for me. I tried on the dress and wasn't surprised it fit perfectly. You couldn't go wrong with Valentino. I opened the rest of the drawers and was surprised he'd even got me sandals, boots, and bags. From Jimmy Choo to Christian Louboutin, I had everything in this closet. From pumps to wedges, handbags to clutches, Burberry to Fendi, YSL to Gucci, it was indeed a boutique. When he said he wanted to place the world at my feet, only if I'd trust him, was he talking about this?

I chose shimmery Christian Louboutin high-heeled sandals to match the shimmers in the gown and selected the black Fendi clutch to go with the attire. There were some high-end European brands that I'd never even heard of, or rather, it was beyond my reach to even think about them.

It was no surprise that the closet/ boutique also had accessories. Boxes of Hermès, Chanel, and other high-end brands for scarves, hair accessories, watches and jewelry filled the lower drawers. If money couldn't buy happiness, it was a flat lie. And I wouldn't lie. These things did make me happy. It made me forget about last night.

"Can I come in?" Adam knocked gently.

"Yes, please." I gathered everything when he stepped inside the closet.

"Is there anything wrong?" He checked my worried face.

"No, umm…It's just—"

"Shhh…" He put his fingers on my lips again to cut me off as if he knew I'd complain again. "I told you this is my way of showing I care. Please, let me do it. Don't take this feeling away from me." He paused for a moment. "You have no idea how scared I was when I realized you'd be no longer. It was as if someone ripped out my heart from my chest." *Oh, I felt the same.* "When I look at you now, alive, I don't desire anything else, Rania. You are all I want, no more, no less." Noticing me holding the dress and undergarments, he smiled. "I can't wait to see you in this."

And I can't wait to tell you how much I love you, Adam. I promised myself that I'd tell everything about my past after the party. Whatever he'd chosen for me, I'd accept it as my fate. But he must know about my feelings.

"What?" he asked, reading my thoughts like a mind reader.

"Umm…nothing." I looked down with confusion, hoping he didn't read my eyes.

"Some ladies are here waiting for you. Please, come down." He took my hand and exited the closet, placing my belongings on the bed.

In the living room, two women awaited us. I still didn't understand why they were here.

"Hello, Miss Rania. Pleasure meeting you. I am Cynthia, your makeup and hair artist, and this is Emma, your masseuse and aesthetician." I blinked at Adam. "Mr. Gibson requested that we pamper you and help you prepare for tonight." She glanced at Adam. "Mr. Gibson, we would appreciate it if you let us know where to set up?"

"Oh yes, please, follow me." Adam, taking my hand, led us upstairs again to his bedroom. The women exchanged a look, an element of surprise dancing in their eyes. "You can start your work in our bedroom. Everything is here." *Our bedroom?* Lowering his head, he whispered, only for my ears. "I know I owe you a foot massage from Quebec." He winked at me. *He still remembers that.* "I'll get ready in the other room. You carry on and enjoy your treat." He kissed my forehead and left.

It was no surprise that they were fully equipped with a mobile spa. Within a few hours, I was massaged, scrubbed, polished, waxed, even manicured and pedicured. One of the ladies shaped my eyebrows, and after all the essential treatments, they asked me to put on the dress I intended to wear tonight. I sat in front of Adam's grand dresser. The ladies treated me like a princess getting ready for a royal ball. The makeup and hair had done wonders for me. I couldn't believe how gorgeous I looked after this treatment.

Adam knocked at the door around six in the evening to check if I was ready.

CHAPTER 25
THE ROYAL BALL

ADAM

As I entered the bedroom and lay my eyes on her, the world around me stopped. The snow outside forgot to fall, the wind stilled, the lakes froze—the entire universe ceased functioning as they witnessed my heart falling for her all over again.

I held my breath as Emma and Cynthia waited for my response. Rania had always looked beautiful, no matter how she'd dressed, but tonight, she looked like an enchantress mistakenly dropped from Heaven, where only perfection resides. I felt an overwhelming urge to tear off her dress and make love to her fervently, but she looked so pure and divine that my sinful thoughts wouldn't even let me pull her into my arms.

This was the first time I'd seen her in a black dress. Her hairdo made her look like a princess from some classic storybook. From my expression, the two women must have surmised that I was more than satisfied. They collected their belongings and fled the room.

I requested her to dress up the way I looked at her—beautiful, breathtaking and remarkable.

Watching me from the mirror, I was sure she could read my intentions. She looked away and took her seat back to face the mirror. I stood behind her, wondering what to say rather than standing dumbstruck like a fool. Her eyes had a certain shine I never noticed before. She had never looked at me like that before, either.

I knelt behind her to reach her level, never breaking my firm gaze.

Placing my hands on her shoulders, I whispered the poetic words of William Wordsworth.

And now I see with eye serene
The very pulse of the machine;
A Being breathing thoughtful breath,
A Traveler between life and death;
The reason firm, the temperate will,
Endurance, foresight, strength, and skill;
A perfect Woman, nobly planned,
To warn, to comfort, and command;
And yet a Spirit still, and bright
With something of angelic light.

She smiled, looking down, her cheeks staining with a blush.

"I feel like a fool who can't formulate words." I shook my head. "I don't know what to say. Poetry was just an excuse. You're always beautiful, and you must have heard from me a thousand times. It's not something new to you." She gave a soft smile. "But when I say no other woman would take this place…you must believe me." I tapped on my heart. "You look like an angel. I have no words to express."

"Thank you," she said with another gorgeous smile.

"I wonder what the angels' reaction was when God made you?" She giggled and shook her head. "They must have argued with Him to keep you." As if playing a beautiful classical piece on a piano, my fingers caressed from her shoulders to her arms, feeling her delicate skin vibrating under my fingertips. The fire last night had shaken both of us, and without confessing our feelings, we'd grown close…very close.

"Cynthia and Emma did a wonderful job," she said. This was her way of avoiding the conversation and changing the topic. "You didn't even thank them. They gave their time on Christmas Eve. That's a huge favour." *Is she changing the subject deliberately?*

"I don't take favours." I rested my palms on her forearms and met her gaze in the mirror. "They were paid to do it." She blinked. "When someone like you, who is already so beautiful, I don't think they'd need to make too much effort."

"They were more like fairy godmothers who dolled up a Cinderella," she giggled. "And this Cinderella already met her Prince Charming."

I rested my chin on her shoulder. "Then perhaps we don't need to go to the ball. No fear of losing your shoe on midnight bell." Gently, I wrapped my arms around her. "This prince is getting insecure. I don't want anyone to look at you and desire you as I do."

She raised her eyebrow. "You gotta be kidding me!"

I pulled out a box from my jacket's pocket. "Cinderella is not supposed to refuse the prince. It will break the spell."

She remained quiet as I took the diamond chain out of the box, the one I wanted to give her the first time we met. Ignoring her gaping mouth and the look of *I-don't-need-it*, I clasped the necklace around her beautiful neckline. She closed her eyes, tilted her head to one side and let me secure the lock. *Fuck. She smells delicious!*

As always, her fragrance diffused through my nerves like an addiction. Her heart pumped audibly when I kissed her softly at the nape. This sensation I get from her, I had never felt this way for any woman. Abandoned in the wilderness, I knew if I didn't control myself, we'd never make it to the party. She hummed softly as I wrapped my arms around her again.

"I'm never going to let you go, Rania. Ever." Her body stiffened at my words, breaking her trance. "Do you trust my words?" She snapped her eyes open and turned around, her eyes welling up as if she was about to burst into tears.

"I trust you more than I trust myself, Adam. But there are a few things you need to know. You don't have to say how you feel about me. I can see it in your eyes, in your words, in your actions. But…" She closed her eyes for a moment, taking a deep breath. "But before anything, I want to tell you about myself. I'm afraid you'll never want to see me again if you know about my past." She placed her hand on my face. "I don't want to lose you."

Is this her way of confessing her love?

"Nothing will change my mind. No matter what you tell me." I kissed her forehead, and a single teardrop fell from her eye.

"It's not what you think, Adam. I'm not what you see." She inhaled sharply. "It's very complex."

"Then tell me tonight." I gently wiped the tear. "Perhaps let's not make Mother wait."

When she got to her feet, she beamed. "You look very handsome, Mr. Gibson." She looked up, fixing my tie. "I'm sure lots of ladies are going to have cardiac arrest at the sight."

I placed my hand on her waist and pulled her close. "Then perhaps we should stay in to combat our insecurities."

She laughed at my words. "And what's Grace's fault in all that?"

I pursed my lips. I wished I could come up with an excuse to skip the party. "You look tall tonight." I checked her footwear.

"That's because Cinderella is wearing her glass slippers." She held up one foot and proudly showed me her sparkling sandals. She indeed looked happy after the makeover.

I took her hand and brought it to my lips. "I don't know what I'd have done if anything had happened to you last night."

She studied my face. "This has brought us closer. Hasn't it?" Yes, we were not friends anymore. We were lovers. As if she could read my mind, she checked the time. "We are late."

"Do you have your phone?" I asked.

"Yes, why?"

"Because Eva is coming," I grunted. "And you know how she is. She'll drag you somewhere, and I should know where to find you." She laughed as she secured her phone in her clutch bag. I handed her a few pre-signed checks, to which I received a sour look. "Keep them. Lots of people ask for donations. I'm sure they'll approach you once they know about my girlfriend. I don't want you to be embarrassed."

"So you think I can't make donations?" She sounded offended. *Not again.*

"You can, but the donations are normally in the thousands, and—"

"And I can't afford them?"

"That's not what I meant, Rania." *It's so hard to explain!* "These types of parties are expected to generate lots of donations. Many wealthy people donate generously just to stay in the limelight. I don't want the media to create any low opinion for you."

"So I flaunt with your money?"

"Whether you like it or not, it's how this world works. The more you donate, the more acknowledgement you get."

"Then what's the point? You don't donate to show off. You donate to help people. And if you want to help, you don't need to tell the world about it. It's like throwing your own good deed down the drain."

"I get your point, but I don't want them to write something bad about you."

"Adam," she huffed. "If I donate these checks, they'd already assume it's your money. The checks are under your company's name."

"Trust me…you'll need them."

She gave me a *I-am-not-buying* look but didn't argue.

Ali drove us to the party. On our drive, she had an exciting conversation about books with him. I didn't know he was also a reader. They talked about some books and authors I didn't know, but I chipped in when they started on *Arabian Nights.*

We reached the venue in twenty minutes. At the entrance to the ballroom, I heard Eva shrieking in excitement like a spoiled toddler.

"Oh my God, Rania!" Her shrilling and deafening voice drew some speculative looks at us. "If looks could kill, Adam must have died by now."

"Trust me, Eva, I'm already having a cardiac arrest," I mumbled.

Rania blushed again at my words. How could I control myself not to kiss her?

"Mum and Dad are waiting." She grabbed Rania's arm and pulled her into the crowd.

Brian and Mom were delighted to see her. They embraced her before acknowledging my presence.

"How lovely you look tonight," Brian exclaimed and turned to me. "You keep an eye on her. Don't blame me if any of my guests hit on her. Look around. She is already turning heads."

I could sense Rania was nervous, so I pulled her close. "Don't worry, Brian. I don't plan to let her out of my sight."

"But that doesn't mean you wouldn't let her dance." Mom took Rania's hand.

"She will not dance with anyone, Mom," I seethed.

"Such a caveman!" Eva interjected.

Mom introduced us to her extended family, who seemed curious about my plus one. I also met people from Brian's side for the first time.

It was a big hall accommodating almost three hundred people. A grand bar greeted guests on one side, with opulent buffet tables arranged on the other. A dance floor centred the area, keeping the guests entertained.

What surprised me were the guests from my father's side. I didn't know Mom was still in touch with them. We were introduced to my cousins, whom I didn't know existed, who were more interested in my love life than me.

Everyone seemed to be smitten by Rania. Like a classic piece of art that draws everyone's attention and yet doesn't bother who the admirer is, Rania was the sun in this universe. Not only the men but also the women were admiring her.

We met my half-brother, Scott, and his wife, Tina. Brian's other son, Nathan, was still missing. Rania beamed when she saw thirteen-month-old Scott Junior. Even the baby seemed to adore her, coming to her instantly when she offered her embrace. I'd be a fool to ignore how men were looking at her. And if they all shared the same thought as me…well…fuck!

It was no surprise that the press was more productive than the servers. They snapped pictures of us whenever they saw the opportunity. Rania didn't shy away. Perhaps she accepted our relationship. The news was already out.

Brian's parents flew from England to attend the party. Brian's father, Edward Moore, was in his eighties, but even at his age, he didn't neglect to praise Rania's beauty.

"My eighty-five years of experience says you hold on to your woman," said Edward Moore. "Especially at gatherings like this." He studied Rania through his thick-rimmed glasses. "And don't do anything stupid to lose her. You won't find anyone like her." Rania looked down, her face blushing again.

"I intend to cherish her forever, Mr. Moore," I said.

"Then, if I last until next Christmas, I hope to see Adam

Junior with you two?"

Luckily, Mrs. Edward Moore interrupted him. "Oh, Edward, stop teasing the poor girl. You're embarrassing her. They are young. They have plenty of time." She took Rania's hands and placed them in mine. "Don't heed the old man. He will drive you crazy otherwise. You two carry on." With that, she grabbed Mr. Moore's arm and led him away.

The thought of marriage and imagining us starting a family stirred something warm inside me. Rania was old school. She'd never agree to share a bed unless we gave a name to this relationship. This made me reconsider my beliefs of staying single. I didn't want to live alone anymore. I wanted to cherish, wanted to spend every living moment with her. I had never thought of marriage before because no woman had ever touched me deep enough to propose.

Rania started twisting the ring on her index finger. It was a sign she was anxious.

"Guess what!" Eva shrieked. "Aunt Marie is here, all the way from Scotland."

"Who's Aunt Marie?" I asked.

"Mom's second cousin. You don't remember, Adam?" Noticing my blank face, she continued, "Oh yeah, how would you know? She is a very famous fortune teller in Scotland. A professional. I've heard she communicates with spirits—dead people and all."

Rania snorted, shaking her head in disbelief. "She must be lying, then. She can't be seeing dead people, Eva. It's not possible."

"No, but that's what she says," argued Eva, her voice clipped. "She conducts séance. She talks to the spirits and then tells the future."

"Then they would be the other spirits." Everyone around us turned their attention to Rania. "Those who are dead, their souls don't wander around in this world."

"What other spirits?" I asked, now curious.

"Djinn, maybe," she shrugged.

"Are you serious?" Eva asked, her mouth hung open. It was odd how nonchalant Rania sounded while talking about Djinns, as if they were her friends.

"Think of yourself, Eva. Can these dead people communicate with their loved ones? No. If they have no power, how would they predict your future?"

"Why don't we meet her and find out?" Eva suggested, grabbing her hand.

"No." Rania stepped back. "I don't indulge in such nonsense." Her expression suddenly darkened.

"Why is that?" I asked out of curiosity.

"I can't show her my hand and ask about my future. Not if she might be contacting the Djinn."

"So you think she is bluffing?" Eva gasped.

"I don't know. If she is working professionally, I'm sure she is right. But…"

"That's fine," Eva said. "You don't show your hand, but let's meet her. I want to see how she runs her séance."

Eva grabbed Rania's arm and dragged her to a room. I followed them. I strongly felt that there was more than what meets the eye.

When we entered the room, many people surrounded a middle-aged woman sitting in the corner. She was reading palms individually, but the setting indeed looked like a séance. The room was shrouded in dim light, featuring dark walls and flickering candles on the verge of dying.

As Eva approached her with Rania by her side, Aunt Marie snapped her eyes open as if Rania's presence broke her trance. She looked darkly at Rania in a way I didn't like. It was a strange feeling.

Sensing an unseen danger, I pulled Rania closer. I felt the

same heavy air I'd often felt when I tried to kiss her. There was nothing intimate or private here, yet I sensed that more eyes were watching us than my eyes could see.

Aunt Marie raised her hand. Those who surrounded her fled the room as if they already knew this was a sign of dismissal.

Eva looked around, noticing it was just four of us. From Aunt Marie's face, she looked displeased. Her eyes were still glued to Rania, who also forgot to blink in return.

"I think we are supposed to leave, too," Eva whispered.

Rania blinked and turned around.

"Rania," Aunt Marie called out. "I didn't ask you to leave."

We froze in our tracks. Did they know each other? Rania once told me her parents studied in Scotland. Had they met before, or was she mistaking Rania with her mother? But how did she know her name?

Rania left my side and approached Aunt Marie. "Drop it," she seethed.

"Finally, we meet," Aunt Marie smirked. "You are more beautiful than the picture he drew of you." Rania's expression darkened, staring at the blank wall like someone was standing there. Eva and I exchanged a silent look, but we didn't dare to speak in the middle of this weird conversation.

"He bluffs sometimes," Rania snorted. *What the hell is going on? Who is she talking about?*

"Let's not talk when we have intruders here." Aunt Marie glared at us.

Rania shook her head and turned around. "Let's go."

"Don't let the shadow chase you, Kiya." At Aunt Marie's words, Rania froze. She turned around to meet her gaze. *Who is Kiya?* "Don't lose your soulmate this time. He is the only one who can pull you out of the darkness."

Aghast by Aunt Marie's sharp words, Rania's face was wretched with dread.

"Don't pretend you don't know who I am talking about," Aunt Marie snickered. She got to her feet and leaned closer to Rania, her whisper still audible. "The one who sneaks into your darkness and guards your nightmares. Why can't you see him?"

Rania's face blanched at Aunt Marie's words. She stared blankly at me as if trying to comprehend her words, but after a moment, she sprinted out of the room. Eva and I stood there, still rooted to the ground. I didn't know why I couldn't move. I wanted to follow Rania, but someone had chained me.

Aunt Marie placed her hand on my heart. "Go and guard her." When she pulled away her hand, I was able to move my feet. *What the fuck!*

I ran after Rania, but she disappeared into the crowd. After a few minutes of searching, I found her running toward the exit. I sprinted after her and caught her by the arm.

"Where are you going?" She hid her face in my chest. Her body was shaking, but I didn't know why. "What's wrong, baby?"

"Please take me home, Adam. I can't stay here."

"Who is that woman? Who is Kiya?"

"I can't tell you." She withdrew. "Why don't you continue? I'll go home with Ali."

"No. I'll take you home," I pressed. "Let's just say goodbye to Mom and Brian. We can't leave without that." She nodded and followed me to see Mom.

A voice drew our attention. "Rania?"

Rania turned around and gasped when she noticed a man.

"Nathan?" She threw her arms to hug him.

"I thought I'd never see you again." He embraced her back, lifting her feet off the ground.

"I can't believe it. Three years, eh?" I cleared my throat to draw her attention. She pulled away and forced a smile. "Oh yes, Nathan. This is—"

"Adam Gibson. Who doesn't know him?" Nathan offered his

hand for a firm handshake. I politely accepted his gesture. This made me realize that Rania had never discussed her personal life with me. I didn't know her friends other than Mike, whom I met coincidentally twice.

"Pleasure meeting you, Nathan." I tried to be courteous, but his presence felt like a sore spot thumb.

"Do you guys know each other?" Rania asked.

"This is my parents' party," Nathan said. "How about you?"

"It's my mother's party, too," I interrupted, though he knew. "And she's with me." I pulled Rania closer, wrapping my arm around her waist with firm decisiveness. Nathan blinked at her, taking in my words.

"You are dating," he said quietly. "Unbelievable!" *Doesn't he follow the news?*

"Is that a problem?" I asked, frowning.

Taking a step ahead, he regarded her. "You're dating *him*?" He shook his head as if in utter disbelief. Rania looked down as if she was embarrassed to admit it. "All these years, I kept thinking it was our cultural differences that came between us. I just can't believe I never mattered to you."

"It's not what you think, Nathan," Rania mumbled, her voice dropping a few decibels. "I was in the middle of my degree program. I wasn't ready for marriage." *What? He proposed to her?*

"You two dated?" I interrupted again.

"Dated? Ha!" Nathan snorted. "Rania does not believe in dates." He turned his gaze to me. "It seems like she made an exception here." He patted my arm. "Lucky man!"

Just in time, Mom barged in. "Nathan, darling." Pulling Nathan in a motherly hug, she kissed him on the forehead. "Did you meet Adam's girlfriend?" Pride glinted in her eyes.

Nathan put his arm around Mom's shoulders. "You remember the girl I told you about from the uni?"

"The one you wanted to marry?" Mom asked.

"Yes, the one we got the ring for." He nodded at Rania. "She's the one."

Mom's mouth hung open. "But she..."

"Right, she refused me, Mom. But your other son got lucky." His jealousy was evident on his face.

I lowered my head to whisper, only for Rania's ears. "You never told me he proposed to you."

"There was nothing to say," she answered, looking utterly uncomfortable.

"If you don't mind, Mr. Gibson, can I steal your *girlfriend* for a few minutes?" Nathan asked rather brazenly. "Some colleagues from the university are here. You wanna see them?"

"Hang on, Nathan," Mom interrupted. "Tell your friends that dinner is served. Rania, Adam, please join us for dinner."

We all sat at the large family table. Rania sat next to me. When Scott Junior began crying in his mother's lap, waving toward Rania, she took the baby and cuddled him, letting him play with her necklace.

"Tina, can I give him mashed potato?" Rania asked Scott's wife.

"Oh, he's a fussy baby," Tina grumbled. "He doesn't eat anything. I try to give him vegetables and mashed fruits, but God, he's a terrible eater."

"Just like his father," Mr. Moore added, making everyone laugh.

Rania mashed green peas and potato and added some butter. Everyone watched her as she started singing the nursery rhyme *row-row-row-the-boat*, to which the baby responded excitedly and opened his mouth. She kept repeating it until the baby had had around twenty mini-spoonful of mashed vegetables.

"I think you'll have to move in with me, Rania. He likes you to feed him." Tina offered to take the baby back, but the child refused to leave Rania. "You should eat now."

"Do you want me to feed you?" I whispered, but unfortunately, my annoying sister heard it.

"Oh my God! Look at the romance." Eva shrieked again. I glared at my sister, but she didn't stop.

"What happened?" Nathan asked, sitting at her other side.

"Adam offered to feed his pretty lady…with his own hands… ooo." *Why is my sister so irritating?* I rolled my eyes, evidently showing my displeasure.

"I'm fine. I will manage," Rania whispered back. The baby was sleeping peacefully, resting his head on her soft breasts, holding her chain in his tiny fingers. She tucked the baby closer, securing him.

"I thought you were a magnet to men only, but damn… babies too?" Nathan popped his head toward her. "Well, I guess …who wouldn't want to sleep like that?" Nathan's remark made me choke on my wine.

"Eva and Nathan, stop teasing," Mr. Moore reprimanded his spoiled kids. "Tina, take the baby from Rania so she can eat." Rania handed the sleeping baby to his mother. No one dared to speak for the rest of the meal.

Finally, when we were finished eating, Nathan offered Rania again to see their friends. Her eyes sparkled at the idea, and I had no excuse for saying no. A moment ago, she wanted to go home, and now, after seeing Nathan, she seemed to forget everything. The way Nathan was looking at her, I was damn sure they had a past. He couldn't have been proposing to her out of the blue. *Why didn't she tell me?* But she'd never told me anything about her past. I'd shared everything about my life with her, but she was still a mystery.

Nathan took Rania's hand and led her into his group of friends. I knew I sounded like an insecure boyfriend, but there was no point in fussing about it. She had spent four years of her academic life with them. After all, we had an entire night after the party.

Settling in the bar, I distracted myself with a glass of whiskey. Though Rania stood at some distance, my eyes couldn't help but track her every move. In the background, they were playing "Amazed." How the song fitted my current feelings! She truly amazed me.

She stole a glance a few times, knowing I was watching her.

Nathan said something to his friends, who all looked in my direction. I assumed they were discussing our relationship. I was in the middle of my drink when Mom joined me.

"How is she doing after last night?" Mom asked with concern.

"Better than yesterday." I shook my head. "I thought I lost her."

"She's here with you now, darling." Mom placed a comforting hand on my shoulder.

"You know what, Mom? I've built many houses and residential properties over the years. I have donated so much to provide shelter to the poor. But the woman I care about most is feeling homeless right now. And there's nothing I can do about it. It's so strange and unfair. Isn't it?"

Mom took a deep breath and said, "God has different ways of doing things. You should be thankful she's safe."

"I am. I have no words to express how much." We both looked toward Rania and Nathan, busy talking.

"The world is very small. I didn't know she was the same girl who captured Nathan's heart." She took a sip of her wine. I turned my head to her. "Nathan told me he was in love with an Arab girl. He even asked me to help him buy her an engagement ring. He wanted to propose before graduation so they could get married right afterward. She refused with an excuse of their cultural differences. That her father would not allow it. I don't know how that goes with you."

"Her father is still not buying the idea of us together. And to tell you the truth, she considers me only a friend."

"Are you serious? Can't you see, Adam, that she is in love with you?"

"Did she tell you that?" I whipped my head at her again.

"Did *you* tell me you love her?" She chuckled. I blinked at her in astonishment. *How does she know?* "No, Adam, you didn't, but you're my son, and I can see it in your eyes. And I see the same spark in her eyes." She placed her hand on my shoulder. "You have lived your life all alone. I'm glad you found someone who is true to you. I know she sees beyond your riches, which makes her special. But just remember one thing. Don't lose the trust you have in her. She is beautiful, wise, and intelligent, and you will come across many men who want to take your place. You need to trust that she's chosen you and not the others. Don't ever let skepticism come between you. If there is doubt in a relationship, then it doesn't stand a chance."

She took another sip, pondering. "I know it makes you unhappy seeing her with Nathan. But don't make your father's mistake and spoil what you have now." I listened to my mother's wise words intently. My father spent the rest of his life trying to make up for that single mistake, but he couldn't. I couldn't let myself do that if I claimed I loved her.

Love requires faith and patience.

Rania seemed to forget that she was my company. Perhaps I should confess my love openly tonight. This alcohol might help kick in some courage. I abandoned my glass of wine and switched on the whiskey.

After a few rounds, I realized I had too much of it since it was getting hot in here. I was heady and breathless, but I had all the courage to confess loudly. Everyone here must know that she solely belonged to me. If anyone had any sinister idea about her, they could drop it now.

Ignoring the crowd, I approached her slowly, trying to make

my feet steady. Good, lord, she looked more seductive after my sloshed brain. The song, 'Save the Last Dance for Me' played in the background. *Yes, I will have a last dance.* No one should take her in his arms.

She looked at me skeptically, perhaps noticing that I was indeed drunk. I wanted her to listen to my heart. I wanted her to know what war was waging inside me and how hard it was for me to control my emotions and not kiss her publicly.

She frowned at me. "Are you drunk, Adam?" She looked utterly displeased.

Yes, I am drunk and in love with you.

But before I could say something in my defence, Nathan grabbed her hand and shrieked. "Rania! Our song!"

I didn't even realize the music had changed. She screamed with him, showing the same level of excitement.

"Let's relive our memory." And without giving us even a chance to exchange a glance, he dragged her onto the dance floor and started dancing with her crazily to *She Bangs*. As if she was drunk herself, Rania laughed heartily, swirling in his arms, not caring whether I was watching.

"I can't believe they remember all the moves, even after three years." One of the men in their circle of friends commented.

"They practiced this one for almost six months," another man added. "That's why they won the competition. It was a breathtaking performance. I always thought they were a couple. Look how they move together when they dance."

Watching Rania and Nathan dance seductively like a perfectly blended couple boiled my blood with rage and envy. He touched her everywhere during the dance, and she swirled in his arms, seeming to let him claim her whole body. The entire crowd watched and clapped at their extraordinary performance. *Why is my heart splitting in two?*

They performed in a competition, and even after all these

years, they still remembered all the moves. The sight of Rania getting so physically close to someone spiked adrenaline in my body. The insecurity, fear and anxiety overwhelmed me, and I headed for the dance floor, drink still in my hand. She was still laughing, utterly ignoring my presence as if she'd escaped to another world where I didn't exist.

When I reached the dance floor, that was when Nathan touched her neckline with his fingers as a part of the dance move, and she closed her eyes in pleasure.

Jealousy consumed me, and I smashed the glass on the floor.

The music stopped, and everyone turned to look at me in shock.

I pulled Rania out of Nathan's filthy hands, grabbed her nape, and kissed her wildly on the lips without even giving her a chance to blink. After a few seconds, I pushed her away, glaring at her with my burning, drunken eyes.

"You. Are. Mine," I yelled. "Do you hear that? Don't you dare dance with anyone. You are fuckin' mine."

Shock masked her face.

I didn't realize my ferocious kiss had bruised her soft lips, and her lower lip was bleeding. She flicked her finger on her wounded lip, and a single tear ran down her cheek as she found the drop of blood on her fingertip.

When she looked around and noticed how everyone was watching us, she hurried toward the exit.

"Asshole," Nathan growled and ran after her.

Suddenly, everything around me turned to ice. I felt like time had halted.

I fell to my knees. As if trying to rewind the clock, I began collecting shards to piece them together. The photographers snapped and clicked at my painful moment until Brian pushed everyone away.

Mom rushed toward me. "Adam, what are you doing? You

have injured your hand." She picked up my hand, soaked in blood.

"I lost her, Mom. I lost her." I examined my injured hands, taking deep, agonized breaths. Mom said nothing to comfort me, but her tears reminded me of my blunder. She knew what I'd done.

My pride, my envy, destroyed everything. I lost everything with my own jealousy. I shook my head in disbelief.

"You warned me, Mom, but I…" Tears clouded my eyes until I could see nothing around me.

Suddenly, something crossed my mind, and I looked to my mother for help.

"Where did she go? Where *would* she go? She has no home. She has no place to live."

Mom blinked at me.

"Everything was burned last night. Mom, find her. Where did she go?"

AUTHOR'S NOTE

I hope you enjoyed **A Silent Prayer**. Adam and Rania's story continues as Rania's mystery unfolds in the sequel, **A Prayer Heeded.**

ABOUT THE AUTHOR

Samreen Ahsan is an international award-winning author. As a bibliophile, she loves visiting old libraries in castles, palaces and monasteries and wishes to own a vast library. As an avid reader, she loves to visit every real place from the books and admires the architecture of historical cities. Her favourite hobbies besides reading are visiting art galleries (which she often shares on her social media). She is a traveller and a history buff at heart. She wishes to run a travel show one day.

She lives in ON, Canada

Visit her website: **samreenahsan.com** for details.